I0784742

Marah Ellis Ryan

That Girl Montana

OK Publishing 2021

Marah Ellis Ryan

That Girl Montana

From the renowned author of In Love's Domain, A Flower of France, The Treasure Trail & The House of the Dawn

Published by

MUSAICUM

Books

- Advanced Digital Solutions & High-Quality book Formatting -

musaicumbooks@okpublishing.info

2021 OK Publishing

ISBN 978-80-272-7574-8

Contents

"That girl the murderer of a man-of Lee Holly! That pretty little girl? Bosh! I don't believe it."

"I did not say she killed him; I said she was suspected. And even though she was cleared, the death of that renegade adds one more to the mysteries of our new West. But I think the mere suspicion that she did it entitles her to a medal, or an ovation of some sort."

The speakers were two men in complete hunting costume. That they were strangers in the Northwest was evidenced by the very lively interest they took in each bit of local color in landscape or native humanity. Of the latter, there was a most picturesque variety. There were the Northern red men in their bright blankets, and women, too, with their beadwork and tanned skins for sale. A good market-place for these was this spot where the Kootenai River is touched by the iron road that drives from the lakes to the Pacific. The road runs along our Northern boundary so close that it is called the "Great Northern," and verily the land it touches is great in its wildness and its beauty.

The two men, with their trophies of elk-horn and beaver paws, with their scarred outfit and a general air of elation gained from a successful "outing," tramped down to the little station after a last lingering view toward far hunting grounds. While waiting for the train bound eastward, they employed their time in dickering with the Indian moccasin-makers, of whom they bought arrows and gaily painted bows of ash, with which to deck the wall of some far-away city home.

While thus engaged, a little fleet of canoes was sighted skimming down the river from that greater wilderness of the North, penetrated at that time only by the prospector, or a chance hunter; for the wealth of gold in those high valleys had not yet been more than hinted at, and the hint had not reached the ears of the world.

Even the Indians were aroused from their lethargy, and watched with keen curiosity the approaching canoes. When from the largest there stepped forth a young girl —a rather remarkable-looking young girl-there was a name spoken by a tall Indian boatman, who stood near the two strangers. The Indians nodded their heads, and the name was passed from one to the other-the name 'Tana —a soft, musical name as they pronounced it. One of the strangers, hearing it, turned quickly to a white ranchman, who had a ferry at that turn of the river, and asked if that was the young girl who had helped locate the new gold find at the Twin Springs.

"Likely," agreed the ranchman. "Word came that she was to cut the diggings and go to school a spell. A Mr. Haydon, who represents a company that's to work the mine, sent down word that a special party was to go East over the road from here to-day; so I guess she's one of the specials. She came near going on a special to the New Jerusalem, she did, not many days ago. I reckon you folks heard how Lee Holly-toughest man in the length of the Columbia-was wiped off the living earth by her last week."

"We heard she was cleared of it," assented the stranger.

"Yes, so she was, so she was-cleared by an alibi, sworn to by Dan Overton. You don't know Dan, I suppose? Squarest man you ever met! And he don't have to scratch gravel any more, either, for he has a third interest in that Twin Spring find, and it pans out big. They say the girl sold her share for two hundred thousand. She doesn't look top-heavy over it, either."

And she did not. She walked between two men-one a short, rather pompous elderly man, who bore a slight resemblance to her, and whom she treated rather coolly.

"Of course I am not tired," she said, in a strong, musical voice. "I have been brought all the way on cushions, so how could I be? Why, I have gone alone in a canoe on a longer trail than we floated over, and I think I will again some day. Max, there is one thing I want in this world, and want bad; that is, to get Mr. Haydon out on a trip where we can't eat until we kill and cook our dinner. He doesn't know anything about real comfort; he wants too many cushions."

The man she called Max bent his head and whispered something to her, at which her face flushed just a little and a tiny wrinkle crept between her straight, beautiful brows.

"I told you not to say pretty things that way, just because you think girls like to hear them. I don't. Maybe I will when I get civilized; but Mr. Haydon thinks that is a long ways ahead, doesn't he?" The wrinkle was gone-vanished in a quizzical smile, as she looked up into the very handsome face of the young fellow.

"So do I," he acknowledged. "I have a strong desire, especially when you snub me, to be the man to take you on a lone trail like that. I will, too, some day."

"Maybe you will," she agreed. "But I feel sorry for you beforehand."

She seemed a tantalizing specimen of girlhood, as she stood there, a slight, brown slip of a thing, dressed in a plain flannel suit, the color of her golden-brown short curls. In her brown cloth hat the wings of a redbird gleamed-the feathers and her lips having all there was of bright color about her; for her face was singularly colorless for so young a girl. The creamy skin suggested a pale-tinted blossom, but not a fragile one; and the eyes-full eyes of wine-brown — looked out with frank daring on the world.

But for all the daring brightness of her glances, it was not a joyous face, such as one would wish a girl of seventeen to possess. A little cynical curve of the red mouth, a little contemptuous glance from those brown eyes, showed one that she took her measurements of individuals by a gauge of her own, and that she had not that guileless trust in human nature that is supposed to belong to young womanhood. The full expression indicated an independence that seemed a breath caught from the wild beauty of those Northern hills.

Her gaze rested lightly on the two strangers and their trophies of the chase, on the careless ferryman, and the few stragglers from the ranch and the cabins. These last had gathered there to view the train and its people as they passed, for the ties on which the iron rails rested were still of green wood, and the iron engines of transportation were recent additions to those lands of the far North, and were yet a novelty.

Over the faces of the white men her eyes passed carelessly. She did not seem much interested in civilized men, even though decked in finer raiment than was usual in that locality; and, after a cool glance at them all, she walked directly past them and spoke to the tall Indian who had first uttered her name to the others.

His face brightened when she addressed him; but their words were low, as are ever the words of an Indian in converse, low and softly modulated; and the girl did not laugh in the face of the native as she had when the handsome young white man had spoken to her in softened tones.

The two sportsmen gave quickened attention to her as they perceived she was addressing the Indian in his own language. Many gestures of her slim brown hands aided her speech, and as he watched her face, one of the sportsmen uttered the impulsive exclamation at the beginning of this story. It seemed past belief that she could have committed the deed with which her name had been connected, and of which the Kootenai valley had heard a great deal during the week just passed. That it had become the one topic of general interest in the community was due partly to the personality of the girl, and partly to the fact that the murdered man had been one of the most notorious in all that wild land extending north and west into British Columbia.

Looking at the frank face of the girl and hearing her musical, decided tones, the man had a reasonable warrant for deciding that she was not guilty.

"She is one of the most strongly interesting girls of her age I have ever seen," he decided. "Girls of that age generally lack character. She does not; it impresses itself on a man though she never speak a word to him. Wish she'd favor me with as much of her attention as she gives that hulking redskin."

"It's a 'case,' isn't it?" asked his friend. "You'll be wanting to use her as a centerpiece for your next novel; but you can't make an orthodox heroine of her, for there must have been some reason for the suspicion that she helped him 'over the range,' as they say out here. There must have been something socially and morally wrong about the fact that he was found dead in her cabin. No, Harvey; you'd better write up the inert, inoffensive red man on his native heath, and let this remarkable young lady enjoy her thousands in modest content-if the ghosts let her."

"Nonsense!" said the other man, with a sort of impatience. "You jump too quickly to the conclusion that there must be wrong where there is suspicion. But you have put an idea into my mind as to the story. If I can ever learn the whole history of this affair, I will make use of it, and I'm not afraid of finding my pretty girl in the wrong, either."

"I knew from the moment we heard who she was that your impressionable nature would fall a victim, but you can't write a story of her alone; you will want your hero and one or two other people. I suppose, now, that very handsome young fellow with the fastidious get-up will about suit you for the hero. He does look rather lover-like when he addresses your girl with the history. Will you pair them off?"

"I will let you know a year from now," returned the man called Harvey. "But just now I am going to pay my respects to the very well-fed looking elderly gentleman. He seems to be the chaperon of the party. I have acquired a taste for trailing things during our thirty days hunt in these hills, and I'm going to trail this trio, with the expectation of bagging a romance."

His friend watched him approach the elder gentleman, and was obviously doubtful of the reception he would get, for the portly, prosperous-looking individual did not seem to have been educated in that generous Western atmosphere, where a man is a brother if he acts square and speaks fair. Conservatism was stamped in the deep corners of his small mouth, on the clean-shaven lips, and the correctly cut side-whiskers that added width to his fat face.

But the journalist proper, the world over, is ever a bit of a diplomat. He has won victories over so many conservative things, and is daunted by few. When Harvey found himself confronted by a monocle through which he was coolly surveyed, it did not disturb him in the least (beyond making it difficult to retain a grave demeanor at the lively interest shown by the Indians in that fashionable toy).

"Yes, sir-yes, sir; I am T. J. Haydon, of Philadelphia," acknowledged he of the glass disc, "but I don't know you, sir."

"I shall be pleased to remedy that if you will allow me," returned the other, suavely, producing a card which he offered for examination. "You are, no doubt, acquainted with the syndicate I represent, even if my name tells you nothing. I have been hunting here with a friend for a month, and intend writing up the resources of this district. I have a letter of introduction to your partner, Mr. Seldon, but did not follow the river so far as to reach your works, though I've heard a good deal about them, and imagine them interesting."

"Yes, indeed; very interesting-very interesting from a sportsman's or mineralogist's point of view," agreed the older man, as he twirled the card in a disturbed, uncertain way. "Do you travel East, Mr. —Mr. Harvey? Yes? Well, let me introduce Mr. Seldon's nephew-he's a New Yorker-Max Lyster. Wait a minute and I'll get him away from those beastly Indians. I never can understand the attraction they have for the average tourist."

But when he reached Lyster he said not a word of the despised reds; he had other matters more important.

"Here, Max! A most annoying thing has happened," he said, hurriedly. "Those two men are newspaper fellows, and one is going East on our train. Worse still-the one knows people I know. Gad! I'd rather lose a thousand dollars than meet them now! And you must come over and get acquainted. They've been here a month, and are to write accounts of the life and country. That means they have been here long enough to hear all about 'Tana and that Holly. Do you understand? You'll have to treat them well,—the best possible-pull wires even if it costs money, and fix it so that a record of this does not get into the Eastern papers. And, above and beyond everything else, so long as we are in this depraved corner of the country, you must keep them from noticing that girl Montana."

The young man looked across at the girl, and smiled doubtfully.

"I'm willing to undertake any possible thing for you," he said; "but, my dear sir, to keep people from noticing 'Tana is one of the things beyond my power. And if she gives notice to all the men who will notice her, I've an idea jealousy will turn my hair gray early. But come on and introduce your man, and don't get in a fever over the meeting. I am so fortunate as to know more of the journalistic fraternity than you, and I happen to be aware that they are generally gentlemen. Therefore, you'd better not drop any hints to them of monetary advantages in exchange for silence unless you want to be beautifully roasted by a process only possible in printer's ink."

The older man uttered an exclamation of impatience, as he led his young companion over to the sportsmen, who had joined each other again; and as he effected the introduction, his mind was sorely upset by dread of the two gentlemanly strangers and 'Tana.

'Tana was most shamelessly continuing her confidences with the tall Indian, despite the fact that she knew it was a decided annoyance to her principal escort. Altogether the evening was a trying one to Mr. T. J. Haydon.

The sun had passed far to the west, and the shadows were growing longer under the hills there by the river. Clear, red glints fell across the cool ripples of the water, and slight chill breaths drifted down the ravines and told that the death of summer was approaching.

Some sense of the beauty of the dying October day seemed to touch the girl, for she walked a little apart and picked a spray of scarlet maple leaves and looked from them to the hills and the beautiful valley, where the red and the yellow were beginning to crowd out the greens. Yes, the summer was dying-dying! Other summers would come in their turn, but none quite the same. The girl showed all the feeling of its loss in her face. In her eyes the quick tears came, as she looked at the mountains. The summer was dying; it was autumn's colors she held in her hand, and she shivered, though she stood in the sunshine.

As she turned toward the group again, she met the eyes of the stranger to whom Max was talking. He seemed to have been watching her with a great deal of interest, and her hand was raised to her eyes, lest a trace of tears should prove food for curiosity.

"It was to one of Akkomi's relations I was talking," she remarked to Mr. Haydon, when he questioned her. "His little grandson is sick, and I would like to send him something. I haven't money enough in my pocket, and wish you would get me some."

After taking some money out of his purse for her, he eyed the tall savage with disfavor.

"He'll buy bad whisky with it," he grumbled.

"No, he will not," contradicted the girl. "If a person treats these Indians square, he can trust them. But if a lie is told them, or a promise broken-well, they get even by tricking you if they can, and I can't say that I blame them. But they won't trick me, so don't worry; and I'm as sure the things will go to that little fellow safely as though I took them."

She was giving the money and some directions to the Indian, when a word from a squaw drew her attention to the river.

A canoe had just turned the bend not a quarter of a mile away, and was skimming the water with the swiftness of a swallow's dart. Only one man was in it, and he was coming straight for the landing.

"Some miner rushing down to see the train go by," remarked Mr. Haydon; but the girl did not answer. Her face grew even more pale, and her hands clasped each other nervously.

"Yes," said the Indian beside her, and nodded to her assuringly. Then the color swept upward over her face as she met his kindly glance, and drawing herself a little straighter, she walked indifferently away.

The stolid red man did not look at all snubbed; he only pocketed the money she had given him, and looked after her with a slight smile, accented more by the deepening wrinkles around his black eyes than by any change about the lips.

Then there was a low rumbling sound borne on the air, and as the muffled whistle of the unseen train came to them from the wilderness to the west, with one accord the Indians turned their attention to their wares, and the white people to their baggage. When the train slowed up Mr. Haydon, barely waiting for the last revolution of the wheels, energetically hastened the young girl up the steps of the car nearest them.

"What's the hurry?" she asked, with a slight impatience.

"I think," he replied quickly, "there is but a short stop made at this station, and as there are several vacant seats in this car, please occupy one of them until I have seen the conductor. There may be some changes made as to the compartments engaged for us. Until that is decided, will you be so kind as to remain in this coach?"

She nodded rather indifferently, and looked around for Max. He was gathering up some robes and satchels when the older man joined him.

"We are not going to make the trip to Chicago in the car with those fellows if it can be helped, Max," he insisted, fussily; "we'll wait and see what car they are booked for, and I'll arrange for another. Sorry I did not get a special, as I first intended."

"But see here; they are first-class fellows-worth one's while to meet," protested Max; but the other shook his head.

"Look after the baggage while I see the conductor. 'Tana is in one of the cars-don't know which. We'll go for her when we get settled. Now, don't argue. Time is too precious."

And 'Tana! She seated herself rather sulkily, as she was told, and looked at once toward the river.

The canoe was landing, and the man jumped to the shore. With quick, determined strides, he came across the land to the train. She tried to follow him with her eyes, but he crossed to the other side of the track.

There was rather a boisterous party in the car-two men and two women. One of the latter, a flaxen-haired, petite creature, was flitting from one side of the car to the other, making remarks about the Indians, admiring particularly one boy's beaded dress, and garnishing her remarks with a good deal of slang.

"Say, Chub! that boy's suit would be a great 'make-up' for me in that new turn-the jig, you know; new, too. There isn't a song-and-dance on the boards done with Indian make-up. Knock them silly in the East, where they don't see reds. Now sing out, and tell me if it wouldn't make a hit."

"Aw, Goldie, give us a rest on shop talk," growled the gentleman called Chub. "If you'd put a little more ginger into the good specialty you have, instead of depending on wardrobe, you'd hit 'em hard enough. It ain't plans that count, girlie-it's work."

The "girlie" addressed accepted the criticism with easy indifference, and her fair, dissipated face was only twisted in a grimace, while she held one hand aloft and jingled the bangles on her bracelets as though poising a tambourine.

"Better hustle yourself into the smoker again, Chubby dear. It will take a half-dozen more cigars to put you in your usual sweet frame of mind. Run along now. Ta-ta!"

The other woman seemed to think their remarks very witty, especially when Chub really did arise and make his way toward the smoker. Goldie then went back to the window, where the Indians were to be seen. The quartet were, to judge by their own frank remarks, a party of variety singers and dancers who had been doing the Pacific circuit, and were now booked for some Eastern houses, of which they spoke as "solid."

Some of the passengers had got out and were buying little things from the Indians, as souvenirs of the country. 'Tana saw Mr. Haydon among them, in earnest conversation with the conductor; saw Max, with his hand full of satchels, suddenly reach out the other hand with a great deal of heartiness and meet the man of the canoe.

He was not so handsome a man as Max, yet would have been noticeable anywhere-tall, olive-skinned, and dark-haired. His dress had not the fashionable cut of the young fellow he spoke to. But he wore his buckskin jacket with a grace that bespoke physical strength and independence; and when he pushed his broad-brimmed gray hat back from his face, he showed a pair of dark eyes that had a very direct glance. They were serious, contemplative eyes, that to some might look even moody.

"There is a fellow with a great figure," remarked the other woman of the quartet; "that fellow with the sombrero; built right up from the ground, and looks like a picture; don't he, Charlie?"

"I can't see him," complained Goldie, "but suppose it's one of the ranchmen who live about here." Then she turned and donated a brief survey to 'Tana. "Do you live in this region?" she asked.

After a deliberate, contemptuous glance from the questioner's frizzed head to her little feet, 'Tana answered:

"No; do you?"

With this curt reply, she turned her shoulder very coolly on the searcher for information.

Vexation sent the angry blood up into the little woman's face. She looked as though about to retort, when a gentleman who had just taken possession of a compartment, and noted all that had passed, came forward and addressed our heroine.

"Until your friends come in, will you not take my seat?" he asked, courteously. "I will gladly make the exchange, or go for Mr. Lyster or Mr. Haydon, if you desire it."

"Thank you; I will take your seat," she agreed. "It is good of you to offer it."

"Say, folks, I'm going outside to take in this free Wild West show," called the variety actress to her companions. "Come along?"

But they declined. She had reached the platform alone, when, coming toward the car, she saw the man of the sombrero, and shrank back with a gasp of utter dismay.

"Oh, good Heaven!" she muttered, and all the color and bravado were gone from her face, as she shrank back out of his range of vision and almost into the arms of the man Harvey, who had given the other girl his seat.

"What's up?" he asked, bluntly.

She only gave a muttered, unintelligible reply, pushed past him to her own seat, where her feather-laden hat was donned with astonishing rapidity, a great cloak was thrown around her, and she sank into a corner, a huddled mass of wraps and feathers. Any one could have walked along the aisle without catching even a glimpse of her flaxen hair.

'Tana and the stranger exchanged looks of utter wonder at the lightning change effected before their eyes.

At that moment a tap-tap sounded on the window beside 'Tana, and, looking around, she met the dark eyes of the man with the sombrero gazing kindly upward at her.

The people were getting aboard the train again-the time was so short-so short! and how can one speak through a double glass? The fingers were all unequal to the fastening of the window, and she turned an imploring, flushed face to the helpful stranger.

"Can you-oh, will you, please?" she asked, breathlessly. "Thank you, I'm very much obliged."

Then the window was raised, and her hand thrust out to the man, who was bareheaded now, and who looked very much as though he held the wealth of the world when he clasped only 'Tana's fingers.

"Oh, it is you, is it?" she asked, with a rather lame attempt at careless speech. "I thought you had forgotten to say good-by to me."

"You knew better," he contradicted. "You knew-you know now it wasn't because I forgot."

He looked at her moodily from under his dark brows, and noticed the color flutter over her cheek and throat in an adorable way. She had drawn her hand from him, and it rested on the window —a slim brown hand, with a curious ring on one finger-two tiny snakes whose jeweled heads formed the central point of attraction.

"You said you would not wear that again. If it's a hoodoo, as you thought, why not throw it away?" he asked.

"Oh —I've changed my mind. I need to wear it so that I will be reminded of something-something important as a hoodoo," she said, with a strange, bitter smile.

"Give it back to me, 'Tana," he urged. "I will-No-Max will have something much prettier for you. And listen, my girl. You are going away; don't ever come back; forget everything here but the money that will be yours for the claim. Do you understand me? Forget all I said to you when-you know. I had no right to say it; I must have been drunk. I —I lied, anyway."

"Oh, you lied, did you?" she asked, cynically, and her hands were clasped closely, so close the ring must have hurt her. He noticed it, and kept his eyes on her hand as he continued, doggedly:

"Yes. You see, little girl, I thought I'd own up before you left, so you wouldn't be wasting any good time in being sorry about the folks back here. It wasn't square for me to trouble you as I did. And —I lied. I came down to say that."

"You needn't have troubled yourself," she said, curtly. "But I see you can tell lies. I never would have believed it if I hadn't heard you. But I guess, after all, I will give you the ring. You might want it to give to some one else-perhaps your wife."

The bell was ringing and the wheels began slowly to revolve. She pulled the circlet from her finger and almost flung it at him.

"'Tana!" and all of keen appeal was in his voice and his eyes, "little girl-good-by!"

But she turned away her head. Her hand, however, reached out and the spray of autumn leaves fluttered to his feet where the ring lay.

Then the rumble of the moving train sounded through the valley, and the girl turned to find Max, Mr. Haydon and a porter approaching, to convey her to the car ahead. Mr. Haydon's face was a study of dismay at the sight of Mr. Harvey closing the window and showing evident interest in 'Tana's comfort.

"So Dan did get down to see you off, 'Tana?" observed Max, as he led her along the aisle. "Dear old fellow! how I did try to coax him into coming East later; but it was of no use. He gave me some flowers for you-wild beauties. He never seemed to say much, 'Tana, but I've an idea you'll never have a better friend in your life than that same old Dan."

Mr. Harvey watched their exit, and smiled a little concerning Mr. Haydon's evident annoyance. He watched, also, the flaxen-haired bundle in the corner, and saw the curious, malignant look with which she followed 'Tana, and to his friend he laughed over his triumph in exchanging speech with the pretty, peculiar girl in brown.

"And the old party looked terribly fussy over it. In fact, I've about sifted out the reason. He imagines me a newspaper reporter on the alert for sensations. He's afraid his stupidly respectable self may be mentioned in a newspaper article concerning this local tragedy they all talk about. Why, bless his pocket-book! if I ever use pen and ink on that girl's story, it will not be for a newspaper article."

"Then you intend to tell it?" asked his friend. "How will you learn it?"

"I do not know yet. The 'how' does not matter; I'll tell you on paper some day."

"And write up that handsome Lyster as the hero?"

"Perhaps."

Then a bend of the road brought them again in sight of the river of the Kootenais. Here and there the canoes of the Indians were speeding across at the ferry. But one canoe alone was moving north; not very swiftly, but almost as though drifting with the current.

Using his field-glass, Harvey found it was as he had thought. The occupant of the solitary canoe was the tall man whose dark face had impressed the theatrical lady so strongly. He was not using the paddle, and his chin was resting on one clenched hand, while in the other he held something to which he was giving earnest attention.

It was a spray of bright-colored leaves, and the watcher dropped his glass with a guilty feeling.

"He brings her flowers, and gets in return only dead leaves," Harvey thought, grimly. "I didn't hear a word he said to her; but his eyes spoke strongly enough, poor devil! I wonder if she sees him, too."

And all through the evening, and for many a day, the picture remained in his mind. Even when he wrote the story that is told in these pages, he could never find words to express the utter loneliness of that life, as it seemed to drift away past the sun-touched ripples of water into that vast, shadowy wilderness to the north.

Chapter I
A Strange Girl

"Well, by the help of either her red gods or devils, she can swim, anyway!"

This explosive statement was made one June morning on the banks of the Kootenai, and the speaker, after a steady gaze, relinquished his field-glass to the man beside him.

"Can she make it?" he asked.

A grunt was the only reply given him. The silent watcher was too much interested in the scene across the water.

Shouts came to them-the yells of frightened Indian children; and from the cone-shaped dwellings, up from the water, the Indian women were hurrying. One, reaching the shore first, sent up a shrill cry, as she perceived that, from the canoe where the children played, one had fallen over, and was being swept away by that swift-rushing, chill water, far out from the reaching hands of the others.

Then a figure lolling on the shore farther down stream than the canoe sprang erect at the frightened scream.

One quick glance showed the helplessness of those above, and another the struggling little form there in the water-the little one who turned such wild eyes toward the shore, and was the only one of them all who was not making some outcry.

The white men, who were watching from the opposite side, could see shoes flung aside quickly; a jacket dropped on the shore; and then down into the water a slight figure darted with the swiftness of a kingfisher, and swam out to the little fellow who had struggled to keep his head above water, but was fast growing helpless in the chill of the mountain river.

Then it was that Mr. Maxwell Lyster commented on the physical help lent by the gods of the red people, as the ability of any female to swim thus lustily in spite of that icy current seemed to his civilized understanding a thing superhuman. Of course, bears and other animals of the woods swam it at all seasons, when it was open; but to see a woman dash into it like that! Well, it sent a shiver over him to think of it.

"They'll both get chilled and drop to the bottom!" he remarked, with irritated concern. "Of course there are enough of the red vagabonds in this new El Dorado of yours, without that particular squaw. But it would be a pity that so plucky a one should be translated."

Then a yell of triumph came from the other shore. A canoe had been loosened, and was fairly flying over the water to where the child had been dragged to the surface, and the rescuer was holding herself up by the slow efforts of one arm, but could make no progress with her burden.

"That's no squaw!" commented the other man, who had been looking through the glass.

"Why, Dan!"

"It's no squaw, I tell you," insisted the other, with the superior knowledge of a native. "Thought so the minute I saw her drop the shoes and jacket that way. She didn't make a single Indian move. It's a white woman!"

"Queer place for a white woman, isn't it?"

The man called Dan did not answer. The canoe had reached that figure in the water and the squaw in it lifted the now senseless child and laid him in the bottom of the light craft.

A slight altercation seemed going on between the woman in the water and the one in the boat. The former was protesting against being helped on board-the men could see that by their gestures. She finally gained her point, for the squaw seized the paddle and sent the boat shoreward with all the strength of her brown arms, while the one in the water held on to the canoe and was thus towed back, where half the Indian village had now swarmed to receive them.

"She's got sand and sense," and Dan nodded his appreciation of the towing process; "for, chilled as she must be, the canoe would more than likely have turned over if she had tried to climb into it. Look at the pow-wow they are kicking up! That little red devil must count for big stakes with them."

"But the woman who swam after him. See! they try to stand her on her feet, but she can't walk. There! she's on the ground again. I'd give half my supper to know if she has killed herself with that ice-bath."

"Maybe you can eat all your supper and find out, too," observed the other, with a shrug of his shoulders, and a quizzical glance at his companion, "unless even the glimpse of a petticoat has chased away your appetite. You had better take some advice from an old man, Max, and swear off approaching females in this country, for the specimens you'll find here aren't things to make you proud they're human."

"An old man!" repeated Mr. Lyster with a smile of derision. "You must be pretty near twenty-eight years old-aren't you, Dan? and just about five years older than myself. And what airs you do assume in consequence! With all the weight of those years," he added, slowly, "I doubt, Mr. Dan Overton, if you have really *lived* as much as I have."

One glance of the dark eyes was turned on the speaker for an instant, and then the old felt hat again shaded them as he continued watching the group on the far shore. The swimmer had been picked up by a stalwart Indian woman, and was carried bodily up to one of the lodges, while another squaw-evidently the mother-carried the little redskin who had caused all the commotion.

"I suppose, by living, you mean the life of settlements-or, to condense the question still more, the life of cities," continued Overton, stretching himself lazily on the bank. "You mean the life of a certain set in one certain city-New York, for instance," and he grinned at the expression of impatience on the face of the other. "Yes, I reckon New York is about the one, and a certain part of the town to live in. A certain gang of partners, who have a certain man to make their clothes and boots and hats, and stamp his name on the inside of them, so that other folks can see, when you take off your coat, or your hat, or your gloves, that they were made at just the right place. This makes you a man worth knowing-isn't that about the idea? And in the afternoon, at just about the right hour, you rig yourself out in a certain cut of coat, and stroll for an hour or so on a certain street! In the evening-if a man wants to understand just what it is to live-he must get into other clothes and drop into the theater, making a point of being introduced to any heavy swell within reach, so you can speak of it afterward, you know. Just as your chums like to say they had a supper with a pretty actress, after the curtain went down; but they don't go into details, and own up that the 'actress' maybe never did anything on a stage but walk on in armor and carry a banner. Oh, scowl if you want to! Of course it sounds shoddy when a trapper outlines it; but it doesn't seem shoddy to the people who live like that. Then, about the time that all good girls are asleep, it is just the hour for a supper to be ordered, at just the right place for the wine to be good, and the dishes served in A1 shape, with a convenient waiter who knows how dim to make the lights, and how to efface himself, and let you wait on your 'lady' with your own hands. And she'll go home wearing a ring of yours-two, if you have them; and you'll wake up at noon next day, and think what a jolly time you had, but with your head so muddled that you can't remember where it was you were to meet her the next night, or whether it was the next night that her husband was to be home, and she couldn't see you at all." Overton rolled over on his face and grunted disdainfully, saying: "That's about the style of thing you call *living*, don't you, sonny?"

"Great Scott, Dan!" and the "sonny" addressed stared at him in perplexity, "one never knows what to expect of you. Of course there is *some* truth in the sketch you make; but-but I thought you had never ranged to the East?"

"Did you? Well, I don't look as if I'd ever ranged beyond the timber, do I?" and he stretched out his long legs with their shabby coverings, and stuck his fingers through a hole in his hat. "This outfit doesn't look as if the hands of a Broadway tailor had ever touched it. But, my boy, the sketch you speak of would be just as true to life among a certain set in any large city of the States; only in the West, or even in the South, those ambitious sports would know enough to buy a horse on their own judgment, if they wanted to ride. Or would bet on the races without hustling around to find some played-out jockey who would give them tips."

"Well, to say the least, your opinion is not very flattering to us," remarked the young man, moodily. "You've got some grudge against the East, I guess."

"Grudge? Not any. And you're all right, Max. You will find thousands willing to keep to your idea of life, so we won't split on that wedge. My old stepdad would chime in with you if he were here. He prates about civilization and Eastern culture till I get weary sometimes. Culture! Wait till you see him. He's all right in his way, of course; but as I cut loose from home when only fifteen, and never ran across the old man again until two years ago-well, you see, I can make my estimates in that direction without being biased by family feeling. And I reckon he does the same thing. I don't know what to expect when I go back this time; but, from signs around camp when I left, I wouldn't be surprised if he presented me with a stepmother on my return."

"A stepmother? Whew!" whistled the other. "Well, that shows there are some white women in your region, anyway."

"Oh, yes, we have several. This particular one is a Pennsylvania product; talks through her nose, and eats with her knife, and will maybe try to make eyes at you and keep you in practice. But she is a good, square woman; simply one of the many specimens that drift out here. Came up from Helena with the 'boom,' and started a milliner store —a milliner store in the bush, mind you! But after the Indians had bought all the bright feathers and artificial flowers, she changed her sign, and keeps an eating-house now. It is the high-toned corner of the camp. She can cook some; and I reckon that's what catches the old man."

"Any more interesting specimens like that?"

"Not like that," returned Overton; "but there are some more."

Then he arose, and stood listening to sounds back in the wild forests.

"I hear the 'cayuse' bell," he remarked; "so the others are coming. We'll go back up to the camp, and, after 'chuck,' we'll go over and give you a nearer view of the tribe on the other shore, if you want to add them to the list of your sight-seeing."

"Certainly I do. They'll be a relief after the squads of railroad section hands we've been having for company lately. They knocked all the romance out of the wildly beautiful country we've been coming through since we left the Columbia River."

"Come back next year; then a boat will be puffing up here to the landing, and you can cross to the Columbia in a few hours, for the road will be completed then."

"And you-will you be here then?"

"Well-yes; I reckon so. I never anchor anywhere very long; but this country suits me, and the company seems to need me."

The young fellow looked at him and laughed, and dropped his hand on the broad shoulder with a certain degree of affection.

"Seems to need you?" he repeated. "Well, Mr. Dan Overton, if the day ever comes when *I'm* necessary to the welfare of a section as large as a good-sized State, I hope I'll know enough to appreciate my own importance."

"Hope you will," said Overton, with a kindly smile. "No reason why you should not be of use. Every man with a fair share of health and strength ought to be of use somewhere."

"Yes, that sounds all right and is easy to grasp, if you have been brought up with the idea. But suppose you had been trained by a couple of maiden aunts who only thought to give you the manners of a gentleman, and leave you their money to get through the world with? I guess, under such circumstances, you, too, might have settled into the feathery nest prepared for you, and thought you were doing your duty to the world if you were only ornamental," and the dubious smile on his really handsome face robbed the speech of any vanity.

"You're all right, I tell you," returned the other. "Don't growl at yourself so much. You'll find your work and buckle down to it, some of these days. Maybe you'll find it out here-who knows? Of course Mr. Seldon would see to it that you got any post you would want in this district."

"Yes, he's a jolly old fellow, and has shown me a lot of favors. Seems to me relatives mean more to folks out here than they do East, because so few have their families or relatives along,

I guess. If it had not been for Seldon, I rather think I would not have had the chance of this wild trip with you."

"Likely not. I don't generally want a tenderfoot along when I've work to do. No offense, Max; but they are too often a hindrance. Now that you have come, though, I'll confess I'm glad of it. The lonely trips over this wild region tend to make a man silent —a bear among people when he does reach a camp. But we've talked most of the time, and I reckon I feel the better of it. I know I'll miss you when I go over this route again. You'll be on your way East by that time."

The "cayuse" bell sounded nearer and nearer, and directly from the dense forest a packhorse came stepping with care over the fallen logs, where the sign of a trail was yet dim to any eyes but those of a woodsman. A bell at its neck tinkled as it walked, and after it four others followed, all with heavy loads bound to their backs. It looked strange to see the patient animals thus walk without guide or driver through the dense timber of the mountains; but a little later voices were heard, and two horsemen came out of the shadows of the wood, and followed the horses upward along the bank of the river to where a little stream of fresh water tumbled down to the Kootenai. There a little camp was located, an insignificant gathering of tents, but one that meant a promising event to the country, for it was to be the connecting point of the boats that would one day float from the States on the river, and the railroad that would erelong lead westward over the trail from which the packhorses were bringing supplies.

The sun was setting and all the ripples of the river shone red in its reflected light. Forests of pine loomed up black and shadowy above the shores; and there, higher up-up where the snow was, all tips of the river range were tinged a warm pink, and where the shadows lay, the lavender and faint purples drifted into each other, and bit by bit crowded the pink line higher and higher until it dared touch only the topmost peaks with its lingering kiss.

Lyster halted to look over the wild beauty of the wilderness, and from the harmony of river and hills and sky his eyes turned to Overton.

"You are right, Dan," he said, with an appreciative smile, a smile that opened his lips and showed how perfect the mouth was under the brown mustache —"you are right enough to keep close to all these beauties. You seem in some way to belong to them-not that you are so much 'a thing of beauty' yourself," and the smile widened a little; "but you have in you all the strength of the hills and the patience of the wilderness. You know what I mean."

"Yes, I guess so," answered Overton. "You want some one to spout verses to or make love to, and there is no subject handy. I can make allowances for you, though. Those tendencies are apt to stick to a man for about a year after a trip to Southern California. I don't know whether it's the girls down there, or the wine that is accountable for it; but whatever it is, you have been back from there only three months. You've three-quarters of a year to run yet-maybe more; for I've a notion that you have a leaning in that direction even in your most sensible moments."

"H'm! You must have made a trip to that wine country yourself sometime," observed Lyster. "Your theory suggests practice. Were there girls and wine there then?"

"Plenty," returned Overton, briefly. "Come on. There's the cook shouting supper."

"And after supper we're to go over to the Kootenai camp. Say! what is the meaning of that name, anyway? You know all their jargons up here; do you know that, too?"

"Nobody does, I reckon; there are lots of theories flying around. The generally accepted one is that they were called the '*Court Nez*' by the French trappers long ago, and that Kootenai is the result, after generations of Indian pronunciation. They named the '*Nez Perces*,' too-the 'pierced noses,' you know; but that name has kept its meaning better. You'll find the trail of the French all through the Indian tribes up here."

"Think that was a Frenchwoman in the river back there? You said she was white."

"Yes, I did. But it's generally the Frenchmen you find among the reds, and not the women; though I do know some square white women across the line who have married educated Indians."

"But they are generally a lazy, shiftless set?"

The tone was half inquiring, and Overton grimaced and smiled.

"They are not behind the rest, when it comes to a fight," he answered. "And as to lazy-well, there are several colors of people who are that, under some circumstances. I have an Indian friend across in the States, who made eight thousand dollars in a cattle deal last year, and didn't sell out, either. Now, when you and I can do as well on capital we've earned ourselves, then maybe we'll have a right to criticise some of the rest for indolence. But you can't do much to improve Indians, or any one else, by penning them up in so many square miles and bribing them to be good. The Indian cattleman I speak of kept clear of the reservation, and after drifting around for a while, settled down to the most natural civilized calling possible to an Indian-stock-raising. Dig in the ground? No; they won't do much of that, just at first. But I've eaten some pretty good garden truck they've raised."

Lyster whistled and arched his handsome brows significantly.

"So your sympathies run in that direction, do they? Is there a Kootenai Pocahontas somewhere in the wilderness accountable for your ideas? That is about the only ground I could excuse you on, for I think they are beastly, except in pictures."

They had reached a gathering of men who were seated at a table in the open air-some long boards laid on trestles.

Overton and his friend were called to seats at the head of the table, where the "boss" of the construction gang sat. The rough pleasantries of the men, and the way they made room for him, showed that the big bronzed ranger was a favorite visitor along the "works."

They looked with some curiosity at his more finely garbed companion, but he returned their regard with a good deal of careless audacity, and won their liking by his independence. But in the midst of the social studies he was making of them, he heard Overton say:

"And you have not heard of a white girl in this vicinity?"

"Never a girl. Are you looking for one? Old Akkomi, the Indian, has gone into camp across the river, and he might have a red one to spare."

"Perhaps," agreed Overton. "He's an old acquaintance of mine —a year old. But I'm not looking for red girls just now, and I'm going to tell the old man to keep the families clear of your gang, too." Then to Lyster he remarked:

"Whether these people know it or not, there is a white girl in the Indian camp —a young girl, too; and before we sleep, we'll see who she is."

Chapter II
In the Lodge of Akkomi

The earliest stars had picked their way through the blue canopy, when the men from the camp crossed over to the fishing village of the Indians; for it was only when the moon of May, or of June, lightened the sky that the red men moved their lodges to the north-their winter resort was the States.

"Dan-umph! How?" grunted a tall brave lounging at the opening of the tepee. He arose, and took his pipe from his lips, glancing with assumed indifference at the handsome young stranger, though, in reality, Black Bow was not above curiosity.

"How?" returned Overton, and reached out his hand. "I am glad to see that the lodges by the river hold friends instead of strangers," he continued. "This, too, is a friend-one from the big ocean where the sun rises. We call him Max."

"Umph! How?" and Lyster glanced in comical dismay at his friend as his hand was grasped by one so dirty, so redolent of cooked fish, as the one Black Bow was gracious enough to offer him.

Thereupon they were asked to seat themselves on the blanket of that dignitary-no small favor in the eyes of an Indian. Overton talked of the fish, and the easy markets there would soon be for them, when the boats and the cars came pushing swiftly through the forests; of the many wolves Black Bow had killed in the winter past; of how well the hunting shirt of deer-skin had worn that Black Bow's squaw had sold him when he met them last on the trail; of any and many things but the episode of the evening of which Lyster was waiting to hear.

As the dusk fell, Lyster fully appreciated the picturesque qualities of the scene before him. The many dogs and their friendly attentions disturbed him somewhat, but he sat there feeling much as if in a theater; for those barbarians, in their groupings, reminded him of bits of stage setting he had seen at some time or another.

One big fire was outside the lodges, and over it a big kettle hung, and the steam drifted up and over the squaws and children gathered there. Some of them came over and looked at him, and several grunted at Overton. Black Bow would order them away once in a while with a lordly "Klehowyeh," much as he did the dogs; and, like the dogs, they would promptly return, and gaze with half-veiled eyes at the elegance of the high boots covering the shapely limbs of Mr. Lyster.

The men were away on a hunt, Black Bow explained; only he and Akkomi, the head chief, had not gone. Akkomi was growing very old and no longer led the hunts; therefore a young chief must ever be near to his call; so Black Bow was also absent from the hunt.

"We stay until two suns rise," and Overton pointed across to the camp of the whites. "To-morrow I would ask that Black Bow and the chief Akkomi eat at our table. This is the kins-man —*tillicums* —of the men who make the great work where the mines are and the boats that are big and the cars that go faster than the horses run. He wants that the two great chiefs of the Kootenais eat of his food before he goes back again to the towns of the white people."

Lyster barely repressed a groan as he heard the proposal made, but Overton was blandly oblivious of the appealing expression of his friend; the thing he was interested in was to bring Black Bow to a communicative mood, for not a sign could he discover of a white woman in the camp, though he was convinced there was or had been one there.

The invitation to eat succeeded. Black Bow would tell the old chief of their visit; maybe he would talk with them now, but he was not sure. The chief was tired, his thoughts had been troubled that day. The son of his daughter had been near death in the river there. He was only a child, and could not swim yet; a young squaw of the white people had kept him from drowning, and the squaw of Akkomi had been making medicines for her ever since.

"Young squaw! Where comes a white squaw from to the Kootenai lakes?" asked Overton, incredulously. "Half white, half red, maybe."

"White," affirmed their host. "Where? Humph! Where come the sea-birds from that get lost when they fly too far from shore? Kootenai not know, but they drop down sometimes by the rivers. So this one has come. She has talked with Akkomi; but he tell nothing; only maybe we will all dance a dance some day, and then she will be Kootenai, too."

"*Adopt* her," muttered Overton, and glanced at Lyster; but that gentleman's attention was given at the moment to a couple of squaws who walked past and looked at him out of the corners of their eyes, so he missed that portion of Black Bow's figurative information.

"I have need to see the chief Akkomi," said Overton, after a moment's thought. "It would be well if I could see him before sleeping. Of these," producing two colored handkerchiefs, "will you give one to him, that he may know I am in earnest, the other will you not wear for Dan?"

The brave grunted a pleased assent, and carefully selecting the handkerchief with the brightest border, thrust it within his hunting shirt. He then proceeded to the lodge of the old chief, bearing the other ostentatiously in his hand, as though he were carrying the fate of his nation in the gaudy bit of silk and cotton weaving.

"What are you trading for?" asked Lyster, and looked like protesting, when Overton answered:

"An audience with Akkomi."

"Great Cæsar! is one of that sort not enough? I'll never feel that my hand is clean again until I can give it a bath with some sort of disinfectant stuff. Now there's another one to greet! I'll not be able to eat fish again for a year. Why didn't luck send the old vagabond hunting with the rest? I can endure the women, for they don't sprawl around you and shake hands with you. Just tell me what I'm to donate for being allowed to bask in the light of Akkomi's countenance? Haven't a thing over here but some cigars."

Overton only laughed silently, and gave more attention to the lodge of Akkomi than to his companion's disgust. When Black Bow emerged from the tent, he watched him sharply as he approached, to learn from the Indian's countenance, if possible, the result of the message.

"If he sends a royal request that we partake of supper, I warn you, I shall be violently and immediately taken ill-too ill to eat," whispered Lyster, meaningly.

Black Bow seated himself, filled his pipe, handed it to a squaw to light, and then sent several puffs of smoke skyward, ere he said:

"Akkomi is old, and the time for his rest has come. He says the door of his lodge is open-that Dan may go within and speak what there is to say. But the stranger-he must wait till the day comes again."

"Snubbed me, by George!" laughed Lyster. "Well, am I then to wait outside the portals, and be content with the crumbs you choose to carry out to me?"

"Oh, amuse yourself," returned Overton, carelessly, and was on his feet at once. "I leave you to the enjoyment of Black Bow."

A moment later he reached the lodge of the old chief and, without ceremony, walked in to the center of it.

A slight fire was there, —just enough to kill the dampness of the river's edge, and over it the old squaw of Akkomi bent, raking the dry sticks, until the flames fluttered upward and outlined the form of the chief, coiled on a pile of skins and blankets against the wall.

He nodded a welcome, said "Klehowyeh," and motioned with his pipe that his visitor should be seated on another pile of clothing and bedding, near his own person.

Then it was that Overton discovered a fourth person in the shadows opposite him-the white woman he had been curious about.

And it was not a woman at all, —only a girl of perhaps sixteen years instead-who shrank back into the gloom, and frowned on him with great, dark, unchildlike eyes, and from under brows wide and straight as those of a sculptor's model for a young Greek god; for, if any beauty of feature was hers, it was boyish in its character. As for beauty of expression, she assuredly did not cultivate that. The curved red mouth was sullen and the eyes antagonistic.

One sharp glance showed Overton all this, and also that there was no Indian blood back of the rather pale cheek.

"So you got out of the water alive, did you?" he asked, in a matter of fact way, as though the dip in the river was a usual thing to see.

She raised her eyes and lowered them again with a sort of insolence, as though to show her resentment of the fact that he addressed her at all.

"I rather guess I'm alive," she answered, curtly, and the visitor turned to the chief.

"I saw to-day your child's child in the waters of the Kootenai. I saw the white friend lifting him up out of the river, and fighting with death for him. It would have been a good thing for a man to do, Akkomi. I crossed the water to-night, to see if your boy is well once more, or if there is any way I can do service for the young white squaw who is your friend."

The old Indian smoked in silence for a full minute. He was a sharp-eyed, shrewd-faced old fellow. When he spoke, it was in the Chinook jargon, and with a significant nod toward the girl, as though she was not to hear or understand his words.

"It is true, the son of my daughter is again alive. The breath was gone when the young squaw reached him, but she was in time. Dan know the young squaw, maybe?"

"No, Akkomi. Who?"

The old fellow shook his head, as if not inclined to give the information required.

"She tell white men if she want white men to know," he observed. "The heart of Akkomi is heavy for her-heavy. A lone trail is a hard one for a squaw in the Kootenai land —a white squaw who is young. She rests here, and may eat of our meat all her days if she will."

Overton glanced again at the girl, who was evidently, from the words of the chief, following some lone trail through the wilderness, —a trail starting whence, and leading whither? All that he could read was that no happiness kept her company.

"But the life of a red squaw in the white men's camps is a bad life," resumed the old man, after a season of deliberation; "and the life of the white squaw in the red man's village is bad as well."

Overton nodded gravely, but said nothing. By the manner of Akkomi, he perceived that some important thought was stirring in the old man's mind, and that it would develop into speech all the sooner if not hurried.

"Of all the men of the white camps it is you Akkomi is gladdest to talk to this day," continued the chief, after another season of silence; "for you, Dan, talk with a tongue that is straight, and you go many times where the great towns are built."

"The words of Akkomi are true words," assented Overton, "and my ears listen to hear what he will say."

"Where the white men live is where this young white squaw should live," said Akkomi, and the listening squaw of Akkomi grunted assent. It was easy to read that she looked with little favor on the strange white girl within their lodge. To be sure, Akkomi was growing old; but the wife of Akkomi had memories of his lusty youth and of various wars she had been forced to wage on ambitious squaws who fancied it would be well to dwell in the lodge of the head chief.

And remembering those days, though so long past, the old squaw was sorely averse to the adoption dance for the white girl who lay on their blankets, and thought it good, indeed, that she go to live in the villages of the white people.

Overton nodded gravely.

"You speak wisely, Akkomi," he said.

Glancing at the girl, Dan noted that she was leaning forward and gazing at him intently. Her face gave him the uncomfortable feeling that she perhaps knew what they were talking of, but she dropped back into the shadows again, and he dismissed the idea as improbable, for white girls were seldom versed in the lore of Indian jargon.

He waited a bit for Akkomi to continue, but as that dignitary evidently thought he had said enough, if Overton chose to interpret it correctly, the white man asked:

"Would it please Akkomi that I, Dan, should lead the young squaw where white families are?"

"Yes. It is that I thought of when I heard your name. I am old. I cannot take her. She has come a long way on a trail for that which has not been found, and her heart is so heavy she does not care where the next trail leads her. So it seems to Akkomi. But she saved the son of my daughter, and I would wish good to her. So, if she is willing, I would have her go to your people."

"If she is willing!" Overton doubted it, and thought of the scowl with which she had answered him before. After a little hesitation, he said: "It shall be as you wish. I am very busy now, but to serve one who is your friend I will take time for a few days. Do you know the girl?"

"I know her, and her father before her. It was long ago, but my eyes are good. I remember. She is good-girl not afraid."

"Father! Where is her father?"

"In the grave blankets-so she tells me."

"And her name-what is she called?"

But Akkomi was not to be stripped of all his knowledge by questions. He puffed at the pipe in silence and then, as Overton was as persistently quiet as himself, he finally said:

"The white girl will tell to you the things she wants you to know, if she goes with your people. If she stays here, the lodge of Akkomi has a blanket for her."

The girl was now face downward on the couch of skins, and when Overton wished to speak to her he crossed over and gently touched her shoulder. He was almost afraid she was weeping, because of the position; but when she raised her head he saw no signs of tears.

"Why do you come to me?" she demanded. "I ain't troubling the white folks any. Huh! I didn't even stop at their camp across the river."

The grunt of disdain she launched at him made him smile. It was so much more like that of an Indian than a white person, yet she was white, despite all the red manners she chose to adopt.

"No, I reckon you didn't stop at the white camp, else I'd have heard of it. But as you're alone in this country, don't you think you'd be better off where other white women live?"

He spoke in the kindliest tone, and she only bit her lip and shrugged her angular shoulders.

"I will see that you are left with good people," he continued; "so don't be afraid about that. I'm Dan Overton. Akkomi will tell you I'm square. I know where there's a good sort of white woman who would be glad to have you around, I guess."

"Is it your wife?" she demanded, with the same sullen, suspicious wrinkle between her brows.

His face paled ever so little and he took a step backward, as he looked at her through narrowing eyes.

"No, miss, it is not my wife," he said, curtly, and then walked back and sat down beside the old chief. "In fact, she isn't any relation to me, but she's the nearest white woman I know to leave you with. If you want to go farther, I reckon I can help you. Anyway, you come along across the line to Sinna Ferry, and I feel sure you'll find friends there."

She looked at him unbelievingly. "She's used to being deceived," decided Overton, as she watched him; but he stood her gaze without flinching and smiled back at her.

"Do you live there?" she asked again, in that abrupt, uncivil way, and turned her eyes to Akkomi, as though to read his countenance as well as that of the white man, —a difficult thing, however, for the head of the old man was again shrouded in his blanket, from which only the tip of his nose and his pipe protruded.

In a far corner the squaw of Akkomi was crouched, her bead-like eyes glittering with a watchful interest, as they turned from one to the other of the speakers, and missed no tone or gesture of the two so strangely met within her tepee. Overton noticed her once, and thought what a subject for a picture Lyster would think the whole thing-at long range. He would want to view it from the door of the tepee, and not from the interior.

But the questioning eyes of the girl were turned to him, and remembering them, he said:

"Live there? Well, as much —a little more than I do anywhere else of late. I am to go there in two days; and if you are ready to go, I will take you and be glad to do it."

"You don't know anything about me," she protested.

He smiled, for her tone told him she was yielding.

"Oh, no-not much," he confessed, "but you can tell me, you know."

"I know I can, but I won't," she said, doggedly. "So I guess you'll just move on down to the ferry without me. He knows, and he says I can live here if I want to. I'm tired of the white people. A girl alone is as well with the Indians. I think so, anyway, and I guess I'll try camping with them. They don't ask a word-only what I tell myself. They don't even care whether I have a name; they would give me one if I hadn't."

"A suitable name-and a nice Indian one-for you would be, 'The Water Rat' or 'The Girl Who Swims.' Maybe," he added, "they will hunt you up one more like poetry in books (the only place one finds poetry in Indians), 'Laughing Eyes,' or 'The One Who Smiles.' Oh, yes, they'll find you a name fast enough. So will I, if you have none. But you have, haven't you?"

"Yes, I have, and it's 'Tana," said the girl, piqued into telling by the humorous twinkle in the man's eyes.

"'Tana? Why, that itself is an Indian name, is it not? And you are not Indian."

"It's 'Tana, for short. Montana is my name."

"It is? Well, you've got a big name, little girl, and as it is proof that you belong to the States, don't you think you'd better let me take you back there?"

"I ain't going down among white folks who will turn up their noses at me, just because you found me among these redskins," she answered, scowling at him and speaking very deliberately. "I know how proud decent women are, and I ain't going among any other sort and that's settled."

"Why, you poor little one, what sort of folks have you been among?" he asked, compassionately. Her stubborn antagonism filled him with more of pity than tears could have done; it showed so much suspicion, that spoke of horrible associations, and she was so young!

"See here! No one need know I found you among the Indians. I can make up some story-say you're the daughter of an old partner of mine. It'll be a lie, of course, and I don't approve of lies. But if it makes you feel better, it goes just the same! Partner dies, you know, and I fall heir to you. See? Then, of course, I pack you back to civilization, where you can-well, go to school or something. How's that?"

She did not answer, only looked at him strangely, from under those straight brows. He felt an angry impatience with her that she did not take the proposal differently, when it was so plainly for her good he was making schemes.

"As to your father being dead-that part of it would be true enough, I suppose," he continued; "for Akkomi told me he was dead."

"Yes-yes, he is dead," she said coldly, and her tones were so even no one would imagine it was her father she spoke of.

"Your mother, too?"

"My mother, too," she assented. "But I told you I wasn't going to talk any more about myself, and I ain't. If I can't go to your Sunday-school without a pedigree, I'll stop where I am-that's all."

She spoke with the independence of a boy, and it was, perhaps, her independence that induced the man to be persistent.

"All right, 'Tana," he said cheerfully. "You come along on your own terms, so long as you get out of these quarters. I'll tell the dead partner story-only the partner must have a name, you know. Montana is a good name, but it is only a half one, after all. You can give me another, I reckon."

She hesitated a little and stared at the glowing embers of the lodge fire. He wondered if she was deciding to tell him a true one, or if she was trying to think of a fictitious one.

"Well?" he said at last.

Then she looked up, and the sullen, troubled, unchildlike eyes made him troubled for her sake.

"Rivers is a good name-Rivers?" she asked, and he nodded his head, grimly.

"That will do," he agreed. "But you give it just because you were baptized in the river this evening, don't you?"

"I guess I give it because I haven't any other I intend to be called by," she answered.

"And you will cut loose from this outfit?" he asked. "You will come with me, little girl, across there into God's country, where you must belong."

"You won't let them look down on me?"

"If any one looks down on you, it will be because of something you will do in the future, 'Tana," he said, looking at her very steadily. "Understand that, for I will settle it that no one knows how I came across you. And you will go?"

"I —will go."

"Come, now! that's a good decision-the best you could have made, little girl; and I'll take care of you as though you were a cargo of gold. Shake hands on the agreement, won't you?"

She held out her hand, and the old squaw in the corner grunted at the symbol of friendship. Akkomi watched them with his glittering eyes, but made no sign.

It surely was a strange beginning to a strange friendship.

"You poor little thing!" said Overton, compassionately, as she half shrank from the clasp of his fingers. The tender tone broke through whatever wall of indifference she had built about her, for she flung herself face downward on the couch, and sobbed passionately, refusing to speak again, though Overton tried in vain to calm her.

Chapter III
The Image-Maker

The world was a night older ere Dan Overton informed Lyster that they would have an addition of one to their party when they continued their journey into the States.

On leaving the village of Akkomi but little conversation was to be had from Dan. In vain did his friend endeavor to learn something of the white squaw who swam so well. He simply kept silence, and looked with provoking disregard on all attempts to surprise him into disclosures.

But when the camp breakfast was over, and he had evidently thought out his plan of action, he told Lyster over the sociable influence of a pipe, that he was going over to the camp of Akkomi again.

"The fact, is, Max, that the girl we saw yesterday is to go across home with us. She's a ward of mine."

"What!" demanded Max, sitting bolt upright in his amazement, "a ward of yours? You say that as though you had several scattered among the tribes about here. So it is a Kootenai Pocahontas! What good advice was it you gave me yesterday about keeping clear of Selkirk Range females? And now you are deliberately gathering one to yourself, and I will be the unnecessary third on our journey home. Dan! Dan! I wouldn't have thought it of you!"

Overton listened in silence until the first outburst was over.

"Through?" he asked, carelessly; "well, then, it isn't a Pocahontas; it isn't an Indian at all. It is only a little white girl whose father was-was an old partner. Well, he's gone 'over the range' —dead, you know-and the girl is left to hustle for herself. Naturally, she heard I was in this region, and as none of her daddy's old friends were around but me, she just made her camp over there with the Kootenais, and waited till I reached the river again. She'll go with me down to Sinna; and if she hasn't any other home in prospect, I'll just locate her there with Mrs. Huzzard, the milliner-cook, for the present. Now, that's the story."

"And a very pretty little one it is, too," agreed Mr. Max. "For a backwoodsman, who is not supposed to have experience, it is very well put together. Oh, don't frown like that! I'll believe she's your granddaughter, if you say so," and he laughed in wicked enjoyment at Overton's flushed face. "It's all right, Dan. I congratulate you. But I wouldn't have thought it."

"I suppose, now," remarked Dan, witheringly, "that by all these remarks and giggles you are trying to be funny. Is that it? Well, as the fun of it is not visible to me yet, I'll just keep my laughter till it is. In the meantime, I'm going over to call on my ward, Miss Rivers, and you can hustle for funny things around camp until I come back."

"Oh, say, Dan, don't be vindictive. Take me along, won't you? I'll promise to be good —'pon honor I will. I'll do penance for any depraved suspicions I may have indulged in. I'll —I'll even shake hands again with Black Bow, there! Beyond that, I can think of no more earnest testimony of repentance."

"I shall go by myself," decided Overton. "So make a note of it, if you see the young lady before to-morrow, it will be because she specially requests it. Understand? I'm not going to have her bothered by people who are only curious; not but that she can take her own part, as you'll maybe learn later. But she was too upset to talk much last night. So I'll go over and finish this morning, and in the meantime, this side of the river is plenty good enough for you."

"Is it?" murmured Mr. Lyster, as he eyed the stalwart form of the retreating guardian, who was so bent on guarding. "Well, it would do my heart good, anyway, to fasten another canoe right alongside of yours where you land over there, and I shouldn't be surprised if I did it."

Thus it happened that while Overton was skimming upward across the river, his friend, on mischief bent, was getting a canoe ready to launch. A few minutes after Overton had disappeared toward the Indian village, the second canoe danced lightly over the Kootenai, and the occupant laughed to himself, as he anticipated the guardian's surprise.

"Not that I care in the least about seeing the dismal damsel he has to look after," mused Lyster. "In fact, I'm afraid she'll be a nuisance, and spoil our jolly good time all the way home.

But he is so refreshingly earnest about everything. And as he doesn't care a snap for girls in general, it is all the more amusing that it is he who should have a charge of that sort left on his hands. I'd like to know what she looks like. Common, I dare say, for the ultra refined do not penetrate these wilds to help blaze trails; and she swam like a boy."

When he reached the far shore, no one was in sight. With satisfied smiles, he fastened his canoe to that of Overton, and then cast about for some place to lie in wait for that selfish personage and surprise him on his return.

He had no notion of going up to the village, for he wanted only to keep close enough to trace Overton. Hearing children's voices farther along the shore, he sauntered that way, thinking to see Indian games, perhaps. When he came nearer, he saw they were running races.

The contestants were running turn about, two at a time. Each victory was greeted with shrill cries of triumph. He also noticed that each victor returned to a figure seated close under some drooping bushes, and each time a hand was reached out and some little prize was given to the winner. Then, with shouts of rejoicing, a new race was planned.

As the stranger stood back of the thick bushes, watching the stretch of level beach and the half-naked, childish figures, he grew curious to see who that one person just out of sight was.

One thing at last he did discover-that the hand awarding the prizes was tanned like the hand of a boy, but that it certainly had white blood instead of red in its veins. What if it should be the ward?

Elated, and full of mischief, he crept closer. If only he could be able to give Overton a description of her when Overton came back to the canoe!

At first all he could see were the hands-hands playing with a bit of wet clay-or so it seemed to him.

Then his curiosity was more fully aroused when out of the mass a recognizable form was apparent —a crudely modeled head and shoulders of a decided Indian character.

Lyster was so close now that he could notice how small the hands were, and to see that the head bent above them was covered with short, brown, loosely curled hair, and that there was just a tinge of reddish gold on it, where the sunlight fell.

A race was just ended, and one of the little young savages trotted up where the image-maker was. The small hand was again reached out, and he could see that the prize the little Indian had raced for was a blue bead of glass. He could see, also, that the owner of the hand had the face of a girl —a girl with dark eyes, and long lashes that touched the rather pale cheeks. Her mouth was deliciously saucy, with its bow-like curve, and its clear redness. She said something he did not understand, and the children scampered away to resume the endless races, while she continued the manipulation of the clay, frowning often when it would not take the desired form.

Then one of the sharp-eyed little redskins left his companions and slipped back to her, and said something in a tone so low it was almost a whisper.

She turned at once and looked directly into the thicket, back of which Lyster stood.

"What are you watching for?" she demanded. "I don't like people who are afraid to show themselves."

"Well, I'll try to change that as quickly as I can," Lyster retorted, and circling the clump of bushes, he stood before her with his hat in his hand, looking smilingly audacious as she frowned on him.

But the frown faded as she looked; perhaps because 'Tana had never seen any one quite so handsome in all her life, or so fittingly and picturesquely dressed, for Mr. Maxwell Lyster was artist enough to make the most of his many good points and to exhibit them all with charming unconsciousness.

"I hope you will like me better here than across there," he said, with a smile that was contagious. "You see, I was too shy to come forward at first, and then I was afraid to interrupt your modeling. It is very good."

"You don't look shy," she said, combatively, and drew the clay image back, where he could not look at it. She was not at all sure that he was not laughing at her, and she covered her worn shoes with the skirt of her dress, feeling suddenly very poor and shabby in the light of his eyes. She had not felt at all like that when Overton looked at her in Akkomi's lodge.

"You would not be so unfriendly if you knew who I am," he ventured meekly. "Of course, I—Max Lyster-don't amount to much, but I happen to be Dan Overton's friend, and with your permission, I hope to continue with him to Sinna Ferry, and with you as well; for I am sure you must be Miss Rivers."

"If you're sure, that settles it, I suppose," she returned. "So he-he told you about me?"

"Oh, yes; we are chums, as you will learn. Then I was so fortunate as to see your brave swim after that child yesterday. You don't look any the worse for it."

"No, I'm not."

"I suppose, now, you thought that little dip a welcome break in the monotony of camp-life, while you were waiting for Dan."

She looked at him in a quick, questioning way he thought odd.

"Oh-yes. While I was waiting for-Dan," she said in a queer tone, and bent her head over the clay image.

He thought her very interesting with her boyish air, her brusqueness, and independence. Yet, despite her savage surroundings, a certain amount of education was visible in her speech and manner, and her face had no stamp of ignorance on it.

The young Kootenais silently withdrew from their races, and gathered watchfully close to the girl. Their nearness was a discomfiting thing to Lyster, for it was not easy to carry on a conversation under their watchful eyes.

"You gave them prizes, did you not?" he asked. "How much wealth must one offer to get them to run?"

"Run where?" she returned carelessly, though quietly amused at the scrutiny of the little redskins. They were especially charmed by the glitter of gold mountings on Mr. Lyster's watch-guard.

"Oh, run races-run anywhere," he said.

From a pocket of her blouse she drew forth a few blue beads that yet remained.

"This is all I had to give them, and they run just as fast for one of these as they would for a pony."

"Good enough! I'll have some races for my own edification and comfort," and he drew out some coins. "Will you run for this-run far over there?"

The children looked at the girl. She nodded her head, said a word or two unintelligible to him, but perfectly clear to them; for, with sharp looks at the coins and pleased yells, they leaped away to their racing.

"Now, this is more comfortable," he said. "May I sit down here? Thanks! Now would you mind telling me whose likeness it is you are making in the clay?"

"I guess you know it's nobody's likeness," she answered, and again thrust it back out of sight, her face flushing that he should thus make a jest of her poor efforts. "You've seen real statues, I suppose, and know how they ought to be, but you don't need to look for them in the Purcell Range."

"But, indeed, I am in earnest about your modeling. Won't you believe me?" and the blue eyes looking into her own were so appealing, that she turned away her head half shyly, and a pink flush crept up from her throat. Miss Rivers was evidently not used to eyes with caressive tendencies and they disturbed her, for all her strangely unchildlike character.

"Of course, your work is only in the rough," he continued; "but it is not at all bad, and has real Indian features. And if you have had no teaching—"

"Huh!" and she looked at him with a mirthless smile. "Where'd any one get teaching of that sort along the Columbia River? Of course, there are some gentlemen-officers and such-about the reservations, but not one but would only laugh at such a big girl making doll babies out of mud. No, I had no teaching to do anything but read, and I did read some in a book about a sculptor, and how he made animals and people's faces out of clay. Then I tried."

As she grew communicative, she seemed so much more what she really was in years —a child; and he noticed, with satisfaction, that she looked at him more frankly, while the suspicion faded almost entirely from her face.

"And are you going to develop into a sculptor under Overton's guardianship?" he asked. "You see, he has told me of his good luck."

She made a queer little sound between a laugh and a grunt.

"I'll bet the rest of the blue beads he didn't call it good luck," she returned, looking at him keenly. "Now, honest Injun-did he?"

"Honest Injun! he didn't speak of it as either good or bad luck; simply as a matter of course, that at your father's death you should look him up, and let him know you were alone. Oh, he is a good fellow, Dan is, and glad, I am sure, to be of use to you."

Her lips opened in a little sigh of content, and a swift, radiant smile was given him.

"I'm right glad you say that about him," she answered, "and I guess you know him well, too. Akkomi likes him, and Akkomi's sharp."

The winner of the race here trotted back for the coin, and Lyster showed another one, as an incentive for all to scatter along the beach again. It looked as though the two white people must pay for the grant of privacy on the river-bank.

Having grown more at ease with him, 'Tana resumed again the patting and pressing of the clay, using only a little pointed stick, while Lyster watched, with curiosity, the ingenious way in which she seemed to feel her way to form.

"Have you ever tried to draw?" he asked.

She shook her head.

"Only to copy pictures, like I've seen in some papers, but they never looked right. But I want to do everything like that-to make pictures, and statues, and music, and-oh, all the lovely things there are somewhere, that I've never seen-never will see them, I suppose. Sometimes, when I get to thinking that I never will see them, I just get as ugly as a drunken man, and I don't care if I never do see anything but Indians again. I get so awful reckless. Say!" she said, again with that hard, short laugh, "girls back your way don't get wild like that, do they? They don't talk my way either, I guess."

"Maybe not, and few of them would be able, either, to do what we saw you do in this river yesterday," he said kindly. "Dan is a judge of such things, you know, and he thought you very nervy."

"Nervy? Oh, yes; I guess he'd be nervy himself if he was needed. Say! can you tell me about the camp, or settlement, at this Sinna Ferry? I never was there. He says white women are there. Do you know them?"

Lyster explained his own ignorance of the place, knowing it as he did only through Dan's descriptions.

Then she, from her bit of Indian knowledge, told him Sinna was the old north Indian name for Beaver. Then he got her to tell him other things of the Indian country, things of ghost-haunted places and strange witcheries, with which they confused the game and the fish. He fell to wondering what manner of man Rivers, the partner of Dan, had been, that his daughter had gained such strange knowledge of the wild things. But any attempt to learn or question her history beyond yesterday was always checked in some way or other.

Chapter IV
Dan's Ward

Mr. Max Lyster was not given to the study of deep problems; his habits of thought did not run in that groove. But he did watch the young stranger with unusual interest. Her face puzzled him as much as her presence there.

"I feel as though I had seen you before," he said at last, and her face grew a shade paler. She did not look up, and when she spoke, it was very curtly:

"Where?"

"Oh, I don't know-in fact, I believe it is a resemblance to some one I know that makes me feel that way."

"I look like some one you know?"

"Well, yes, you do —a little —a lady who is a little older than you —a little more of a brunette than you; yet there is a likeness."

"Where does she live-and what is her name?" she asked, with scant ceremony.

"I don't suppose her name would tell you much," he answered. "But it is Miss Margaret Haydon, of Philadelphia."

"Miss Margaret Haydon," she said slowly, almost contemptuously. "So you know her?"

"You speak as though you did," he answered; "and as if you did not like the name, either."

"But you think it's pretty," she said, looking at him sharply. "No, I don't know such swells-don't want to."

"How do you know she is a swell?"

"Oh, there's a man owns big works across the country, and that's his name. I suppose they are all of a lot," she said, indifferently. "Say! are there any girls at Sinna Ferry, any family folks? Dan didn't tell me-only said there was a white woman there, and I could live with her. He hasn't a wife, has he?"

"Dan?" and he laughed at the idea, "well, no. He is very kind to women, but I can't imagine the sort of woman he would marry. He is a queer fish, you know."

"I guess you'll think we're all that up in this wild country," she observed. "Does he know much about books and such things?"

"Such things?"

"Oh, you know! things of the life in the cities, where there's music and theaters. I love the theaters and pictures! and-and-well, everything like that."

Lyster watched her brightening face, and appreciated all the longing in it for the things he liked well himself. And she loved the theaters! All his own boyish enthusiasm of years ago crowded into his memory, as he looked at her.

"You have seen plays, then?" he asked, and wondered where she had seen them along that British Columbia line.

"Seen plays! Yes, in 'Frisco, and Portland, and Victoria-big, real theaters, you know; and then others in the big mining camps. Oh, I just dream over plays, when I do see them, specially when the actresses are pretty. But I mostly like the villains better than the heroes. Don't know why, but I do."

"What! you like to see their wickedness prosper?"

"No —I think not," she said, doubtfully. "But I tell you, the heroes are generally just too good to be live men, that's all. And the villain mostly talks more natural, gets mad, you know, and breaks things, and rides over the lay-out as though he had some nerve in him. Of course, they always make him throw up his hands in the end, and every man in the audience applauds-even the ones who would act just as he does if such a pretty hero was in their way."

"Well, you certainly have peculiar ideas of theatrical personages-for a young lady," decided Lyster, laughing. "And why you have a grievance against the orthodox handsome hero, I can't see."

"He's too good," she insisted, with the little frown appearing between her brows, "and no one is ever started in the play with a fair chance against him. He is always called Willie, where the villain would be called Bill-now, isn't he? Then the girl in the story always falls in love with him at first sight, and that's enough to rile any villain, especially when he wants her himself."

"Oh!" and the face of the young man was a study, as he inspected this wonderful ward of Dan. Whatever he had expected from the young swimmer of the Kootenai, from the welcomed guest of Akkomi, he had not expected this sort of thing.

She was twisting her pretty mouth, with a schoolgirl's earnestness, over a problem, and accenting thus her patient forming of the clay face. She built no barriers up between herself and this handsome stranger, as she had in the beginning with Overton. What she had to say was uttered with all freedom-her likes, her thoughts, her ambitions. At first the fineness and perfection of his apparel had been as grandeur and insolence when contrasted with her own weather-stained, coarse skirt of wool, and her boy's blouse belted with a strap of leather. Even the blue beads-her one feminine bit of adornment-had been stripped from her throat, that she might give some pleasure to the little bronze-tinted runners on the shore. But the gently modulated, sympathetic tones of Lyster and the kindly fellowship in his eyes, when he looked at her, almost made her forget her own shabbiness (all but those hideous coarse shoes!) for he talked to her with the grace of the people in the plays she loved so, and had not once spoken as though to a stray found in the shelter of an Indian camp.

But he did look curious when she expressed those independent ideas on questions over which most girls would blush or appear at least a little conscious.

"So, you would put a veto on love at first sight, would you?" he asked, laughingly. "And the beauty of the hero would not move you at all? What a very odd young lady you would have me think you! I believe love at first sight is generally considered, by your age and sex, the pinnacle of all things hoped for."

A little color did creep into her face at the unnecessary personal construction put on her words. She frowned to hide her embarrassment and thrust out her lips in a manner that showed she had little vanity as to her features and their attractiveness.

"But I don't happen to be a young lady," she retorted; "and we think as we please up here in the bush. Maybe your proper young ladies would be very odd, too, if they were brought up out here like boys."

She arose to her feet, and he saw more clearly then how slight she was; her form and face were much more childish in character than her speech, and the face was looking at him with resentful eyes.

"I'm going back to camp."

"Now, I've offended you, haven't I?" he asked, in surprise. "Really, I did not mean to. Won't you forgive me?"

She dug her heel in the sand and did not answer; but the fact that she remained at all assured him she would relent. He was amused at her quick show of temper. What a prospect for Dan!

"I scarcely know what I said to vex you," he began; but she flashed a sullen look at him.

"You think I'm odd-and-and a nobody; just because I ain't like fine young ladies you know somewheres-like Miss Margaret Haydon," and she dug the sand away with vicious little kicks. "Nice ladies with kid slippers on," she added, derisively, "the sort that always falls in love with the pretty man, the hero. Huh! I've seen some men who were heroes-real ones-and I never saw a pretty one yet."

As she said it, she looked very straight into the very handsome face of Mr. Lyster.

"A young Tartar!" he decided, mentally, while he actually colored at the directness of her gaze and her sweepingly contemptuous opinion of "pretty men."

"I see I'd better vacate your premises since you appear unwilling to forgive me even my unintentional faults," he decided, meekly. "I'm very sorry, I'm sure, and hope you will bear no malice. Of course I —nobody would want you to be different from what you are; so you must not think I meant that. I had hoped you would let me buy that clay bust as a memento of this morning, but I'm afraid to ask favors now. I can only hope that you will speak to me again to-morrow. Until then, good-by."

She raised her eyes sullenly at first, but they dropped, ashamed, before the kindness of his own. She felt coarse and clumsy, and wished she had not been so quick to quarrel. And he was turning away! Maybe he would never speak nicely to her again, and she loved to hear him speak.

Then her hand was thrust out to him, and in it was the little clay model.

"You can have it. I'll give it to you," she said, quite humbly. "It ain't very pretty, but if you like it —"

Thus ended the first of many differences between Dan's ward and Dan's friend.

When Daniel Overton himself came stalking down among the Indian children, looking right and left from under his great slouch hat, he halted suddenly, and with his lips closed somewhat grimly, stood there watching the rather pretty picture before him.

But the prettiness of it did not seem to appeal to him strongly. He looked on the girl's half smiling, drooped face, on Lyster, who held the model and his hat in one hand and, with his handsome blonde head bared, held out his other hand to her, saying something in those low, deferential tones Dan knew so well.

Her hand was given after a little hesitation. When they beheld Dan so near them, the hands were unclasped and each looked confused.

Mr. Lyster was the first to recover, and adjusting his head covering once more, he held up the clay model to view.

"Thought you'd be around before long," he remarked, with a provoking gleam in his eyes. "I really had no hope of meeting Miss Rivers before you this morning; but fortune favors the brave, you know, and fortune sent me right along these sands for my morning walk —a most indulgent fortune, for, look at this! Did you know your ward is an embryo sculptress?"

The older man looked indifferently enough at the exalted bit of clay.

"I leave discoveries of that sort to you. They seem to run in your line more than mine," he answered, briefly. Then he turned to the girl. "Akkomi told me you were here with the children, 'Tana. If you had other company, Akkomi would have made him welcome."

He did not speak unkindly, yet she felt that in some way he was not pleased; and perhaps-perhaps he would change his mind and leave her where he found her! And if so, she might never see-either of their faces again! As the thought came to her, she looked up at Dan in a startled way, and half put out her hand.

"I —I did not know. I don't like the lodges. It is better here by the river. It is *your* friend that came, and I —"

"Certainly. You need not explain. And as you seem to know each other, I need not do any introducing," he answered, as she seemed to grow confused. "But I have a little time to talk to you this morning and so came early."

"Which means that I can set sail for the far shore," added Lyster, amiably. "All right; I'm gone. Good-by till to-morrow, Miss Rivers. I'm grateful for the clay Indian, and more grateful that you have agreed to be friends with me again. Will you believe, Dan, that in our short acquaintance of half an hour, we have had time for one quarrel and 'make up'? It is true. And now that she is disposed to accept me as a traveling companion, don't you spoil it by giving me a bad name when my back is turned. I'll wait at the canoes."

With a wave of his hat, he passed out of sight around the clump of bushes, and down along the shore, singing cheerily, and the words floated back to them:

> "Come, love! come, love!
> My boat lies low;
> She lies high and dry
> On the Ohio."

Overton stood looking at the girl for a little time after Lyster disappeared. His eyes were very steady and searching, as though he began to realize the care a ward might be, especially when the antecedents and past life of the ward were so much of stubborn mystery to him.

"I wonder," he said, at last, "if there is any chance of your being my friend, too, in so short a time as a half-hour? Oh, well, never mind," he added, as he saw the red mouth tremble, and tears show in her eyes as she looked at him. "Only don't commence by disliking, that's all; for unfriendliness is a bad thing in a household, let alone in a canoe, and I can be of more downright use to you, if you give me all the confidence you can."

"I know what you mean-that I must tell you about-about how I came here, and all; but I won't!" she burst out. "I'll die here before I do! I hated the people they said were my people. I was glad when they were dead-glad-glad! Oh, you'll say it's wicked to think that way about relatives. Maybe it is, but it's natural if they've always been wicked to you. I'll go to the bad place, I reckon, for feeling this way, and I'll just have to go, for I can't feel any other way."

"'Tana —'*Tana!*" and his hand fell on her shoulder, as though to shake her away from so wild a mood. "You are only a girl yet. When you are older, you will be ashamed to say you ever hated your parents-whoever they were-your mother!"

"I ain't saying anything about her," she answered bitterly. "She died before I can mind. I've been told she was a lady. But I won't ever use the name again she used. I —I want to start square with the world, if I leave these Indians, and I can't do it unless I change my name and try to forget the old one. It has a curse on it-it has."

She was trembling with nervousness, and her eyes, though tearless, were stormy and rebellious.

"You'll think I'm bad, because I talk this way," she continued, "but I ain't —I ain't. I've fought when I had to, and-and I'd swear-sometimes; but that's all the bad I ever did do. I won't any more if you take me with you. I —I can cook and keep house for you, if you hain't got folks of your own, and —I do want to go with you."

> "Come, love! come!
> Won't you go along with me?
> And I'll take you back
> To old Tennessee!"

The words of the handsome singer came clearly back to them. Overton, about to speak, heard the words of the song, and a little smile, half-bitter, half-sad, touched his lips as he looked at her.

"I see," he said, quietly, "you care more about going to-day, than you did when I talked to you last night. Well, that's all right. And I reckon you can make coffee for me as long as you like. That mayn't be long, though, for some of the young fellows will be wanting you to keep house for them before many years, and you'll naturally do it. How old are you?"

"I'm —past sixteen," she said, in a deprecating way, as though ashamed of her years and her helplessness. "I'm old enough to work, and I will work if I get where it's any use trying. But I won't keep house for any one but you."

"Won't you?" he asked, doubtfully. "Well, I've an idea you may. But we'll talk about that when the time comes. This morning I wanted to talk of something else before we start-you and Max and I —down into Idaho. I'm not asking the name of the man you hate so; but if I am to acknowledge him as an old acquaintance of mine, you had better tell me what business he was in. You see, it might save complications if any one should run across us some day and know."

"No one will know me," she said, decidedly. "If I didn't know that, I'd stay right here, I think. And as to him, my fond parent," and she made a grimace —"I guess you can call him a prospector and speculator-either of those would be correct. I think they called him Jim, when he was christened."

"Akkomi said last night you had been on the trail hunting for some one. Was it a friend, or-or any one I could help you look for?"

"No, it wasn't a friend, and I'm done with the search and glad of it. Did you," she added, looking at him darkly, "ever put in time hunting for any one you didn't want to find?"

Without knowing it, Miss Rivers must have touched on a subject rather sensitive to her guardian, for his face flushed, and he gazed at her with a curious expression in his eyes.

"Maybe I have, little girl," he said at last. "I reckon I know how to let your troubles alone, anyway, if I can't help them. But I must tell you, Max-Max Lyster, you know-will be the only one very curious about your presence here-as to the route you came, etc. You had better be prepared for that."

"It won't be very hard," she answered, "for I came over from Sproats' Landing, up to Karlo, and back down here."

"Over from Sproats-you?" he asked, looking at her nervously. "I heard nothing of a white girl making that trip. When, and how did you do it?"

"Two weeks ago, and on foot," was the laconic reply. "As I had only a paper of salt and some matches, I couldn't afford to travel in high style, so I footed it. I had a ring and a blanket, and I traded them up at Karlo for an old tub of a dugout, and got here in that."

"You had some one with you?"

"I was alone."

Overton looked at her with more of amazement than she had yet inspired in him. He thought of that indescribably wild portage trail from the Columbia to the Kootenai. When men crossed it, they preferred to go in company, and this slip of a girl had dared its loneliness, its dangers alone. He thought of the stories of death, by which the trail was haunted; of prospectors who had verged from that dim path and had been lost in the wilderness, where their bones were found by Indians or white hunters long after; of strange stories of wild beasts; of all the weird sounds of the jungles; of places where a misstep would send one lifeless to the jagged feet of huge precipices. And through that trail of terror she had walked-alone!

"I have nothing more to ask," he said briefly. "But it is not necessary to tell any of the white people you meet that you made the trip alone."

"I know," she said, humbly, "they'd think it either wasn't true-or-or else that it oughtn't to be true. I know how they'd look at me and whisper things. But if-if you believe me —"

She paused uncertainly, and looked up at him. All the rebellion and passion had faded out of her eyes now: they were only appealing. What a wild, changeable creature she was with those quick contrasts of temper! wild as the name she bore-Montana-the mountains. Something like that thought came into his mind as he looked at her.

He had gathered other wild things from his trips into the wilderness; young bears with which to enliven camp life; young fawns that he had loved and cared for, because of the beauty of eyes and form; even a pair of kittens had been carried by him across into the States, and developed into healthy, marauding panthers. One of these had set its teeth through the flesh of his hand one day ere he could conquer and kill it, and his fawns, cubs and smaller pets had drifted from him back to their forests, or else into the charge of some other prospector who had won their affections.

He remembered them, and the remembrance lent a curious character to the smile in his eyes, as he held out his hand to her.

"I do believe you, for it is only cowards who tell lies; and I don't believe you'd make a good coward-would you?"

She did not answer, but her face flushed with pleasure, and she looked up at him gratefully. He seemed to like that better than words.

"Akkomi called you 'Girl-not-Afraid,'" he continued. "And if I were a redskin, too, I would look up an eagle feather for you to wear in your hair. I reckon you've heard that only the braves dare wear eagle feathers."

"I know, but I —"

"But you have earned them by your own confession," he said, kindly, "and some day I may run across them for you. In the meantime, I have only this."

He held out a beaded belt of Indian manufacture, a pretty thing, and she opened her eyes in glad surprise, as he offered it to her.

"For me? Oh, Dan! —Mr. Overton —I —"

She paused, confused at having called him as the Indians called him; but he smiled understandingly.

"We'll settle that name business right here," he suggested. "You call me Dan, if it comes easier to you. Just as I call you 'Tana. I don't know 'Mr. Overton' very well myself in this country, and you needn't trouble yourself to remember him. Dan is shorter. If I had a sister, she'd call me Dan, I suppose; so I give you license to do so. As to the belt, I got it, with some other plunder, from some Columbia River reds, and you use it. There is some other stuff in Akkomi's tepee you'd better put on, too; it's new stuff —a whole dress-and I think the moccasins will about fit you. I brought over two pairs, to make sure. Now, don't get any independent notions in your head," he advised, as she looked at him as though about to protest. "If you go to the States as my ward, you must let me take the management of the outfit. I got the dress for an army friend of mine, who wanted it for his daughter; but I guess it will about fit you, and she will have to wait until next trip. Now, as I've settled our business, I'll be getting back across the river, so until to-morrow, *klahowya*."

She stood, awkward and embarrassed, before him. No words would come to her lips to thank him. She had felt desolate and friendless for so long, and now when his kindness was so great, she felt as if she should cry if she spoke at all. Just as she had cried the night before at his compassionate tones and touch.

Suddenly she bent forward for the belt, and with some muttered words he could not distinguish, she grasped his big hand in her little brown fingers, and touching it with her lips, twice-thrice-turned and ran away as swiftly as the little Indians who had run on the shore.

The warm color flushed all over Dan's face, as he looked after her. Of course, she was only a little girl, but he was devoutly glad Max was not in sight. Max would not have understood aright. Then his eyes traveled back to his hand, where her mouth had touched it. Her kiss had fallen where the scar of the panther's teeth was.

And this, also, was a wild thing he was taking from the forests!

Chapter V
At Sinna Ferry

"It has been young wolves, an' bears, an' other vicious pets-every formed thing, but snakes or redskins, and at last it's that!"

"Tush, tush, captain! Now, it's not so bad. Why, I declare, now, I was kind of pleased when I got sight of her. She's white, anyway, and she's right smart."

"Smart!" The captain sniffed, dubiously. "We'll get a chance to see about that later on, Mrs. Huzzard. But it's like your-hem! tender heart to have a good word for all comers, and this is only another proof of it."

"Pshaw! Now, you're making game, I guess. That's what you're up to, captain," and Mrs. Huzzard attempted a chaste blush and smile, and succeeded in a smirk. "I'm sure, now, that to hem a few neckties an' sich like for you is no good reason for thinking I'm doing the same for every one that comes around. No, indeed; my heart ain't so tender as all that."

The captain, from under his sandy brows, looked with a certain air of satisfaction at the well rounded personality of Mrs. Huzzard. His vanity was gently pleased-she was a fine woman!

"Well, I mightn't like it so well myself if I thought you'd do as much for any man," he acknowledged. "There's too many men at the Ferry who ain't fit even to eat one of the pies you make."

Mrs. Huzzard was fluting the edge of a pie at that moment, and looked across the table at the captain, with arch meaning.

"Maybe so; but there's a right smart lot of fine-looking fellows among them, too; there's no getting around that."

The unintelligible mutter of disdain that greeted her words seemed to bring a certain comfort to her widowed heart, for she smiled brightly and flipped the completed pie aside, with an airy grace.

"Now-now, Captain Leek, you can't be expecting common grubbers of men to have all the advantages of manners that you've got. No, sir; you can't. They hain't had the bringing up. They hain't had the schooling, and they hain't had the soldier drills to teach them to carry themselves like gentlemen. Now, you've had all that, and it's a sight of profit to you. But don't be too hard on the folks that ain't jest so finished like as you. There's that new Rivers girl, now-she ain't a bad sort, though it is queer to see your boy Dan toting such a stranger into camp, for he never did seem to take to girls much-did he?"

"It's not so easy to tell what he's taken to in his time," returned the captain, darkly. "You know he isn't my own boy, as I told you before. He was eight years old when I married his mother, and after her death he took the bit in his own teeth, and left home. No great grief to me, for he wasn't a tender boy to manage!" And Captain Leek heaved a sigh for the martyrdom he had lived through.

"Oh, well, but see what a fine man he's turned out, and I'm sure no own son could be better to you," for Mrs. Huzzard was one of the large, comfortable bodies, who never see any but the brightest side of affairs, and a good deal of a peacemaker in the little circle where she had taken up her abode. "Indeed, now, captain, you'll not meet many such fine fellows in a day's tramp."

"If she'd even been a real Indian," he continued, discontentedly, "it would have been easier to manage her-to-to put her in some position where she could earn her own living; for by Dan's words (few enough, too!) I gather that she has no money back of her. She'll be a dead weight on his hands, that's what she'll be, and an expensive savage he'll find her, I'll prophesy."

"Like enough. Young ones of any sort do take a heap of looking after. But she's smart, as I said before, and I do think it's a sight better to make room for a likely young girl than to be scared most to death with young wolves and bears tied around for pets. I was all of a shiver at night on account of them. I'll take the girl every time. She won't scratch an' claw at folks, anyway."

"Maybe not," added the captain, who was too contented with his discontent to let go of it at once. "But no telling what a young animal like that may develop into. She has no idea whatever of duty, Mrs. Huzzard, or of-of veneration. She contradicted me squarely this morning when I made some comment about those beastly redskins; actually set up her ignorance against my years of service under the American flag, Mrs. Huzzard. Yes, madame! she did that," and Captain Leek arose in his wrath and tramped twice across the room, halting again near her table and staring at her as though defying her to justify that.

When he arose, one could see by the slight unsteadiness in his gait that the cane in his hand was for practical use. His limp was not a deformity-in fact, it made him rather more interesting because of it; people would notice or remember him when nothing else in his personality would cause them to do so.

For Captain Alphonso Leek was not a striking-looking personage. His blue eyes had a washed-out, querulous expression. His sandy whiskers had the appearance of having been blown back from his chin, and lodged just in front of his ears. An endeavor had been made to train the outlying portions of his mustache in line with the lengthy, undulating "mutton chops;" but they had, for well-grounded reasons, failed to connect, and the effect was somewhat spoiled by those straggling skirmishers, bristling with importance but waiting in vain for recruits. The top of his head had got above timber line and glistened in the sun of early summer that streamed through the clear windows of Mrs. Huzzard's back room.

But as that head was generally covered by a hat that sported a cord and tassel, and as his bulging breastbone was covered by a dark-blue coat and vest, on which the brass buttons shone in real military fashion-well, all those things had their weight in a community where few men wore a coat at all in warm weather.

Mrs. Huzzard, in the depths of her being, thought it would be a fine thing to go back to Pennsylvania as "Mrs. Captain," even if the captain wasn't as forehanded as she'd seen men.

Even the elegant way in which he could do nothing and yet diffuse an air of importance, was impressive to her admiring soul. The clerical whiskers and the military dress completed the conquest.

But Mrs. Huzzard, having a bit of native wisdom still left, knew he was a man who would need managing, and that the best way was not to let his opinion rule her in all things; therefore, she only laughed cheerily at his indignation.

"Well, captain, I can't say but she did flare up about the Indians, when you said they were all thieves and paupers, stealing from the Government, and all that. But then, by what she says, she has knowed some decent ones in her time-friends of hers; an' you know any one must say a good word for a friend. You'd do that yourself."

"Maybe; I don't say I wouldn't," he agreed. "But I do say, the friends would not be redskins. No, madame! They're no fit friends for a gentleman to cultivate; and so I have told Dan. And if this girl owns such friends, it shows plainly enough that the class she belongs to is not a high one. Dan's mother was a lady, Mrs. Huzzard! She was my wife, madame! And it is a distress for me to see any one received into our family who does not come up to that same level. That is just the state of the case, and I maintain my position in the matter; let Dan take on all the temper he likes about it."

The lady of the pies did not respond to his remarks at once. She had an idea that she herself might fall under the ban of Captain Leek's discriminating eyes, and be excluded from that upper circle of chosen humanity to which he was born and bred. He liked her pies, her flap-jacks, and even the many kinds of boiled dinners she was in the habit of preparing and garnishing with "dumplings." So far as his stomach was concerned, she could rule supreme, for his digestion was of the best and her "filling" dishes just suited him. But Lorena Jane Huzzard had read in the papers some romances of the "gentle folk" he was fond of speaking of in an intimate way. The gentle folk in her kind of stories always had titles, military or civil, and were generally English lords and ladies; the villains, as generally, were French or Italian. But think as she might over the whole list, she could remember none in which the highbred scion of blue blood had married either a cook or a milliner. One might marry the milliner if she was very young and madly beautiful, but Lorena Jane was neither. She remembered also that beautiful though the milliner or bailiff's daughter, or housekeeper's niece might be, it was only the villain in high life who married her. Then the marriage always turned out at last to be a sham, and the milliner generally died of a broken heart.

So Mrs. Huzzard sighed and, with a thoughtful face, stirred up the batter pudding.

Captain Leek had given her food for reflection of which he was little aware, and it was quite a little while before she remembered to answer his remarks.

"So Mr. Dan is showing temper, too, is he? Well-well-that's a pity. He's a good boy, captain. I wouldn't waste my time to go against him, if I was you, and there he is now. Good-morning, Mr. Dan! Come right in! Breakfast over, but I'll get you up a bite at any time, and welcome. It does seem right nice for you to be back in town again."

Overton entered at her bidding, and smiled down from his tall stature to the broad, good-natured face she turned to him.

"Breakfast! Why, I'm thinking more about dinner, Mrs. Huzzard. I was up in the hills last night, and had a camp breakfast before you city folks were stirring. Where's 'Tana?"

A dubious sniff from Captain Leek embarrassed Mrs. Huzzard for a moment. She thought he meant to answer and hesitated to give him a chance. But the sniff seemed to express all he wanted to say, and she flushed a little at its evident significance.

"Well, what's the matter now?" demanded the younger man, impatiently, "where is she-do you know?"

"Oh-why, yes-of course we do," said Mrs. Huzzard hurriedly. "I didn't mean to leave you without an answer-no, indeed. But the fact is, the captain is set against something I did this morning, but I do hope you won't be. Whatever they know or don't know in sussiety, the girl was ignorant of it as could be when she asked to go, and so was I when I let her. That's the gospel truth, and I do hope you won't have hard feeling against me for it."

He came a step nearer them both, and looked keenly from one to the other-even a little threateningly into the watchful eyes of Captain Leek.

"Let her go! What do you mean? Where-Out with it!"

"Well, then, it was on the river she went, in one of them tiltuppy Indian boats that I'm deathly afraid of. But Mr. Lyster, he did promise faithfully he'd take good care of her. And as she'd seemed a bit low-spirited this morning, I thought it 'ud do her good, and I part told her to run along. And to think of its being improper for them to go together-alone! Well, then, I never did-that's all!"

"Is it?" and Overton drew a long breath as of relief and laughed shortly. "Well, you are perfectly right, Mrs. Huzzard. There is nothing wrong about it, and don't you be worried into thinking there is. Max Lyster is a gentleman-didn't you ever happen to know one, dad? Heavens! what a sinner you must have been in your time, if you can't conceive two young folks going out for an innocent boat ride. If any 'sky pilot' drifts up this way, I'll explain your case to him-and ask for some tracts. Why, man, your conscience must be a burden to you! I understand, now, how it comes I find your hair a little scarcer each time I run back to camp."

He had seated himself, and leaning back, surveyed the irate captain as though utterly oblivious of that gentleman's indignation, and then turned his attention to Mrs. Huzzard, who was between two fires in her regret that the captain should be ridiculed and her joy in Overton's commendation of herself. The captain had dismayed her considerably by a monologue on etiquette while she was making the pies, and she had inwardly hoped that the girl and her handsome escort would return before Overton, for vague womanly fears had been awakened in her heart by the opinions of the captain. To be sure, Dan never did look at girls much, and he was as "settled down" as any old man yet. The girl was pretty, and there was a bit of mystery about her. Who could tell what her guardian intended her for? This question had been asked by Captain Leek. Dan was very close-lipped about her, and his reticence had intensified the mystery regarding his ward. Mrs. Huzzard had seen wars of extermination started for a less worthy reason than pretty Montana, and so she had done some quiet fretting over the question until 'Tana's guardian set her free from worries by his hearty words.

"Don't you bother your precious head, or 'Tana's, with ideas of what rules people live by in a society of the cities thousands of miles away," he advised her. "It's all right to furnish guards or chaperons where people are so depraved as to need them."

This with a turn of his eyes to the captain, who was gathering himself up with a great deal of dignity.

"Good-morning, Mrs. Huzzard," he said, looking with an unapproachable air across Dan's tousled head. "If my stepson at times forgets what is due a gentleman in your house, do not fancy that I reflect on you in the slightest for it. I regret that he entertains such ideas, as they are totally at variance with the rules by which he was reared. Good-morning, madame."

Mrs. Huzzard clasped her hands and gazed with reproach at Overton, but at the same time she could not repress a sigh of relief.

"Well, now, he is good-natured to take it like that, and speak so beautiful," she exclaimed, admiringly; "and you surely did try any man's patience, Mr. Dan. Shame on you!"

But Dan only laughed and held up his finger warningly.

"You'll marry that man some day, if I don't put a stop to this little mutual admiration society I find here on my return," he said, and caught her sleeve as she tried to pass him. "Now don't you do it, Mrs. Huzzard. You are too nice a woman and too much of a necessity to this camp for any one man to build up a claim for you. Just think what will happen if you do marry him! Why, you'll be my stepmother! Doesn't the prospect frighten you?"

"Oh, stop your nonsense, Mr. Dan! I declare you do try a body's patience. You are too big to send to bed without your supper, or I vow I'd try it and see if it would tame you any. The captain is surely righteous mad."

"Then let him attend to his postoffice instead of interfering with your good cooking. Jim Hill said yesterday he guessed the postoffice had moved to your hotel, and the boys all ask me when the wedding is to be."

She blushed with a certain satisfaction, but tossed her head provokingly.

"Well, now, you can just tell them it won't be this week, Mr. Dan Overton; so you can quit your plaguing. Who knows but they may be asking the same about you, if you keep fetching such pretty girls into camp? Oh, I guess you don't like bein' plagued any more than other folks."

For Overton's smile had vanished at her words, and a tiny wrinkle crept between his brows. But when she commented on it, he recovered himself, and answered carelessly:

"But I don't think I will keep on bringing pretty girls into camp-that is, I scarcely think it will grow into a steady habit," he said, and met her eyes so steadily that she dismissed all idea of any heart interest in the girl. "But I'd rather 'Tana didn't hear any chaff of that sort. You know what I mean. The boys, or any one, is like enough to joke about it at first; but when they learn 'for keeps,' that I'm not a marrying man, they'll let up. As she grows older, there'll be enough boys to bother her in camp without me. All I want is to see that she is looked after right; and that's what I'm in here to talk about this morning."

"Well, now, I'm right glad to help you all I can-which ain't much, maybe, for I never did have a sight of schooling. But I can learn her the milliner trade-though it ain't much use at the Ferry yet; but it's always a living, anyway, for a woman in a town. And as to cookin' and bakin' —"

"Oh, yes; they are all right; she will learn such things easily, I think! But I wanted to ask about that cousin of yours-the lady who, you said, wanted to come out from Ohio to teach Indians and visit you. Is she coming?"

"Well, she writes like it. She is a fine scholar, Lavina is; but I kind o' let up on asking her to come after I struck this camp, for she always held her head high, I hear, and wouldn't be noways proud of me as a relation, if she found me doing so much downright kitchen work. I hain't seen her since she was grow'd up, you know, and I don't know how she'd feel about it."

"If she's any good, she'll think all the more of you for having pluck to tackle any honest work that comes," said Overton, decidedly. "We all do-every man in the settlement. If I didn't, I wouldn't be asking you to look after this little girl, who hasn't any folks-father or mother-to look after her right. I thought if that lady teacher would just settle down here, I would make it worth her while to teach 'Tana."

"Well, now, that would be wise," exclaimed Mrs. Huzzard, delightedly. "An' I'll write her a letter this very night. Or, no-not to-night," she added, "for I'll be too busy. To-night the dance is to be."

"What dance?"

"Well, now, I clean forgot to tell you about that. But it was Mr. Lyster planned it out after you left yesterday. As he's to go back East in a few days, he is to give a supper and a dance to the boys, and I just thought if they were going to have it, they might as well have it right and so it's to be here."

Overton twisted his hat around in silence for a few moments.

"What does 'Tana think of it?" he asked, at last.

"She? Why, land's sakes! She's tickled a heap over it. Indeed, to go back to the commencement, I guess it was to please her he got it up. At least, that's the way it looked to me, for she no sooner said she'd like to see a dance with this crowd at the Ferry than he said there should be one, and I should get up a supper. I tell you that young chap sets store by that little girl of yours, though she does sass him a heap. They're a fine-looking young couple, Mr. Dan."

Mr. Dan evidently agreed, for he nodded his head absently, but did not speak. He did not look especially pleased over the announcement of the dance.

"Well, I suppose she's got to learn soon or late whom to meet and whom to let alone here," he said at last, in a troubled way, "and she might as well learn now as later. Yet I wish Max had not been in such a hurry. And he promised to take good care of her on the river, did he?" he added, after another pause. "Well, he's a good fellow; but I reckon she can guide him in most things up here."

"No, indeed," answered Mrs. Huzzard, with promptness, "I heard her say myself that she had never been along this part of the Kootenai River before."

"Maybe not," he agreed. "I'm not speaking of this immediate locality. I mean that she has good general ideas about finding ways, and trails, and means. She's got ideas of outdoor life that girls don't often have, I reckon. And if she can only look after herself as well in a camp as she can on a trail, I'll be satisfied."

Mrs. Huzzard looked at him as he stared moodily out of the window.

"I see how it is," she said, nodding her head in a kindly way. "Since she's here, you're afraid some of the folks is most too rough to teach her much good. Well, well, don't you worry. We'll do the best we can, and that dead partner o' yours-her father, you know-will know you do your best; and no man can do more. I had a notion about her associates when I let her go out on the river this morning. 'Just go along,' thought I, 'if you get into the way of making company out of real gentlemen, you'll not be so like to be satisfied with them as ain't —"

"Good enough," Dan assented, cheerily. "You have been doing a little thinking on your own account, Mrs. Huzzard? That's all right, then. I'll know that you are a conscientious care-taker, no matter how far out on a trail I am. There's another thing I wanted to say; it's this: Just you let her think that the help she gives you around the house more than pays for her keeping, will you?"

"Why, of course I will; and I'm willing enough to take her company in change for boarding, if that's all. You know I didn't want to take the money when you did pay it."

"I know; that's all right. I want you to have the money, only don't let her know she is any bill of expense to me. Understand! You see, she said something about it yesterday-thought she was a trouble to me, or some such stuff. It seemed to bother her. When she gets older, we can talk to her square about such things. But now, till she gets more used to the thought of being with us, we'll have to do some pious cheating in the matter. I'll take the responsibilities of the lies, if we have to tell any. It-it seems the only way out, you see."

He spoke a little clumsily, as though uttering a speech prepared beforehand and by one not used to memorizing, and he did not look at Mrs. Huzzard as he talked to her.

But she looked at him and then let her hand fall kindly on his shoulder. She had not read romances for nothing. All at once she fancied she had found a romance in the life of Dan Overton.

"Yes, I see, as plain as need be," she said. "I see that you've brought care for yourself with that little mischief in her Indian dress; an' you take all the care on your shoulders as though it was a blessed privilege. And she's never to know what she owes you. Well, there's my hand. I'm your friend, Dan Overton. But don't waste your days with too much care about this new pet you've brought home. That's all I've got to say. She'll never think more of you for it. Girls don't; they are as selfish as young wolves."

Chapter VI
Mrs Huzzard's Suspicions

Overton sat silent and thoughtful for a little while after Mrs. Huzzard's words. Then he glanced up and smiled at her.

"I've just been getting an idea of the direction your fancies are taking," he said mockingly, "and they're very pretty, but I reckon you'll change them to oblige me; what I'm doing for her is what I'd do for any other child left alone. But as this child doesn't happen to be a boy, I can't take it on the trail, and a ranger like me is not fit to look after her, anyway. I think I told you before, I'm not a marrying man, and she, of course, would not look at me if I was; so what does it matter about her thinking of me? Of course, she won't —it ain't my intention. Even if she leaves these diggings some day and forgets all about me, just as the young wolves or wildcats do-well, what difference? I've helped old bums all over the country, and never heard or wanted to hear of them again, and I'm sure it's more worth one's while to help a young girl. Now, you're a nice little woman, Mrs. Huzzard, and I like you. But if you and I are to keep on being good friends, don't you speak like that about the child and me. It's very foolish. If she should hear it, she'd leave us some fine night, and we'd never learn her address."

Then he put on his hat, nodded to her, and walked out of the door as though averse to any further discussion of the subject.

"Bums all over the country!" repeated Mrs. Huzzard, looking after him darkly. "Well, Mr. Dan Overton, it's well for you that ward of yours, as you call her, wasn't near enough to hear that speech. And you're not a marrying man, are you? Well, well, I guess there's many a man and woman, too, goes through life and don't know what they might be, just because they never meet with the right person who could help them to learn, and you're just of that sort. Not a marrying man! Humph! When there's not a better favored one along this valley-that there ain't."

She fidgeted about the dinner preparations, filled with a puzzled impatience as to why Dan Overton should thus decidedly state that he was not one of the men to marry, though all the rest of the world might fall into the popular habit if they chose.

"It's the natural ambition of creation," she declared in confidence to the dried peach-pie she was slipping from the oven. "Of course, being as I'm a widow myself, I can't just make that statement to men folks promiscuous like. But it's true, and every man ought to know it's true, and why Dan Overton —"

She paused in the midst of her soliloquy, and dropped into the nearest chair, while a light of comprehension illuminated her broad face.

"To think it never came in my mind before," she ejaculated. "That's it! Poor boy! he's had a girl somewhere and she's died, I suppose, or married some other fellow; and that's why he's a bachelor at nearly thirty, I guess," she added, thoughtfully. "She must have died, and that's why he never looks as gay or goes on larks with the other boys. He just goes on a lone trail mostly, Dan does. Even his own stepfather don't seem to have much knowledge about him. Well, well! I always did feel that he had some sort of trouble lookin' out of them dark eyes of his, and his words to-day makes it plain to me all at once. Well, well!"

The pensive expression of her face, as it rested on her fat hand, was evidence that Lorena Jane Huzzard had, after all, found a romance in real life suited to her fancy, and the unconscious hero was Dan Overton. Poor Dan!

The grieving hero to whom her thoughts went out was at that moment walking in a most prosaic, lazy fashion down the main thoroughfare of the settlement. The road led down to the Ferry from seemingly nowhere in particular, for from the Ferry on both sides of the river the road dwindled into mere trails that slipped away into the wildernesses-trails traveled by few of the white race until a few short years ago, and then only by the most daring of hunters, or the most persevering of the gold-seekers.

In the paths where gold is found the dwellings of man soon follow, and the quickly erected shanties and more pretentious buildings of Sinna Ferry had grown there as evidence that the precious metals in that region were no longer visionary things of the enthusiasts, but veritable facts. The men who came to it along the water, or over the inland trails, were all in some way connected with the opening up of the new mining fields.

Overton himself had drifted up there as an independent prospector, two years before. Then, when works were got under way all along that river and lake region, when a reliable man was needed by the transfer company to get specie to their men for pay-days, it was Overton to whom was given the responsibility.

Various responsible duties he had little by little shouldered, until, as Lyster said, he seemed a necessity to a large area, yet he had not quite abandoned the dreams with which he had entered those cool Northern lands. Some day, when the country was more settled and transportation easier, it was his intention to slip again up into the mountains, along some little streams he knew, and work out there in quietness his theories as to where the gold was to be found.

Meantime, he was contented enough with his lot. No vaulting ambition touched him. He was merely a ranger of the Kootenai country, and was as welcome in the scattered lodges of the Indians as he was in the camps of the miners. He even wore clothes of Indian make, perhaps for the novelty of them, or perhaps because the buckskin was better suited than cloth to the wild trails over which he rode. And if, at times, he drifted into talk of existence beyond the frontier, and gave one an idea that he had drunk of worldly life deep enough to be tired of it, those times were rare; even Lyster had but once known him to make reference to it-that one evening after their ride along the falls of the Kootenai.

But however tired he might at some time have grown of the life of cities, he was not at all too *blasé* to accommodate himself to Sinna Ferry. If poor Mrs. Huzzard had seen the very hearty drink of whisky with which he refreshed himself after his talk with her, she would not have been so apt to think of him with such pensive sympathy.

The largest and most popular saloon was next door to the postoffice, the care of which Dan had secured for his stepfather, as the duties of it were just about as arduous as any that gentleman would deign to accept. The mail came every two weeks, and its magnitude was of the fourth-class order. No one else wanted it, for a man would have to possess some other means of livelihood before he could undertake it, but the captain accepted it with the attitude of a veteran who was a martyr to his country. As to the other means of livelihood, that did not cause him much troubled thought, since he had chanced to fall in Dan's way just as Dan was starting up to the Kootenai country, and Dan had been the "other means" ever since.

The captain watched Overton gulp down the "fire-water," while he himself sipped his with the appreciation of a gentleman of leisure.

"You didn't use to drink so early in the day," the captain remarked, with a certain watchful malice in his face. "Are your cares as a guardian wearing on your nerves, and bringing a need of stimulants?"

Overton wheeled about as though to fling the whisky-glass across at the speaker; but the gallant captain, perceiving that he had overreached his stepson's patience, promptly dodged around the end of the bar, squatting close to the floor. Overton, leaning over to look at him, only laughed contemptuously, and set the glass down again.

"You're not worth the price of the glass," he decided, amused in spite of himself at the fear in the pale-blue eyes. Even the flowing side-whiskers betrayed a sort of alarm in their bristling alertness. "And if it wasn't that one good woman fancied you were true metal instead of slag, I'd —"

He did not complete the sentence, leaving the captain in doubt as to his half-expressed threat.

"Get up there!" Dan suddenly exclaimed. "Now, you think you will annoy me about that guardianship until I'll give it up, don't you?" he said, more quietly, as the captain once more stood erect, but in a wavering, uncertain way. "Well, you're mightily mistaken, and you might as well end your childish interference right here. The girl is as much entitled to my consideration as you are-more! So if any one is dropped out of the family circle, it will not be her. Do you understand? And if I hear another word of your insinuations about her amusements, I'll break your neck! Two, Jim."

This last was to the barkeeper, and had reference to a half-dollar he tossed on the counter as payment for his own drink and that of the captain; and again he stalked into the street with his temper even more rumpled than when he left Mrs. Huzzard's.

Assuredly it was not a good morning for Mr. Overton's peace of mind.

Down along the river he came in sight of the cause of his discontent, the most innocent-looking cause in the world. She was teaching Lyster to paddle the canoe with but one paddle, as the Indians do, and was laughing derisively at his ineffectual attempts to navigate in a straight line.

"You-promised-Mrs. Huzzard-you'd —take-care-of-me," she said, slowly and emphatically, "and a pretty way you're doing it. Suppose I depended on you getting me in to shore for my dinner, how many hours do you think I'd have to go without eating? Just about sixteen. Give me that paddle, and don't upset the canoe when you move."

These commands Mr. Lyster obeyed with alacrity.

"What a clever little girl you are!" he said, admiringly, as she sent the canoe skimming straight as a swallow for the shore. "Now, Overton would appreciate your skill at this sort of work" —and then he laughed a little —"much more than he would your modeling in clay."

A dark flush crept over her face, and her lips straightened.

"Why shouldn't he look down on that sort of pottering around?" she demanded. "*He* isn't the sort of man who has time to waste on trifles."

"Why that emphasis on the *he?*" asked her tormentor. "Do you mean to insinuate that I do waste time on trifles? Well, well! is that the way I get snubbed, because I grow enthusiastic over your artistic modeling and your most charming voice, Miss 'Tana?"

She flashed one sulky, suspicious look at him, and paddled on in silence.

"What a stormy shadow lurks somewhere back of your eyes," he continued, lazily. "One moment you are all sugar and cream to a fellow, and the next you are an incipient tornado. I think you might distribute your frowns a little among the people you know, and not give them all to me. Now, there's Overton —"

"Don't you talk about him," she commanded, sharply. "You do a lot of making fun about folks, but don't you go on making fun of him, if that's what you're trying to do. If it's *me* —pooh!" and she looked at him, saucily. "I don't care much what you think about me; but Dan —"

"Oh! Dan, then, happens to-day to be one of the saints in your calendar, and plain mortals like myself must not take his name in vain-is that it? What a change from this time yesterday! —for I don't think you sent him to the hills in a very angelic mood. And you! —well, I found you with a clay Indian crumbled to pieces in your destroying hands; so I don't imagine Dan's talk to you left a very peaceful impression."

He laughed at her teasingly, expecting to see her show temper again, but she did not. She only bent her head a little lower, and when she lifted it, she looked at him with a certain daring.

"He was right, and I was silly, I guess. He was good-so good, and I'm mostly bad. I was bad to him, anyway, but I ain't too much of a baby to say so. And if he's mad at me when he comes back, I'll just pack my traps and take another trail."

"Back to Akkomi?" he asked, gaily. "Now, you know we would not hear to that."

"It ain't your affair, only Dan's."

"Oh, excuse me for living on the same earth with you and Dan! It is not my fault, you know. I suppose now, if you did desert us, it would be to act as a sort of guardian angel to the tribes along the river, turn into a whole life-saving service yourself, and pick up the superfluous reds who tumble into the rivers. I wondered for a whole day why you made so strong a swim for so unimportant an article."

"His mother thought he was important," she answered. "But I didn't know he had a mother just then; all I thought as I started for him was that he was so plucky. He tried his little best to save himself, and he never said one word; that was what I liked about him. It would have been a pity to let that sort of a boy be lost."

"You think a heap of that-of personal bravery-don't you? I notice you gauge every one by that."

"Maybe I do. I know I hate a coward," she said, indifferently.

Then, as the canoe ran in to the shore, she for the first time saw Overton, who was standing there waiting for them. She looked at him with startled alertness as his eyes met hers. He looked like a statue —a frontier sentinel standing tall and muscular with folded arms and gazing with curious intentness from one to the other of the canoeists.

In the bottom of the boat a string of fish lay, fine speckled fellows, to delight the palate of an epicure. She stooped and picking up the fish, walked across the sands to him.

"Look, Dan!" she said, with unwonted humility. "They're the best I could find, and-and I'm sorry enough for being ugly yesterday. I'll try not to be any more. I'll do anything you want-yes, I will!" she added, snappishly, as he smiled dubiously, she thought unbelievingly. "I'd —dress like a boy, and go on the trails with you, paddle your canoe, or feed your horse —I would, if you like."

Lyster, who was following, heard her words, and glanced at Overton with curious meaning. Overton met the look with something like a threat in his own eyes —a sort of "laugh if you dare!"

"But I don't like," Dan said, briefly, to poor 'Tana, who had made such a great effort to atone for ugly words spoken to him the day before.

She said no more; and Lyster, walking beside her, pulled one of her unruly curls teasingly, to make her look at him.

"Didn't I tell you it was better to give your smiles to me instead of to Overton?" he asked, in a bantering way, as he took the string of fish. "I care a great deal more about your good opinion than he does."

"Oh-you —" she began, and shrugged her shoulders for a silent finish to her thought, as though words were useless.

"Oh, *me*! Of course, me. Now, if you had offered to paddle a canoe for me, I'd —"

"You'd loll in the bottom of the boat and let me," she flashed out. "Of course you would; you're made just that way."

"Sh —h, 'Tana," said Overton, while to himself he smiled in an indulgent way, and thought: "That is like youth; they only quarrel when there is a listener." Then turning to the girl, he said aloud:

"You know, 'Tana, I want you to learn other things besides paddling a canoe. Such things are all right for a boy; but —"

"I know," she agreed; but there was a resentful tone in her voice. "And I guess I'll never trouble you to do squaw's work for you again."

She looked squaw-like, but for her brown, curly hair, for she still wore the dress Overton had presented to her at the Kootenai village; and very becoming it was with its fancy fringes and dots of yellow, green, and black beads. Only the hat was a civilized affair-the work of Mrs. Huzzard, and was a wide, pretty "flat" of brown straw, while from its crown some bunches of yellow rosebuds nodded-the very last "artificial" blossoms left of Sinna Ferry's first millinery store. The young face looked very piquant above the beaded collar; not so pinched or worn a face as when the men had first seen her. The one week of sheltered content had given her cheeks a fullness and color remarkable. She was prettier than either man had imagined she would be. But it was not a joyous, girlish face even yet. There was too much of something like suspicion in it, a certain watchful attention given to the people with whom she came in contact; and this did not seem to abate in the least. Overton had noticed it, and decided that first night that she must have been treated badly by people to have distrust come so readily to her. He noticed, also, that any honest show of kindness soon won her over; and that to Lyster, with his graceful little attentions and his amused interest, she turned from the first hour of their acquaintance as to some chum who was in the very inner circle of those to whom her favor was extended. Overton, hearing their wordy wars and noting their many remarks of friendship, felt old, as though their light enjoyment of little things made him realize the weight of his own years, for he could no longer laugh with them.

Looking down now at the clouded young face under the hat, he felt remorsefully like a "kill-joy;" for she had been cheery enough until she caught sight of him.

"And you will never do squaw work for me again, little squaw?" Dan questioned, banteringly. "Not even if I asked you?"

"You never will ask me," she answered, promptly.

"Well, then, not even if I should get sick and need a nurse?"

"You!" and she surveyed him from head to foot with pronounced unbelief. "*You'll* never be sick. You're strong as a mountain lion, or an old king buffalo."

"Maybe," he agreed, and smiled slightly at the dubious compliment. "But you know even the old king buffaloes die sometime."

"Die? Oh, yes, in a fight, or something of that sort; but they don't need much medicine!"

"And even if you did," said Lyster, addressing Overton, "I'm going to give you fair warning you can't depend on 'Tana, unless you mend your ways. She threatened to-day to leave us, if you allow the shadow of your anger to fall on her again. So take heed, or she will swim back to Akkomi."

Overton looked at her sharply, and saw that back of Lyster's badinage there was something of truth.

"You did?" he asked, reproachfully. "I did not know I had been so bad a friend to you as that."

But no answer was made to him. She was ashamed, and she looked it. She was also angry at Lyster, and he was made aware of it by a withering glance.

"Now *I'm* in her bad books," he complained; "but it was only my fear of losing her that urged me to give you warning. I hope she does not take revenge by refusing me all the dances I am looking forward to to-night. I'd like to get you, as her guardian, on my side, Overton."

The girl looked up, expectantly, and rested her slim fingers on the arms of the two men.

"I could not be of much use, unless I had an invitation myself to the dance," Dan remarked, dryly; "mine has evidently been delayed in the mail."

"You don't like it?" said the girl, detecting the fact in his slight change of tone. "You don't want me to go to dances?"

"What an idea!" exclaimed Lyster. "Of course, he is not going to spoil our good time by objecting-are you, Dan? I never thought of that. You see, you were away; but, of course, I fancied you would like it, too. I'll write you out a flourishing request for your presence, if that's all."

"It isn't necessary; I'll be there, I reckon. But why should you think I mean to keep you from jollifications?" he asked, looking kindly at 'Tana. "Don't get the idea in your head that I'm a sort of 'Bad Man from Roaring River,' who eats a man or so for breakfast every day, and all the little girls he comes across. No, indeed! I'll whistle for you to dance any time; so get on your war-paint and feathers when it pleases you."

The prospect seemed to please her, for she walked closer to him and looked up at him with more content.

"Anyway, you ain't like Captain Leek," she decided. "He's the worst old baby! Why, he just said all sorts of things about dances. Guess he must be a heavy swell where he comes from, and where all the fandangoes are got up in gilt-edged style. I'd like to spoil the gilt for him a little. I will, too, if he preaches any more of his la-de-da society rules to me. I'll show him I'm a different boy from Mrs. Huzzard."

"Now, what would you do?" asked Lyster. "He wouldn't trust himself in a boat with you, so you can't drown him."

"Don't want to. Huh! I wouldn't want to be lynched for *him*. All I'd like to hit hard would be his good opinion of himself. I could, too, if Dan wouldn't object."

"If you can, you're a wonder," remarked Dan. "And I'll give you license to do what I confess I can't. But I think you might take us into your confidence."

This she would not do, and escaped all their questions, by taking refuge in Mrs. Huzzard's best room, and much of her afternoon was spent there under that lady's surveillance, fashioning a party gown with which to astonish the natives. For Mrs. Huzzard would not consent to her appearing in the savageness of an Indian dress, when the occasion was one of importance-namely, the first dance in the settlement held in the house of a respectable woman.

And as 'Tana stitched, and gathered, and fashioned the dress, according to Mrs. Huzzard's orders, she fashioned at the same time a little plan of her own in which the personality of Captain Leek was to figure.

If Mrs. Huzzard fancied that her silent smiles were in anticipation of the dancing festivities, she was much mistaken.

Chapter VII
A Game of Poker

Mr. Max Lyster, in his hasty plans for an innocent village dance, had neglected to make allowance for a certain portion of the inhabitants whose innocence was not of the quality that allowed them to miss anything, no matter who was host. They would shoot the glass out of every window in a house, if the owner of the house should be in their bad books for any trifling slight, and would proceed to "clean out" any establishment where their own peculiar set was ignored.

There were, perhaps, seven or eight women in the place who were shown all respect by men in general. They were the wives and daughters of the city fathers-the first of the "family folks" to give the stamp of permanency to the little camp by the river. These ladies and their husbands, together with the better class of the "boys," were the people whom Mr. Lyster expected to meet and to partake of his hospitality in the cheery abode of Mrs. Huzzard.

But Overton knew there were one or two other people to consider, and felt impatient with Lyster for his impulsive arrangements. Of course, 'Tana could not know and Mrs. Huzzard did not, but Lyster had at least been very thoughtless.

The fact was that the well-ordered establishment of Mrs. Huzzard was a grievance and a thorn in the side of certain womankind, who dwelt along the main street and kept open drinking saloons seven days in the week. They would have bought ribbons and feathers from her, and as a milliner thought no more about her, or even if she had opened a hotel, with a bar attached, they would have been willing to greet her as a fellow worker, and all would have had even chances. But her effrontery in opening an eating house, where only water-pure or adulterated with tea or coffee-was drunk-Well, her immaculate pretensions, to use the vernacular of one of the disgusted, "made them sick."

It may have been their dislike was made more pronounced because of the fact that the more sober-minded men turned gladly to the irreproachable abode of Mrs. Huzzard, and the "bosses" of several "gangs" of workmen had arranged with her for their meals. Besides, the river men directed any strangers to her house; whereas, before, the saloons had been the first point of view from which travelers or miners had seen Sinna Ferry. All these grievances had accumulated through the weeks, until the climax was capped when the report went abroad that a dance was to take place at the sickeningly correct restaurant, and that only the *elité* of the settlement were expected to attend.

Thereupon some oaths had been exchanged in a desultory fashion over the bars at Mustang Kate's and Dutch Lena's; and derisive comments made as to Mrs. Huzzard and her late charge, the girl in the Indian dress. Some of the boys, who owned musical instruments —a banjo and a mouth organ-were openly approached by bribery to keep away from the all too perfect gathering, so that there might be a dearth of music. But the boys with the musical instruments evaded the bribes, and even hinted aloud their desire to dance once anyway with the new girl of the curly hair and the Indian dress.

This decision increased somewhat the muttering of the storm brewing; and when Dutch Lena's own man indiscreetly observed that he would have to drop in line, too, if all the good boys were going, then indeed did the cyclone of woman's wrath break over that particular branch of Hades. Lena's man was scratched a little with a knife before quiet was restored, and there had been some articles of furniture flung around promiscuously; also some violent language.

Overton divined somewhat of all this, knowing as he did the material of the neighborhood, though no actual history of events came to his ears. And 'Tana, presenting herself to his notice in all the glory of her party dress, felt her enthusiasm cool as he looked at her moodily. He would have liked to shut her away from all the vulgar gaze and comment he knew her charming face would win for her. His responsibilities as a guardian forced on him so many new phases of thought. He had never before given the social side of Sinna Ferry much consideration; but he thought fast and angrily as he looked down on the slim, girlish, white-draped figure and the lovely appealing face turned upward to him.

"You don't like it-you don't think it is pretty?" she asked, and her mouth was a little tremulous. "I tried so hard. I sewed part of it myself, and Mrs. Huzzard said —"

Lyster arose from a seat by the window. He had entered the room but a moment before, and now lounged toward her with critical eyes.

"Mrs. Huzzard said you were enchanting in your new gown-is not that it?" he asked, and then frowned at Overton in a serio-comic way. "And lives there a man with soul so dead that he cannot perceive the manifold beauties arranged for his inspection? Well, you know I told you I appreciate you much more than he will ever do; so —"

"What nonsense you are talking!" said Overton, irritably. "Of course, the dress is all right. I don't know much about such things, though; so my opinion is not worth much. But I don't think little girls should be told so much of their charms, Lyster. They are too likely to be made think that prettiness is the only thing worth living for."

He smiled at 'Tana to soften the severity of his speech; but she was not looking at him just then, and so missed the softening accompaniment. She felt it was herself who was taken to task instead of Lyster, and stood with drooped, darkening face until the door closed behind Overton.

"That is your fault," she burst out. "He-he might have thought it was nice, if you hadn't been here with your fool speeches. You just go around laughing at everything, Mr. Max Lyster, and you're just as empty as that china cat on the mantel, and it's hollow. I'd like to hit you sometimes when you say your nice, tantalizing words-that's what *I'd* like to do; and maybe some day I will."

"I shouldn't be surprised if you did," he agreed, and stepped back out of range of her clenched brown hands. "Whew! what a trial you'd be to a guardian who had nerves. You are spoiling your pretty face with that satanic expression. Now, why should you make war on me? I'm sure I am one of your most devoted servants."

"You are your own devoted servant," she retorted, "and you'll never be any other person's."

"Well, now, I'm not so sure of that," he said, and looked at her smilingly. All her anger did not keep him from seeing what a wondrous difference all that white, billowy lawn made in the girl whom he had taken for a squaw that first day when he saw her swimming the Kootenai.

She looked taller, slighter, with such lovable curves in the girlish form, and the creamy neck and arms gleaming through the thin material. No ornaments or ribbons broke the whiteness of her garb-nothing but the Indian belt of beads that Overton had given her, and in it were reddish tints and golden brown the color of her hair.

To be sure, the cheeks were a little tanned by the weather, and the little hand was browner than need be for beauty; but, for all that, he realized, as Overton had seemingly not done, that the girl, when dressed as dainty girlhood should be, was very pretty, indeed.

"I am willing to sign myself your bond slave from this hour, if that will lessen your anger against me," he protested. "Just think, I leave Sinna Ferry to-morrow. How shall I do penance until then?"

> "'It may be for years, and it may be forever,
> Then why art thou silent, O voice of my heart?'"

She pouted and frowned a little at his warbling, though a smile eventually touched her lips, and speculation shone in her eyes.

"I *will* make you do penance," she declared, "and right now, too. I haven't any money, but I'll put up my moccasins against five dollars in a game of poker."

"You-play poker?"

"I'll try," she said briefly, and her eyes sparkled; "I'll play you and ask no favors."

"Your moccasins are not worth five."

"Maybe not. Call it two-fifty then and promise me two hands at that."

"How sure you are to win!" he laughed, well pleased that she was diverted from her quick displeasure. "We'll call it five against the moccasins. Here are the cards. And what am I to do with those little moccasins, even if I do win them?"

"Oh, I'll take care of the moccasins!" she said, easily. "I guess they'll not trouble you much, Mr. Lyster. Cut for deal?"

He nodded, and they commenced their game there alone in Mrs. Huzzard's most respectable *café*. Mrs. Huzzard herself did not approve of card playing. No one but Captain Leek had, as yet, been allowed that privilege. His playing she had really begun to look upon as almost moral in its effects, since he pursued it as the most innocent of pastimes, never betting more than a few dimes, and since it secluded him effectually from the roaring lion of iniquity to which so many men fell victims in the lively little settlement. But 'Tana, knowing that card playing by a girl would not be a thing within Mrs. Huzzard's understanding, glanced warily at the door leading to the second floor of the establishment and comforted herself that the mistress of the domain was yet employed by her toilet for the evening.

'Tana dealt, and did it so deftly that Lyster looked at her in surprise, even irritation. What business had she touching the bits of pasteboard like that-like some old gambler. Such a slight slip of a thing, with all the beauty of early youth in her face, and all the guilelessness of a vestal in the pure white of her garb. He fancied he would have felt different if he had seen her playing cards in that Indian dress; it would not have brought such a discord with it. And it was not merely that she played, but it was the way she played that brought vexation to him-that careless, assured handling of the cards. It seemed almost professional, —it seemed —

"I'll just take that little five," remarked his opponent easily, and spread out the cards before him. "I know what you've got, and it won't touch this flush, and if you play again I'd advise you to gather your wits and not play so wild-that is, if you want to win."

He stared at her in astonishment. It was quite true-while his thoughts had been with her personality and her incongruous occupation, her thoughts had been centered very decidedly on the points of the game. She, at least, had not played "wild." A doubt even came into his mind, as to whether she played honestly.

"I don't think I cared about winning," he answered, "I'd rather have given you the stakes than to have had you play for them that way-yes, 'Tana, double the stakes."

"Oh, would you?" she asked, with saucy indifference. "Well, I ain't asking favors. I guess I can win all I want."

"No doubt you can," he assented, gravely. "But as young ladies do not generally depend on their skill with cards to earn their pocket money, I'm afraid Overton would have a lecture ready for you, if he learned of your skill."

"Let him," she said, recklessly. "I've tried to be good, and tried to be nice, and-and even pretty," she added, touching the dainty sleeve and skirt of her dress, "but what use is it? He just stands off and stares at me, and even speaks sharp as if he's sorry he ever brought me down here. I didn't think he'd be like that. He was nicer in Akkomi's village; and now —"

She hesitated, and, seeing that Lyster's eyes were watching her attentively, she laughed in a careless way, and curled the five-dollar bill around her finger.

"So I might as well be bad, don't you see? and I'm going to be, too. I want this five dollars to gamble with, and for nothing else in the world. I'm going to get square with some one."

"Which means you are going to worry some one else, just because Overton has annoyed you," decided Lyster. "That is a woman's idea of retaliation, I believe. Am I the selected victim?"

"Of course you're not, or I wouldn't have told you. All I wanted of you was to give me a start."

"Exactly; your frankness is not very flattering; but, in spite of it, I'd like to give you a start in a different way-toward a good school, for instance. How would you like that?"

She looked at him for a moment suspiciously, she was so used to raillery from him; then she answered briefly:

"But you are not my guardian, Mr. Max Lyster."

"Then you prefer card playing?"

"No, I don't. I'd like it, but my income can't cover such luxuries, and I have booked myself to play for a time this evening, if I can get the man I want to play with."

"But that is what you must not do," he said, hastily. "With Overton or myself, of course, a game would not do you any special harm; but you simply must not indulge in such pastime with this promiscuous gathering of people-of men."

"But it isn't men-it's only one man I want to play-do you see?"

"I might if I knew who it was; but you don't know any men here but Dan and me."

"Yes, I do, too. I know Captain Alphonso Leek."

"Perhaps, but —" Lyster smiled, and shook his head dubiously.

"But he won't play with me, because he don't like me; that's what you would say, if you were not too polite-isn't it? He doesn't approve of me, and can't understand why I'm on the face of the earth, and especially why Dan should take any responsibility but Captain Leek on his hands. Huh! Can't I see? Of course I do. I heard him call me *'that'* this morning. And so, I want to play a game of poker with him."

She looked impishly at him from under her brows, and twirled the money.

"Won't you be a messenger of peace and fix the game for me?" she asked, insinuatingly. "You know you promised to do penance."

"Then I forswear all rash promises for the future," he declared.

"But you did promise."

"Well, then, I'll keep my word, since you are such a little Shylock. And if it is only the captain —"

She laughed after he had gone out, and sat there shuffling the cards and building them into various forms. She was thus employed when Overton again passed the window and entered the room ere she could conceal them. He observed her attempt to do so and smiled indulgently.

"Playing with the cards, are you?" he asked, in a careless way. "They are expensive toys sometimes. But I'll teach you 'seven-up' some day; it's an easy game."

"Is it?" she said; but did not look up at him. His indifference to the pretty dress had not yet ceased to annoy her.

"Yes. And see here, 'Tana! I forgot to give you a present I brought you a little while ago. It's a ring a fellow from the upper lake region worried me into buying, as he was dead broke. He bought it from an Indian up near Karlo. Queer for an Indian to have, isn't it?"

"Near Karlo?" she said, and reached out her hand for it.

There was a strange look on her face, a strange choking sound in her throat. He noticed it, and his voice was very kindly as he spoke again.

"You don't like even to hear of that region, do you? You must have been very miserable somewhere up there. But never mind, little girl; we'll try to forget all that. And if the ring fits you, wear it, no matter what country it comes from."

She tried to thank him, but the words would not come easily, and her outstretched hand in which the ring lay was tremulous.

"Oh, that's all right," he said hastily, afraid, no doubt, she was going to cry, as he had seen her do before at kind words. "Never mind about the thanks. If you care to wear it, that's all that's necessary; though a snake ring is not the prettiest of ornaments for a girl. It fits, doesn't it?"

"Yes, it fits," she returned, and slipped it on her finger. "It is very nice," but she shivered as with cold, and her hand shook.

It was curious enough to attract notice anywhere, a silver and a gold snake twined together with their heads meeting, and in the flattened gold head, eyes of garnet gleamed, while the silver head had eyes of emerald. Not a girlish looking ornament, surely.

"I'll wear it," she said, and dropped the hand to her side. "But don't tell the rest where it came from. I may want to tease them."

Chapter VIII
The Dance

"Ain't it lovely, Ora?" and 'Tana danced past Ora Harrison, the doctor's pretty daughter, as if her feet had wings to them. And as Ora's bright face smiled an answer, it was clear that the only two young girls in the settlement were enjoying Lyster's party to the full.

For it was a pronounced success. Every "boy" invited was there in as much of festive outfit as circumstances would allow. All the "family" people were there. And the presence of Doctor Harrison-the only "professional" man in the town-and his wife and daughter gave a stamp of select society to the gathering in Mrs. Huzzard's rooms.

Mrs. Huzzard beamed with pleasure at the great success of it all. She would have liked to dance, too, and refused most unwillingly when Lyster tried to persuade her. But a supercilious glance from the captain made her refusal decided. The doubt as to whether ladies in "sussiety" ever did dance after forty years, and one hundred and sixty-three pounds weight, deterred her. Now, if the captain had asked her to dance, she would have been more assured.

But the captain did not; and, after a while, he was not to be seen. He had vanished into the little back sitting room, and she was confident he was engaged in his innocent pastime of a friendly game of cards with the doctor.

"Go and dance with 'Tana, or that nice little girl of the doctor's," she said to Lyster, when he was trying to inveigle her into a quadrille —"that's the sort of partner for you."

"But 'Tana has disappeared mysteriously; and as Miss Ora is 'bespoke,' I can't dance with her unless I want a duel with her partner."

"'Tana disappeared! Well, now, I haven't seen her for two dances," said Mrs. Huzzard, looking around searchingly, "though I never missed her till this minute."

"Beg pardon, ma'am," said a voice at her elbow; "but is it the-the young lady with the white dress you are looking for?"

"Yes, it is," answered Mrs. Huzzard, and turned around to face the speaker, who was an apologetic-looking stranger with drab-colored chin whiskers, and a checkered shirt, and a slight impediment in his speech.

"Well, ma'am, I saw her go into that room there quite a spell ago," and he nodded toward the back sitting room. "She hasn't passed out again, as I've seen."

Then, as Mrs. Huzzard smiled on him in a friendly way, he ventured further:

"She's a very pretty girl, as any one can see. Might I ask her name?"

"Oh, yes! Her name is Rivers-Miss Tana Rivers," said Mrs. Huzzard. "You must be a stranger in the settlement?"

"Yes, ma'am, I am. My name is Harris-Jim Harris. I come down from the diggings with Mr. Overton this morning. He allowed it would be all right for me to step inside, if I wanted to see the dancing."

"To be sure it is," agreed Mrs. Huzzard, heartily. "His friends are our friends, and civil folks are always right welcome."

"Thank, you, ma'am; you're kind, I'm sure. But we ain't just friends, especial. Only I had business in his line, so we picked up acquaintance and come into camp together; and when I saw the pretty girl in white, I did think I'd like to come in a spell. She looks so uncommon like a boy I knew up in the 'big bend' country. Looks enough like him to be a twin; but he wasn't called Rivers. Has-has this young lady any brothers or cousins up there?"

"Well, now, as for cousins, they are far out, and we hain't ever talked about them; but as for brothers or sisters, father or mother, that she hasn't got, for she told me so. Her pa and Mr. Dan Overton they was partners once; and when the pa died he just left his child to the partner's care; and he couldn't have left her to a squarer man."

"That's what report says of him," conceded the stranger, watching her with guarded attention. "Then Mr. Overton's partner hasn't been dead long?"

"Oh, no-not very long; not long enough for the child to get used to talking of it to strangers, I guess; so we don't ask her many questions about it. But it troubles her yet, I know."

"Of course-of course; such a pretty little girl, too."

Then the two fell into quite a pleasant chat, and it was not until he moved away from beside her, to make room for the doctor's wife, that Mrs. Huzzard observed that one arm hung limply beside him, and that one leg dragged a little as he walked. He was a man who bore paralysis with him.

She thought, while he was talking to her, that he looked like a man who had seen trouble. A weary, drawn look was about his eyes. She had seen dissipated men who looked like that; yet this stranger seemed in no ways a man of that sort. He was so quiet and polite; and when she saw the almost useless limbs, she thought she knew then what that look in his face meant.

But there were too many people about for her to study one very particularly, so she lost sight of the stranger, Harris, and did not observe that he had moved near the door of the sitting room, or that the door was open.

But it was; and just inside of it Lyster stood watching, with a certain vexation, a game of cards played there. The doctor had withdrawn, and was looking with amusement at the two players — 'Tana and Captain Leek. The captain was getting the worst of it. His scattered whiskers fairly bristled with perplexity and irritation. Several times he displayed bad judgment in drawing and discarding, because of his nervous annoyance, while she seemed surprisingly skillful or lucky, and was not at all disturbed by her opponent's moods. She looked smilingly straight into his eyes, and when she exhibited the last winning hand, and the captain dashed his hand angrily into the pack, she waited for one civil second and then swept the stakes toward her.

"What! Don't you want to play any more, captain?" she asked, maliciously. "I would really like to have another dance, yet if you want revenge —"

"Go and dance by all means," he said, testily. "When I want another game of poker, I'll let you know, but I must say I do not approve of such pastime for young ladies."

"None of us would, if in your place, captain," laughed the doctor. "And, for my part, I am glad I did not play against her luck."

The captain mumbled something about a difference between luck and skill, while 'Tana swept the money off the table and laughed-not a pleasant laugh, either.

"One-two-three-four! —twenty dollars-that is about a dollar a minute, isn't it?" she asked provokingly. "Well, captain, I guess we are square up to to-night, and if you want to open another account, I'm ready."

She spoke with the dash and recklessness of a boy. Lyster noticed it again, and resented it silently. But when she turned, she read the displeasure in his eyes.

"Oh, it's you, is it?" she inquired airily. "Is it time for our dance? You see, the captain wanted some amusement, and, as the doctor was nearly asleep over the cards, I came in and helped them out."

"Beautifully," agreed the doctor.

But Lyster borrowed no cheeriness from their smiles.

"I think it is our dance," Lyster observed. "And if you will come —"

"Certain," she said, with a nod; but at the door she paused. "Won't you keep this money for me?" she asked. "I've no pocket. And just put a five in a locked pocket 'for keeps,' please; I owe it to you."

"To me? You won that five."

"No, I didn't; I cheated you," she whispered. "Keep it, please do."

She pushed the money into his hand. One piece of it fell and rolled to the feet of the stranger, who leaned carelessly against the doorway, but in such a position that he could easily see into the sitting room.

He stooped and picked up the money.

"Yours, miss?" he said, courteously, and she smilingly reached out her hand for it-the hand on which Overton's gift, the strange ring, glittered.

The paralytic stranger barely repressed an exclamation as he noticed it, and from it his eyes went swiftly, questioningly, to the girl's face.

"Yes, it's mine," she said, with a nod of thanks. Then she smiled a little as she saw where his attention was given. "Are you wondering if the snakes you see are the result of odd drinks? Well, they are not; they are of metal and won't hurt you."

"Beg pardon, miss. Guess I did look at your pretty ring sharp; and it is enough to make a man shake if he's been drinking. But a little drink will do me a long time."

Then Lyster and the girl passed on, the girl smiling at the little exchange of words with the stranger. But Lyster himself was anything but well pleased at the entire affair. He resented the fact that he had found her there gambling, that she had shown such skill, that she had turned to the seedy-looking stranger and exchanged words, as men might do, but as a girl assuredly should not do. All these things disturbed him. Why, he could scarcely have told. Only that morning she had been but a little half-savage child, who amused him by her varying moods and sharp speech. But to-night, in her graceful white gown, she seemed to have grown taller and more womanly and winsome. The glances and homage of the most acceptable youths about revealed to him the fact that she was somewhat more than the strong swimmer or clever canoeist. She was deemed charming by others, in a very different fashion than he had thought of her, and she appeared rather too conscious of the fact. He fancied that she even delighted in letting him see that others showed deference to her, when he had only that day teased her as carelessly as he would have teased a boy into a rage.

Then to stop and jest like that with the insignificant stranger by the door! Mr. Lyster said a bad word in his mind, and decided that the presuming masculinity of the settlement would be allowed few chances for favors the remainder of the evening. He intended to guard her himself—a formidable guard for the purpose, as a man would need a good deal of self-reliance to try for favor if so handsome a personality as Lyster's was an opponent.

But the rather shabby stranger, standing by the inner door, scarcely noticed the noticeable young fellow. All his attention was given to the girl who had spoken to him so frankly. She passed on and did not observe his excessive interest. But his eyes lighted up when he heard her voice speaking to him, and his face flushed with color as he stroked his beard with his well hand and gazed after her.

"So this is where the trail begins, is it?" he whispered to the trembling hand at his lips. "Well, I would have looked for it many another place before commencing with a partner of Mr. Dan Overton-law-and-order man. He must have gulled this whole territory beautifully to have them swear by him as they do. And 'Monte' is his *protégée*! Well, Miss-or Mr. Monte-whichever it is-your girl's toggery is more becoming than the outfit I saw you wear last; but though your hair is a little darker, I'd swear to you anywhere-yes, and to the ring, too. Well, I think I'll rest my weary body in this 'burgh' for a few weeks to come. If the devil hasn't helped his own, and cheated me, this partner-Mr. 'Rivers'—is yet alive and in the flesh. If so, there is one place he will drift sooner or later, and that is to this young gambler. And then-then death will be no sham for him, for I will be here, too."

To 'Tana-jubilant with her victory over her instinctive antagonist, the captain-all the evening was made for her pleasure, and she floated in the paradise of sixteen years; and the world where people danced was the only world worth knowing.

"I will be good now—I can be as good as an angel since I've got even with the captain."

She whispered those words to Lyster, whose hand was clasping hers, whose arm was about her waist, as they, drifted around the rather small circle, to a waltz played on a concertina and a banjo.

She looked up at him, mutely asking him to believe her. Her desire for revenge satisfied, she could be a very good girl now.

It was just then that Overton, who stood outside the window, glanced in and saw her lovely upturned face-saw the red lips move in some pouting protest, to which Lyster smiled but looked doubtfully down at her. To the man watching them from without, the two seemed always so close-so confidential. At times he even wondered if Lyster had not learned more than himself of her life before that day at Akkomi's camp.

All that evening Dan had not once entered the room where they danced, or added in any way to their merry-making. He had stood outside the door most of the time, or sometimes rested a little way from it on a store box, where he smoked placidly, and inspected the people who gathered to the dance.

All the invited guests came early, and perfect harmony reigned within. A few of the unsavory order of citizens had sauntered by, as though taking note of the pleasures from which they were excluded. But it was not until almost twelve o'clock-just after Overton had turned away from watching the waltz-that a pistol shot rang out in the street, and several dancers halted.

Some of the men silently moved to the door, but just then the door was opened by Overton, who looked in.

"It was only my gun went off by accident," he said, carelessly. "So don't let me stampede the party. Go on with your music."

The stranger, Harris, was nearest the door, and essayed to pass out, but Overton touched him on the arm.

"Not just yet," he said hurriedly. "Don't come out or others will follow, and there'll be trouble. Keep them in some way."

Then the door closed. The concertina sobbed and shrieked out its notes, and drowned a murmur of voices on the outside. One man lay senseless close to the doorstep, and four more men with two women stood a little apart from him.

"If another shot is fired, your houses will be torn down over your heads to-morrow," said Overton, threateningly; "and some of you will not be needing an earthly habitation by that time, either."

"Fury! It is Overton!" muttered one of the men to another. "They told us he wasn't in this thing."

"What for you care?" demanded the angry tones of a Dutch woman. "What difference that make-eh? If so be as we want to dance-well, then, we go in and dance-you make no mistake."

But the men were not so aggressive. The most audacious was the senseless one, who had fired the revolver and whom Overton had promptly and quietly knocked down.

"I don't think you men want any trouble of this sort," he remarked, and ignored the women entirely. "If you've been told that I'm not in this, that's just where some one told you a lie; and if it's a woman, you should know better than to follow her lead. If these women get through that door, it will be when I'm an angel. I'm doing you all a good turn by not letting the boys in there know about this. No religion could save you, if I turned them loose on you; so you had better get away quiet, and quick."

The men seemed to appreciate his words.

"That's so," mumbled one.

And as the other woman attempted a protest, one of the men put his hand over her mouth, and, picking her up bodily, walked down the street with her, she all the time kicking and making remarks of a vigorous nature.

The humor of the situation appealed to the delicate senses of her companions, until they laughed right heartily, and the entire tone of the scene was changed from a threat of battle to an excuse for jollity. The man on the ground reeled upward to his feet with the help of a shake from Overton.

"Where's my gun?" he asked, sulkily.

Blood trickling from a cut brow compelled him to keep one eye shut.

"Overton has it," explained one of his friends. "Come on, and don't try another racket."

"I want my gun-it was him hit me," growled the wounded one, whose spirits had not been enlivened by the spectacle the rest had witnessed.

"You are right-it was him," agreed the other, darkly; "and if it hadn't been for breaking up the dance, I guess he'd a-killed you. Come on. You left a ball in his arm by the looks of things, and all he did was to knock you still. He may want to do more to-morrow. But as you have no gun, you'd better wait till then."

The door had been opened, and the light streamed out. Men talked in a friendly, jovial fashion on and about the doorstep. They saw the forms moving away in the shadows, but no sign of disturbance met them.

Overton stood looking in the window at the dancers. The waltz was not yet finished, and 'Tana and Lyster drifted past within a few feet of him. The serenity of their evening had not been disturbed. Her face held all of joyous content-so it seemed to the watcher. She laughed as she danced; and hearing the music of her high, girlish tones, he forgot for a time the stinging little pain in his arm, until his left hand, thrust into his coat pocket, slowly filled with blood. Then Dan turned to the man nearest him.

"If Doctor Harrison is still in there, would you do me the favor of asking him to come outside for a few minutes?" he asked, and the man addressed stepped closer.

"There is a back way into the house. Hadn't you better just step in that way, and have him fix you up? He's in the back room, alone, smoking."

Overton turned with an impatient exclamation, and a sharp, questioning look. It was the half-paralyzed stranger-Harris.

"Oh, I ain't interfering!" he said, amiably. "But as I slipped out through the back door before your visitors left, I dropped to the fact that you had some damage done to that left arm. Yes, I'll carry any message you like to your doctor, for I like your nerve. But I must say it's thankless work to stand up as a silent target for cold lead, just so some one else may dance undisturbed. Take an old man's advice, sonny, do some of the dancing yourself."

Chapter IX
The Stranger's Warning

That one festive night decided the immediate future of 'Tana. All her joy in it did not prevent a decision that it should be the last in her experience, for a year to come, at least.

It was Lyster who broached the subject, and Overton looked at him closely while he talked.

"You are right," he decided, at last; "a school is the easiest path out of this jungle, I reckon. I thought of a school, but didn't know where —I'm not posted on such things. But if you know the trail to a good one, we'll fix it. She has no family folks at all, so —"

"I'd like to ask, if it's allowable —"

"Don't ask me about her people," said the other, quickly; "she wouldn't want me to talk of them. You see, Max, all sorts get caught in whirlpools of one sort or another, when ventures are made in a new country like this, and often it's a thoroughbred that goes under first, while a lot of scrub stock will pull through an epidemic and never miss a feed. Well, her folks belonged to the list that has gone under-speculating people, you know, who left her stranded when they started 'over the range,' and she's sensitive about it-has a sort of pride, too, and doesn't want to be pitied, I guess. Anyway, I've promised she sha'n't be followed by any reminder of her misfortunes, and I can't go into details."

"Oh, that's all right; I'm not curious to know whether her folks had a palace or a cabin to live in. But she has brightness. I like her well enough to give up some useless pastimes that are expensive, and contribute the results to a school fund for her, if you say yes. But I should like to know if her people belonged to the class we call ladies and gentlemen-that is all."

Overton did not answer at once. His eyes were turned toward his bandaged arm, and a little wrinkle grew between his brows.

"The man is dead, and I don't think there's anything for me to say as to his gentlemanly qualities," he said at last. "He was a prospector and speculator, with an equal amount of vice and virtue in him, I suppose; just about like the rest of us. Her mother I never saw, but have reason to think she was a lady."

"And you say every word of that as if they were drawn from you with forceps," said Lyster, cheerily. "Well, I'll not bother you about it again. But, you see, there is a cousin of mine at the school I spoke of, and I wanted to know because of that. It's all right, though; my own instincts would tell me she came of good stock. But even good stock will grow wild, you know, if it doesn't get the right sort of training. You know, old fellow, I'm downright in earnest about wanting to help you about her."

"Yes, I know. You have, too," said the other. "You've pointed out the school and all, and we see she can't be left here."

"Not when you are ranging around the hills, and never a man to take your place as a guard," agreed Lyster. "I feel about two years old ever since I heard of how you kept annoyances from us last night while we were so serenely unconscious of your trials. 'Tana will scarcely look at me this morning, for no reason but that I did not divine the state of affairs and go to help you. That girl has picked up so much queer knowledge herself that she expects every one to be gifted with second sight."

Then he told, with a good deal of amusement, the episode of the poker game and the discomfiture of the captain.

Overton said little. He was not so much shocked or vexed over it as Lyster had been, because he had lived more among people to whom such pastimes were not unusual.

"And I offered to teach her 'seven-up,' because it was easy," he remarked grimly. "Yes, the school is best. You see, even if I am on the ground, I'm not a fit guardian. Didn't I give her leave to get square with the old man? While, if I'd been the right sort of a guardian, she would have been given a moral lecture on the sinfulness of revenge. I guess we'd better begin to talk school right away."

"I imagine she'll object at first, through force of habit, and protest that she knows enough for one girl."

But she did not. She listened with wonder in her eyes, and something of shamed contrition in her face, and knew so well-so very well that she did not deserve it. She had wanted-really wanted to vex him when she played the cards, when she had danced past, and never let on she saw him looking somberly in at the window the night before. But in the light of morning and with the knowledge of his wounded arm, all her resentment was gone. She could scarcely speak even the words she meant to say.

"I can't do that-go, I mean. It will cost so much, and I have no money. I can't make any here, and-and you are not rich enough to lend it to me, even if I could pay it back some day, so —"

"Never mind about the money; it will be got. I'm to start up north of this soon, and this doesn't seem a good place to school you in, anyway. So, for a year or so, you go to that school down in Helena. Max knows the name of it; I forget. When you get all rigged out with an education, and have a capital of knowledge, you can talk then about the money and paying it, if it makes you feel more comfortable. But just now you be a good little girl; go down there with Max to the school, study hard, so that if I drop into a chasm some night, or am picked off by a bullet, you'll have learned, anyway, how to look after yourself in the right way."

"Oh, it's Mr. Max, then, that's planning this, is it?" she asked suddenly, and her face flushed a little-he must have thought in anger, for he said:

"Why-yes; that is-mostly. You see, 'Tana, I've drifted out from the ways of the world while Max has kept up with them. So he proposed-well, no matter about the plan. I'm to suggest it to you, and as it's no loss and all gain to you, I reckon you'll be sensible enough to say yes."

"I will," she answered, quietly; "it is very kind of you both to be so good to me, for I haven't been good to you-to either of you, I'm sorry —I —maybe I'll be better when I come back-and-maybe I can pay you some day."

"Me? Oh, you won't owe me anything, and I reckon you'd better not make plans about coming back here! The books and things you learn will likely turn you toward other places-finer places. This is all right for men who have money to make; but you —"

"I'm coming back here," she said, nodding her head emphatically. "Maybe not for always-but I'll come back some time —I will."

She was twisting her fingers in a nervous way, and, as he watched her, he noticed that her little brown hands were devoid of all ornament.

"Where is the ring?" he asked. "Have you lost it already?"

"No, it's here-in my pocket," and she drew it out that he might see. "I —I took it off this morning when I saw you were shot. You'll laugh, I suppose; but I thought the snakes brought bad luck."

"So you are superstitious?"

"Oh, I don't know! I'm not afraid very often; but sometimes I think there are signs that are true. I've heard old folks say so, and talk of things unlucky. I took the ring off when I saw your arm."

"But the arm was only scratched-not worth a thought from a little girl like you," he said; "and surely not worth throwing off your jewelry for. But some day-some day of good luck, I may find you a prettier ring-one more like a girl's ring, you know; one you can wear and not be afraid."

"If I'm afraid, it isn't for myself," she said, with that old, unchildlike look he had not seen in her eyes of late. "But I'll tell you what I'm afraid of. Have you ever heard of people who were 'hoodoos'? I guess you have. Well, sometimes I'm afraid I'm just that-like the snakes in that ring. I'm afraid I bring bad luck to people-people I like. It isn't the harm to me that ever frightens me. I guess I can fight that; but no one can fight a 'hoodoo,' I guess; and your arm —"

"Oh, see here! Wake up, 'Tana, you're dreaming! Who put that cussed nonsense into your head? 'Hoodoo!' Pshaw! I will have patience with you in anything but that. Did any one look at you last night as if you were a 'hoodoo'? Here comes Max; we'll ask him."

But she did not smile at their badinage.

"I was in earnest, and you think it only funny," she said. "Well, maybe you won't always laugh at it. Men who know a heap believe in 'hoodoos.'"

"But not 'hoodoos' possessed of the *tout ensemble* of Miss Rivers," objected Lyster. "You are simply trying to scare us-me, out of the journey I hoped to make with you to Helena. You are trying to evade a year of scholastic training we have planned for you, and you would like to prophesy that the boat will blow up or the cars run off the track if you embark. But it won't. You will say good-by to your ogre of a guardian to-morrow. You will be guarded by no less a personage than my immaculate self to the door of your academy; from which you will emerge, later on, with never a memory of 'hoodoos' in your wise brain; and you will live to a green old age and make clay busts of us both when we are gray haired. There! I think I'm a good healthy sort of a prophet; and as a reward will you go with me to-morrow?"

"With you? Then it is you who —"

"Who has planned the whole brilliant scheme? Exactly-the journey part of it at all events; and I'm not so modest as our friend here. I'll take the blame of my share, and his, too, if he doesn't speak up for himself. Here comes your new friend, Dan. Where did you pick him up?"

It was the man Harris, and beside him was the captain. They were talking with some animation of late Indian raids to the westward.

"I doubt if it was Indians at all who did the thieving," remarked Harris; "there are always a lot of scrub whites ready to take advantage of war signals, and do devilment of that sort, made up as reds."

"Oh, yes-some say so! That man Holly used to get the credit of that sort of renegade work. Handsome Holly he was called once. But now that he's dead, maybe we'll see he was not the only one to work mischief between the whites and reds."

"Holly? Lee Holly?" asked Lyster. "Why, didn't we hear a rumor that he wasn't dead at all, but had been seen somewhere near Butte?"

"I didn't," returned Overton, who was the one addressed, "though it may be so. He's a very slippery specimen and full of schemes, from what I hear. But he doesn't seem to range over this territory, so I've never run across him. It would be like him, though, to play dead when the Government men grew warm on his trail, and he'd no doubt get plenty of help from his Indian allies."

Harris was watching him keenly, and the careless honesty of the speaker's face and tone evidently perplexed him, for he turned with a baffled look to the girl, who stood with down-dropped eyes, and twisted a spray of leaves nervously around her fingers. He noticed one quick, troubled glance she gave Overton, but even to his suspicious eyes it did not seem a regard given a fellow-conspirator.

"I believe it was the doctor I heard speak of the rumor that Holly was yet above ground," said Lyster. "The mail came up yesterday, and perhaps he found it in the papers. Don't think I had heard of the man before. Is he one of the important people up here?"

"Rather," remarked Overton, "an accomplished crook who has dabbled in several trades in the Columbia River region. The latest was a wholesale horse steal from a ranch over in Washington-Indian work, with him as leader. The regulars from the fort got after them, there was an ugly fight, and the reds reported Holly as killed. That is the last I heard of him. You were asking me yesterday if he ever prospected in our valley, didn't you?" he asked, turning to Harris.

"A man made undue importance of by the stupid Indians," declared Captain Leek. "He humored their superstitions and played medicine man with them, I've heard; and he had a boy for a partner —a young slip the gamblers called 'Monte' down in Cœur d'Alene. Some said it was his son."

"A fine instructor for youth," observed Lyster. "Who could expect anything but vice from a man who had such a boyhood?"

"But you would," said 'Tana, suddenly, "if you knew that boy when he grew to be a man. If he was bad, you'd want him to get off the earth where you walked; and you never once would stop to ask if he was brought up right or not-you know you wouldn't —nobody does, I guess.

I don't know why it is, but it seems all wrong to me. Maybe, though, when I go to school, and learn things, I will think like the rest, and not care."

Lyster shrugged his shoulders and looked after her as she vanished into the regions where Mrs. Huzzard was concocting dishes for the mid-day meal.

"I doubt if she thinks like the rest," he remarked. "How fiery she is, and how independent in her views of things."

But Overton smiled at her curt speech.

"Poor 'Tana has lived among rough scenes until she learns to judge quickly, and for herself," he said. "Her words are true enough, too; she may have known just such boys as Holly's clever little partner and seen how hard it was for them to be any good. I wonder now what has become of young 'Monte' since Holly disappeared. He would be a good one to follow, if there is doubt as to Holly's death being a fact. I believe there was a reward out for him some time ago, to stimulate lagging justice. Don't know if it's withdrawn or not."

"Square," decided Harris, in silent communion with himself, as he surveyed Overton; "dead square, and don't scent the trail. I'd like to know what their little game is with him. Some devilment, sure."

On one pretext and another he kept close to Overton. He was studying the stalwart, easy-going keeper of the peace, and Dan, who had a sort of compassion for all who were halt, or blind, or homeless, took kindly enough to the semi-paralyzed stranger. Harris seemed to belong nowhere in particular, yet knew each trail of the Kootenai and Columbia country, knew each drift where the yellow sands were found-each mine where the silver hunt paid best returns.

"You've prospected some, I see, even if you don't get over the ground very fast," Dan remarked; "and with it all, I reckon you've staked out some pay claims for yourself?"

The face of Harris contracted in a swift frown; he drew a long breath, and his clasped hands tightened on each other.

"I did," he said, in a choked, nervous sort of way; "I did. If I could tell you of it, I would. You're the sort of man I'd —But never mind. I'm not well yet-not strong enough to get excited over it. I've got to take things easy for a spell, or another stroke of this paralysis will come as my share. That handicaps me considerable. I was-was upset by something unexpected last night, and I've had a queer, shaky feeling ever since; can't articulate clear. Did you notice? The-the only thing under God's heaven I'm afraid of is that paralysis-that it will catch me again before I get my work done; and to-day —"

"Don't talk of it," advised Overton, as he noticed how the man's voice hesitated and trembled, how excitable he was over the subject of his mineral finds and his threatened helplessness. "Don't think of it, and you'll come out all right yet. If I can do anything for you —"

The other man laughed in a spasmodic, contemptuous fashion.

"For me?" he said. "You can't. I thought you could, but I was on a blind trail-you can't. I can give you a lift, though-yes, I can. It's about-about that girl. You-you tried to guard her last night, as if she was a flower the rough wind must not blow on. I know —I watched you. I've been there, and know."

"Know what? You're an infernal fool!" burst out Dan, with all his good nature out of sight. "No hints about the girl, or-or anything else! I won't have it!"

"It's no hint; facts are all I'd mention to you, and I'd do that just because I think you're square. And they-they are playing you. See? For he ain't dead. I don't know what their game is with you, but he ain't dead; and there-there's no telling what scheme he's got her into this-this territory for. So I want you to know. I don't want you to be caught in any trap of theirs. She-she looks all right; but he's a devil —a thing infernal —a —"

Overton caught him by one arm, and swung him around like a child.

"Speak clear. No more of your blasted stuttering or beating away from points; who is the man you talk of? Who is playing with me? Now speak."

"Why, Monte, the girl; Monte and Lee Holly. He's somewhere alive-that's what I'm trying to tell you. I was hunting for him when I found her laying low here, don't you understand? You stare so. It is Lee Holly and — Ah-my-God!"

The last words were gurgled in his throat; his face whitened, and he sank to the ground as though his bones had suddenly been converted into jelly —a strange, shapeless heap of humanity as he lay at Overton's feet. Overton bent over him, and after a moment of blank amaze, lifted the helpless head, and almost dropped it again, when the eyes, appealing and keenly conscious, met his own. There was a queer chuckling sound in the man's throat; he was trying to speak, but could not. The secret he was trying to tell was buried back of those speechless lips, and one more stroke of the doom he feared had overtaken him.

Chapter X
The Stranger's Love Story

'Tana sat alone in her room a few hours later, and from the window watched the form of Ora Harrison disappear along the street. The latter had been sent by her father with some medicine for the paralyzed stranger, and the girls had chatted of the school 'Tana was to attend, and of the schools Ora had gone to and all the friends she remembered there, who now sent her such kind letters. Ora told 'Tana of the lovely time she expected to have when the steamers would come up from Bonner's Ferry to the Kootenai Lake region, for then her friends were to come in the summers, and the warm months were to be like holidays.

All this girlish frankness, all the cheery friendship of the doctor's family filled 'Tana with a wild unrest against herself-against the world.

"It would be easy to be good if a person lived like that always," she thought, "in a nice home, with a mother to kiss me and a father I was not ashamed of. I felt stupid when they talked to me. I could only think how happy they were, and that they did not seem to know it. And Ora was sweet and sorry for me because my parents were dead. Huh!" she grunted, disdainfully, in the Indian fashion peculiar to her at times. "If she knew how I felt about it she'd hate me, I suppose. They'd all think I was bad clear through. They wouldn't understand the reason-no nice women like them could. Oh, if the school would only make me nice like that! But I suppose it's got to be born in people, and I was born different."

Even this reason did not render her more resigned; and, to add to her disquiet, there came to her the memory of eyes whose gaze made her shiver-the eyes of the stranger whom Overton had carried into the house for dead, but whose brain was yet alive. He had looked at her with a strange, wild stare, and Overton himself had turned his eyes toward her in moody questioning when she came forward to help. He had accepted the help, but each time she raised her eyes she saw that Dan was looking at her with a new watchfulness; all his interest in the stricken stranger did not keep him from that.

"If any one is accountable for this, I guess I'm the man," he confessed, ruefully. "He told me he was afraid of this, yet I was fool enough to lose my temper and turn him around rough. It might have struck him, anyway; but my conscience doesn't let me down easy. He'll be my care till some one comes along with a stronger claim."

"Maybe there is some one somewhere," said 'Tana. "There might be letters, if it would be right to look."

"If there are relatives anywhere in the settlements, I guess they'd be glad enough if I'd look," decided Overton. "There is no way to get permission from him, though," and he looked in the helpless man's eyes. "I don't know what you'd say to this if you could speak, stranger," he said; "but to go through your pockets seems the only way to locate you or your friends; so I'll have to do it."

It was not easy to do, with those eyes staring at him in that horrible way. But he tried to avoid the eyes, and thrust his hand into the inner pocket, drawing out an ordinary notebook, some scraps of newspaper folded up in it, and two letters addressed to Joe Hammond; one to Little Dalles, and the other had evidently been delivered by a messenger, for no destination was marked on it. It was an old letter and the envelope was worn through all around the edges. Another paper was wrapped around it, and the writing was of a light feminine character. Overton touched it with a certain reverence and looked embarrassed.

"I think, Mrs. Huzzard, I will ask you to read this, as it seems a lady's letter, and if there is any information in it, you can give it to us; if not, I'll just put it back in his pocket and hope luck will tell us what the letter doesn't."

But Mrs. Huzzard demurred: "And me that short-sighted that even specs won't cure it! No, indeed. I'm no one to read important papers. But here's 'Tana, with eyes like a hawk for sighting things. She'll read it fast enough."

Overton looked undecided, remembering those strange insinuations of the now helpless man, and feeling that the man himself might not be willing.

"I —well —I guess not," he said, at last. "It ain't just square to send a little girl blindfold like that into a stranger's claim. We'll let some one over twenty-one read the letters. You'll do, Max, and if it ain't all right, you can stop up short."

So Lyster read the treasured message, all in the same feminine writing. His sensitive face grew grave, and he turned compassionate glances toward the helpless man as he read the letters, according to their dates. The oldest one was the only one not sad. Its postmark was a little town many miles to the south.

"Dear Old Joe: It's awful to be this near you, and know you are sick, without being able to get to you. I just arrived, and your partner has met me, and told me all about it. But I'll go up with him, just the same; and when you are able to travel we can come down to a town and be married, instead of to-day, as we had set on. So that's all right, and don't you worry. Your partner, John Ingalls, is as nice as he can be to me. Why did you not tell me how good looking he was? Maybe you never discovered it-you slow, prosy old Joe! When you wrote to me of that rich find you stumbled on, I was sorry you had picked up a partner; for you always did trust folks too much, and I was afraid you'd be cheated by the stranger you picked up. But I guess that I was wrong, Joe; for he is a very nice gentleman-the nicest I ever met, I think. And he talks about you just as if he was your brother, and thought a heap of you. He tried to tease me some, too-asked how you ever came to catch such a pretty girl as me! Then I told him, Joe, that you never had to catch me-that I was little, and hadn't any folks, and how you got your folks to give me a home when you was only a boy; and that you was always like a big brother to me till you made some money in the mines. Then you wrote and asked me to come out and marry you. He just laughed, Joe, and said it was not a brother's love that a wife wanted; but I don't think he knows anything about that-do you? And, Joe, I came pretty near telling him all about that richest find you made-the one you said you wanted me to be the first to see. I thought, of course, you had told your partner, just as you told me when you sent me the plan of it-what for, I don't know, Joe, for I never could find it in the wide world, even if there was any chance of my hunting for it alone. Your partner asked me point blank if you had written to me of any late find of yours, or of any special location where you found good signs. I tried to look innocent, and said maybe you had, but I couldn't remember. I didn't like to tell a story. I wanted to tell him all the truth, and how rich you said we would be. I knew you would want to tell him yourself, so I managed to keep quiet in time. But whenever he looks at me I feel guilty. And he looks at me so kindly, and he is so good. He says we can't begin our journey to you right away, because he has provisions and things to get first; but we will set out in three days. So I send this letter that you will know I am on the road; maybe we'll reach you first. He is going to take me riding around this camp this evening —I mean Mr. Ingalls. He says I must get some enjoyment before I go up there to the mountains, where no one lives. He is the nicest stranger I ever met. But, of course, I never was away from home much to meet folks; I guess, though, I might travel a long ways and not meet any one so nice. He just brought me a pretty purse made by the Indians. I hope you wear a big hat like he does, and big, high boots. I never saw folks wear them back home; but they do look nice. Now, good-by, Joe, for a few days.

"Yours affectionately,
"Fannie."

"Well, that letter is plain sailing," remarked Overton, "but there is only one name in it we could follow up-the partner, John Ingalls. But I don't think I've heard of him."

"Wait! there is another letter-two more," said Lyster; and the others were silent as he read:

> "Joe: I hope you'll hate me now. I can stand that better than to know you still like me. I can't help it. I am going with him-your partner. He loves me, too, Joe-not in the brotherly way you did, but in a way that makes me think of him and no one else. So I can't marry any one but him. Maybe it's a sin to be false to you, Joe; but I never could go to you now. And I can't help going where he wants me to go. Don't be mad at him; he can't help it either, I suppose. He says he will always be good to me, and I am going. But my heart is heavy as I write to you. I am not happy-maybe because I love him too much. But I am going. Try and forget me.
>
> "Fannie."

In dead silence Lyster unfolded the third paper. The drama of this stranger's life was a pathetic thing to the listeners, who looked at him with pity in their eyes, but could utter no words of sympathy to the man who sat there helpless and looked at them. Then the last, a penciled sheet, was read.

> "Joe: I am dying, I think. The Indian woman with me says so; and I hope it is true. He came to me to-day —the first time in weeks. He never married me, as he promised. He cursed me to-day because my baby face led him away from a fortune he knows you found. I never told him, though it is a wonder. All he knows of it he heard you say in your sleep when you were sick that time. To-day he told me you were paralyzed, Joe-that you are helpless still-that he has taken Indians with him there to your old claim, and searched every foot of ground for the gold vein he thinks you know of. But it is of no use, and he is furious over it, and so taunts me of your helplessness alone in the wilderness.
>
> "Joe, I still have the plan you made of the river and the two little streams and the marked tree. Can't I make amends some way for the wrong I did you? Is there anywhere a friend you could trust to work the find and take care of you? For if you are too helpless to write yourself, and can get only the name of the person to me, I will send the plan some way to him. I know I am not to live long. I am in a perfect fever to hear from you, and tell you that my sin against you weighs me down to despair.
>
> "I can't tell you of my life with him; it is too horrible. I do not even know who he is, for Ingalls is not his name. We are with Indians and they call him 'Medicine,' and seem to know him well. He has left me here, to-day, and I feel I will never see him again. He tells me he has sent for a young white boy who is to be brought to camp, and who will help care for me. Anything would be better than the sly red faces about me; they fill me with terror. My one hope is that the boy may get this letter sent to you, and that some word may come to me from you before my life ends. It has taken me all this day to write to you.
>
> "Good-by. I am dying miserably, and I deserve it. I can't even tell you where to write me; only we are with Indians camped by a big river. Not far away is a wall of rock, like a hill, beside the river, and Indian writing is cut on the wall, and holes and things are cut all along it."

"The Arrow lakes of the Columbia!" interrupted Overton —

> "If the boy comes, and is to be trusted at all, he may tell me more; that is my only hope of this reaching you. If you are not able to make another plan (and he says

your hands are powerless) remember, I have the one you did make. If you can send me one word-one name of a friend —I will try-try so hard. He would kill me if he knew, and I would be glad of it, if I could only help you first. I feel that I will never see you again.

"Fannie."

Mrs. Huzzard was crying and whispering, "Poor dear! —poor child!" and even the voice of Lyster was not quite steady as he read. Those straggling, weak pencil marks had a pathos of their own to him. The letter, crossed and recrossed by the lines, was on two pages, evidently torn from the back of a book.

"It seems a sacrilege to dive into a man's feelings and secrets like this," he said, ruefully. "It *is*! My only consolation is that I did it with good intent."

"And, after all, not a plain trail found that will help us locate this man or his friends," decided Overton —"not a name we can really fasten to but the name on the envelope-Joe Hammond. It is too bad. Why, 'Tana! Good God! *'Tana!*"

For the girl, who had uttered no word, but had listened to that last letter with whitened face and staring eyes, leaned against the wall at its close, and a little gasp from her drew their attention.

She fell forward on her face ere Overton could reach her.

"Tana, my girl, what is it? Speak!" he entreated.

But the girl only whispered: "I know now! Joe-Joe Hammond!" and fainted dead away at the feet of the paralyzed man.

Chapter XI
'Tana and Joe

"Just like a part in a play, captain-that's just the way it struck me," said Mrs. Huzzard, recounting the affair for the benefit of the postmaster of Sinna Ferry. "The man a-sitting there like a statue, with only his eyes looking alive, and that poor, scared dear a-falling down on the floor beside him, and looking as white as milk! I never had a notion she was so easy touched by people's troubles. It surely was a sorry story read from them three letters. I tell you, sir, men leave women with aching hearts many's the time," and she glanced sentimentally toward her listener; "though if there is one place more heart-rending to be deserted in than another, I think an Indian village would be the very worst. Just to think of that poor dear dying there in a place she didn't even know the name of."

"Humph! I've an idea you are giving your sympathy to the wrong individual," decided the captain. "It must be easier even to die in some unknown corner than for a living soul to be shut up in a dead body, after the manner of this Harris, or Hammond, or whatever his name is. I guess, from the looks of things, he must have collapsed when that second letter reached him; had a bad stroke, and was just recovering somewhat when he strayed into this camp. Yes, madame, I've an idea he's had a harder row to hoe than the girl; and, then, it doesn't look as though he'd deserved it so much."

"Mr. Dan is mightily upset over it, ain't he?"

"Mr. Dan is just as likely to get upset over any other vagabond who strays in his direction," grumbled the captain. "Folks are always falling in his way to be looked after. He has the worst luck! He never did a bit of harm to this stranger-nothing but drop a hand on his shoulder; and all at once the man falls down helpless. And Dan feels in duty bound to take care of him. Then the girl 'Tana has to flop over in the same way, just when I thought we were to get rid of her. And she's another charge to look after. He'll be wanting to hire your house for a hospital next thing, Mrs. Huzzard."

"And welcome he'd be to it for 'Tana," declared Mrs. Huzzard, valiantly. "She's been a bit saucy to you at times, and I know it; but, indeed, it's only because she fancies you don't like her."

"Like her, madame! A girl who plays poker, and-and —"

"And wins," added Mrs. Huzzard, with a twinkle in her eyes. "Ah, now, didn't Mr. Max tell me the whole story! She is a clip, and I know it; but I think she only meant that game as a bit of a joke."

"A twenty-dollar joke, Mrs. Huzzard, is too expensive to be funny," growled the captain, with natural discontent. "But if I could only convince myself that the money was honestly won, I would not feel so annoyed over it; but I can't —no, madame. I am confident there was a trick in that game-some gambler's trick she has picked up among her promiscuous acquaintances. And I am annoyed-more than ever annoyed now that there is a chance of her remaining longer under Dan's care. She's a dangerous *protégée* for a boy of his age, that's all."

"Dangerous! Oh, now, I've my doubts of that," said Mrs. Huzzard, shaking her head, emphatically. "You take my word for it, if she's dangerous as a girl to any one in this camp, it's not Mr. Dan's peace of mind she's disturbing, but that of his new friend."

"You mean Lyster? Ridiculous! A gentleman of culture, used to the best society, give a thought to such an unclassed individual? No, madame! —don't you believe it. His interest about the school affair was doubtless to get her away from camp, and to keep her from being a responsibility on Dan's hands."

"Hum! maybe. But, from all the dances he danced with her, and the way he waited on her, I'd a notion that he did not think her a great responsibility at all."

This conversation occurred the morning after those letters had been read. The owner of them was installed in the best room Mrs. Huzzard had to offer, and miners from all sections were cordially invited to visit the paralyzed man, in the vain hope that some one would chance to remember his face, or help establish the lost miner's identity; for he seemed utterly lost from all record of his past-all but that he had loved a girl whom an unknown partner had stolen. And Overton remembered that he seemed especially interested in the whereabouts of the renegade, Lee Holly.

The unknown Lee Holly's name had suddenly attained the importance of a gruesome ghost to Overton. He had stared gloomily at the paralytic, as though striving to glean from the living eyes the secrets held close by the silenced lips. 'Tana and Monte and Lee Holly! —his little girl and those renegades! Surely these persons could have nothing to do with each other. Harris was looney-so Overton decided as he stalked back and forth beside the house, glancing up once in a while to a window above him —a window where he hoped to see 'Tana's face; for all one day had gone, and the evening come again, yet he had never seen her since he had lifted her unconscious form from beside the chair of Harris. Her words, "I know now! Joe-Joe Hammond!" were yet whispering through his senses. Did those words mean anything? or was the child simply overwrought by that tragedy told in the letters? He did not imagine she would comprehend all the sadness of it until she had fallen in that faint.

The night he had talked with her first in Akkomi's tepee, and afterward in the morning by the river, he had promised to be satisfied with what she chose to tell him of herself, and ask no questions of her past. But since the insinuations of Harris and her own peculiar words and manner, he discovered that the promise was not easy to keep-especially when Lyster besieged him with questions; for 'Tana had spent the day utterly alone, but for the ministrations of Mrs. Huzzard. She would not see even the doctor, as she said she was not sick. She would not see Overton, Lyster, or any one else, because she said she did not want to talk; she was tired, and that reason must suffice. It did for Lyster, especially after he had received a nod, a smile, and a wave of her hand from her window —a circumstance he related hopefully to Overton, as it banished the lingering fear in his mind that her exile was one caused by absolute illness.

"I candidly believe, Dan, that she is simply ashamed of having fainted before us last evening-fancies it looks weak, I suppose; and she does pride herself so on her ungirlish strength. I've no doubt she will emerge from her seclusion to-morrow morning, and expect us to ignore her sentimental swoon. How is your other patient?"

"Better."

"Much?"

"Well, just the difference of turning his eyes quickly toward a thing, instead of slowly, as at first. The doctor just told me he is able to move his head slightly, so I guess he is not to go under this trip. But he'll never be a well man again."

"Rather heavy on you, old fellow, that you feel bound to look after him. I can't see the necessity of it. Why don't you let the rest of the camp —"

But Overton had turned away and resumed his walk. Lyster stared at him in wonder for a moment and then laughed.

"All right, Rothschild," he observed. "You know the depth of your own purse best. But, to tell the truth, you don't act like your own responsible self to-day. You go moping around as though the other fellow's stroke had touched you, too. You are a great fellow, Dan, to take other people's loads on your shoulders; but it is a bad habit, and you'd better reform."

"I will, when I have time," returned Overton, with a grim smile. "Just now I have other things to think of. Don't mind me."

"I sha'n't. I confess I don't mind any of you very much since I saw the cheery vision of your *protégée* at the window-and waving her hand to me, too; the first bit of sunshine I've seen in camp to-day. For the average specimen I've run across has looked to me like you-glum."

Receiving no reply whatever to this criticism, he strolled away after a smiling glance upward to 'Tana's window. But no girlish hand waved greeting to him this time, and he comforted himself by humming, "My Love is but a Lassie Yet." This was a mischievous endeavor to attract Overton's attention and make him say something, even though the something should prove uncomplimentary to the warbler.

But it was a failure. Overton only thrust his hands a little deeper in his pockets as he stared after the handsome, light-hearted fellow. Of course, it would be Max to whom she would wave her hand; and he was glad somebody felt like singing, though he himself could not. His mind was too much tormented by the thoughts of those two who formed a nucleus for the hospital already contemptuously alluded to by the captain.

And those two?

One sat almost motionless, as he had been for the twenty-four hours. But as Mrs. Huzzard and the captain left his room, each spoke hopefully of his appearance. Mrs. Huzzard especially was very confident his face showed more animation than she had observed at her noonday visit; and the fact that he could move his head and nod in reply to questions certainly did seem to promise recovery.

In the adjoining room, close to the very thin partition, 'Tana lay with ears strained to catch each word of the conversation. But when her door was opened by Mrs. Huzzard, all semblance of interest was gone, and she lay on the little bed with closed eyes.

"I'm right glad she's taking a nap at last," said the good soul as she closed the door softly. "That child scarce slept a bit all night, and I know it. Curious how nervous she got over that man's troubles. But, of course, he did look awful at first, and nigh about scared me."

'Tana lay still till the steps died away on the stairs, and the voices were heard more faintly on the lower floor. All the day she had waited for the people to leave the stranger in the next room alone; and, for the first time, no voice of visitors broke the silence of the upper floor.

She slipped to the door and listened. Her movements were stealthy as that of some forest animal evading a hunter. She turned the knob softly, and with still swiftness was inside the stranger's room, and the door closed behind her.

He certainly was more alert, for his eyes met hers instantly. His look was almost one of fear, and she was trembling visibly.

"I had to come," she said, nervously, in a half whisper, "I heard the letters read, and I have to tell you something I've thought all night-all day-and I have to tell you. Do you understand? Try to understand. Nod your head if you do. Do you?"

Her speech was rapid and impatient, while she listened each moment lest a step sound on the stairs again. But in all her eagerness to hear she never looked away from his face, and she uttered a low exclamation of gladness when the man's head bent slowly in assent.

"Oh, I am so glad-so glad! You will get well; you must! Listen! I know you now, and why you looked at me so. You think you saw me up at Revelstoke —I think I remember your face there-and you don't trust me. You are looking for that man-the man that took her away from you. You think I could find a trail to him; but you are wrong. He is dead, and I know she is —I *know*! Your name was the last word she said —'Joe.' She wanted you to forgive her, and not cross *his* path. You don't believe me, perhaps; but it is all true. I went to the camp with-with the boy she wrote of. She talked of you to me. I had word to give you if we ever met. But how was I to know that Jim Harris was the man-the same man? Do you hear-do you believe me?"

Those burning eyes-eyes in which all of life in him seemed concentrated-looked out on her from the pale, strange face; looked on her until her own cheeks grew colorless, for there was something awful in the searching regard of the man who was but half alive.

"See!" she said, and slipped from her belt a package in which paper rustled, "I've had that plan of the gold find ever since-since she died. She gave it to me, in case you should be-as you are, and no one to look after it for you. Or, if you should go under, she said, I was to look it up. And I started to look it up-yes, I did; but things were against me, and I let it go for a while. But now, listen! If you get well, it means money must do it. See? Dan hasn't very much-not enough to float you long. Now, I've thought it all out. You give up the notion of looking for that man, who wasn't worth a shot of powder when he was alive, and worth less now. It's that notion that's been eating the life out of you. Oh, I've thought it all out! Now you just turn honest prospector, like you was when that man Ingalls first spotted you. I'm only a girl, but I'll try to help make amends for the wrongs he did you. I'll go partners with you.

Look! here is the plan; and I'm almost sure I know where the two little streams meet. I've thought of it a heap; but the face of-of that dead girl, kept me from doing anything till I had either found you or knew you were dead. No one knows I have the plan-though *he* would have cut throats for it. Now do you trust me?"

She held the plan up so he could see it —a queer puzzle of lines and dots; but a glance sufficed, and he turned his eyes again to the face of the girl. Her eagerness, her intensity, awakened him to trust and sympathy. He looked at her and nodded his head.

"Oh, I knew you would!" she breathed, thankfully. "And I'll stand by you-you'll see! I've wanted a chance like this —a chance to make up for some of the devilment he's done to folks-and some he's made me help at. You know who I am, but none of the rest do-and they sha'n't. I'm a new girl now. I want to make up for some of the badness that has been. It's all over; but sometimes I hate the blood in my veins because-you know! And if I can only do *some* good —"

She paused, for the eyes of the paralyzed man had moved from her face, and were resting on something back of her.

It was Overton! He entered and closed the door, and stood looking doubtful and astonished, while 'Tana rose to her feet trembling and a little pale.

"How long-were you there?" she demanded, angrily.

He looked at her very steadily before making reply-such a curious, searching look that she moved uneasily because of it; but her face remained defiant.

"I just now opened the door," he said at last, speaking in a slow, deliberate way. "I slipped here as quietly as I could, because they told me you were asleep, and I must not make a noise. I got here just as you were telling this man that no one but him should know who you were before you came among us-that is all, I guess."

She had sat down on a seat close to Harris, and dropped her face in her hands.

Overton stood with his back against the door, looking down at her. In his eyes was a keen sorrow as she sat down in that despairing fashion, and crept close to the stranger as though for refuge from *him*.

"I might have avoided telling what I heard," he continued; "but I don't think that would be quite square among friends. Then, as I see you have found a new acquaintance here, I thought maybe you would have something to tell me if you knew what I heard you say to him."

But, kindly as his words were, she seemed to shrink from them.

"No; I can't. Oh, Mr. Dan, I can't —I can't," she muttered, with her head still bowed on the arm of the chair occupied by Harris. "If you can't trust me any more, I can't blame you. But I can't tell you-that's all."

"Then I'll just go down stairs again," he decided, "and you can finish your talk with Harris. I'll keep the rest of the folks from interrupting you as I did. But if you want me, little girl, you know I'll not be far away."

The tears came in her eyes. His persistent kindness to her made her both ashamed and glad, and she reached out her hand.

"Wait," she said, "maybe I have something to tell you," and she unfolded the paper again and showed it to Harris.

"Shall I tell him? Would you rather he would be the man to do the business?" she asked. "You know I'm willing, but I don't know enough myself. Do you want him to be the man?"

Harris nodded his head.

With a look of relief on her face, she turned to Overton, who watched them wonderingly.

"What sort of man is it you want? or what is it you want to tell me?"

"Only that I've found a plan of the ground where he made that rich find the letter told of," she answered, with a bit of a tremble in her voice. "He's never been able to look after it himself, and was afraid to trust any one. But now —"

"And you have the plan —*you*, 'Tana?"

"Yes, I have it. I think I even know where the place is located. But-don't ask me anything about how I got the plan. He knows, and is satisfied-that is all."

"But, 'Tana, I don't understand. You are giving me surprises too thick this evening. If he has found a rich yield of ore, and has taken you into partnership, it means that you will be a rich woman. A streak of pay ore can do more for you than a ranger like myself; so I guess you can afford to drop me."

Her face fell forward in her hands again. The man in the chair looked at her and then turned his eyes pleadingly to the other man, who remained standing close to the door.

Overton recognized the pleading quality of the glance, and was filled with amazement by it. Witchery seemed to have touched the stranger when paralysis touched him, else he would not so quickly have changed from his suspicion of the girl into that mute pleading for her.

She was trying so hard to keep back the tears, and in the effort her jaws were set and her brows drawn together stormily. She looked to him as she had looked in the lodge of Akkomi.

"You don't trust me," she said at last; "that's why you won't help us. But you ought to, for I've never lied to you. If it's because I'm in it that you won't have anything to do with the mine, I'll leave. I won't bother you about that school. I won't bother you about anything. I'll help locate the place if-if Joe here is willing; and then you two can be partners, and I'll be out of it, for I can trust you to take care of him, and see that the money does what it can for him. I can trust you if you can't me. So you are the one to speak up. What is your answer?"

Chapter XII
Partners

"Well, I've been a 'hoodoo' all my, life; and if I only lead some one into luck now-good luck-oh, wouldn't I learn a sun-dance, and dance it!"

The world was two weeks older, and it was 'Tana who spoke; not the troubled 'Tana who had crouched beside the paralytic and cowered under her fear of Overton's distrust, but a girl grown lighter-hearted by the help of work to be done-work in which she was for once to stand side by side with Overton himself, for his decision about the prospecting had been in her favor. He had "spoken up," as she had asked him to do, and a curious three-cornered partnership had been arranged the next day; a very mysterious partnership, of which no word was told to any one. Only 'Tana suddenly decided that the schooling must wait a little longer. Lyster would have to make the trip to Helena without her; she was not feeling like it just then, and so forth.

Therefore, despite the very earnest arguments of Mr. Lyster, he did have to go alone. During all the journey, he was conscious of a quite unreasonable disappointment, an impatience with even Overton, for not enforcing his authority as guardian, and insisting that she at once commence the many studies in which she was sadly deficient.

But Overton had stood back and said nothing. Lyster did not understand it, and could not succeed in making either of them communicative.

"You'll be back here in less than a month," said Overton. "We will send her then, if she feels equal to it. In the meantime, we'll take the best care we can of her here at the Ferry. I find I will have time to look after her a little until then. I have only one short trip to make up the river; so don't get uneasy about her. She'll be ready to go next run you make, sure."

So Lyster wondered, dissatisfied, and went away. He was even a little more dissatisfied with his last memory of the girl —a vision of her bending over that unknown, helpless miner. His sympathies were with the man. He was most willing to assist, in a financial way, toward taking care of one so unfortunate. But the thing he was not willing to do was to see 'Tana devote herself without restraint to the welfare of a stranger —a man they knew nothing of —a fellow who, of course, could have no appreciation of the great luck he was in to have her constantly beside him. It was a clean waste of exceptionable sympathy; and a squaw, or some miner out of work, would do as well in this case.

He even offered to pay for a squaw, or for any masculine nurse; but the girl had very promptly suggested that he busy himself with his own duties, if he had any. She stated further that he had no control whatever over her actions, and she could not understand —

"I know I have none," he retorted, with some impatience, and yet a good deal of fondness in his handsome eyes. "That is why I'm complaining. I wish I had. And if I had, wouldn't I whisk you away from this uncouth life! I wonder if you will ever let me do so, Tana?"

"I think you'd better be packing your plunder," she remarked, coolly. "If you don't, you'll keep the whole outfit waiting."

And that was how they let even Lyster go away. Not a hint was he given of the all-engrossing plan that bound both 'Tana and Overton to the interests of the passive stranger, who looked at them with intelligence, but who could not speak.

Their partnership was a curious affair, and the arrangement for interests in it was conducted on the one side by nods or shakes of the head, while the other two offered suggestions, and asked questions, until a very clear understanding was arrived at.

Only one knotty discussion had arisen. Overton offered to give one month of time to the search, on condition that one half of the find, if there was any made, should belong to 'Tana, while the original finder should have the other half. He himself would give that much time to helping them out in a friendly way; but more than that he could not give, because of other duties.

To this the man Harris shook his head with all possible vigor, while 'Tana was quite as emphatic in an audible way. Harris desired that all shares be equal, and Overton count himself in for a third. 'Tana approved the plan, insisting that she would not accept an ounce of the dust if he did not. So Dan finally agreed and ended the discussion concerning the division of the gold they might never find.

"And don't be so dead sure that the dirt will pan out well, even if we do find the place," he said, warningly, to 'Tana. "Why, my girl, if the average of dust had been as high as my average of hope over strikes I've made myself, I would have been a billionaire long ago."

"I never heard you talk of prospecting," remarked 'Tana. "All the rest do here, and not you—how is that?"

"Oh, prospecting strikes one like a fever; sometimes a man recovers from it, or seems to for a while. I had the fever bad about two years ago—out in Nevada. Well, I left there. I sunk my stock of capital in a very big hole, and lost my enthusiasm for a while. Maybe I will find it again, drifting along the Kootenai; but as yet it has not struck me hard. From what I can gather, this fellow must simply have dropped on a nugget or little pocket, and something must have made him distrust his partner to such an extent that he kept the secret find to himself. So there evidently has been no testing of the soil, no move toward development. We may never find an ounce of metal, for such disappointments have been even where very large nuggets have been found. You must not expect too much of this search. Golden hope lets you down hard when you do fall with it."

But, despite his warnings, he made arrangements for their river journey with all speed possible. The three of them were to go; and, as chaperon, Mrs. Huzzard was persuaded to join their queer "picnic" party, for that was the idea given abroad concerning their little trip to the north. It was to be a venture in the interests of Harris—supposedly the physical interests; though Captain Leek did remark, with decided emphasis, that it was the first time he ever knew of a man being sent out to live in the woods as a cure for paralysis.

But the preparations were made; even the fact that Mrs. Huzzard was seized with an unreasonable attack of rheumatism on the eve of departure did not deter them at all.

"Unless you need me to stay here and look after you, we'll go just the same," decided 'Tana. "A squaw won't be much of a substitute for you; but she'll be better than no one, and we'll go."

So the squaw was secured, through the agency of her husband, whom Overton knew, and who was to take their camp outfit up the river for them. This was one reason why Mrs. Huzzard, as she watched them depart, was a little thankful for the visitation of rheumatism.

Their camp was only a day old when 'Tana announced her willingness to dance if only good fortune would come to her.

It seemed a thing probable, for as Overton poured water slowly from a tin pan into the shallow little stream, there were left in the bottom of the pan, as the last sifting bit of soil was washed out, some tiny bits of yellow the size of a pin-head, and one as large as a grain of wheat.

'Tana gave a little ecstatic cry as she bent over it and touched the particles with her finger.

"Oh, Dan—it is the gold! —the real gold! and we are millionaires! —millionaires, and you would not believe it!"

He raised his finger warningly, and shook his head.

"Wait until we are millionaires before you commence to shout," he advised. "It is a good show here—yes; but, after all, it may be only a chance washing from hills far enough away. Show them to Harris, though; he may be interested, though he appears to me very indifferent about the matter."

"He don't seem to care," she agreed. "He just looks at us as though we were a couple of children he had found a new plaything for. But don't you think he looks brighter?"

"Well, yes; the river trip has done him good, instead of the harm the Ferry folks prophesied. But you run along and show him the 'yellow,' and don't draw the squaw's attention to it."

The squaw was wrapped neck and heels in a blanket, although the day was one of the warmest of summer; and stretched asleep in the sun, she gave no heed to the quick, light step of the girl.

Neither did Harris, at whose tent door she lay. He must have thought it was the stoical, indifferent Indian, for he gave her a quick, startled glance as he heard her surprised "Oh!" at the door. Then she walked directly to him, lifted his right hand, and let go again. It fell on his knee in the old, helpless way.

"But you did raise it," she said, accusingly. "I saw you as I came to the door. You stretched out your hand."

He looked at her and nodded very slightly, then looked at his hand and appeared trying to lift it; but gave up, and shook his head sadly.

"You mean you moved it a little once, but can't do it again?" she asked, and he nodded assent.

"Oh, well, that's all right," she continued, cheerfully. "You are sure to get along all right, now that you have commenced to manage your hands if ever so little. But just at first, when I saw you, I had a mighty queer notion come into my head. I thought you were getting over that stroke faster than you let us know. But I'm too suspicious, ain't I? Maybe it's a bad thing for folks to trust strangers too much in this world; but it is just as bad for a girl to grow up where she can't trust any one. Don't you think so?"

The man nodded. They had many conversations like that, and she had grown not to notice his lack of speech nearly so much as at first. He was so good a listener, and she had become so used to his face gradually gaining again expressive power, that she divined his wishes more readily than the others.

"But trusting don't cut any figure in what I came to speak to you about," she continued. "No 'trust and hope on, brethren,' about this, I guess," and she held the grains of yellow metal before his eyes. "There it is-the gold! Dan found it in the little hollow where the spring is. Is that where you found it?"

He shook his head, but looked pleased at the show they had found.

"Was it bigger bundles of it than this you struck?"

He nodded assent.

"Bigger than this! Well, it must have been rich. These lumps are enough in size if they only turn out enough in number. Oh, how I wish you had put the very spot on that plan of the ground and the rivers! Still, I suppose you were right to be cautious. And if I hadn't been on a lone trail through this country last spring, and got lost, and happened to notice the two little streams running into the river so close to each other, we might have had a year's journey along the Kootenai before we could have found the particular little stream and followed the right one to its source. I think we are close on the trail now, Joe."

He shook his head energetically when she called him Joe.

"Well, I forget," she said. "You see, I've been thinking for months about finding Joe Hammond; and now that I've found you, I can't get used to thinking you are Jim Harris. What's the use of your changing your name, anyway? You did it so you could trail him, your partner, better. But what was the use, with him well and strong, and with devils back of him, and you alone and barely able to crawl? Your head was wrong, Joe-Jim, I mean. If you hadn't been looney, you'd just have settled down and worked your claim, got rich, and then looked for your man."

He shook his head impatiently, and looked at her with as much of a frown as his locked muscles would allow, and a very queer, hard smile about his eyes and mouth.

"Ah!" and 'Tana shivered a little; "don't look like that, Joe. You wouldn't get any Sunday-school prizes for a meek and lowly spirit if the manager saw you fix your face in that fashion. I guess I know how you felt. If you had just so much strength, and couldn't hope for more, you wouldn't waste it looking for gold while he was above ground. Now, ain't I about right?"

He gave no assent, but smiled in a more kindly way at the shrewdness of her guess.

"You won't own up, but I know I am right," she said; "and the way I know it is because I think I'd feel just like that myself if some one hurt me bad. I wonder if girls often feel that way. I guess not. I know Ora Harrison, the doctor's girl, don't. She says her prayers every night, and asks God to let her enemies have good luck. U'm! I can't do that."

The man watched her as she sat silent for a little, looking out into the still, warm sunshine. The squaw slumbered on, and the girl stared across her, and her face grew sad and moody with some hard thought.

"It's awful to hate," she said, at last. "Don't you think it is? —to hate so that you can't breathe right when the person you hate comes near where you are-to be able to *feel* if he comes near, even when you don't see or hear him, to feel a devil that rises up in your breast and makes you want to get a knife and cut-cut deep, until the blood you hate runs away from the face you hate, and leaves it white and cold. Ah! it's bad, I reckon, to have some one hate you; but it's a thousand times worse to hate back. It makes the prettiest day black when the devil tells you of the hate you must remember, and you can't pray it away, and you can't forget it, and you can't help it! Oh, dear!"

She put her hands over her eyes and leaned her head against his hand. He felt her tears, but could not comfort her.

"You see, I know-how you felt," she said, trying to speak steadily. "Girls shouldn't know; girls should have love and good thoughts taught to them. I —I've dreamed dreams of what a girl's life ought to be like; something like Ora's home, where her mother kisses her and loves her, and her father kisses and loves them both. I went to their home once, and I never could go again. I was starving for the kind of home she has, and I knew I never would get it. That is the hardest part of it-to know, no matter how hard you try to be good, all your life, you can't get back the good thoughts and the love that should have been yours when you were little-the good thoughts that would have kept hate from growing in your heart, until it is stronger than you are. Oh, it's awful!"

The squaw, who did not understand English, but did understand tears, rolled over and peered out from her blanket at the girl who knelt there as at the feet of a confessor. But the girl did not see her; she still knelt there, almost whispering now.

"And the worst of it is, Joe, after they are dead-the ones you hate-then the devil in you commences to torment you by making you think of some good points among the bad ones; some little kind word that would have made the hate in your heart less if it had not been for your own terrible wickedness. And it gnaws and torments you just like a rat gnawing the heart out of a log for a nest. And hate is terrible! whether it is live hate, or dead, it is terrible. Maybe I won't feel so bad now that I've said out loud to some one how I feel-how much harder my heart is than it ought to be. I couldn't tell any one else. But you hate, too, you know. Maybe you know, too, that dead hate hurts worst-that it haunts like a ghost."

She looked up at him, and saw again that queer, wise smile about his lips.

"You don't believe he's dead!" she said, and her face grew paler. "You think he's still alive, and that is why you don't want folks to use your old name. You are laying for him yet, and you so helpless you can't move!"

The man only looked at her grimly. He would not deny; he would not assent.

"But you are wrong," she persisted. "He is dead. The Indians told me so-Akkomi told me so. Would they lie to me? Joe, can't you let the hate go by, now that he is dead-dead?"

But no motion answered her, though his eyes rested on her kindly enough. Then the squaw arose and slouched away to pick up firewood in the forest, and the girl arose, too, and touched his hand.

"Well, whether you can or not, I am glad I told you what I did. Maybe it won't worry me so much now; for sometimes, just when I'm almost happy, the ghost of that bad hate seems to whisper, whisper, and there ain't any more good times for me. I'm glad I told you. I would not have, though, if you could talk like other folks, but you can't."

She got him a drink of water, slipped their first find of the gold into his pocket, and then stood at the tent door, watching for Overton.

But he did not come, and after a little she picked up the pan again and started for the small stream where she had left him.

The man in the chair watched her go, and when she was out of sight, that right hand was again slowly raised from the chair.

"C —an't I?" he whispered, in a strange, indistinct way. "Poor lit-tle girl! poor little-girl!"

Chapter XIII
The Track in the Forest

Their camp was about a mile from the Kootenai River, and close to a stream of depth sufficient to carry a canoe; while, a little way north of their camp, a beautiful spring of clear water gurgled out from under a little bank, and added its portion to the larger stream that flowed eastward to the river.

There was a little peculiarity about the spring, which made it one to remember-or, rather, two to remember, for it was really a twin, and its sister stream slipped from the other side of the narrow ledge and ran north for a little way, and then turned to the east and emptied into the Kootenai, not a hundred yards from the stream into which its mate had run.

The two springs were not twenty feet apart, and lay direct north and south from each other. Then their wide curves, in opposite directions, left within their circle a tract of land like an island, for the streams bounded it entirely except for that narrow neck of rock and soil joining it to the bigger hills to the west.

It was in the vicinity of the two springs that the rude sketch of Harris bade them search; but more definite directions than that he had not given. He had marked a tree where the north stream joined the river; and finding that as a clew, they followed the stream to its source. When they reached the larger stream, navigable for a mile, they concluded to move their tents there, for no lovelier place could be found.

It was 'Tana and Overton who tramped over the lands where the streams lay, and did their own prospecting for location. He was surprised to find her knowledge of the land so accurate. The crude drawing was as a solved problem to her; she never once made a wrong turn.

"Well, I've thought over it a heap," she said, when he commented on her clever ideas. "I saw that marked tree as we went down to the Ferry, and I remembered where it was; and the trail is not hard if you only get started on it right. It's getting started right that counts-ain't it, Dan?"

There seemed fewer barriers between them in the free, out-of-door life, where no third person's views colored their own. They talked of Lyster, and missed him; yet Dan was conscious that if Lyster were with them, he would have come second instead of first in her confidences, and her friendly, appealing ways.

Whether he trusted her or not, she did not know. He had not asked a question as to how that survey of the land came to her; but he watched Harris sometimes when the girl paid him any little attention, and he could read only absolute trust in the man's eyes.

Overton was not given to keen analysis of people or motives; a healthy unconcern pervaded his mind as to the affairs of most people. But sometimes the girl's character, her peculiar knowledge, her mysterious past, touched him with a sense of strange confusion, yet in the midst of the confusion-the deepest of it-he had put all else aside when she appealed to him, and had followed her lead into the wilderness.

And as she ran from him with the particles of gold, and carried them, as he bade her, to Harris, he followed her with his gaze until she disappeared through the green wall of the bushes. Once he started to follow her, and then stopped, suddenly muttered something about a "cursed fool," and flung himself face down in the tall grass.

"It's got to end here," he said, aloud, as men grow used to thinking when they live alone in the woods much. Then he raised himself on his elbows and looked over the little grassy dip of the land to where the stream from the hills sparkled in the warm sun; and then away beyond to where the evergreens raised their dark heads along the heights, looking like somber guardians keeping ward over the sunny valley of the twin springs. Over them all his gaze wandered, and then up into the deep forest above him —a forest unbroken from there to the swift Columbia.

The perfect harmony of it all must have oppressed him until he felt himself the one discordant note, for he closed his eyes with a sigh that was almost a groan.

"I'll see it all again-often, I suppose," he muttered; "but never quite as it is now-never, for it's got to end. The little bits of gold I found are a warning of the changes to come here-that is the way it seems to me. Queer how a man will change his idea of life in a year or so! There have been times when I would have rejoiced over the prospect of wealth there is here; yet all I am actually conscious of is regret that everything must change-the place-the people-all where gold is king. Pshaw! what a fool I would seem to any one else if he knew. Yet-well, I have dreamed all my days of a sort of life where absolute happiness could be lived. Other men do the same, I suppose-yes, of course. I wonder if others also come in reach of it too late. I suppose so. Well, reasoning won't change it. I marked out my own path-marked it out with as little thought as many another fool; but I've got to walk in it just the same, and cursing back don't help luck. But I had to have a little pow-wow all alone and be sorry for myself, before turning my back on the man I'd like to be-and-the rest of my dreams that have come in sight for a little while but can never come nearer-There she comes again! I'm glad of it, for she will at least keep me from drifting into dreams alone."

But she appeared to be dreaming a little herself. At any rate, the scene she had passed through in the tent left memories too dark with feeling to be quickly dispelled, and he noticed at once the change in her face, and the traces of tears left about her eyes.

"What has hurt you?" he asked.

She shook her head and said:

"Nothing."

"Oh! So you leave here jolly enough, and run around to camp, and cry about nothing-do you?" he asked, with evident unbelief. "Were you crying for joy over those little grains of gold-or over your loneliness in being so far from the Ferry folks?"

She laughed at the mere idea of either-and laughter dispels tear traces so quickly from faces that are young. "Lonely!" she exclaimed: "lonely here? why, I feel a heap more satisfied here than down at the Ferry, where the whole place smelled like saw-mills and new lumber. I always had a grudge against saw-mills, for they spoil all the lovely woods. That is why I like all this," and she made a sweep of her arm, embracing all the territory in sight; "for in here not a tree has been touched with an ax. Lonely here! Why, Dan, I've been so perfectly happy that I'm afraid-yes, I am. Didn't you ever feel like that-just as if you were too happy to last, and you were afraid some trouble would come and end it all?"

But Overton stooped to lift the pick he had been using, and so turned his face away from her.

"Well, I'm glad you are not getting blue over lack of company," he remarked; "for we have only commenced prospecting, you know, and it will be at least a week before we can hope to send for any one else to join us."

"A week! Do you intend to send for other folks, then?" and her tone was one of regret. "Oh, it would be all different, then. My pretty camp would be spoiled for me if folks should come talking and whistling up our creek. Don't let any one know so soon!"

"You don't know what you are talking of," he answered, a little roughly. "This is a business trip. We did not come up here just because we were looking for a pretty picture of a place to camp in."

"Oh!" and surprise and dismay were in the exclamation. "Then you don't care for it-you want other people just as soon as you find the rich streak where the gold is? Well" —and she looked again over their little chosen valley —"I almost hope you won't find it very soon-not for several days. I would like to live just like this for a whole week. And I thought —I was so sure you liked it, too."

"Oh, yes," he answered, indifferently enough, evidently giving his whole attention to examining the soil he had commenced to dig up again, "I like the camp all right, but we can't just stand around and admire it, if we want to accomplish what we came for. And see here, 'Tana," he said, and for the first time he looked at her with a sort of unwillingness, "you must know that this gold is going to make a big change in things for you. You can't live out in the woods with a couple of miners and an Indian squaw, after your fortune is made-don't you see that? You must go to school, and live out in the world where your money will help you to-well, the right sort of society for a girl."

"What is the use of having money if it don't help you to live where you please?" she demanded. "I thought that was what money was for. I'd a heap rather stay poor here in the woods, with—with the folks I know, instead of going where I'll have to buy friends with money. Don't think I'd want the sort of friends who have to be baited with money, anyway."

He stared at her helplessly. She was saying to him the things he had called himself a fool for thinking. But he could not call her a fool. He could only stifle an impatient groan, and wonder how he was to reason her into thinking as other girls would think of wealth and its advantages.

"Why were you so wild about finding the gold, if you care so little for the things it brings?" he demanded, and she pointed toward the tents.

"It was for him I thought at first—of how the money would, maybe, help to make him well—get him great doctors, and all that. The world had been rough on him—people had brought him trouble, and—and I thought, maybe, I could help clear it away. That was what I had in my mind at first."

"You need things, too, don't you? —not doctors, but education—books, beautiful things. You want pictures, statues, fine music, theaters—all such things. Well, the money will help you get them, and get people to enjoy them with you. I've heard you talk to Max about how you would like to live, and what you would like to see; and I think you can soon. But, 'Tana, you will live then where people will be more critical than we are here —"

"More like Captain Leek?" she asked, with a deep wrinkle between her brows; "for if they are, I'll stay here."

"N —no; not like him; and yet they will think considerable of his sort of ideas, too," he answered, blunderingly. "One thing sure is this: When your actual work here is over, you must go at once back to Mrs. Huzzard. It was necessary for you to come, else I wouldn't have allowed it. But, little girl, when you get among those fine friends you are going to have, I don't want them to think you had a guardian up here who didn't take the first bit of civilized care of you. And that's what they would think if I let you stay here, just as though you were a boy. So you see, 'Tana, I just felt I'd have to tell you plain that you would have to try and fit yourself to city ways of living. And when you are a millionairess, as you count on being, we three partners can't keep on living in tents in the Kootenai woods."

She pulled handfuls of the plumy grasses beside her, and stared sulkily ahead of her. Evidently it was a great deal for her to understand at once.

"Would they blame you —*you* for it, if they knew?" she asked at last.

"Yes, they would—if they knew," he said, savagely; and turning away, he walked across the little grassy level to where the abrupt little wall or ledge commenced—the one from under which the springs flowed.

She thought he was simply out of patience with her. He was going to the woods—anywhere to be rid of her and her stupid ideas; and swift as a bird, she slipped after him.

"Then I'll go, Dan," she said reassuringly, catching his arm. "So don't be vexed at me for being stubborn. Come! let me look for the gold with you, and then—then I'll go when you say."

"It's a bargain," he said, briefly, and drew his arm away. "And if we are going to do any more prospecting this evening, we had better begin."

He stood facing her, with his back to the bank that was the first tiny step toward the mountain that rose dark and shadowy far above. He had walked along there before, looking with a miner's attention to the lay of the land. Suddenly he uttered an exclamation, and a light of comprehension brightened his eyes.

"I've got a clew to it, sure, 'Tana!" he said, eagerly. "Do you know where we are standing? Well, if I don't make a big mistake, a good-sized river once rolled along just where we are now. The little creek is all that's left of it. This soil is all a comparatively recent deposit, and it and the gold dust in it have been washed down from the mountain. Which means that this little valley is only a gateway, and the dust we found is only a trail we are to follow up to the mine from which it came. Do you understand?"

"Yes, I think so," she answered, looking at the green-covered banks, and trying to realize how they looked when a mountain river had cut its way through and covered all the pretty level where the spring stream slipped now. "But doesn't that make the gold seem farther away-much farther? Will we have to move up higher in the mountains?"

"That is a question I need time to answer, but if I am right-if there is a backing of gold ore somewhere above this old river bed, it means a much surer thing than an occasional bit of dust washed out of the mud here. But we won't ignore our little placer digging either. There is an advantage to a poor prospector in having a claim he can work without any machinery but a pick, shovel, and pan; while the gold ore needs a fortune to develop it. Let us go back and talk to Harris, to see if his evidence substantiates my theory. If not, we will just stake out our claims on the level, and be thankful. Later we will investigate the hills."

The girl walked slowly beside him back to their camp. The shadows were commencing to lengthen. It was nearing supper time, and their day had been a busy, tiring one, for they had moved their camp many miles since dawn.

"You are very nearly worn out, aren't you?" he asked, as he noticed her tired eyes and her listless step. "You see, you would tramp along the shore this morning when I wanted you to stay in the boat."

"Yes, I know," she answered; "but I don't think that made me tired. Maybe it's the gold we are to find. How queer it is, Dan, that a person will want and want some one thing all his life, and he thinks it will make him so happy; and yet, when at last he gets in sight of it, he isn't happy at all. That is the way I feel about our gold. I suppose I ought to be singing and laughing and dancing for joy. I said I would, too. Yet here I am feeling as stupid as can be, and almost afraid of the fine life you say I must go to. Oh, bother! I won't think over it any more. I am going to get supper."

For while 'Tana would accept the squaw as an assistant and a gatherer of fuel, she decidedly declined to have her installed as head cook. She herself filled that office with a good deal of girlish conceit, encouraged by the praise of Overton and the approving nods of Harris.

There had been a fifth member of their party, Flap-Jacks' husband. 'Tana had bestowed that name on the squaw in the very beginning of their acquaintance. But Overton had sent him on an errand back to Sinna Ferry, not wishing to have his watchful eyes prying into their plans in the very beginning of their prospecting. And it was not until he had started on his journey that the pick and pan had disclosed the golden secret of the old river bed.

Harris watched the two approach, and his keen gray eyes turned with a certain fondness from one to the other. They were as guardian angels to him, and their mutual care of him had brought them closer to each other there in the wilderness than they ever had been in the little settlement farther down the river.

"Squaw not here yet?" asked 'Tana, and at once set to work preparing things for the supper.

Harris shook his head, but at that moment their hand-maiden did return, carrying a great load of sticks for fire, and then brought to the girl a number of fine trout she had caught almost at their door. She built the fire outside, where two forked sticks had been driven into the ground, and across them a pole lay, from which kettles could be hung. As 'Tana set the coffee pot on the hot coals, the Indian woman spoke to her in that low voice which is characteristic of the red people.

"More white men to come into camp?" she asked.

"White men? No. Why do you ask?"

"I see tracks-not Dan's tracks-not yours."

"Made when?"

"Now-little while back-only little."

Overton heard their voices, though not their words; and as 'Tana re-entered the wigwam, he glanced around at her with a dubious smile.

"That is the first time I ever heard you actually talking Chinook," he observed; "though I've had an idea you could, ever since the evening in Akkomi's village. It is like your poker playing, though you have been very modest about it."

"I was not the night I played the captain," she answered; "and I think you might let me alone about that, after I gave him back his money."

"That is just the part I can not forgive you for," he said. "He will never get over the idea, now, that you cheated him, and that your conscience got the better of you to such an extent that you tried to wipe a sin away by giving the money back."

"Perhaps I did," she answered, quietly. "I had to settle his conceit some way, for he did bother me a heap sometimes. But I'm done with that."

She seemed rather thoughtful during the frying of the fish and the slicing down of Mrs. Huzzard's last contribution—a brown loaf.

She was disturbed over the footprints seen by the Indian woman-the track of a white man so close to their camp that day, yet who had kept himself from their sight! Such actions have a meaning in the wild countries, and the meaning troubled her. While it would have been the most simple thing in the world to tell Overton and have him make a search, something made her want to do the searching herself-but how?

"I was right in my theory about the old river bed," he said to her, as she poured his coffee. "Harris backs me up in it, and it was ore he found, and not the loose dirt in the soil. So the thing I am going to strike out for is the headquarters where that loose dust comes from."

"Oh! then it was ore you found?" she asked.

Harris nodded his head.

"Ore on the surface-and near here."

That news made her even more anxious about that stranger who had prowled around. Perhaps he, too, was searching for the hidden wealth.

When the supper was over, and the sun had slipped back of the mountain, she beckoned to the squaw, and with the water bucket as a visible errand, they started toward the spring.

But they did not stop there. She wanted to see with her own eyes those footprints, and she followed the Indian down into the woods already growing dusky in the dying day.

The birds were singing their good-night songs, and all the land seemed steeped in repose. Only those two figures, gliding between the trees, carried with them the spirit of unrest.

They reached an open space where no trees grew very close —a bit of marsh land, where the soil was black and tall ferns grew. The squaw led her straight to a place where two of the fern fronds were bent and broken. She parted the green lances, and there beside it was a scraping away of the earth, as though some one walking there had slipped, and in the black sandy loam a shoe had sunk deep. The Indian was right; it was the mark of a white man, for the reds of that country had not yet adopted the footgear of their more advanced neighbors.

"It turn to camp," said the squaw. "Maybe some white thief, so I tell you. Me tell Dan?"

"Wait," answered the girl; and, kneeling down, she studied the slender outline of the foot attentively. "Any more tracks?"

"No more-only leaves stirred nearer to camp; he go that way."

The full moon rose clear and warm in the east, while yet the sun's light lingered over the wilderness. Beautiful flowers shone white and pink and yellow in the opaline light of the evening; and 'Tana mechanically plucked a few that touched her as she passed, but she gave little notice to their beauty. All her thought was on the slender footprint of the man in the woods, and her face looked troubled.

They walked on, looking to right and left in any nook where deep shadows lay, but never a sign could they see of aught that was human besides themselves, until they neared the springs again, when the squaw laid her hand on the arm of the girl.

"Dan," she said, in her low, abrupt way.

The girl, looking up, saw him a little way ahead of them, standing there straight, strong, and surely to be trusted; yet her first impulse was to tell him nothing.

"Take the water and go," she said to the Indian, and the woman disappeared like a mere wraith of a woman in the pale shadows.

"Don't go so far next time when you want to pick flowers in the evening," said Overton, as 'Tana came nearer to him. "You make me realize that I have nerves. If you had not come in sight the instant you did, I should have been after you."

"But nothing will harm us; I am not afraid, and it is pretty in the woods now," she answered lamely, and toyed with the flowers. But the touch of her fingers was nervous, and the same quality trembled in her voice. He noticed it and reaching out took her hand in his very gently, and yet with decision that forced her to look up at him.

"Little girl-what is it? You are sick?"

She shook her head.

"No, I am not —I am not sick," and she tried to free her hand, but could not.

"'Tana," and his teeth closed for a moment on his lip lest he say all the warm words that leaped up from his heart at sight of her face, which looked startled and pale in the moonlight —"'Tana, you won't need me very long; and when you go away, I'll never try to make you remember me. Do you understand, little girl? But just now, while we are so far off from the rest of the world, won't you trust me with your troubles-with the thoughts that worry you? I would give half of my life to help you. Half of it! Ah, good God! all of it! 'Tana —"

In his voice was all the feeling which compels sympathy, or else builds up a wall that bars it out. But in the eyes of the girl, startled though she was, no resistance could be read. Her hand was in his, her face lifted to him, and alight with sudden gladness. In his eyes she read the force of an irresistible power taking possession of a man's soul and touching her with its glory.

"'Tana!" he said very softly, in a tone she had never before heard Dan Overton use —a tone hushed and reverent and appealing. "*'Tana!*"

Did he guess all the stormy emotions locked alone in the girl's heart, and wearing out her strength? Did he guess all the childish longing to feel strong, loving arms around her as a shield? His utterance of her name drew her to him. His arm fell around her shoulders, and her head was bowed against his breast. The hat she wore had fallen to the ground, and as he bent over her, his hand caressed her hair tenderly, but there was more of moody regret than of joy in his face.

"'Tana, my girl! poor little girl!" he said softly.

But she shook her head.

"No-not so poor now," she half whispered and looked up at him —"not so very poor."

Then she uttered a half-strangled scream of terror and broke away from him; for across his shoulder she saw a face peering at her from the shadows of the over-hanging bushes above them, a white, desperate face, at sight of which she staggered back and would have fallen had Overton not caught her.

He had not seen the cause of her alarm, and for one instant thought it was himself from whom she shrank.

"Tell me-what is it?" he demanded. "'Tana, speak to me!"

She did not speak, but a rustle in the bushes above them caught his ear; and looking up, he saw a form pass lightly through the shadows and away from them. He could not tell whether it was an Indian, a white man, or even an animal scampering off that way through the bushes. But anything that spied like that and ran when discovered was a thing to shoot at. He dropped his hand to his revolver, but she caught his arm.

"No, Dan! Oh, don't —don't shoot him!"

He stared at her, conscious that it was no ordinary fear that whitened her face. What did it mean? She herself had just come from the woods-pale, agitated, and with only a semblance of flower gathering to explain her absence. Had she met some one there-some one who —

He let go of her and started to run up the side of the steep bank; but swiftly as he moved, she caught him and clung to him, half sobbing.

"Don't go! Oh, Dan, let him go!" she begged, and her grasp made it impossible for him to go unless he picked her up and carried her along.

He stooped, took her head roughly in his hands, and turned her face up, so that the light would fall upon it.

"*Him!* Then you know who it is?" he said, grimly. "What sort of business is this, 'Tana? Are you going to tell me?"

But she only crouched closer to him, and, sobbing, begged him not to go. Once he tried to break away but lost his footing, and the soil and bits of boulders went clattering down past her.

With a muttered oath of impatience, he gave up the pursuit, and stared down at her with an expression more bitter than any she had ever seen on his face before.

"So you are bound to protect him, are you?" he asked, coldly. "Very well. But if you value him so highly you had better keep him clear of this camp, else he'll find himself ready for a box. Come! get up and go to the tents. That is a better place for you than here. Your coming out here this evening has been a mistake all around-or else mine has. I wish to Heaven I could undo it all."

She stood a little apart from him, but her hand was still outstretched and clasping his arm.

"All, Dan?" she asked, and her mouth trembled. But his own lips were firm enough, as he nodded his head and looked at her.

"All," he said briefly. "Go now; and here are your flowers for which you hunted so long in the woods."

He stooped to pick them up for her from where they had fallen-the white, fragrant things he had thought so beautiful as she came toward him with them in the moonlight.

But as he lifted them from the bank, where they were scattered, he saw something else there which was neither beautiful nor fragrant, but over which he bent with earnest scrutiny. An ordinary looking piece of shale or stone it would have seemed to an inexperienced eye, a thing with irregular veins of a greenish appearance, and the green dotted plainly with yellow-so plainly as to show even in the moonlight the nature of the find.

He turned to the girl and reached it to her with the flowers.

"There! When my foot slipped I broke off that bit of 'float' from the ledge," he said curtly. "Show it to Harris. We have found the gold ore, and I'll stake out the claims to-night. You can afford to leave for civilization now as soon as you please, I reckon, for your work in the Kootenai country is over. Your fortune is made."

Chapter XIV
New-Comers

Many days went by after that before more time was given to the hunting of gold in that particular valley of the Kootenai lands; for before another day broke, the squaw spoke at the door of Overton's tent and told him the girl was sick with fever, that she talked as a little child babbles and laughs at nothing.

He went with her, and the face he had seen so pale in the moonlight was flushed a rosy red, and her arms tossed meaninglessly, while she muttered-muttered! Sometimes her words were of the gold, and of flowers. He even heard his name on her lips, but only once; and then she cried out that he hurt her. She was ill-very ill; he could see that, and help must be had.

He went for it as swiftly as a boat could be sped over the water. During the very short season of waiting for the doctor and Mrs. Huzzard, he wrote to Lyster, and secured some Indians for work needed. If the doctor thought her able for the journey, he meant to have her brought back in a boat to Sinna Ferry, where she would have something more substantial than canvas walls about her.

But the doctor did not. He was rather mystified by her sudden illness, as there had been no forewarnings of it. That it was caused by some shock was possible; and that it was serious was beyond doubt.

The entire party, and especially Mrs. Huzzard, were taken aback by finding a newly arrived, self-imposed guardian at the door of Tana's tent. It was the blanket-draped figure of old Akkomi, and his gaily painted canoe was pulled up on the bank of the creek.

"I heard on the wind the child was sick," he said briefly to Overton. "I come to ask if you needed help."

But Overton looked at him suspiciously. It was impossible that he could have heard of her illness so soon, though he might have heard of her presence there.

"Were any of your people here at nightfall yesterday?" he asked. The old fellow shook his head.

"No, none of my people," he said briefly; then he puffed away at his pipe, and looked approvingly at Mrs. Huzzard, who tried to pass him without turning her back to him at all, and succeeded in making a circuit bearing some relation to progress made before a throne, though the relationship was rather strained. His approving eyes filled her with terror; for, much as she had reveled in Indian romances (on paper) in her youth, she had no desire to take any active part in them in her middle age.

And so, with the help of the doctor and Mrs. Huzzard, they commenced the nursing of 'Tana back to consciousness and health. Night after night Dan walked alone in the waning moonlight, his heart filled with remorse and blame for which he could find no relief. The gathering of the gold had no longer allurements for him.

But he moved Harris' tent on to one of the claims, and he cut small timber, and in a day and a half had a little log house of two rooms put up and chinked with dry moss and roofed with bark, that 'Tana might have a home of her own, and have it close to where the ore streaked with gold had been found. Then he sent the Indians up the river again, and did with his own hands all labor needed about the camp.

"You'll be sick yourself, Overton," growled the doctor, who slept in the tent with him, and knew that scarce an hour of the night passed that he was not at the door of 'Tana's cabin, to learn if any help was needed, or merely to stand without and listen to her voice as she spoke.

"For mercy's sake, Mr. Dan, do be a little careful of yourself," entreated Mrs. Huzzard; "for if you should get used up, I don't know what I ever would do here in this wilderness, with 'Tana and the paralyzed man and you to look after-to say nothing of the fear I'm in every hour because o' that nasty beast of an Indian that you say is a chief. He is here constant!"

"Proof of your attractive powers," said Overton, reassuringly. "He comes to admire you, that is all."

"And enough, too! And if it wasn't for you that's here to protect me, the good Lord only knows whether I'd ever see a milliner shop or a pie again, as long as I lived. So I am set on your taking more care of yourself-now won't you?"

"Wait until you have cause, before you worry," he advised, "I don't look like a sick man, do I?"

"You don't look like a well one, anyway," she said, looking at him carefully; "and you don't look as I ever saw you look before. You are as hollow eyed as though you had been sick yourself for a month. Altogether, I think your coming out here to camp in the wild woods has been a big mistake."

"It looks like it just now," he agreed, and his eyes, tired and troubled, looked past her into the cabin where 'Tana lay. "Does she seem better?"

"Just about the same. Eight days now since she was took down; and the doctor, he said to-morrow would be the day to hope for a change, either for the better or —"

But the alternative was not a thing easy for the good soul to contemplate, and she left the sentence unfinished and disappeared into the cabin again, while the man outside dropped his head in his hands, feeling the most helpless creature in all the world.

"Better to-morrow, or-worse;" that was what Mrs. Huzzard meant, but could not utter. Better or worse! And if the last, she might be dying now, each minute! And he was powerless to help her-powerless even to utter all the regret, the remorse, the heart-aching sorrow that was with him, for her ears were closed to the sense of words, and his lips were locked by some key of some past.

His own judgment on himself was not light as he went over in his mind each moment of their hours together. Poor little 'Tana! poor little stray!

"I promised not to question her; yes, I promised that, or she would never have left the Indians with me. And I —I was savage with her, just because she would not tell me what she had a perfect right to keep from me if she chose. Even if it was —a lover, what right had I to object? What right to hold her hands-to say all the things I said? If she were a woman, I could tell her all I think-all, and let her judge. But not as it is-not to a girl so young-so troubled-so much of a stray. Oh, God! she shall never be a stray again, if only she gets well. I'd stay here digging forever if I could only send her out in the world among people who will make her happy. And she-the child, the child! said she would rather live here as we did than to have the gold that would make her rich. God! it is hard for a man to forget that, no matter what duty says."

So his thoughts would ramble on each day, each night, and his restlessness grew until Harris took to watching him with a great pity in his eyes, and mutely asked each time he entered if hope had grown any stronger.

By the request of Mrs. Huzzard they had moved Harris into the other room of the cabin, because of a rain which fell one night, and reminded them that his earthen floor might prove injurious to his health. Mrs. Huzzard declared she was afraid, with that room empty; and Harris, though having a partially dead body, had at least a living soul, and she greatly preferred his presence to the spiritless void and the fear of Indian occupancy.

So she shared the room with 'Tana, and the doctor and Overton used one tent, while the squaw used the other. All took turns watching at night beside the girl, who never knew one from the other, but who talked of gold-gold that was too heavy a load for her to carry-gold that ran in streams where she tried to find water to drink and could not-gold that Dan thought was better than friends or their pretty camp. And over those woes she would moan until frightened from them by ghosts, the ghosts she hated, and which she begged them so piteously to keep out of her sight.

So they had watched her for days, and toward the evening of the eighth Overton was keeping an ever-watchful ear for the Indian and the doctor who had gone personally to fetch needed medicines from the settlement.

Akkomi was there as usual. Each day he would come, sit in the doorway of the Harris cabin for hours, and contemplate the helpless man there. When evening arrived he would enter his canoe and go back to his own camp, which at that time was not more than five miles away.

Overton, fearing that Harris would be painfully annoyed by the presence of this self-invited visitor, offered to entertain him in his own tent, if Harris preferred. But while Harris looked with no kindly eye on the old fellow, he signified that the Indian should remain, if he pleased. This was a decision so unexpected that Overton asked Harris if he had ever met Akkomi before.

He received an affirmative nod, which awakened his curiosity enough to make him question the Indian.

The old fellow nodded and smoked in silence for a little while before making a reply; then he said:

"Yes, one summer, one winter ago, the man worked in the hills beyond the river. Our hunters were there and saw him. His cabin is there still."

"Who was with him?"

"White man, stranger," answered Akkomi briefly. "This man stranger, too, in the Kootenai country-stranger from away somewhere there," and he pointed vaguely toward the east. "Name-Joe-so him called."

"And the other man?"

"Other man stranger, too-go way-never come back. This one go away, too; but he come back."

"And that is all you know of them?"

"All. Joe not like Indian friends," and the old fellow's eyes wrinkled up in the semblance of laughter; "too much tenderfoot, maybe."

"But Joe's partner," persisted Overton, "he was not tenderfoot? He had Indian friends on the Columbia River."

"Maybe," agreed the old fellow, and his sly, bead-like eyes turned toward his questioner sharply and were as quickly withdrawn, "maybe so. They hunt silver over there. No good."

Just inside the door Harris sat straining his ears to catch every word, and Akkomi's assumption of bland ignorance brought a rather sardonic smile to his face, while his lips moved in voiceless mutterings of anger. Impatience was clearly to be read in his face as he waited for Overton to question further, and his right hand opened and closed in his eagerness.

But no other questions were asked just then; for Overton suddenly walked away, leaving the crafty-eyed Akkomi alone in his apparent innocence of Joe's past or Joe's partner.

The old fellow looked after him kindly enough, but shook his head and smoked his dirty black pipe, while an expression of undivulged knowledge adorned his withered physiognomy.

"No, Dan, no," he murmured. "Akkomi good friend to little sick squaw and to you; but he not tell-not tell all things."

Then his ears, not so keen as in years gone by, heard sounds on the water, sounds coming closer and closer. But Dan's younger ears had heard them first, and it was to learn the cause that he had left so abruptly and walked to the edge of the stream.

It was the doctor and the Indian boatman who came in sight first around the bend of the creek. Back of them was another canoe, but a much larger, much more pretentious one. In this was Lyster and a middle-aged gentleman of rather portly build, who dressed in a fashion very fine when compared with the average garb of the wilderness.

Overton watched with some surprise the approach of the man, who was an utter stranger to him, and yet who bore a resemblance to some one seen before. A certain something about the shape of the nose and general contour of the face seemed slightly familiar. He had time to notice, also, that the hair was auburn in color, and inclined to curl, and that back of him sat a female form. By the time he had made these observations, their boat had touched the shore, and Lyster was shaking his hand vigorously.

"I got your letter, telling me of your big strike. It caught me before I was quite started for Helena, so I just did some talking for you where I thought it would do the most good, old fellow, and turned right around and came back. I've been wild to hear about 'Tana. How is she? This is my friend, Mr. T. J. Haydon, my uncle's partner, you know. He has made this trip to talk a little business with you, and when I learned you were not at the settlement, but up here in camp, I thought it would be all right to fetch him along."

"Of course it is all right," answered Overton, assuringly. "Our camp has a welcome for your friend even if we haven't first-class accommodations for him. And is this lady also a friend?"

For Lyster, forgetful of his usual gallantry, had allowed the doctor to assist the other voyager from the canoe —a rather tall lady of the age generally expressed as "uncertain," although the certainty of it was an indisputable fact.

A rather childish hat was perched upon her thin but carefully frizzed hair, and over her face floated a white veil, that was on a drawing string around the crown of the hat and drooped gracefully and chastely over the features beneath, after the fashion of 1860. A string of beads adorned the thin throat, and the rest of her array was after the same order of elegance.

The doctor and Lyster exchanged glances, and Lyster was silently proclaimed master of ceremonies.

"Oh, yes," he said, easily. "Pardon me that I am neglectful, and let me introduce you to Miss Slocum-Miss Lavina Slocum of Cherry Run, Ohio. She is the cousin of our friend, Mrs. Huzzard, and was in despair when she found her relative had left the settlement; so we had the pleasure of her company when she heard we were coming direct to the place where Mrs. Huzzard was located."

"She will be glad to see you, miss," said Overton, holding out his hand to her in very hearty greeting. "Nothing could be more welcome to this camp just now than the arrival of a lady, for poor Mrs. Huzzard has been having a sorry siege of care for the last week. If you will come along, I will take you to her at once."

Gathering up her shawl, parasol, a fluffy, pale pink "cloud," and a homemade and embroidered traveling bag, he escorted her with the utmost deference to the door of the log cabin, leaving Lyster without another word.

That easily amused gentleman stared after the couple with keen appreciation of the picture they presented. Miss Slocum had a queer, mincing gait which her long limbs appeared averse to, and the result was a little hitchy. But she kept up with Overton, and surveyed him with weak blue eyes of gratitude. He appeared to her a very admirable personage —a veritable knight of the frontier, possibly a border hero such as every natural woman has an ideal of.

But to Lyster, Dan with his arms filled with female trappings and a lot of pink zephyr blown about his face and streaming over his shoulder, like a veritable banner of Love's color, was a picture too ludicrous to be lost. He gazed after them in a fit of delight that seemed likely to end in apoplexy, because he was obliged to keep his hilarity silent.

"Just look at him!" he advised, in tones akin to a stage whisper. "Isn't he a great old Dan? And maybe you think he would not promenade beside that make-up just as readily on Broadway, New York, or on Chestnut street, Philadelphia? Well, sir, he would! If it was necessary that some man should go with her, he would be the man to go, and Heaven help anybody he saw laughing! If you knew Dan Overton twenty years you would not see anything that would give you a better key to his nature than just his manner of acting cavalier to that-wonder."

But Mr. Haydon did not appear to appreciate the scene with the same degree of fervor.

"Ah!" he said, turning his eyes with indifference to the two figures, and with scrutiny over the little camp-site and primitive dwellings. "Am I to understand, then, that your friend, the ranger, is a sort of modern Don Juan, to whom any order of femininity is acceptable?"

"No," said Lyster, facing about suddenly. "And if my thoughtless manner of speech would convey such an idea of Dan Overton, then (to borrow one of Dan's own expressions) I deserve to be kicked around God's footstool for a while."

"Well, when you speak of his devotion to any sort of specimen —"

"Of course," agreed Lyster. "I see my words were misleading-especially to one unaccustomed to the life and people out here. But Dan, as Don Juan, is one of the most unimaginable things! Why, he does not seem to know women exist as individuals. This is the only fault I have to find with him; for the man who does not care for some woman, or never has cared for any woman, is, according to my philosophy, no good on earth. But Dan just looks the other way if they commence to give him sweet glances-and they do, too! though he thinks that collectively they are all angels. Yes, sir! let the worst old harridan that ever was come to Overton with a tale of virtue and misfortune, and he will take off his hat and divide up his money, giving her a good share, just because she happens to be a woman. That is the sort of devotion to women I had reference to when I spoke first; the wonder to me is that he has not been caught in a matrimonial noose long ere this by some thrifty maid or matron. He seems to me guileless game for them, as his sympathy is always so easily touched."

"Perhaps he is keeping free from bonds that he may marry this ward of his for whom he appears so troubled," remarked Mr. Haydon.

Lyster looked anything but pleased at the suggestion.

"I don't think he would like to hear that said," he returned. "Tana is only a little girl in his eyes-one left in his charge at the death of her own people, and one who appeals to him very strongly just now because of her helplessness."

"Well," said Mr. Haydon, with a slight smile, "I appear to be rather unfortunate in all my surmises over the people of this new country, especially this new camp. I do not know whether it is because I am in a stupid mood, or because I have come among people too peculiar to be judged by ordinary standards. But the thing I am interested in above and beyond our host and his *protégée* is the gold mine he wrote you to find a buyer for. I think I could appreciate that, at least, at its full value, if I was allowed a sight of the output."

The doctor had hurried to the cabin even before Overton and Miss Slocum, so the two gentlemen were left by themselves, to follow at their leisure. Mr. Haydon seemed a trifle resentful at this indifferent reception.

"One would think this man had been making big deals in gold ore all his life, and was perfectly indifferent as to whether our capital is to be used to develop this find of his," he remarked, as they approached the cabin. "Did you not tell me he was a poor man?"

"Oh, yes. Poor in gold or silver of the United States mint," agreed Lyster, with a strong endeavor to keep down his impatience of this magnate of the speculative world, this wizard of the world of stocks and bonds, whom his partners deferred to, whose nod and beck meant much in a circle of capitalists. "I myself, when back East," thought Lyster to himself, "considered Haydon a wonderful man, but he seems suddenly to have grown dwarfed and petty in my eyes, and I wonder that I ever paid such reverence to his judgment."

He smiled dubiously to himself at the consciousness that the wide spirit of the West must have already changed his own views of things somewhat, since once he had thought this marketer of mines superior.

"But no one out here would think of calling Dan Overton poor," he continued, "simply because he is not among the class that weighs a man's worth by the dollars he owns. He is considered one of the solid men of the district-one of the best men to know. But no one thinks of gauging his right to independence by the amount of his bank account."

Mr. Haydon shrugged his shoulders, and tapped his foot with the gold-headed umbrella he carried.

"Oh, yes. I suppose it seems very fine in young minds and a young country, to cultivate an indifference to wealth; but to older minds and civilization it grows to be a necessity. Is that object over there also one of the solid men of the community?"

It was Akkomi he had reference to, and the serene manner with which the old fellow glanced over them, and nonchalantly smoked his pipe in the doorway, did give him the appearance of a fixture about the camp, and puzzled Lyster somewhat, for he had never before met the ancient chief.

He nodded his head, however, saying "How?" in friendly greeting, and the Indian returned the civility in the same way, but gave slight attention to the speaker. All the attention of his little black eyes was given to the stranger, who did not address him, and whose gaze was somewhat critical and altogether contemptuous.

Then Mrs. Huzzard, without waiting for them to reach the door, hurried out to greet Lyster.

"I'm as glad as any woman can be to see you back again," she said heartily, "though it's more than I hoped for so soon, and-Yes, the doctor says she's a little better, thank God! And your name has been on her lips more than once-poor dear! —since she has been flighty, and all the thanks I feel to you for bringing Lavina right along I can never tell you; for it seems a month since I saw a woman last. I just can't count the squaw! And do you want to come in and look at our poor little girl now? She won't know you; but if you wish —"

"May I?" asked Lyster, gratefully. Then he turned to the stranger.

"Your daughter back home is about the same age," he remarked. "Will you come in?"

"Oh, certainly," answered Mr. Haydon, rather willing to go anywhere away from the very annoying old redskin of the pipe and the very-very scrutinizing eyes.

The doctor and Overton had passed into the room where Harris was, and Mrs. Huzzard halted at the door with her cousin, so that the two men approached the bed alone. The dark form of Akkomi had slipped in after them like a shadow, but a very alert one, for his head was craned forward that his eyes might lose never an expression of the fine stranger's face.

'Tana's eyes were closed, but her lips moved voicelessly. The light was dim in the little room, and Lyster bent over to look at her, and touched her hot forehead tenderly.

"Poor little girl! poor 'Tana!" he said, and turned the covering from about her chin where she had pulled it. He had seen her last so saucy, so defiant of all his wishes, and the change to this utter helplessness brought the quick tears to his eyes. He clasped her hand softly and turned away.

"It is too dark in here to see anything very clearly," said the stranger, who bent toward her slightly, with his hat in his hand.

Then Akkomi, who had intercepted the light somewhat, moved from the foot of the bed to the stranger's side, and a little sunshine rifted through the small doorway and outlined more clearly the girl's face on the pillow.

The stranger, who was quite close to her, uttered a sudden gasping cry as he saw her face more clearly, and drew back from the bed.

The dark hand of the Indian caught his white wrist and held him, while with the other hand he pointed to the curls of reddish brown clustering around the girl's pale forehead, and from them to the curls on Mr. Haydon's own bared head. They were not so luxuriant as those of the girl, but they were of the same character, almost the same color, and the vague resemblance to something familiar by which Overton had been impressed was at once located by the old Indian the moment the stranger lifted the hat from his head.

"Sick, maybe die," said Akkomi, in a voice that was almost a whisper —"die away from her people, away from the blood that is as her blood," and he pointed to the blue veins on the white man's wrist.

With an exclamation of fear and anger, Mr. Haydon flung off the Indian's hand.

Lyster, scarce hearing the words spoken, simply thought the old fellow was drunk, and was about to interfere, when the girl, as though touched by the contest above her, turned mutteringly on the pillow and opened her unconscious eyes on the face of the stranger.

"See!" said the Indian. "She looks at you."

"Ah! Great God!" muttered the other and staggered back out of the range of the wide-open eyes.

Lyster, puzzled, astonished, came forward to question his Eastern friend, who pushed past him rudely, blindly, and made his way out into the sunshine.

Akkomi looked after him with a gratified expression on his dark, wrinkled old face, and bending over the girl, he muttered in a soothing way words in the Indian tongue, as though to quiet her restlessness with Indian witchery.

Chapter XV
Something Worse than a Gold Crisis

"What is the matter with your friend?" asked Overton, as Lyster stood staring after Mr. Haydon, who walked alone down the way they had come from the boats. "Is one glimpse of our camp life enough to drive him to the river again?"

"No, no-that is-well, I don't just know what ails him," confessed Lyster, rather lamely. "He went in with me to see 'Tana, and seems all upset by the sight of her. She does look very low, Dan. At home he has a daughter about her age, who really resembles her a little-as he does —a girl he thinks the world of. Maybe that had something to do with his feelings. I don't know, though; never imagined he was so impressionable to other people's misfortunes. And that satanic-looking old Indian helped make things uncomfortable for him."

"Who-Akkomi?"

"Oh, that is Akkomi, is it? The old chief who was too indisposed to receive me when I awaited admittance to his royal presence! Humph! Well, he seemed lively enough a minute ago-said something to Haydon that nearly gave him fits; and then, as if satisfied with his deviltry, he collapsed into the folds of his blanket again, and looks bland and innocent as a spring lamb at the present speaking. Is he grand chamberlain of your establishment here? Or is he a medicine man you depend on to cure 'Tana?"

"Akkomi said something to Mr. Haydon?" asked Overton, incredulously. "Nonsense! It could not have been anything Haydon would understand, anyway, for Akkomi does not speak English."

Lyster looked at him from the corner of his eyes, and whistled rather rudely.

"Now, it is not necessary for any reason whatever, for you to hide the accomplishments of your noble red friend," he remarked. "You are either trying to gull me, or Akkomi is trying to gull you-which is it?"

"What do you mean?" demanded Overton, impatiently. "You look as though there may be a grain of sense in the immense amount of fool stuff you are talking. Akkomi, maybe, understands English a little when it is spoken; but, like many another Indian who does the same, he will not speak it. I have known him for two years, in his own camp and on the trail, and I have never yet heard him use English words."

"Well, I have not had the felicity of even a two-hour acquaintance with his royal chieftain-ship," remarked Lyster, "but during the limited space of time I have been allowed to gaze on him I am confident I heard him use five English words, and use them very naturally."

"Can you tell me what they were?"

"Certainly; and I see I will have to-and maybe bring proof to indorse me before you will quite credit what I tell you," answered Lyster, with an amused expression. "You can scarcely believe a tenderfoot has learned more of your vagabond reds than you yourself knew, can you? Well, I distinctly heard him say to Mr. Haydon: 'See! She looks at you.' But his other mutterings did not reach my ears; they did Haydon's, however, and drove him out yonder. I tell you, Dan, you ought to chain up your medicine men when capitalists brave the wilds of the Kootenai to lay wealth at your doorstep, for this pet of yours is not very engaging."

Overton paid little heed to the chaffing of his friend. His gaze wandered to the old Indian, who, as Lyster said, was at that moment a picture of bland indifference. He was sunning himself again at the door of Harris' cabin, and his eyes followed sleepily the form of Mr. Haydon, who had stopped at the creek, and with hands clasped back of him, was staring into the swift-flowing mountain stream.

"Oh, I don't doubt you, Max," said Overton, at last. "Don't speak as if I did. But the idea that old Akkomi really expressed himself in English would suggest to me a vital necessity, or else that he was becoming weak in his old age; for his prejudice against his people using any of the white men's words has been the most stubborn thing in his whole make-up. And what strong necessity could there be for him to address Mr. Haydon, an utter stranger?"

"Don't know, I am sure-unless it is that his interest in 'Tana is very strong. You know she saved the life of his little grandchild-the future chief, you said. And I think you are fond of asserting that an Indian never forgets a favor; so it may be that his satanic majesty over there only wanted to interest a seemingly influential stranger in a poor little sick girl, and was not aware that he took an uncanny way of doing it. Had we better go down and apologize to Haydon?"

"You can-directly. Who is he?"

"Well, he is the great moneyed mogul at the back of the company for whom you have been doing some responsible work out here. I guess he is what you call a silent partner; while Mr. Seldon-my relation, you know-has been the active member in the mining deals. They have been friends this long time. I have heard that Seldon was to have married Haydon's sister years ago. Wedding day set and all, when the charms of a handsome employee of theirs proved stronger than her promise, and she was found missing one morning; also the handsome clerk, as well as a rather heavy sum of money, to which the clerk had access. Of course, they never supposed that the girl knew she was eloping with a thief. But her brother-this one here-never forgave her. An appeal for help came to him once from her-there was a child then-but it was ignored, and they never heard from her again. Haydon was very fond of her, I believe-fond and proud, and never got over the disgrace of it. Seldon never married, and he did what he could to make her family forgive her, and look after her. But it was no use, though their regard for him never lessened. So you see they are partners from away back; and while Haydon is considerable of an expert in mineralogy, this is the first visit he has ever made to their works up in the Northwest. In fact, he had not intended coming so far north just now; he was waiting for Seldon, who was down in Idaho. But when I got your letter, and impressed on his mind the good business policy of having the firm investigate at once, he fell in with the idea, and-here we are! Now, that is about all I can tell you of Haydon, and how he came here."

"Less would have been plenty," said Overton, with a pretended sigh of relief. "I didn't ask to be told his sister's love affairs or his brother-in-law's failings. I was asking about the man himself."

"Well, I don't know what to tell you about him; there doesn't seem to be anything to say. He is T. J. Haydon, a man who inherited both money and a genius for speculation. Not a plunger, you know; but one of those pursy, far-seeing fellows who always put their money on the right number and wait patiently until it wins. I might tell you that he was sentimental once in his life, and got married; and I might tell you of a pretty daughter he has (and whom he used to be very much afraid I would make love to), but I suppose you would not be interested in those exciting details, so I will refrain. But as to the man himself and his trip here, I can only say, if you have made a strike up here, he is the very best man I know to get interested. Better even than Seldon, for Seldon always defers to Haydon, while Haydon always acts on his own judgment. And say, old fellow, long as we have talked, you have not yet told me one word of the new gold mine. I suspected none of the Ferry folks knew of it, from the general opinion that your trip here was an idiotic affair. Even the doctor said there was no sane reason why you should have dragged Harris and 'Tana into the woods as you did. I kept quiet, remembering the news in your letter, for I was sure you did not decide on this expedition without a good reason. Then the contents of that letter I read the night Harris collapsed-well, it stuck in my mind, and I got to wondering if your bonanza was the one he had found before. Oh, I've been doing some surmising about it. Am I right?"

"Pretty nearly," assented Overton. "Of course I knew some of the folks would raise a howl because I let 'Tana come along; but it was necessary, and I thought it would be best for her in the end, else you may be sure-be very sure —I would not have had her come. She-was to have gone back-at once-the very next day; but when the next day came, she was not able. I have done what I could, but nothing seems to count. She does not get well, and the gold doesn't play much of a figure in this camp just now. One-third of the find is hers, and the same for Harris and me; but I'd give my share cheerfully this minute if it would buy back health for her and let me see her laughing and bright again."

Lyster reached out his hand and gave Overton's arm an affectionate pressure.

"Don't I know it, Dan?" he asked kindly. "Can't I see that you have just worked and worried yourself sick over her illness-blaming yourself, perhaps —"

"Yes, that is it-blaming myself for-many things," he agreed, brokenly, and then he checked himself as Lyster's curious glance was turned on him. "So you see I am in no fit condition to talk values with this Mr. Haydon. All my thoughts are somewhere else. Doctor says if she is not better to-night she will not get well. That means she will not live. Tell your friend that something worse than a gold crisis is here just now, and I can't talk to him till it is over. Don't mind if I'm even a bit careless with you, Max. Look after yourselves as well as you can. You are welcome-you know that; but-what's the use of words? Perhaps 'Tana is dying!"

And turning his back abruptly on his friend, he walked away, while Lyster looked after him with some surprise.

"I seem to be dropped by everybody," he remarked, "first Haydon and now Dan. But I don't believe there is danger of her dying. I *won't* believe it! Dan has worried himself sick and fearful during these terrible days, but I'll do my share now and let him get some rest and sleep. 'Tana die! I can't think it. But I care ten times more for Dan, just because of his devotion to her. I wonder what he would think if he knew why I wanted her to go to school, or how much she was in my mind every hour I was gone. I felt like telling him just now, but better not-not yet. He thinks she is only a little child yet. Dear old Dan!"

He entered the cabin and spoke to Harris, whom he had not seen before, and who looked with pleasure at him, though, as ever, speechless and moveless, but for that nod of his head and the bright, quick glance of his eyes.

From him he went again to 'Tana; but she lay still and pale, with closed eyes and no longer muttering.

"There ain't a blessed thing you can do, Mr. Max," said Mrs. Huzzard, in a wheezing whisper; "but if there is, you may be sure I'll let you know and glad to do it. Lavina says she's going to help me to a rest; and you must help Dan Overton, for slept he has not, and I know it, these eight nights since I've been here. And if that ain't enough to kill a man!"

"Sure enough. But now that I am here, we will not have any night watches on his part," decided Lyster. "Between Miss Slocum and myself I think we can manage to do some very creditable nursing."

"I am willing to do my best," said Miss Lavina, with a shrinking glance toward Flap-Jacks, who just slouched past with a bucket of water; "but I must confess I do feel a timidity in the presence of these sly-looking Indians. And if at night I can only be sure none of them are very close, I may be able to watch this poor girl instead of watching for them with their tomahawks."

"Never fear while I am detailed as guard," answered Lyster, reassuringly. "They will reach you only over my dead body."

"Oh, but —" and the timid one arose as if for instant flight, but was held by Mrs. Huzzard.

"Now, now!" she said reprovingly to the young fellow, "it's noways good-natured of you to make us more scared of the dirty things than we are naturally. But, Lavina, I'll go bail that he never yet has seen a dead body of their killing since he came in the country. Lord knows, they don't look as if they would kill a sheep, though they might steal them fast enough. It ain't from Dan Overton that you ever learned to scare women, Mr. Max; you wouldn't catch him at such tricks."

"Now I beg that whatever you do, Mrs. Huzzard, you will not compare me to that personage," objected Lyster; "for I am convinced that anything human would in your eyes suffer by such a comparison. Great is Dan in the camp of the Kootenais!"

Mrs. Huzzard only laughed at his words, but Miss Lavina did not. She even let her eyes wander again to Akkomi, in order to show her disapproval of frivolous comment on Mr. Overton; a fact Lyster perceived and was immensely amused by.

"She has set her covetous maidenly eyes on him, and if she doesn't marry him before the year is over, he will have to be clever," he decided, as he left them and went to look up Haydon.

"Serves Dan right if she did, for he never gives any other fellow half a chance with the old ladies. The rest of us have to be content with the young ones."

Chapter XVI
Through the Night

The soft dusk of the night had fallen over the northern lands, and the pale stars had gleamed for hours on the reflecting waves of mountain streams. It was late-near midnight, for the waning sickle of the moon was slipping from its dark cover in the east and hanging like a jewel of gold just above the black crown of the pines. Breaths from the heights sifted down through the vast woods, carrying sometimes the dreary twitter of a bird disturbed, or the mellow call of insects singing to each other of the summer night. All sounds of the wilderness were as echoes of rest and utter content.

And in the camp of the Twin Springs, shadows moved sometimes with a silence that was scarce a discord in the wood songs of repose. A camp fire glimmered faintly a little way up from the stream, and around it slept the Indian boatman, the squaw, and old Akkomi, who, to the surprise of Overton, had announced his intention of remaining until morning, that he might know how the sickness went with the little "Girl-not-Afraid."

A dim light showed through the chinks of 'Tana's cabin, where Miss Lavina, the doctor, and Lyster were on guard for the night. The doctor had grown sleepy and moved into Harris' room, where he could be comfortable on blankets. Lyster, watching the girl, was trying to make himself think that their watching was all of no use; her sleep seemed so profound, so healthfully natural, that he could not bring himself to think, as Dan did, that the doctor's worst prophecy could come true-that out of that sleep she might awake to consciousness, or that, on the other hand, she might drift from sleep to lethargy and thus out of life.

Outside a man stood peering in through a chink from which he had stealthily pulled the moss. He could not see the girl's face, but he could see that of Lyster as he bent over, listening to her breathing, and he watched it as if to glean some reflected knowledge from the young fellow's earnest glances.

He had been there a long time. Once he slipped away for a short distance and stood in the deeper shadows, but he had returned, and was listening to the low, disjointed converse of the watchers within, when suddenly a tall form loomed up beside him and a heavy hand was dropped on his shoulder.

"Not a word!" said a voice close to his ear. "If you make a noise, I'll strangle you! Come along!"

To do otherwise was not easy, for the hand on his shoulder had a helpful grip. He was almost lifted over the ground until they were several yards from the cabin, and out in the clearer light of the stars.

"Well, I protest, Mr. Overton, that your manner is not very pleasant," remarked the captive, as he was released and allowed to speak. "Is-is this sort of threats a habit of yours with strangers in your camp?"

Overton, seeing him now away from the thick shadows of the cabin, gave a low exclamation of astonishment and irritation.

"*You* —Mr. Haydon! Well, you must confess that if my threats are not pleasant, neither is it pleasant to find some one moving like a spy around that little girl's cabin. If you don't want to be treated like a spy, don't act like one."

"Well, it does look queer, maybe," said the other, lamely. "I —I could not get asleep, and as I was walking around, it seemed natural to look in the cabin, though I did not want to disturb them by going in. I think I heard them say she was improving."

"Did they say that-lately?" asked Overton, earnestly, everything else forgotten for the moment in his strong desire for her recovery. "Who said it-Miss Slocum? Well, she seems like a sensible woman, and I hope to God she is right about this! Don't mind my roughness just now. I was too quick, maybe; but spies around a new gold mine or field are given pretty harsh treatment up here sometimes; and you were liable to suspicion from any one."

"No doubt-no doubt," agreed the other, with visible relief. "But to be a suspected character is a new rôle for me —a bit amusing, too. However, now that you have broached the subject of this new find of yours, I presume Lyster made clear to you that I came up here for the express purpose of investigating what you have to offer, with a view to making a deal with you. And as my time here will be limited —"

"Perhaps to-morrow we can talk of it. I can't to-night," answered Overton. "To that little girl in there one-third of the stock belongs; another third belongs to that paralyzed man in the other cabin. I have to look after the interests of them both, and need to have my head clear to do it. But with her there sick-dying maybe —I can't think of dollars and cents."

"You mean to tell me that the young girl is joint owner of a gold find promising a fortune? Why, I understood Max to say she was poor-in fact, indebted to you for all care."

"Max is too careless with his words," answered Overton, coldly. "She is in my care-yes; but I do not think she will be poor."

"She has a very conscientious guardian, anyway," remarked Mr. Haydon, "when it is impossible for a man even to look in her cabin without finding you on his track. I confess I am interested in her. Can you tell me how she came in this wild country? I did not expect to find pretty young white girls in the heart of this wilderness."

"I suppose not," agreed the other.

They had reached the little camp fire by this time, and he threw some dry sticks on the red coals. As the blaze leaped up and made bright the circle around them, he looked at the stranger and said, bluntly:

"What did Akkomi tell you of her?"

"Akkomi?"

"Yes; the old Indian who went in with you to see her."

"Oh, that fellow? Some gibberish."

"I guess he must have said that she looks like you," decided Overton. "I rather think that was it."

"Like *me*! Why-how —" and Mr. Haydon tried to smile away the absurdity of such a fancy.

"For there is a resemblance," continued the younger man, with utter indifference to the stranger's confusion. "Of course it may not mean anything —a chance likeness. But it is very noticeable when your hat is off, and it must have impressed the old Indian, who seems to think himself a sort of godfather to her. Yes, I guess that was why he spoke to you."

"But her-her people? Are there only you and these Indians to claim her? She must have some family —"

"Possibly," agreed Overton, curtly. "If she ever gets able to answer, you can ask her. If you want to know sooner, there is old Akkomi; he can tell you, perhaps."

But Mr. Haydon made a gesture of antipathy to any converse with that individual.

"One meets so many astonishing things in this country," he remarked, as though in extenuation of something. "The mere presence of such a savage in the sick girl's room is enough to upset any one unused to this border life-it upset me completely. You see, I have a daughter of my own back East."

"So Max tells me," replied Overton, carelessly, all unconscious of the intended honor extended to him when Mr. Haydon made mention of his own family to a ranger of a few hours' acquaintance.

"Yes," Haydon continued, "and that naturally makes one feel an interest in any young girl without home or-relatives, as this invalid is; and I would be glad of any information concerning her-or any hint of help I might be to her, partly for-humanity's sake, and partly for Max."

"At present I don't know of any service you could render her," said Overton, coldly, conscious of a jarring, unpleasant feeling as the man talked to him. He thought idly to himself how queer it was that he should have an instinctive feeling of dislike for a person who in the slightest degree resembled 'Tana; and this stranger must have resembled her much before he grew stout and broad of face; the hair, the nose, and other points about the features, were very much alike.

He did not wonder that Akkomi might have been startled at it, and made comments. But as he himself surveyed Mr. Haydon's features by the flickering light of the burning sticks, he realized how little the likeness of outlines amounted to after all, since not a shadow of expression on the face before him was like that of the girl whose sleep was so carefully guarded in the cabin.

And then, with a feeling of thankfulness that it was so, there flashed across his mind the import of the stranger's closing words—"for the sake of Max."

"For Max, you said. Well, maybe I am a little more stupid than usual to-night, but I must own up I can't see how a favor to 'Tana could affect Max very much."

"You do not?"

"I tell you so," said Overton curtly, not liking the knowing smile in the eyes of the speaker. He did not want to be there talking to him, anyway. To walk alone under the stars was better than the discord of a voice unpleasant. Under the stars she had come to him that once-once, when she had been clasped close-close! when she had whispered words near to his heart, and their hands had touched in the magnetism of troubled joy. Ah! it was best to remember that, though death itself follow after! A short, impatient sigh touched his lips as he tried to listen to the words of the stranger while his thoughts were elsewhere.

"And Seldon would do something very handsome for Max if he married to suit him," Haydon was saying, thoughtfully. "Seldon has no children, you know, and if this girl was sent to school for a while, I think it would come out all right-all right. I would take a personal interest to the extent of talking to Seldon of it. He will think it a queer place for Max to come for a wife; but when-when I talk to him, he will agree. Yes, I can promise it will be all right."

"What are you talking of?" demanded Overton, blankly. He had not heard one-half of a very carefully worded idea of Mr. Haydon's. "Max married! To whom?"

"You are not a very flattering listener," remarked the other, dryly, "and don't show much interest in the love affairs of your *protégeé*; but it was of her I was speaking."

"You-you would try to marry her to Max Lyster-marry her!" and his voice sounded in his own ears as strange and far away.

"Well, it is not an unusual prophecy to make of a young girl, is it?" asked Mr. Haydon, with an attempt to be jocular. "And I don't know where she could find a better young fellow. From his discourses concerning her on our journey here and his evident devotion since our arrival, I fancy the idea is not so new to him as it seems to be to you, Mr. Overton."

"Nonsense! when she is well, they quarrel as often as they agree-oftener."

"That is no proof that he is not in love with her-and why not? She is a pretty girl, a bright girl, he says, and of good people—"

"He knows nothing about her people," interrupted Overton.

"But you do?"

"I know all it has been necessary for me to know," and, in spite of himself, he could not speak of 'Tana to this man without a feeling of anger at his persistence. "But I can't help being rather surprised, Mr. Haydon, that you should so quickly agree that a wise thing for your partner's nephew to do is to turn from all the cultured, intelligent girls he must know, and look for a wife among the mining camps of the Kootenai hills. And, considering the fact that you approve of it, without ever having heard her speak, without knowing in the least who or what her family have been—I must say it is an extraordinarily impulsive thing for a man of your reputation to do—a cool-headed, conservative business man."

Mr. Haydon found himself scrutinized very closely, very coldly by the ranger, who had all the evening kept away from him, and whom he had mentally jotted down as a big, careless, improvident prospector, untaught and a bit uncouth.

But his words were not uncouth as he launched them at the older man, and he was no longer careless as he watched the perturbation with which they were received. But Haydon shrugged his shoulders and attempted to look indifferent.

"I remarked just now that this was a land of astonishing things," he said, with a tolerant air, "and it surely is so when the most depraved-looking redskin is allowed admittance to a white girl's chamber, while the most harmless of Caucasians is looked on with suspicion if he merely shows a little human interest in her welfare."

"Akkomi is a friend of her own choosing," answered Overton, "and a friend who would be found trusty if he was needed. As to you-you have no right, that I know of, to assume any direction of her affairs. She will choose her own friends-and her own husband-when she wants them. But while she is sick and helpless, she is under my care, and even though you were her father himself, your ideas should not influence her future unless she approved you."

With a feeling of relief he turned away, glad to have in some way given vent to the irritation awakened in him by the prosperous gentleman from civilization.

The prosperous gentleman saw his form grow dim in the starlight, and though his face flushed angrily at first, the annoyance gave place to a certain satisfaction as he seated himself on a log by the fire, and repeated Overton's final words:

"'*Even though you were her father himself!*' Well, well, Mr. Overton! Your uncivil words have told me more than you intended-namely, that your own knowledge as to who her father was, or is, seems very slight. So much the better, for one of your unconventional order is not the sort of person I should care to have know. 'Even though you were her father himself.' Humph! So he does me the doubtful honor to suppose I may be? It is a nasty muddle all through. I never dreamed of walking into such a net as this. But something must be done, and that is clear; no use trying to shirk it, for Seldon is sure to run across them sooner or later up here-sure. And if he took a hand in it-as he would the minute he saw her-well, I could not count on his being quiet about it, either. I've thought it all out this evening. I've got to get her away myself-get her to school, get her to marry Max, and all so quietly that there sha'n't be any social sensation about her advent into the family. I hardly know whether this wealth they talk of will be a help or a hindrance; a help, I suppose. And there need not be any hitch in the whole affair if the girl is only reasonable and this autocratic ranger can be ignored or bought over to silence. It would be very annoying to have such family affairs talked of-annoying to the girl, also, when she lives among people who object to scandals. Gad! how her face did strike me! I felt as if I had seen a ghost. And that cursed Indian!"

Altogether, Mr. Haydon had considerable food for reflection, and much of it was decidedly annoying; or so it seemed to Akkomi, who lay in the shadow and looked like a body asleep, as were the others. But from a fold of his blanket he could see plainly the face of the stranger and note the perplexity in it.

The first tender flush of early day was making the stars dim when the doctor met Overton between the tents and the cabins, and surveyed him critically from his slouch hat to his boots, on which were splashes of water and fresh loam.

"What, in the name of all that's infernal, has taken possession of you, Overton?" he demanded, with assumed anger and real concern. "You have not been in bed all night. I know, for I've been to your tent. You prowl somewhere in the woods when you ought to be in bed, and you are looking like a ghost of yourself."

"Oh, I guess I'll last a day or two yet, so quit your growling; you think you'll scare me into asking for some of your medicines; but that is where you will find yourself beautifully left. I prefer a natural death."

"And you will find it, too, if you don't mend your ways," retorted the man of the medicines. "I thought at first it was the care of 'Tana that kept you awake every hour of every night; but I see it is just the same now when there are plenty to take your place; worse-for now you go tramping, God only knows where, and come back looking tired, as though you had been racing with the devil."

"You haven't told me how she is," was all the answer he made to this tirade. "You said-that by daylight —"

"There would be a change-yes, and there is; only a shadow of a change as yet, but the shadow leans the right way."

"The *right* way," he half whispered, and walked on toward her cabin. He felt dizzy and the tears crept up in his eyes, and he forgot the doctor, who looked after him and muttered statements damaging to Dan's sanity.

All the long night he had fought with himself to keep away, to let the others care for her-the others, who fancied they were giving him a wished-for rest. And all the while the desire of his heart was to bar them out-to wait, alone with her, for the life or death that was to come. He had walked miles in his restlessness, but could not have found again the paths he walked over. He had talked with some of the people who were wakeful in the night, but could scarce have told of any words he had said.

He had felt dazed by the dread of what the new day would bring, and now he looked up at the morning star with a great thankfulness in his heart. The new day had come, and with it a breath of hope.

Miss Lavina met him at the door, and whispered that the doctor thought the fever had taken the hoped-for turn for the better. 'Tana had opened her eyes but a moment before, and looked at Miss Slocum wonderingly, but fell asleep again; she had looked rational, but very weak.

"Well, old fellow, I am proud of myself," said Lyster, as Overton entered. "It took Miss Slocum and me only one night to bring 'Tana around several degrees nearer health. We are the nurses! And if she only wakes conscious —"

His words, or else the intense, wistful gaze of the man at the foot of the bed, must have aroused her, for she moved and opened her eyes and looked around aimlessly, passing over the faces of Miss Slocum, of the squaw, and of Overton, until Lyster, close beside her, whispered her name. Then her lips curved ever so little in a smile as her eyes met his.

"Max!" she said, and put out her hand to him. As his fingers clasped it, she turned her face toward him, and fell contentedly asleep again, with her cheek against his hand.

And Mr. Haydon, who came in with the doctor a moment later, glanced at the picture they made, and smiled meaningly at Overton.

"You see, I was right," he observed. "And do you not think it would be a very exacting guardian who could object?"

Overton only looked at Max, whose face had flushed a little, knowing how significant his attitude must appear to others. But his hand remained in hers, and his eyes turned to Dan with a half embarrassed confession in them —a confession Dan read and understood.

"Yes, you may well be proud, Max," he said, answering Lyster's words. "You deserve all gratitude; and I hope —I hope nothing but good luck will come your way."

Mr. Haydon, who watched him with critical eyes, could read nothing in his words but kindliest concern for a friend.

The doctor, who had suddenly got a ridiculous idea in his head that Dan Overton was wearing himself out on 'Tana's account, changed his mind and silently called himself a fool. He might have known Dan had more sense than that. Yet, what was it that had changed him so?

Twenty-four hours later he thought he knew.

"So it was a gold mine that dragged you people up into this wilderness? Well, I've puzzled my mind a good deal to understand your movements lately; but the finding of a vein as rich as your free gold promises is enough to turn any man's head for a while. Well, well; you are a lucky fellow, Overton."

"Yes, I've no doubt that between good luck and bad luck, I've as much luck as anybody," answered Overton, with a grimace, "but a week or so ago you did not think me lucky-you thought me 'looney.'"

"You are more than half right," agreed the doctor; "appearances justified me. My wife and I stormed at you-behind your back-for carrying 'Tana with you on your fishing trip; it was such an unheard-of thing to my folks, you know. Humph! I wonder what they will say when it is known that she was on a prospecting trip, and that the venture will result in a gain to her of dollars that will be counted by the tens of thousands. By George! it seems incredible! Just like a chapter from the old fairy tales."

"Yes. I find myself thinking about it like that sometimes," said Overton; "a little afraid to lay plans, for fear that after all it may be a dream. I never hoped much for it; I came under protest, and the luck seems more than I deserved."

"Maybe that is the reason you accept it in such a sulky fashion," observed the doctor, "for, upon my soul, I think I am more elated over your good fortune than you are. You don't appear to get up a particle of enthusiasm because of it."

"Well, I have not had an enthusiastic lot of partners, either. Harris, here, not able to move; 'Tana not expected to live; and I suddenly face to face with all this responsibility for them. It gave me considerable to think about."

"You are right. I only wonder you are not gray-haired. A new gold-field waiting for you to make it known, and you guarding it at the same time, perhaps, from red tramps who come spying around. But you are lucky, Dan; everything comes your way, even a capitalist ready at your word to put up money on the strength of the ore you have to show. Why, man, many a poor devil of a prospector has stood a long siege with starvation, even with gold ore in sight, just because no one with capital would buy or back him."

"I know. I realize that; and, for the sake of the other two, I am very glad there need be no waiting for profits."

"Do you know, Dan, I fancy little 'Tana is in the way of being well cared for, even without this good fortune," observed the doctor, looking at the other in a questioning way. "It just occurred to me yesterday that that fine young fellow, Lyster, is uncommonly fond of her. It may be simply because she is ill, and he is sorry for her; but his devotion appeared to me to have a sentimental tinge, and I thought what a fine thing it would be."

"Very," agreed Overton; "and you are sentimental enough yourself to plan it all out for them. I guess Haydon helped to put that notion into your head, didn't he?"

The doctor laughed.

"Well, yes, he did speak of Lyster's devotion to your *protégée*," he acknowledged; "and you think we are a couple of premature match-makers, don't you?"

"I think maybe you had better leave it for 'Tana to decide," answered Overton, "and I also think schools will be the first thing considered by her. She is very young, you know."

"Seventeen, perhaps," hazarded the doctor; but Overton did not reply.

He was watching the canoe just launched by their Indian boatmen. They were to take Mr. Haydon back again to the Ferry. He was to send up workmen, and Overton was to manage the work for the present-or, at least, until Mr. Seldon could arrive and organize the work of developing the vein that Mr. Haydon had found was of such exceeding richness that his offer to the owners had been of corresponding magnitude. Overton had promptly accepted the terms offered; Harris agreed to them; and even if 'Tana should not, Dan decided that out of his own share he could make up any added sum desired by her for her share, though he had little idea that she would find fault with his arrangements. She! who had thought, that day of the gold find, that it was better to have their little camp unshared by the many whom gold would bring to them-that it was almost better to be poor than to have their happy life changed.

And it was all over now. Other people had come and were close about her, while he had not seen her since the morning before, when she had awakened and turned to Max. Well, he should be satisfied, so he told himself. She was going to get well again. She was going to be happy. More wealth than they had hoped for had come to her, and with it she would, of course, leave the hills, would go into the life of the cities, and by and by would be glad to forget the simple, primitive life they had shared for the few days of one Kootenai summer. Well, she would be happy.

And here on the spot where their pretty camp had been, he would remain. No thought of leaving came to him. It would all be changed, of course; men and machinery would spoil all the beauty of their wilderness. But as yet no plan for his own future had occurred to him. That he himself had wealth sufficient to secure him from all toil and that a world of pleasure was within his reach, did not seem to touch him with any alluring sense. He was going to remain until the vein of the Twin Springs had a big hole made in it; and the rich soil of the old river he had staked out as a reserve for himself and his partners, to either work or sell. Through his one-sided conversations with Harris he learned that he, too, wanted to remain in the camp where their gold had been found. Doctors, medicines, luxuries, could be brought to him, but he would remain.

Mrs. Huzzard had at once been offered a sum that in her eyes was munificent, for the express purpose of managing the establishment of the partners-when it was built. Until then she was to draw her salary, and act as either nurse or cook in the rude dwellings that for the present had to satisfy all their dreams of luxury.

An exodus from Sinna Ferry was expected; many changes were to be made; and Overton and the doctor went down to the canoe to give final directions to their Indian messenger.

Lyster was there, too, with a most exhausting list of articles which Mr. Haydon was to send up from Helena.

"Dan, some of these things I put down for 'Tana, as I happened to think of them," he said, and unfolded a little roll made from the leaves of a notebook stuck together at the ends with molasses. "You look it over and see if it's all right. I left one sheet empty for anything you might want to add."

Dan took it, eying dubiously the length of it and the great array of articles mentioned.

"I don't think I had better add anything to it until heavier boats are carrying freight on the Kootenai," he remarked, and then commenced reading aloud some of the items:

Eiderdown pillows.

Rugs and hammocks.

A guitar.

Hot water bottle.

Some good whisky.

Toilet soap.

Bret Harte's Poems.

A traveling dress for a girl. (Here followed measurements and directions to the dressmaker.) Then the whole was scratched out, and the following was substituted: Brown flannel or serge-nine yards.

"I had to get Mrs. Huzzard to tell me some of the things," said Lyster, who looked rather annoyed at the quizzical smiles of Dan and the doctor.

"I should imagine you would," observed Overton. "I would have needed the help of the whole camp to get together that amount of plunder. A good shaving set and a pair of cork insoles, No. 8, are they for 'Tana, too?"

But Lyster disdained reply, and Overton, after reading, "All the late magazines," and "A double kettle for cooking oatmeal," folded up the paper and gave it back.

"As I have read only a very small section of the list, I do not imagine you have omitted anything that could possibly be towed up the river," he said. "But it is all right, my boy. I would never have thought of half that stuff, but I've no doubt they will all be of use, and 'Tana will thank you."

"How soon do you expect she will be able to walk, or be moved?" asked Mr. Haydon of the doctor.

"Oh, in two or three weeks, if nothing interferes with her promised recovery. She is a pretty sick girl; but I think her good constitution will help her on her feet by that time."

"And by that time I will be back here," said Haydon, addressing Lyster.

He took a sealed envelope from an inner pocket and gave it to the young fellow.

"When she gets well enough to read that, give it to her, Max," he said, in a low tone. "It's something that may surprise her a little, so I trust your discretion as to when she is to see it. From what I hear of her, she must be a rather level-headed, independent little girl. And as I have something to tell her worth her knowing, I have decided to leave the letter. Now, don't look so puzzled. When I come back she will likely tell you what it means, but you may be sure it is no bad news I send her. Will you attend to it?"

"Certainly. But I don't understand —"

"And there is no need for you to understand-just yet. Take good care of her, and help Overton in all possible ways to look after our interests here. There will be a great deal to see to until Seldon or I can get back."

"Oh, Dan is a host in himself," said Lyster. "He won't want me in his way when it comes to managing his men. But I can help Flap-Jacks carry water, or help old Akkomi smoke, for he comes here each day for just that purpose-that and his dinner-so never fear but that I will make myself useful."

Miss Slocum from the cabin doorway-the door was a blanket-watched the canoe skim down the little stream, and sighed dolefully when it disappeared entirely.

"Now, Lavina," remonstrated Mrs. Huzzard, "I do hope that you ain't counting on making part of the next load that leaves here; for now that you have got here, I'd hate the worst kind to lose you. Gold mines are fine things to live alongside of, I dare say; but I crave some human beings within hail-yes, indeed."

"Exactly my own feelings, Cousin Lorena," admitted Miss Slocum, "and I regret the departure of any member of our circle-all except the Indians. I really do not think that any amount of living among them would teach me to feel lonely at their absence. And that dreadful Akkomi!"

"Yes, isn't he a trial? Not that he ever does any harm; but he just keeps a body in mortal dread, for fear he might take a notion to."

"Yet Mr. Overton seems to think him entirely friendly."

"Humph! yes. But if 'Tana should pet a rattlesnake, Mr. Overton would trust it. That's just how constant he is to his friends."

"Well, now," said Miss Lavina, with mild surprise in her tone, "I really have seen nothing in his manner that would indicate any extreme liking for the girl, though she is his ward. Now, that bright young gentleman, Mr. Lyster —"

"Tut, tut, Lavina! Max Lyster is all eyes and hands for her just now. He will fan her and laugh with her; but it will be Dan who digs for her and takes the weight of her care on his shoulders, even if he never says a word about it. That is just Dan Overton's way."

"And a very fine way it is, Lorena," said Miss Slocum, while her eyes wandered out to where he stood talking to Lyster. "I've met many men of fine manners in my time, but I never was more impressed at first sight by any person than by him when he conducted me personally to you on my arrival. The man had never heard my name before, yet he received me as if this camp had been arranged on purpose for my visit, and that he himself had been expecting me. If that did not contain the very essence of fine manners, I never saw any, Lorena Jane."

"I —I s'pose it does, Lavina," agreed Mrs. Huzzard; "though I never heard any one go on much about his manners before. And as for me-well," and she looked a bit embarrassed, "I ain't the best judge myself. I've had such a terrible hard tussle to make a living since my man died, that I hain't had time to study fine manners. I'll have time enough before long, I suppose, for Dan Overton surely has offered me liberal living wages. But, Lavina, even if I did want to learn now, I wouldn't know where to commence."

"Well, Lorena, since you mention it, there is lots of room for improvement in your general manner. You've been with careless people, I suppose, and bad habits are gathered that way. Now I never was much of a genius-couldn't trim a bonnet like you to save my life; but I did have a most particular mother; and she held that good manners was a recommendation in any land. So, even if her children had no fortune left them, they were taught to show they had careful bringing up. One of my ideas in coming out here was that I might teach deportment in some Indian school, but not much of that notion is left me. Could I ever teach Flap-Jacks to quit scratching her head in the presence of ladies and gentlemen? No."

"I don't think," said Mrs. Huzzard, in a meditative way, "that I mind the scratching so much as I do the dratted habit she has of carrying the dish-cloth under her arm when she don't happen to be using it. That just wears on my nerves, it does. But I tell you what it is, Lavina-if you are kind of disappointed on account of not getting Indian scholars that suit just yet, I'm more than half willing you should teach me the deportment, if you'd be satisfied with one big white scholar instead of a lot of little red ones."

"Yes, indeed, and glad to do it," said Miss Slocum, frankly. "Your heart is all right, Lorena Jane; but a warm heart will not make people forget that you lean your elbow on the table and put your food into your mouth with your knife. Such things jar on other people just as Flap-Jacks and the dish-cloth jar on you. Don't you understand? But your desire to improve shows that you are a very remarkable woman, Lorena, for very few people are willing to learn new habits after having followed careless ones for forty years."

"Thirty-nine," corrected Lorena Jane, showing that, however peculiar and remarkable her wisdom might be in some directions, it did not prevent a natural womanly feeling regarding the number of years she had lived.

"You see," she continued, after a little, as Miss Lavina kept a discreet silence, "this here gold fever is catching; and if any one gets started on the right track, there is no telling what day he may stumble over a fortune. One might come my way-or yours, Lavina. And, just as you say, fine manners is a heap of help in sassiety. And thinking of it that way makes me feel I'd like to be prepared to enjoy, in first-class style, any amount of money I might get a chance at up here. For I tell you what it is, Lavina, this Western land is a woman's country. Her chances in most things are always as good, and mostly better than a man's."

"Yes, if she does not die from fright at the creepy looks of the friendly Indians," said Miss Slocum, with a shivering breath. "I have not slept sound for a single minute since I saw that old smoking wretch who never seems a rod from this cabin. Now down there at Sinna Ferry I thought it might be kind of nice, though we stopped only a little while, and I was not up in the street. Any real genteel people there?"

"Well-yes, there is," answered Lorena Jane, after a slight hesitation as to just how much it would be wise to say of the genteel gentleman who resided in Sinna Ferry, and was in her eyes a model of culture and disdainful superiority. Indeed, that disdain of his had been a first cause in her desire to reach the state of polish he himself enjoyed-to rise above the vulgar level of manners that had of old seemed good enough to her. "Yes, there is some high-toned folks there; the doctor's wife and family, for one; and then there is a very genteel man there-Captain Leek. He is an ex-officer in the late war, you know; a real military gentleman, with a wound in his leg. Limps some, but not enough to make him awkward. He keeps the postoffice. But if this Government looked after its heroes as it ought to, he'd be getting a good pension-that's just what he would. I'm too sound a Union woman not to feel riled at times when I see the defenders of the Constitution go unrewarded."

"Don't say 'riled,' Lorena," corrected Miss Slocum. "You must drop that and 'dratted' and 'I'll swan'; for I don't think you could tell what any of them mean. I couldn't, I'm sure. But I used to know a family of Leeks back in Ohio. They were Democrats, though, and their boys joined the Confederate Army, though I heard they wasn't much good to the cause. But of course it is not likely to be one of them."

"I should think not," agreed Mrs. Huzzard, stoutly. "I never heard him talk politics much; but I do know that he wears nothing but the Union blue to this day, and always that military sort of hat with a cord around it-so-so dignified like."

"No, I did not suppose it could be the one I knew," said her cousin; "the military uniform decides that."

Chapter XVIII
Awakening

"Flap-Jacks," said 'Tana, softly, so as to reach no ear but that of the squaw, who came in from Harris' cabin to find the parasol of Miss Slocum, who was about to walk in the sunshine. To the red creature of the forest this parasol seemed the most wonderfully beautiful thing of all the strange things which the white squaws made use of. "Flap-Jacks, are they gone?"

Three weeks had gone by, three weeks of miraculous changes in the beauty of their wild nook along the trail of the old river.

"Twin Springs," the place was called now-Twin Spring Mines. Already men were at work on the new lode, and doing placer digging for the free gold in the soil. Wooden rails were laid to the edge of the stream, and over it the small, rude car was pushed with the new ore down to a raft on which a test load had been drifted to the immense crusher at the works on Lake Kootenai. And the test had resulted so favorably that the new strike at Twin Springs was considered by far the richest one of the year.

Through all the turbulence that swept up the little stream to their camp, two of the discovering party were housed, sick and silent, in the little double cabin. The doctor could see no reason why 'Tana was so slow in her recovery; he had expected so much more of her-that she would be carried into health again by the very force of her ambition, and her eager delight in the prospects which her newly acquired wealth was opening up to her.

But puzzling to relate, she showed no eagerness at all about it. Her ambitions, if she had any, were asleep, and she scarcely asked a question concerning all the changes of life and people around her. Listless she lay from one day to another, accepting the attention of people indifferently. Max would read to her a good deal, and several times she asked to be carried into the cabin of Harris, where she would sit for hours talking to him, sometimes in a low voice and then again sitting close beside him in long silences, which, strangely enough, seemed more of companionship to her than the presence of people who laughed and talked. They wearied her at times. When she was able to walk out, she liked to go alone; even Max she had sent back when he followed her.

But she never went far. Sometimes she would sit for an hour by the stream, watching the water slip past the pebbles and the grasses, and on to its turbulent journey toward a far-off rest in the Pacific. And again, she would watch some strange miner dig and wash the soil in his search for the precious "yellow." But her walks were ever within the limits of the busy diggings; all her old fondness for the wild places seemed sleeping-like her ambitions.

"She needs change now. Get her away from here," advised the doctor, who no longer felt that she needed medicines, but who could not, with all his skill, build her up again into the daring, saucy 'Tana, who had won the game of cards from the captain that night at the select party at Sinna Ferry.

But when Overton, after much hesitation, broached the subject of her going away, she did look at him with a touch of the old defiance in her face, and after a bit said:

"I guess the camp will have to be big enough for you and me, too, a few days longer. I haven't made up my mind as to when I want to go."

"But the summer will not last long, now. You must commence to think of where you want to go; for when the cold weather comes, 'Tana, you can't remain here."

"I can if I want to," she answered.

After one troubled, helpless look at her pale face, he walked out of the cabin; and Lyster, who had wanted to ask the result of the interview, could not find him all that evening. He had gone somewhere alone, up on the mountain.

She had answered him with a great deal of cool indifference; but when the two cousins entered her room, she was on the bed with her face buried in the pillows, weeping in an uncontrollable manner that filled them with dismay. The doctor decided that while Dan was a good fellow in most ways, he evidently had not a soothing influence on 'Tana, possibly not realizing the changed mental condition laid on her by her sickness. The doctor further made up his mind that, without hurting Dan's feelings, he must find some other mouthpiece for his ideas concerning her or reason with her himself.

But, so far, she would only say she was not ready to go yet. Dan, wishing to make her stay comfortable as possible, went quietly to all the settlements within reach for luxuries in the way of house-furnishing, and had Mrs. Huzzard use them in 'Tana's cabin. But when he had done all this, she never asked a question as to where the comforts came from-she, who, a short month before, had valued each kind glance received from him.

Mrs. Huzzard was sorely afraid that it was pride, the pride of newly acquired wealth, that changed her from the gay, saucy girl into a moody, dreamy being, who would lie all alone for hours and not notice any of them coming and going. The good soul had many a heartache over it all, never guessing that it was an ache and a shame in the heart of the girl that made the new life that was given her seem a thing of little value.

'Tana had watched the squaw wistfully at times, as if expecting her to say something to her when the others were not around, but she never did. When 'Tana heard the ladies ask Lyster to go with them to a certain place where beautiful mosses were to be found, she waited with impatience until their voices left the door.

The squaw shook her head when asked in that whispering way of their departure; but when she had carried out the parasol and watched the party disappear beyond the numerous tents now dotting the spaces where the grass grew rank only a month before, then she slipped back and stood watchful and silent inside the door.

"Come close," said the girl, motioning with a certain nervousness to her. She was not the brave, indifferent little girl she had been of old. "Come close-some one might listen, some-where. I've been so sick —I've dreamed so many things that I can't tell some days what is dream and what is true. I lie here and think and think, but it will not come clear. Listen! I think sometimes you and I hunted for tracks —a white man's tracks-across there where the high ferns are. You showed them to me, and then we came back when the moon shone, and it was light like day, and I picked white flowers. Some days I think of it-of the tracks, long, slim tracks, with the boot heel. Then my head hurts, and I think maybe we never found the tracks, maybe it is only a dream, like-like other things!"

She did not ask if it were so, but she leaned forward with all of eager question in her eyes. It was the first time she had shown strong interest in anything. But, having aroused from her listlessness to speak of the ghosts of fancy haunting her, she seemed quickened to anxiety by the picture her own words conjured up.

"Ah! those tracks in the black mud and that face above the ledge!"

"It is true," said the squaw, "and not a dream. The track of the white man was there, and the moon was in the sky, as you say."

"Ah!" and the evidently unwelcome truth made her clench her fingers together despairingly; she had hoped so that it was a dream. The truth of it banished her lethargy, made her think as nothing else had. "Ah! it was so, then; and the face-the face was real, was —"

"I saw no face," said the squaw.

"But I did-yes, I did," she muttered. "I saw it like the face of a white devil!"

Then she checked herself and glanced at the Indian woman, whose dark, heavy face appeared so stupid. Still, one never could tell by the looks of an Indian how much or how little he knows of the thing you want to know; and after a moment's scrutiny, the girl asked:

"Did you learn more of the tracks? —learn who the white man was that made them?"

The woman shook her head.

"You sick-much sick," she explained. "All time Dan he say: 'Stay here by white girl's bed. Never leave.' So I not get out again, and the rain come wash all track away."

"Does Dan know? —did you tell him?"

"No, Dan never ask-never talk to me, only say, 'Take care 'Tana,' that all."

The girl asked no more, but lay there on her couch, filled with dry moss and covered with skins of the mountain wolf. Her eyes closed as though she were asleep; but the squaw knew better, and after a little, she said doubtfully:

"Maybe Akkomi know."

"Akkomi!" and the eyes opened wide and slant. "That is so. I should have remembered. But oh, all the thoughts in my brain have been so muddled. You have heard something, then? Tell me."

"Not much-only little," answered the squaw. "That night-late that night, a white stranger reached Akkomi's tent, to sleep. No one else of the tribe got to see him, so the word is. Kawaka heard on the river, and it was that night."

"And then? Where did the stranger go?"

The squaw shook her head.

"Me not know. Kawaka not hear. But I thought of the track. Now many white men make tracks, and one no matter."

"Akkomi," and the thoughts of the girl went back to the very first she could remember of her recovery; and always, each day, the face of Akkomi had been near her. He had not talked, but would look at her a little while with his sharp, bead-like eyes, and then betake himself to the sunshine outside her door, where he would smoke placidly for hours and watch the restless Anglo-Saxon in his struggle to make the earth yield up its riches.

Each day Akkomi had been there, and she had not once aroused herself to question why; but she would.

Rising, she passed out and looked right and left; but no blanketed brave met her gaze. Only Kawaka, the husband of Flap-Jacks, worked about the canoes by the water. Then she entered Harris' cabin, where the sight of his helpless form, and his welcoming smile, made her halt, and drop down on the rug beside him. She had forgotten him so much of late, and she touched his hand remorsefully.

"I feel as if I had just got awake, Joe," she said, and stretched out her arms, as though to drive away the last vestige of sleep. "Do you know how that feels? To lie for days, stupid as a chilled snake, and then, all at once, to feel the sun creeping around where you are and warming you until you begin to wonder how you could have slept so many days away. Well, just now I feel almost well again. I did not think I would get well; I did not care. All the days I lay in there I wished they would just let me be, and throw their medicines in the creek. I think, Joe, that there are times when people should be allowed to die, when they grow tired-tired away down in their hearts; so tired that they don't want to take up the old tussle of living again. It is so much easier to die then than when a person is happy, and-and has some one to like them, and —"

She left the sentence unfinished, but he nodded a perfect understanding of her thoughts.

"Yes, you have felt like that, too, I suppose," she continued, after a little. "But now, Joe, they tell me we are rich-you and Dan and I —so rich we ought to be happy, all of us. Are we?"

He only smiled at her, and glanced at the cozy furnishing of his rude cabin. Like 'Tana's, it had been given a complete going over by Overton, and rugs and robes did much to soften its crude wood-work. It had all the luxury obtainable in that district, though even yet the doors were but heavy skins.

She noticed the look but shook her head.

"Thick rugs and soft pillows don't make troubles lighter," she said, with conviction; and then: "Maybe Dan is happy. He-he must be. All he thinks of now is the gold ore."

She spoke so wistfully, and her own eyes looked so far, far from happy, that the face of the man was filled with longing to comfort her-the little girl who had tramped so long on a lone trail-how lonely none knew so well as he. His fingers closed and unclosed, as if with the desire to clasp her hand, —to make some visible show of friendship.

She saw the slight movement, and looked up at him with a new interest.

"Oh, I forgot, Joe! I never once have asked how you have got along while I have been so sick. Can you use your hands any at all? You could once, a little bit that day-the day we found the gold."

But he shook his head, and just then a step was heard outside, and Lyster looked in.

A shade of surprise touched his face, as he saw 'Tana there, with so bright an expression in her eyes.

"What has Harris been telling you that has aroused you to interest, Tana?" he asked, jestingly. "He has more influence than I, for I have scarcely been able to get you to talk at all."

"You don't need me; you have Miss Slocum," she answered. "Have you dropped her in the creek and run back to camp? And have you seen Akkomi lately? I want him."

"Of course you do. The moment I make my appearance, you want to get rid of me by sending me for some other man. No, I am happy to say I have not seen that royal loafer for the past hour. And I am more happy still to find that you really want some one-any one-once more. Do you realize, my dear girl, how very many days it is since you have condescended to want anything on this earth of ours? Won't you accept me as a substitute for Akkomi?"

"I don't want you."

But her eyes smiled on him kindly, and he did not believe her.

"Perhaps not; but won't you pretend you do for a little while, long enough to come with me for a little walk-or else to talk to me in your cabin?"

"To talk to you? I don't think I can talk much to any one yet. I just told Joe I feel as if I was only waking up."

"So I see; that is the reason I am asking an audience. I will do the talking, and it need not be a very long talk, if you are too tired."

"I believe I will go," she said, at last. "I was thinking it would be nice to float in a canoe again-just to float lazy on the current. Can't we do that?"

"Nothing easier," he answered, entirely delighted that she was again more like the 'Tana of two months before. She seemed to him a little paler and a little taller, but as they walked together to the canoe, he felt that they would again come to the old chummy days of Sinna Ferry, when they quarreled and made up as regularly as the sun rose and set.

"Well, why don't you talk?" she asked, as their little craft drifted away from the tents and the man who washed the soil by the spring run. "What did you do with the women folks?"

"Gave them to Overton. They concluded not to risk their precious selves with me, when they discovered that he, for a wonder, was disengaged. Really and truly, that angular schoolmistress will make herself Mrs. Overton if he is not careful. She flatters him enough to spoil an average man; looks at him with so much respectful awe, you know, though she never does say much to him."

"Saves her breath to drill Mrs. Huzzard with," observed the girl, dryly. "That poor, dear woman has a bee in her muddled old head, and the bee is Captain Leek and his fine manners. I can see it, plain as day. Bless her heart! I hear her go over and over words that she always used to say wrong, and she does eat nicer than she used to. Humph! I wonder if Dan Overton will take as kindly to being taught, when the school-teacher begins with him."

There was a mirthless, unlovely smile about her lips, and Lyster reached over and clasped her hand coaxingly.

"'Tana, what has changed you so?" he asked. "Is it your sickness-is it the gold-or what, that makes you turn from your old friends? Dan never says a word, but I notice it. You never talk to him, and he has almost quit going to your cabin at all, though he would do anything for you, I know. My dear, you will find few friends like him in the world."

"Oh, don't —don't bother me about him," she answered, irritably. "He is all right, of course. But I —"

Then she stopped, and with a determined air turned the subject.

"You said you had something to talk to me about. What was it?"

"You don't know how glad I am to hear you speak as you used to," he said, looking at her kindly. "I would be rejoiced even to get a scolding from you these days. But that was not exactly what I brought you out to tell you, either," and he drew from his pocket the letter he had carried for three weeks, waiting until she appeared strong enough to accept surprises. "I suppose, of course, you have heard us talk a good deal about the Eastern capitalist who was here when you were so sick, and who, unhesitatingly, made purchase of the Twin Spring Mines, as it is called now."

"You mean the very fine Mr. Haydon, who had curly hair and looked like me?" she asked, ironically. "Yes, I've heard the women folks talking about him a good deal, when they thought me asleep. Old Akkomi scared him a little, too, didn't he?"

"So, you *have* heard?" he asked, in surprise. "Well, yes, he does look a little like you; it's the hair, I think. But I don't see why you utter his name with so much contempt, 'Tana."

"Maybe not; but I've heard the name of Haydon before to-day, and I have a grudge against it."

"But not this Haydon."

"I don't know which Haydon. I never saw any of them-don't know as I want to. I guess this one is almost too fine for Kootenai country people, anyway."

"But that is where you are wrong, entirely wrong, 'Tana," he hastened to explain. "He was very much interested in you-very much, indeed; asked lots of questions about you, and-and here is what I wanted to speak of. When he went away, he gave me this letter for you. I imagine he wants to help make arrangements for you when you go East, have you know nice people and all that. You see, 'Tana, his daughter is about your age, and looks just a little as you do sometimes; and I think he wants to do something for you. It's an odd thing for him to take so strong an interest in any stranger; but they are the very best people you could possibly know if you go to Philadelphia."

"Maybe if you would let me see the letter myself, I could tell better whether I wanted to know them or not," she said, and Lyster handed it to her without another word.

It was a rather long letter, two closely-written sheets, and he could not understand the little contemptuous smile with which she opened it. Haydon, the great financier, had seemed to him a very wonderful personage when he was 'Tana's age.

The girl was not so indifferent as she tried to appear. Her fingers trembled a little, though her mouth grew set and angry as she read the carefully kind words of Mr. Haydon.

"It is rather late in the day for them to come with offers to help me," she said, bitterly. "I can help myself now; but if they had looked for me a year ago-two or three years ago —"

"Looked for you!" he exclaimed, with a sort of impatient wonder. "Why, my dear girl, who would even think of hunting for little white girls in these forests? Don't be foolishly resentful now that people want to be nice to you. You could not expect attention from people before they were aware of your existence."

"But they did know of my existence!" she answered, curtly. "Oh! you needn't stare at me like that, Mr. Max Lyster! I know what I'm talking about. I have the very shaky honor of being a relation of your fine gentleman from the East. I thought it when I heard the name, but did not suppose he would know it. And I'm not too proud of it, either, as you seem to think I ought to be."

"But they are one of our best families —"

"Then your worst must be pretty bad," she interrupted. "I know just about what they are."

"But 'Tana-how does it come —"

"I won't answer any questions about it, Max, so don't ask," and she folded up the letter and tore it into very little pieces, which she let fall into the water. "I am not going to claim the relationship or their hospitality, and I would just as soon you forgot that I acknowledged it. I didn't mean to tell, but that letter vexed me."

"Look here, 'Tana," and Lyster caught her hand again. "I can't let you act like this. They can be of much more help to you socially than all your money. If the family are related to you, and offer you attention, you can't afford to ignore it. You do not realize now how much their attention will mean; but when you are older, you will regret losing it. Let me advise you-let me —"

"Oh, hush!" she said, closing her eyes, wearily. "I am tired-tired! What difference does it make to you-why need you care?"

"May I tell you?" and he looked at her so strangely, so gravely, that her eyes opened in expectation of-she knew not what.

"I did not mean to let you know so soon, 'Tana," and his clasp of her hand grew closer; "but, it is true —I love you. Everything that concerns you makes a difference to me. Now do you understand?"

"You! —Max —"

"Don't draw your hand away. Surely you guessed —a little? I did not know myself how much I cared till you came so near dying. Then I knew I could not bear to let you go. And-and you care a little too, don't you! Speak to me!"

"Let us go home," she answered in a low voice, and tried to draw her fingers away. She liked him-yes; but —

"Tana, won't you speak? Oh, my dear, dear one, when you were so ill, so very ill, you knew no one else, but you turned to me. You went asleep with your cheek against my hand, and more than once, 'Tana, with your hand clasping mine. Surely that was enough to make me hope-for you did like me a little, then."

"Yes, I —liked you," but she turned her head away, that he could not see her flushed face. "You were good to me, but I did not know —I could not guess —" and she broke down as though about to cry, and his own eyes were full of tenderness. She appealed to him now as she had never done in her days of brightness and laughter.

"Listen to me," he said, pleadingly. "I won't worry you. I know you are too weak and ill to decide yet about your future. I don't ask you to answer me now. Wait. Go to school, as I know you intend to do; but don't forget me. After the school is over you can decide. I will wait with all patience. I would not have told you now, but I wanted you to know I was interested in the answer you would give Haydon. I wanted you to know that I would not for the world advise you, but for your best interests. Won't you believe —"

"I believe you; but I don't know what to say to you. You are different from me-your people are different. And of my people you know nothing, nothing at all, and —"

"And it makes no difference," he interrupted. "I know you have had a lot of trouble for a little girl, or your family have had trouble you are sensitive about. I don't know what it is, but it makes no difference-not a bit. I will never question about it, unless you prefer to tell of your own accord. Oh, my dear! if some day you could be my wife, I would help you forget all your childish troubles and your unpleasant life."

"Let us go home," she said, "you are good to me, but I am so tired."

He obediently turned the canoe, and at that moment voices came to them from toward the river-ringing voices of men.

"It is possibly Mr. Haydon and others," he exclaimed, after listening a moment. "We have been expecting them for days. That was why I could no longer put off giving you the letter."

"I know," she said, and her face flushed and paled a little, as the voices came closer. He could see she nervously dreaded the meeting.

"Shall I get the canoe back to camp before they come?" he asked kindly; but she shook her head.

"You can't, for they move fast," she answered, as she listened. "They would see us; and, if he is with them, he-would think I was afraid."

He let the canoe drift again, and watched her moody face, which seemed to grow more cold with each moment that the strangers came closer. He was filled with surprise at all she had said of Haydon and of the letter. Who would have dreamed that she-the little Indian-dressed guest of Akkomi's camp-would be connected with the most exclusive family he knew in the East? The Haydon family was one he had been especially interested in only a year ago, because of Mr. Haydon's very charming daughter. Miss Haydon, however, had a clever and ambitious mamma, who persisted in keeping him at a safe distance.

Max Lyster, with his handsome face and unsettled prospects, was not the brilliant match her hopes aspired to. Pretty Margaret Haydon had, in all obedience, refused him dances and affected not to see his efforts to be near her. But he knew she did see; and one little bit of comfort he had taken West with him was the fancy that her refusals were never voluntary affairs, and that she had looked at him as he had never known her to look at another man.

Well, that was a year ago, and he had just asked another girl to marry him —a girl who did not look at him at all, but whose eyes were on the swift-flowing current-troubled eyes, that made him long to take care of her.

"Won't you speak to me at all?" he asked. "I will do anything to help you, 'Tana-anything at all."

She nodded her head slowly.

"Yes-now," she answered. "So would Mr. Haydon, Max."

"'Tana! do you mean —" His face flushed hotly, and he looked at her for the first time with anger in his face.

She put out her hand in a tired, pleading way.

"I only mean that now, when I have been lucky enough to help myself, it seems as if every one thinks I need looking after so much more than they used to. Maybe because I am not strong yet-maybe so; I don't know." Then she smiled and looked at him curiously.

"But I made a mistake when I said 'every one,' didn't I? For Dan never comes near me any more."

Then the strange canoes came in sight and very close to them, as they turned a bend in the creek. There were three large boats-one carrying freight, one filled with new men for the works, and in the other-the foremost one-was Mr. Haydon, and a tall, thin, middle-aged stranger.

"Uncle Seldon!" exclaimed Lyster, with animation, and held the canoe still in the water, that the other might come close, and in a whisper he said:

"The one to the right is Mr. Haydon."

He glanced at her and saw she was making a painful effort at self-control.

"Don't worry," he whispered. "We will just speak, and drift on past them."

But when they called greeting to each other, and the Indian boatman was told to send their craft close to the little camp canoe, she raised her head and looked very levelly across the stranger, who had hair so like her own, and spoke to the Indian who paddled their boat as though he were the only one there to notice.

"Plucky!" decided Mr. Haydon, "and stubborn;" but he kept those thoughts to himself, and said aloud: "My dear young lady, I am indeed pleased to see you so far recovered since my last visit. I presume you know who I am," and he looked at her in a smiling, confidential way.

"Yes, I know who you are. Your name is Haydon, and-there is a piece of your letter."

She picked up a fragment of paper that had fallen at her feet, and flung it out from her on the water. Mr. Haydon affected not to see the pettish act, but turned to his companion.

"Will you allow me, Miss Rivers, to introduce another member of our firm? This is Mr. Seldon. Seldon, this is the young girl I told you of."

"I knew it before you spoke," said the other man, who looked at her with a great deal of interest, and a great deal of kindness. "My child, I was your mother's friend long ago. Won't you let me be yours?"

She reached out her hand to him, and the quick tears came to her eyes. She trusted without question the earnest gray eyes of the speaker, and turned from her own uncle to the uncle of Max.

Chapter XIX
The Man in Akkomi's Cloak

"My dear fellow, there is, of course, no way of thanking you sufficiently for your care of her; but I can only say I am mighty glad to know a man like you."

It was Mr. Seldon who said so, and Dan Overton looked embarrassed and deprecating under the praise he had to accept.

"It is all right for you to make a fuss over it, Seldon," he returned; "but you know, as well as you know dinner time, that you would have done no less if you had found a young girl anywhere without a home-and especially if you found her in an Indian camp."

"Did she give you any information as to how she came to be there?"

Overton looked at him good-naturedly, but shook his head.

"I can't give you any information about that," he answered. "If you want to know anything of her previous to meeting her here, she will have to tell you."

"But she won't. I can't understand it; for I can see no need of mystery. I knew her mother when she was a girl like 'Tana, and —"

"You did?"

"Yes, I did. So now, perhaps, you will understand why I take such an interest in her-why Mr. Haydon takes an interest in her. Simply because she is his niece."

"Oh, she is-is she? And he came here, found her dying, or next door to it, and never claimed her."

"No; that is a little way of his," acknowledged his partner. "If she had really died, he never would have said a word about it, for it would have caused him a lot of troublesome explanation at home. But I guess he knew I would be likely to come across her. She is the very image of what her mother was. He told me the whole story of how he found her here, and all. And now he wants to do the proper thing and take her home with him."

"The devil he does!" growled Overton. "Well, why do you come to me about it?"

"Your influence with her was one thing," answered Mr. Seldon, with a dubious smile at the dark face before him. "This *protégée* of yours has a will of her own, it seems, and refuses utterly to acknowledge her aristocratic relations, refuses to be a part of her uncle's household; and we want your influence toward changing her mind."

"Well, you'll never get it," and the tone was decided as the words. "If she says she is no relation to anybody, I'll back her up in it, and not ask her her reasons, either. If she doesn't want to go with Mr. Haydon, she is the only one I will allow to decide, unless he brings a legal order from some court, and I might try to hinder him even then. She willingly came under my guardianship, and when she leaves it, it must be willingly."

"Oh, of course there will be no coercion about the matter," explained Mr. Seldon, hastily. "But don't you, yourself, think it would be a decided advantage for her to live for a while with her own relatives?"

"I am in no position to judge. I don't know her relatives. I don't know why it is that she has not been taken care of by them long ago; and I am not asking any questions. She knows, and that is enough; and I am sure her reasons for not going would satisfy me."

"Well, you are a fine specimen to come to for influence," observed the other. "She has a grudge against Haydon, that is the obstacle —a grudge, because he quarreled with her mother long ago. I thought that as you have done so much for her, your word might have weight in showing her the folly of it."

"My word would have no more weight than yours," he answered, curtly. "All I have done for her amounts to nothing; and I've an idea that if she wanted me to know her family affairs, she would tell me."

"Which, interpreted, means that I had better be at other business than gossiping," said Mr. Seldon, with much good humor. "Well, you are a fine pair, and something alike, too-you goldfinders! She snubbed Max for trying to persuade her, and you snub me. As a last resort, I think I shall try to get that old Indian into our lobbying here. He is her next great friend, I hear."

"I haven't seen him in camp to-day, for a wonder; but he is sure to be around before night."

"But, you see, we are to go on up to the new works on the lake to-day, and be back day after to-morrow. I wish you, too, could go up to-morrow, for I would like your judgment about some changes we expect to make. Could you leave here for twenty-four hours?"

"I'll try," promised Overton. "But the new men from the Ferry will be up to-day or to-morrow, so I may not reach there until you are about ready to start back."

"Come anyway, if you can, I don't seem to get much chance to talk to you here in camp-maybe I could on the river. You may be in a more reasonable mood about 'Tana by that time, and try to influence her to partake of civilization."

"'Civilization!' Oh, yes, of course, you imagine it all lies east of the Appalachian range," remarked Overton, slightingly. "I expect that from a man of Haydon's stamp, but not from you."

Seldon only laughed.

"One would think you had been born and bred out here in the West," he remarked, "while you are really only an importation. But what is that racket about?"

For screeches were sounding from the cabin-cries, feminine and frightened.

Overton and Seldon started for it, as did several of the workmen, but their haste slackened as they saw 'Tana leaning against a doorway and laughing, while the squaw stood near her, chuckling a little as a substitute for merriment.

But there were two others within the cabin who were by no means merry-the two cousins, who were standing huddled together on the couch, uttering spasmodic screeches at every movement made by a little gray snake on the floor.

It had crept in at a crevice, and did not know how to make its escape from the noisy shelter it had found. Its fright was equal to that of the women, for it appeared decidedly restless, and each uneasy movement of it was a signal for fresh screams.

"Oh, Mr. Overton! I beg of you, kill the horrible reptile!" moaned Miss Slocum, who at that moment was as indifferent to the proprieties as Mrs. Huzzard, and was displaying considerable white hosiery and black gaiter tops.

"Oh, lawsy! It is coming this way again. Ooh-ooh —h!" and Mrs. Huzzard did a little dance from one foot to the other, in a very ecstasy of fear. "Oh, Lavina, I'll never forgive myself for advising you to come out to this Idaho country! Oh, Lord! won't somebody kill it?"

"Why, there is no need to fear that little thing," said Overton. "Really, it is not a snake to bite-no more harm in it than in a mouse."

"A *mouse*!" they both shrieked. "Oh, please take it away."

Just then Akkomi came in through the other cabin, and, hearing the shrieks, simply stooped and picked up the little stranger in his hand, holding it that they might see how harmless it was.

But, instead of pacifying them, as he had kindly intended, they only cowered against the wall, too horrified even to scream, while they gazed at the old Indian, as at something just from the infernal regions.

"Lord, have mercy on our souls," muttered Lavina, in a sepulchral tone, and with pallid, almost moveless, lips.

"Forever and ever, amen," added Lorena Jane, clutching her drapery a little closer, and a little higher.

And not until Overton persuaded Akkomi to throw the frightened little thing away did they consent to move from their pedestal. Even then it was with fear and trembling, and many an awful glance toward the placid old Indian, who smoked his pipe and never glanced toward them.

"Never again will I sleep in that room-not if I die for it!" announced Mrs. Huzzard, and Miss Slocum was of the same mind.

"But the cabin is as safe as a tent," said 'Tana, persuasively, "and, really, it was not a dangerous snake."

"Ooh —h! I beg that you will not mention it," shivered Miss Slocum. "For my part, I don't expect to sleep anywhere after this terrible experience. But I'll go wherever Lorena Jane goes, and do what I can to comfort and protect her, while she rests."

Akkomi sat on Harris' doorstep, and smoked, while they argued on the dangers around them, and were satisfied only when Overton put a tent at their disposal. They proceeded to have hammocks swung in it on poles set for the purpose, as they could feel safe on no bed resting on the ground.

"But, really, my conscience troubles me about leaving you here alone, 'Tana," said Mrs. Huzzard, and Overton also looked at her as if interested in her comfort.

"Well, your conscience had better give itself a rest, if that is all it has to disturb it," she answered. "I don't care the least bit about staying alone —I rather like it; though, if I need any one, I'll have Flap-Jacks stay."

So Overton left them to their arrangements, and said nothing to 'Tana; but as Seldon and Haydon were about to embark, he spoke to the former.

"I may not be able to get up there after all, as I may feel it necessary to be here at night, so don't wait for me."

"All right, Overton; but we'd like to have you."

After the others had left the cabin, Akkomi still remained, and the girl watched him uneasily but did not speak. She talked to Harris, telling him of the funny actions of the two frightened women, but all the time she talked and tried to entertain the helpless man, it was with an evident effort, for the dark old Indian's face at the door was constantly drawing her attention.

When she finally entered her own room, he appeared at the entrance, and, after a careful glance, to see that no one was near, he entered and spoke:

"'Tana, it is now two suns since we talked. Will you go to-day in my boat for a little ways?"

"No," she said, angrily. "Go home to your tepee, Akkomi, and tell the man there I am sorry he is not dead. I never will see him again. I go away from this place now-very soon-maybe this week. What becomes of him I do not care, and it will be long before I come back."

He muttered some words of regret, and she turned to him more kindly.

"Yes, I know, Akkomi, you are my good friend. You think it is right to do what you are doing now. Maybe it is; maybe I am wrong. But I will not be different in this matter-never-never!"

"If he should come here —"

"He would not dare. There are people here he had better fear. Give him the names of Seldon and of Haydon."

"He knows; but it is the new miners he fears most; they come from all parts. He wants money."

"Let him work for it, like an honest man," she said, curtly. "Don't talk of it again. I will not go outside the camp alone, and I will not listen to any more words about it. Now mind that!"

In the other cabin, Harris listened intently to each word uttered. His eyes fairly blazed in his eagerness to hear 'Tana's final decision. But when Akkomi slouched past his door, and peered in, with his sharp, quick eyes, he had relapsed again into the apathetic state habitual to him. To all appearances he had not heard their words, and the old Indian walked thoughtfully past the tents and out into the timber.

Lyster called some light greeting to him, but he barely looked up and made no reply whatever. His thoughts were evidently on other things than camp sociabilities.

It was dark when he returned, and his fit of thoughtfulness was yet upon him, for he spoke to no one. Overton, who had been talking to Harris, noticed him smoking beside the door as he came out.

"You had better bring your camp down here," he remarked, ironically. "Well, for to-night you will have to spread your blanket in this room if Harris doesn't object. That is what I am to do, for I've given up my quarters to the ladies, who are afraid of snakes."

Akkomi nodded, and then Overton moved nearer the door again.

"Jim, I may not be back for an hour or so. I am going either on the water or up on the mountain for a little while. Don't lie awake for me, and I'll send a fellow in to look after you."

Harris nodded, and 'Tana, in her own room, heard Overton's steps die away in the night. He was going on the water or on the mountains-the places she loved to go, and dared not.

She felt like calling after him to wait to take her with him once more, and did rise and go to the door, but no farther.

Lights were gleaming all along the little stream; laughter and men's voices came to her across the level. Her own corner of the camp looked very dark and shadowy in comparison. But she turned back to it with a sigh.

"You may go, Flap-Jacks," she said to the squaw. "I don't mind being alone, but first fix the bed of Harris."

She noticed Akkomi outside the door, but did not speak to him. She heard the miner enter the other cabin and assist Harris to his couch and then depart. She wondered a little that the old Indian still sat there smoking, instead of spreading his blanket, as Overton had invited him to do.

A book of poems, presented to her by Lyster, was so engrossing, however, that she forgot the old fellow, until a movement at the door aroused her, and she turned to find the silent smoker inside her cabin.

But it was not Akkomi, though it was the cloak of Akkomi that fell from his shoulders.

It was a man dressed as an Indian, but his speech was the speech of a white man, as he frowned on her white, startled face.

"So, my fine lady, I've found you at last, even if you have got too high and mighty to come when I sent for you," he said, growlingly. "But I'll change your tune very quick for you."

"Don't forget that I can change yours," she retorted. "A word from me, and you know there is not a man in this camp wouldn't help land you where you belong-in a prison, or at the end of a rope."

"Oh, no," and he grimaced in a sardonic way. "I'm not a bit afraid of that-not a bit in the world. You can't afford it. These high-toned friends you've been making might drop off a little if they heard your old record."

"And who made it for me?" she demanded. "You! You've been a curse to every one connected with you. In that other room is a man who might be strong and well to-day but for you. And there is that girl buried over there by the picture rocks of Arrow Lake. Think of my mother, dragged to death through the slums of 'Frisco! And me —"

"And you with a gold mine, or the price of one," he concluded —"plenty of money and plenty of friends. That is about the facts of your case-friends, from millionaires down to that digger I saw you with the other night."

"Don't you dare say a word against him!" she exclaimed, threateningly.

"Oh, that's the way the land lies, is it?" he asked, with an ugly leer at her. "And that is why you were playing 'meet me by moonlight alone,' that night when I saw you together at the spring. Well, I think your money might help you to some one besides a married man."

"A married man?" she gasped. "Dan!"

"Dan, it is," he answered, insolently. "But you needn't faint away on that account. I have other use for you —I want some money."

"You are telling that lie about him because you think it will trouble me," she said, regarding his painted face closely and giving no heed to his demand. "You know it is not true."

"About the marriage? I'll swear —"

"I would not believe your oath for anything."

"Oh, you wouldn't? Well, now, what if I prove to you, right in this camp, that I know his wife?"

"His wife?" She sat down on the side of the couch, and all the cabin seemed whirling around her.

"Well —a girl he married. You may call her what you please. She had been called a good many things before he picked her up. Humph! Now that he has struck it rich, some one ought to let her know. She'd make the dollars fly."

"It is not true! It is not *true!*" she murmured to herself, as if by the words she could drive away the possibility of it.

He appeared to enjoy the sensation he had created.

"It is true," he answered —"every word of it, and he has been keeping quiet about it, has he? Well, see here. You don't believe me-do you? Now, while I was waiting there at the door, a man came in to put your paralyzed partner to bed. The man was Jake Emmons-used to hang out at Spokane. He knew Lottie Snyder before this Overton did-and after Overton married her, too, I guess. You ask him anything you want to know of it. He can tell you-if he will."

She did not answer. She feared, as he talked, that it was true; and she longed for him to go away, that she could think alone. The hot blood burned in her cheeks, as she remembered that night by the Twin Springs. The humiliation of it, if it proved true!

"But, see here, 'Tana. I didn't come here to talk about your virtuous ranger. I want some money-enough to cut the country. It ain't any more than fair, anyway, that you divide with me, for if it hadn't been for that sneaking hound in the other room, half of this find would have been mine a year ago."

"It will do more good where it is," she answered. "He did right not to trust you. And if he were able to walk, you would not be allowed to live many minutes within reach of him."

"Oh, yes; I know he was trailing me," he answered, indifferently, "but it was no hard trick to keep out of his road. I suppose you let him know you approve of his feelings toward me."

"Yes, I would load a gun for him to use on you if he were able to hold it," she answered, and he seemed to think her words amusing.

"You have mighty little regard for your duty to me," he observed.

"Duty? I can't owe you any duty when I never received any from you. I am nearly seventeen, and in all the years I remember you, I can't recall any good act you have ever done for me."

"Nearly seventeen," and he smiled at her in the way she hated. "Didn't your new uncle, Haydon, tell you better than that? You are nearly eighteen years old."

"Eighteen!" and she rose in astonishment. "I?"

"You-though you don't look it. You always were small for your age, so I just told you a white lie about it in order to manage you better. But that is over; I don't care what you do in the future. All I want of you is money to get to South America; so fix it up for me."

"I ought to refuse, and call them in to arrest you."

"But you won't," he rejoined. "You can't afford it."

He watched her, though, with some uncertainty, as she sat silent, thinking.

"No, I can't afford it," she said, at last. "I will be doing wrong to help you, just as if I let a poison snake loose where people travel-for that is what you are. But I am not strong enough to let these friends go and start over again; so I will help you away this once."

He drew a breath of relief, and gathered up his blanket.

"That is the way to talk. You've got a level head —"

"That will do," she said, curtly. "I don't want praise from a coward, a thief, or a murderer. You are all three. I have no money here. You will have to come again for it to-morrow night."

"A trick-is it?"

"It is no trick. I haven't got it, that is all. Maybe I can't get it in money, but I will get it in free gold by to-morrow at dusk. I will put it here under the pillow, and will manage to keep the rest away at that time. You can come as you came this evening, and get it; but I will neither take it nor send it to you. You will have to risk your freedom and your life to come for it. But while I can't quite decide to give you up or to kill you, myself, I hope some one else will."

"Hope what you please," he returned, indifferently. "So long as you get the dust for me, I can stand your opinion. And you will have it here?"

"I will have it here."

"I trust you only because I know you can't afford to go back on me," he said, as he wrapped the blanket around him, and dropped his taller form to the height of Akkomi. "It is a bargain, then, my dear. Good-night."

"I don't wish you a good-night," she answered. "I hope I shall never see you alive again."

And she never did.

Chapter XX
'Tana's Engagement

"And she wants a thousand dollars in money or free gold—a thousand dollars to-day?"

"No use asking me what for, Dan, for I don't know," confessed Lyster. "I can't see why she don't tell you herself; but you know she has been a little queer since the fever-childish, whimsical, and all that. Maybe as she has not yet handled any specie from your bonanza, she wants some only to play with, and assure herself it is real."

"Less than a thousand in money and dust would do for a plaything," remarked Overton. "Of course she has a right to get what she wants; but that amount will be of no use to her here in camp, where there is not a thing in the world to spend it for."

"Maybe she wants to pension off some of her Indian friends before she leaves," suggested Max—"old Akkomi and Flap-Jacks, perhaps. I am a little like Miss Slocum in my wonder as to how she endures them, though, of course, the squaw is a necessity."

"Oh, well, she was not brought up in the world of Miss Slocum-or your world, either," answered Overton. "You should make allowance for that."

"Make allowance—I?" and Lyster looked at him curiously. "Are you trying to justify her to me? Why, man, you ought to know by this time what keeps me here a regular lounger around camp, and there is no need to make excuses for her to me. I thought you knew."

"You mean you-like her?"

"Worse than that," said Max, with his cheery, confident smile. "I'm trying to get her to say she likes me."

"And she?"

"Well, she won't meet me as near half-way as I would like," he confessed; "talks a lot of stuff about not being brought up right, and not suited to our style of life at home, and all that. But she did seem rather partial to me when she was ill and off guard. Don't you think so? That is all I have to go on; but it encourages me to remember it."

Overton did not speak, and Lyster continued speculating on his chances, when he noticed his companion's silence.

"Why don't you speak, Dan? I did hope you would help me rather than be indifferent."

"Help you!" and Lyster was taken aback at the fierce straightening of the brows and the strange tone in which the words were uttered. The older man could not but see his surprised look, for he recovered himself, and dropped his hand in the old familiar way on Lyster's shoulder.

"Not much chance of my helping you when she employs you as an agent when she wants any service, rather than exchange words with me herself. Now, that is the way it looks, Max."

"I know," agreed Lyster. "And to tell the truth, Dan, the only thing she does that really vexes me is her queer attitude toward you of late. I can't think she means to be ungrateful, but—"

"Don't bother about that. Everything has changed for her lately, and she has her own troubles to think of. Don't you doubt her on my account. Just remember that. And if-she says 'yes' to you, Max, be sure I would rather see her go to you than any other man I know."

"That is all right," observed Lyster, laughingly; "but if you only had a love affair or two of your own, you could perhaps get up more enthusiasm over mine."

Then he sauntered off to report the financial interview to 'Tana, and laughed as he went at the impatient look flung at him by Overton.

He found 'Tana visiting at the tent of the cousins, who were using all arguments to persuade her to share their new abode. Each was horrified to learn that she had dismissed the squaw at sleeping time, and had remained in the cabin alone.

"Not quite alone," she corrected, "for Harris was just on the other side of the door."

"Much protection he would be."

"Well, then, Dan Overton was with him. How is he for protection?"

"Thoroughly competent, no doubt," agreed Miss Lavina, with a rather scandalized look. "But, my dear, the propriety?"

"Do you think Flap-Jacks would help any one out in propriety?" retorted 'Tana. "But we won't stumble over that question long, for I want to leave the camp and go back to the Ferry."

"And then, 'Tana?"

"And then—I don't know, Mrs. Huzzard, to school, maybe-though I feel old for that, older than either of you, I am sure-so old that I care nothing for all the things I wanted less than a year ago. They are within my reach now, yet I only want to rest—"

She did not finish the sentence.

Mrs. Huzzard, noticing the tired look in her eyes and the wistfulness of her voice, reached out and patted her head affectionately.

"You want, first of all, to grow strong and hearty, like you used to be-that is what you need first, then the rest will all come right in good time. You'll want to see the theaters, and the pictures, and hear the fine music you used to talk of. And you'll travel, and see all the fine places you used to dream about. Then, maybe, you'll get ambitious, like you used to be, about making pictures out of clay. For you can have fine teaching now, you know, and you'll find, after a while, that the days will hardly seem long enough for all the things you want to do. That is how it will be when you get strong again."

'Tana tried to smile at the cheerful picture, but the smile was not a merry one. Her attention was given to Lyster and Overton, whom she could see from the tent door.

How tall and strong Dan looked! Was she to believe that story of him heard last night? The very possibility of it made her cheeks burn at the thought of how she had stood with his arm around her. And he had pitied her that night. "Poor little girl!" he had said. Was his pity because he saw how much he was to her, while he himself thought only of some one else? One after another those thoughts had come to her through the sleepless night, and when the day came she could not face him to speak to him of the simplest thing. And of the money she must have, she could not ask him at all. She wished she could have courage to go to him and tell him the thing she had heard; but courage was not strong in her of late. The fear that he might look indifferently on her and say, "Yes, it is true-what then?"—the fear of that was so great that she had walked by the water's edge, as the sun rose, and felt desperate enough to think of sleep under the waves, as a temptation. For if it was true—

The two older women watched her, and decided that she was not yet strong enough to think of long journeys. Her hands would tremble at times, and tears, as of weakness, would come to her eyes, and she scarcely appeared to hear them when they spoke.

She never walked through the woods as of old, though sometimes she would stand and look up at the dark hills with a perfect hunger in her eyes. And when the night breeze would creep down from the heights, and carry the sweet wood scents of the forest to her, she would close her eyes and draw in long breaths of utter content. The strong love for the wild places was as second nature to her; yet when Max would ask her to go with him for flowers or mosses, her answer was always "no."

But she would go to the boat sometimes, though no longer having strength to use the paddle. It was a good place to think, if she could only keep the others from going, too, so she slipped away from Max and the women and went down. A chunky, good-looking fellow was mending one of the canoes, and raised his head at her approach, nodding to her and evidently pleased when she addressed him.

"Yes, it is a shaky old tub," he agreed, "but I told Overton I thought it could be fixed to carry freight for another trip; so he put me at it."

"You are new in camp, aren't you?" she asked, not caring at all whether he was or not. She was always friendly with the workmen, and this one smiled and bowed.

"We are all that, I guess," he said. "But I came up the day Haydon and Seldon came. I lived with Seldon down the country, and was staggered a little, I tell you, when I found Overton was in charge, and had struck it rich. But no man deserves good luck more."

"No," she agreed. "Then you knew him before?"

"Yes, indeed-over in Spokane. He don't seem quite the same fellow, though. We thought he would just go to the dogs after he left there, for he started to drink heavily. But he must have settled in his own mind that it wasn't worth while; so here he is, straight as a string, and counting his dollars by the thousands, and I'm glad to see it."

"Drink! He never drinks to excess, that we know of," she answered. "Doesn't seem to care for that sort of thing."

"No, he didn't then, either," agreed this loquacious stranger, "but a woman can drive as good men as him to drink; and that is about the way it was. No one thought any worse of Overton, though-don't think that. The worst any one could say was that he was too square-that's all."

Too square! She walked away from him a little way, all her mind aflame with his suggestions. He had taken to drink and dissipation because of some woman. Was it the woman whose name she had heard last night? The key to the thing puzzling her had been dropped almost at her feet, yet she feared to pick it up. No teaching she had ever received told her it was unprincipled to steal through another the confidence he himself had not chosen to give her. But some instinct of justice kept her from further question.

She knew the type of fellow who was rigging up the canoe, a light-headed, assuming specimen, who had not yet learned to keep a still tongue in his head, but he did not impress her as being a deliberate liar. Then, all at once, she realized who he must be, and turned back. There was no harm in asking that, at any rate.

"You are the man whom Overton sent to put Harris to bed last night, are you not?" she asked. He nodded, cheerfully.

"And your name is Jake Emmons, of the Spokane country?"

"That's who," he assented; "that's where I came across Lottie Snyder, Overton's wife, you know. I was running a little stage there for a manager, and she —"

"I am not asking you about-about Mr. Overton's affairs," she said, and she sat down, white and dizzy, on the overturned canoe. "And he might not like it if he knew you were talking so free. Don't do it again."

"All right," he agreed. "I won't. No one here seems to know about the bad break he made over there; but, Lord! there was excuse enough. She is one of those women that look just like a little helpless baby; and that caught Overton. Young, you know. But I won't whisper her name in camp again, for it is hard on the old man. But, as you are partners, I guessed you must know."

"Yes," she said, faintly; "but don't talk, don't —"

"Say! You are sick, ain't you?" he demanded, as her voice dropped to a whisper. "Say! Look here, Miss Rivers! Great snakes! She's fainted!"

When she opened her eyes again, the rough roof of her cabin was above her, instead of the blue sky. The women folks were using the camp restorative-whisky-on her to such good purpose that her hands and face and hair were redolent of it, and the amount she had been forced to swallow was strangling her.

The face she saw first was that of Max-Max, distressed and anxious, and even a little pale at sight of her death-like face.

She turned to him as to a haven of refuge from the storm of emotion under which she had fallen prostrate.

It was all settled now-settled forever. She had heard the worst, and knew she must go away-away from where she must see that one man, and be filled with humiliation if ever she met his gaze. A man with a wife somewhere —a man into whose arms she had crept!

"Are you in pain?" asked Miss Lavina, as 'Tana groaned and shut her eyes tight, as if to bar out memory.

"No-nothing ails me. I was without a hat, and the sun on my head made me sick, I suppose," she answered, and arose on her elbow. "But I am not going to be a baby, to be watched and carried around any more. I am going to get up."

Just outside her door Overton stood; and when he heard her voice again, with its forced independent words, he walked away content that she was again herself.

"I am going to get up," she continued. "I am going away from here to-morrow or next day-and there are things to do. Help me, Max."

"Best thing you can do is to lie still an hour or two," advised Mrs. Huzzard, but the girl shook her head.

"No, I'm going to get up," she said, with grim decision; and when Lyster offered his hand to help her, she took it, and, standing erect, looked around at the couch.

"That is the last time I'm going to be thrown on you for any such fool cause," she said, whimsically. "Who toted me in here-you?"

"I? Not a bit of it," confessed Lyster. "Dan reached you before any of the others knew you were ill. He carried you up here."

"He? Oh!" and she shivered a little. "I want to talk to Harris. Max, come with me."

He went wonderingly, for he could see she was excited and nervous. Her hand trembled as it touched his, but her mouth was set so firmly over the little white teeth that he knew it was better to humor her than fret her by persuading her to rest.

But once beside Harris, she sat a long time in silence, looking out from the doorway across the level now active with the men of the works. Not until the two cousins had walked across to their other shelter did she speak, and then it was to Harris.

"Joe, I am sick," she confessed; "not sick with the fever, but heartsick and headsick. You know how and maybe why."

He nodded his head, and looked at Lyster questioningly.

"And I've come in here to tell you something. Max, you won't mind. He can't talk, but knows me better than you do, I guess; for I've come to him before when I was troubled, and I want to tell him what you said to me in the boat."

Max stared at her, but silently agreed when he saw she was in earnest. He even reached out his hand to take hers, but she drew away.

"Wait till I tell him," she said, and turned to the helpless man in the chair. "He asked me to marry him-some day. Would it be right for me to say yes?"

"'Tana!" exclaimed Lyster; but she raised her hand pleadingly.

"I haven't any other person in the world I could go to and ask," she said. "He knows me better than you do, Max, and I —Oh! I don't think I should be always contented with your ways of living. I was born different —a heap different. But to-day it seems as if I am not strong enough to do without-some one-who likes me, and I do want to say 'yes' to you, yet I'm afraid it is only because I am sick at heart and lonely."

It was a declaration likely to cool the ardor of most lovers, but Lyster reached out his hand to her and laughed.

"Oh, you dear girl," he said, fondly. "Did your conscience make it necessary for you to confess in this fashion? Now listen. You are weak and nervous; you need some one to look after you. Doesn't she, Harris? Well, take me on trial. I will devote myself to your interests for six months, and if at the end of that time you find that it was only sickness and loneliness that ailed you, and not liking me, then I give you my word I'll never try to hold you to a promise. You will be well and strong by that time, and I'll stand by the decision you make then. Will you say 'yes,' now?"

She looked at Harris, who nodded his head. Then she turned and gave her hand to Max.

"Yes," she said. "But if you should be sorry —"

"Not another word," he commanded; "the 'yes' is all I want to hear just now; when I get sorry I'll let you know."

And that is the way their engagement began.

Chapter XXI
Lavina and the Captain

As the day wore on, 'Tana became more nervous and restless. With the dark, that man was to come for the gold she had promised.

Lyster brought it to her, part in money, part in free gold, and as he laid it on the couch, she looked at him strangely.

"How much you trust me when you never even ask what I am to do with all this!" she said. "Yet it is enough to surprise you."

"Yes, it is," he agreed. "But when you are ready you will tell me."

"No, I will not tell you," she answered, "but it is the last thing —I think-that I will keep from you, Max. It is a debt that belongs to days before I knew you. What did Overton say?"

"Not much, maybe he will leave for the upper works this evening or to-morrow morning."

"Did you-did you tell him —"

"That you are going to belong to me? Well, no, I did not. You forgot to give me permission."

Her face flushed shyly at his words.

"You must think me a queer girl, Max," she said. "And you are so good and patient with me, in spite of my queer ways. But, never mind; they will not last always, I hope."

"Which? —my virtues or your queerness?" he asked.

She only smiled and pushed the gold under the pillow.

"Go away now for a little while. I want to rest."

"Well, rest if you like; but don't think. You have been fretting over some little personal troubles until you fancy them heavy enough to overbalance the world. But they won't. And I'm not going to try and persuade you into Haydon's house, either, now that you've been good to me; unless, of course, you fall in love with Margaret, and want to be with her, and it is likely to happen. But Uncle Seldon and my aunts will be delighted to have you, and you could live as quiet as you please there."

"So I am likely to fall in love with Margaret, am I?" she asked. "Why? Does everybody? Did you-Max? Now, don't blush like that, or I'll be sure of it. I never saw you blush so pretty before. It made you almost good looking. Now go; I want to be alone."

"Sha'n't I send one of the ladies up?"

"Not a soul! Go, Max. I am tired."

So he went, in all obedience, and he and the cousins had a long talk about the girl and the danger of leaving her alone another night. Her sudden illness showed them she was not strong enough yet to be allowed to guide herself.

"I shall try hard to get her to leave to-morrow, or next day," said Lyster. "Where is Dan? I would like to talk to him about it, but he has evidently disappeared."

"I don't know what to think of Dan Overton," confessed Mrs. Huzzard. "He isn't ever around, chatty and sociable, like he used to be. When we do see him, he is nearly always busy; and when he isn't busy, he strikes for the woods."

"Maybe he is still searching for new gold mines," suggested Miss Lavina. "I notice he does seem very much engaged in thought, and is of a rather solitary nature."

"Never was before," protested her cousin. "And if these gold finds just twist a person's nature crosswise, or send them into a fever, then I hope the good Lord'll keep the rest of them well covered up in future."

"Lorena Jane," said Miss Lavina, in a reproachful tone, "it is most essential that you free yourself from those very forcible expressions. They are not a bit genteel."

"No, I reckon they ain't, Lavina; and the more I try the more I'm afraid I never will be. Land sakes, if folks would only teach their young ones good manners when they are young, what a sight of mortified feelings would be saved after a while!"

Lyster left them in the midst of the very earnest plea for better training, for he espied a new boat approaching camp. As it came closer, he found that among the other freight it carried was the autocrat of Sinna Ferry-Captain Leek.

"What a God-forsaken wilderness!" he exclaimed, and looked around with a supercilious air, suggesting that he would have given the Creator of the Kootenai country valuable points if he had been consulted. "Well, my dear young fellow, how you have managed to exist here for three weeks I don't know."

"Well, we had Mrs. Huzzard," explained Max, with a twinkle in his eye; "and she is a panacea for many ills. She has made our wilderness very endurable."

"Yes, yes; excellent woman," agreed the other, with a suspicious look. "And 'Tana? How is she-the dear girl! I really have been much grieved to hear of her illness; and at the earliest day I could leave my business I am here to inquire in person regarding her health."

"Oh!" and Max struggled with a desire to laugh at the change in the captain's attitude since 'Tana was a moneyed individual instead of a little waif. Poor 'Tana! No wonder she looked with suspicion on late-coming friends.

"Yes, she is better-much better," he continued, as they walked up from the boat. "I suppose you knew that a cousin of Mrs. Huzzard, a lady from Ohio, has been with us-in fact, came up with our party."

"So I heard-so I heard. Nice for Mrs. Huzzard. I was not in town, you know, when you rested at the Ferry. I heard, however, that a white woman had come up. Who is she?"

They had reached the tent, and Mrs. Huzzard, after a frantic dive toward their very small looking glass, appeared at the door with a smile enchanting, and a courtesy so nicely managed that it nearly took the captain's breath away. It was the very latest of Lavina's teachings.

"Well, now, I'm mighty-hem! —I'm extremely pleased that you have called. Have a nice trip?"

But the society tone of Mrs. Huzzard was so unlike the one he had been accustomed to hearing her use, that the captain could only stare, and before he recovered enough to reply, she turned and beckoned Miss Slocum, with the idea of completing the impression made, and showing with what grace she could present him to her cousin.

But the lately acquired style was lost on him this time, overtopped by the presence of Miss Lavina, who gazed at him with a prolonged and steady stare.

"And this is your friend, Captain Leek, of the Northern Army, is it?" she asked, in her very sharpest voice —a voice she tried to temper with a smile about her lips, though none shone in her eyes. "I have no doubt you will be very welcome to the camp, Captain Leek."

Mrs. Huzzard had surely expected of Lavina a much more gracious reception. But Mrs. Huzzard was a bit of a philosopher, and if Lavina chose to be somewhat cold and unresponsive to the presence of a cultured gentleman, well, it gave Lorena Jane so much better chance, and she was not going to slight it.

"Come right in; you must be dead tired," she said, cordially. "Mr. Max, you'll let Dan know he's here, won't you-that is, when he does show up again, but no one knows how long that will be."

"Yes, I am tired," agreed the captain, meekly, and not quite at his ease with the speculative eyes of Miss Slocum on him. "I —I brought up a few letters that arrived at the Ferry. I can't make up my mind to trust mail with these Indian boatmen Dan employs."

"They are a trial," agreed Mrs. Huzzard, "though they haven't the bad effect on our nerves that one or two of the camp Indians have-an awful squaw, who helps around, and an ugly old man, who only smokes and looks horrible. Now, Lavina-she ain't used to no such, and she just shivers at them."

"Yes-ah-yes," murmured the captain.

"Lavina says she knew folks of your name back in Ohio," continued Mrs. Huzzard, cheerfully, in order to get the two strangers better acquainted. "I thought at first maybe you'd turn out to know each other; but she says they was Democrats," and she turned a sharp glance toward him, as if to read his political tendencies.

"No, I never knew any Captain Leek," said Miss Slocum, "and the ones I knew hadn't any one in the Union Army. Their principles, if they had any, were against it, and there wasn't a Republican in the family."

"Then, of course, that would settle Captain Leek belonging to them," decided Mrs. Huzzard, promptly. "I don't know much about politics, but as all our men folks wore the blue clothes, and fought in them, I was always glad I come from a Republican State. And I guess all the Republicans that carried guns against the Union could be counted without much arithmetic."

"I —I think I will go and look for Dan myself," observed the captain, rising and looking around a little uncertainly at Miss Slocum. "I brought some letters he may want."

He made his bow and placed the picturesque corded hat on his head as he went out. But Mrs. Huzzard looked after him somewhat anxiously.

"He's sick," she decided as he vanished from her view; "I never did see him walk so draggy like. And don't you judge his manners, either, Lavina, from this first sight of him, for he ain't himself to-day."

"He didn't look to me as though he knew who he was," remarked Lavina; and after a little she looked up from the tidy she was knitting. "So, Lorena Jane, that is the man you've been trying to educate yourself up to more than for anybody else-now, tell the truth!"

"Well, I don't mind saying that it was his good manners made me see how bad mine were," she confessed; "but as for training for him —"

"I see," said Miss Lavina, grimly, "and it is all right; but I just thought I'd ask."

Then she relapsed into deep thought, and made the needles click with impatience all that afternoon.

The captain came near the tent once, but retreated at the vision of the knitter. He talked with Mrs. Huzzard in the cabin of Harris, but did not visit her again in her own tent; and the poor woman began to wonder if the air of the Kootenai woods had an erratic influence on people. Dan was changed, 'Tana was changed, and now the captain seemed unlike himself from the very moment of his arrival. Even Lavina was a bit curt and indifferent, and Lorena Jane wondered where it would end.

In the midst of her perplexity, 'Tana added to it by appearing before her in the Indian dress Overton had presented her with. Since her sickness it had hung unused in her cabin, and the two women had fashioned garments more suitable, they thought, to a young girl who could wear real laces now if she chose. But there she was again, dressed like any little squaw, and although rather pale to suit the outfit, she said she wanted a few more "Indian hours" before departing for the far-off Eastern city that was to her as a new world.

She received Captain Leek with an unconcern that was discouraging to the pretty speeches he had prepared to utter.

Dan returned and looked sharply at her as she sat whittling a stick of which she said she meant to make a cane —a staff for mountain climbing.

"Where do you intend climbing?" he asked.

She waved the stick toward the hill back of them, the first step of the mountain.

"It is only a few hours since I picked you up down there, looking as if you were dead," he said, impatiently; "and you know you are not fit to tramp."

"Well, I'm not dead yet, anyway," she answered, with a shrug of her shoulders; "and as I'm going to break away from this camp about to-morrow, I thought I'd like to see a bit of the woods first."

"You-are going-to-morrow?"

"I reckon so."

"'Tana! And you have not said a word to me of it? That was not very friendly, little girl."

She did not reply, but bent her head low over her work.

After observing her for a while in silence, he arose and put on his hat.

"Here is my knife," he remarked. "You had better use it, if you are determined to haggle at that stick. Your own knife is too dull for any use. You can leave it here in the cabin when you are done with it."

She accepted it without a word, but flushed red when he had gone, and she found the eyes of Harris regarding her sadly.

"'Not very friendly,'" she said, going over Overton's words —"you think that, too-don't you? You think I'm ugly, and saucy, and awful, I know! You look scoldings at me; but if you knew all, maybe you wouldn't —if you knew that my heart is just about breaking. I'm going out where there is no one to talk to, or I'll be crying next."

The two cousins and the captain were in 'Tana's cabin. Mrs. Huzzard was determined that Miss Slocum and the captain should become acquainted, and, getting sight of the girl, who was walking alone across the level, she at once followed her, thinking that the two left behind would perhaps become more social if left entirely to themselves. And they did; that is, they talked, and the captain spoke first.

"So you-you bear a grudge-don't you, Lavina?"

"Well, I guess if I owed you a very heavy one, I've got a good chance to pay it off now," she remarked, grimly.

He twirled his hat in a dejected way, and did not speak.

"You an officer in the Union Army?" she continued, derisively. "You a pattern of what a gentleman should be; you to set up as superior to these rough-handed miners; you to act as if this Government owes you a pension! Why, how would it be with you, Alf Leek, if I'd tell this camp the truth of how you went away, engaged to me, twenty-five years ago, and never let me set eyes on you since-of how I wore black for you, thinking you were killed in the war, till I heard that you had deserted. I took off that mourning quick, I can tell you! I thought you were fighting on the wrong side; yet if you had a good reason for being there, you should have staid and fought so long as there was breath in you. And if I was to tell them here that you haven't a particle of right to wear that blue suit that looks like a uniform, and that you were no more 'captain' of anything than I am-well, I guess Lorena Jane wouldn't have much to say to you, though maybe Mr. Overton would."

He grew actually pale as he listened. His fear of some one overhearing her was as great as his own mortification.

"But you-you won't tell-will you, Lavina?" he said pleadingly. "I haven't done any harm! I —"

"Harm! Alf Leek, you never had enough backbone to do either harm or help to any one in this world. But don't you suppose you did me harm when you spoiled me for ever trusting any other man?"

"I —I would have come back, but I thought you'd be married," he said, in a feeble, hopeless way.

"Likely that is now, ain't it?" she demanded. And, woman-like, now that she had reduced him to meekness and humiliation, she grew a shade less severe, as if pretty well satisfied. "I had other things to think of besides a husband."

"You won't tell-will you, Lavina? I'll tell you how it all happened, some day. Then I'll leave this country."

"You'll not," she contradicted. "You'll stay right here as long as I do, and I won't tell just so long as you keep from trying to make Lorena Jane believe how great you are. But at the first word of your heroic actions, or the cultured society you were always used to —"

"You'll never hear of them," he said eagerly, "never. I knew you wouldn't make trouble, Lavina, for you always were such a good, kind-hearted girl."

He offered his hand to her, sheepishly, and she gave it a vixenish slap.

"Don't try any of your skim-milk praise on me," she said, tartly. "Huh! You, that Lorena thought was a pillar of cultured society! When, the Lord knows, you wouldn't have known how to read the addresses on your own letters if I hadn't taught you!"

He moved to the door in a crestfallen manner, and stood there a moment, moistening his lips, and apparently swallowing words that could not be uttered.

"That's so, Lavina," he said, at last, and went out.

"There!" she muttered aggrievedly —"that's Alf Leek, just as he always was. Give him a chance, and he'd ride over any one; but get the upper hand of him, and he is meeker than Moses. Not that much meekness is needed to come up to Moses, either." Then, after an impatient tattoo, she exclaimed:

"Gracious me! I do wish he hadn't looked so crushed, and had talked back a little."

Chapter XXII
The Murder

That evening, as the dusk fell, a slight figure in an Indian dress slipped to the low brush back of the cabin, and thence to the uplands.

It was 'Tana, ready to endure all the wilds of the woods, rather than stay there and meet again the man she had met the night before. She had sent the squaw away; she had arranged in Mrs. Huzzard's tent a little game of cards that would hold the attention of Lyster and the others; and then she had slipped away, that she might, for just once more, feel free on the mountain, as she had felt when they first located their camp in the sweet grass of the Twin Springs.

The moon would be up after a while. She could not walk far, but she meant to sit somewhere up there in the high ground until the moon should roll up over the far mountains.

The mere wearing of the Indian dress gave her a feeling of being herself once more, for in the pretty conventional dress made for her by Mrs. Huzzard, she felt like another girl —a girl she did not know very well.

In the southwest long streaks of red and yellow lay across the sky, and a clear radiance filled the air, as it does when a new moon is born after the darkness. She felt the beauty of it all, and stretched out her arms as though to draw the peaks of the hills to her.

But, as she stepped forward, a form arose before her —a tall, decided form, and a decided voice said:

"No, 'Tana, you have gone far enough."

"Dan!"

"Yes-it is Dan this time, and not the other fellow. If he is waiting for you to-night, I will see that he waits a long time."

"You-you!" she murmured, and stepped back from him. Then, her first fright over, she straightened herself defiantly.

"Why do you think any one is waiting for me?" she demanded. "What do you know? I am heartsick with all this hiding, and-and deceit. If you know the truth, speak out, and end it all!"

"I can't say any more than you know already," he answered —"not so much; but last night a man was in your cabin, a man you know and quarreled with. I didn't hear you; don't think I was spying on you. A miner who passed the cabin heard your voices and told me something was wrong. You don't give me any right to advise you or dictate to you, 'Tana, but one thing you shall not do, that is, steal to the woods to meet him. And if I find him in your cabin, I promise you he sha'n't die of old age."

"You would kill him?"

"Like a snake!" and his voice was harsher, colder, than she had ever heard it. "I'm not asking you any questions, 'Tana. I know it was the man whom you-saw that night at the spring, and would not let me follow. I know there is something wrong, or he would come to see you, like a man, in daylight. If the others here knew it, they would say things not kind to you. And that is why it sha'n't go on."

"Sha'n't? What right have you-to-to —"

"You will say none," he answered, curtly, "because you do not know."

"Do not know what?" she interrupted, but he only drew a deep breath and shook his head.

"'Tana, don't meet this man again," he said, pleadingly. "Trust me to judge for you. I don't want to be harsh with you. I don't want you to go away with hard thoughts against me. But this has got to stop-you must promise me."

"And if I refuse?"

"Then I'd look for the man, and he never would meet you again."

A little shiver ran over her as he spoke. She knew what he meant, and, despite her bitter words last night to her visitor, the thought was horrible to her that Dan —

She covered her face with her hands and turned away.

"Don't do that, little girl," he said, and laid his hand on her arm. "'Tana!"

She flung off his hand as though it stung her, and into her mind flashed remembrance of Jake Emmons from Spokane-of him and his words.

"Don't touch me!" she half sobbed. "Don't you say another word to me! I am going away to-morrow, and I have promised to marry Max Lyster."

His hand dropped to his side, and his face shone white in the wan glimmer of the stars.

"You have promised that?" he said, at last, drawing his breath hard through his shut teeth. "Well-it is right, I suppose-right. Come! I will take you back to him now. He is the best one to guard you. Come!"

She drew away and looked from him across to where the merest rim of the rising moon was to be seen across the hills. The thought of that other night came to her, the night when they had stood close to each other in the moonlight. How happy she had been for that one little space of time! And now-Ah! she scarcely dare allow him to speak kindly to her, lest she grow weak enough to long for that blind content once more.

"Come, Tana."

"Go. I will follow after a little," she answered, without turning her head.

"I may never trouble you to walk with you again," he said, in a low, constrained tone; "but this time I must see you safe in the tent before I leave."

"Leave! Going! Where to?" she asked, and her voice trembled in spite of herself. She clasped her hands tightly, and he could see the flash of the ring he had given her. She had put it on with the Indian dress.

"That does not matter much, does it?" he returned; "but somewhere, far enough up the lake not to trouble you again while you stay. Come."

She walked beside him without another word; words seemed so useless. She had said words over and over again to herself all that day-words of his wrong to her in not telling her of that other woman, words of reproach, bitter and keen; yet none of her reasoning kept her from wanting to touch his hand as he walked beside her.

But she did not. Even when they reached the level by the springs, she only looked her farewell to him, but did not speak.

"Good-by," he said, in a voice that was not like Dan's voice.

She merely bowed her head, and walked away toward the tent where she heard Mrs. Huzzard laughing.

She halted near the cabin, and then hurried on, dreading to enter it yet, lest she should meet the man she was trying to avoid.

Overton watched her until she reached the tent. The moon had just escaped the horizon, and threw its soft misty light over all the place. He pulled his hat low over his eyes, and, turning, took the opposite direction.

Only a few minutes elapsed when Lyster remembered he had promised Dan to look after Harris, and rose to go to the cabin.

"I will go, too," said 'Tana, filled with nervous dread lest he encounter some one on her threshold, though she had all reason to expect that her disguised visitor had come and gone ere that.

"Well, well, 'Tana, you are a restless mortal," said Mrs. Huzzard. "You've only just come, and now you must be off again. What did you do that you wanted to be all alone for this evening? Read verses, I'll go bail."

"No, I didn't read verses," answered 'Tana. "But you needn't go along to the cabin."

"Well, I will then. You are not fit to sleep alone. And, if it wasn't for the beastly snakes! —"

"We will go and see Harris," said the girl, and so they entered his cabin, where he sat alone with a bright light burning.

Some newspapers, brought by the captain, were spread before him on a rough reading stand rigged up by one of the miners.

He looked pale and tired, as though the effort of perusing them had been rather too much for him.

Listen as she might, the girl could hear never a sound from her own cabin. She stood by the blanket door, connecting the two rooms, but not a breath came to her. She sighed with relief at the certainty that he had come and gone. She would never see him again.

"Shall I light your lamp?" asked Lyster; and, scarce waiting for a reply, he drew back the blanket and entered the darkness of the other cabin.

Two of the miners came to the door just then, detailed to look after Harris for the night. One was the good-natured, talkative Emmons.

"Glad to see you are so much better, miss," he said, with an expansive smile. "But you scared the wits nearly out of me this morning."

Then they heard the sputter of a match in the next room, and a sharp, startled cry from Lyster, as the blaze gave a feeble light to the interior.

He staggered back among the rest, with the dying match in his fingers, and his face ashen gray.

"Snakes!" half screamed Mrs. Huzzard. "Oh, my! oh, my!"

'Tana, after one look at Lyster, tried to enter the room, but he caught and held her.

"Don't, dear! —don't go in there! It's awful-awful!"

"What's wrong?" demanded one of the miners, and picked up a lamp from beside Harris.

"Look! It is Akkomi!" answered Lyster.

At the name 'Tana broke from him and ran into the room, even before the light reached it.

But she did not take many steps. Her foot struck against something on the floor, an immovable body and a silent one.

"Akkomi-sure enough," said the miner, as he saw the Indian's blanket. "Drunk, I suppose-Indian fashion."

But as he held the light closer, he took hold of the girl's arm, and tried to lead her from the scene.

"You'd better leave this to us, miss," he added, in a grave tone. "The man ain't drunk. He's been murdered!"

'Tana, white as death itself, shook off his grasp and stood with tightly clasped hands, unheeding the words of horror around her, scarce hearing the shriek of Mrs. Huzzard, as that lady, forgetful even of the snakes, sank to the floor, a very picture of terror.

'Tana saw the roll of money scattered over the couch; the little bag of free gold drawn from under the pillow. He had evidently been stooping to secure it when the assassin crept behind him and left him dead there, with a knife sticking between his shoulders.

"The very knife you had to-day!" said Lyster, horror-stricken at the sight.

The miner with the lamp turned and looked at her strangely, and his eyes dropped from her face to her clasped hands, on which the ring of the snakes glittered.

"Your knife?" he asked, and others, attracted by Mrs. Huzzard's scream, stood around the doors and looked at her too.

She nodded her head, scarce understanding the significance of it, and never taking her eyes from the dead man, whose face was yet hidden.

"He may not be dead," she said, at last. "Look!"

"Oh, he's dead, safe enough," and Emmons lifted his hand. "Was he trying to rob you?"

"I —no —I don't know," she answered, vaguely.

Then another man turned the body over, and utter surprise was on every face; for, though it was Akkomi's blanket, it was a much younger man who lay there.

"A white man, by Heavens!" said the miner who had first entered. "A white man, with brown paint on his face and hands! But, look here!" and he pulled down the collar of the dead man's shirt, and showed a skin fair as a child's.

"Something terribly crooked here," he continued. "Where is Overton?"

Overton! At the name her very heart grew cold within her. Had he not threatened he would kill the man who visited her at night? Had he come straight to the cabin after leaving her? Had he kept his word? Had he —

"I think Overton left camp after supper-started for the lake," answered some one.

"Well, we'll do our best to get it straight without him, then. Some of you see what time it is. This man has been dead about a half hour. Mr. Lyster, you had better write down all about it; and, if any one here has any information to give, let him have it."

His eyes were on the girl's face, but she said nothing, and he bent to wipe off the stain from the dead man's face. Some one brought water, and in a little while was revealed the decidedly handsome face of a man about forty-five years old.

"Do any of you know him?" asked the miner, who, by circumstance, appeared to have been given the office of speaker —"look-all of you."

One after another the men approached, but shook their heads; until an old miner, gray-haired and weather-beaten, gave vent to a half-smothered oath at sight of him.

"Know him?" he exclaimed. "Well, I do, though it's five years since I saw him. Heavens! I'd rather have found him alive than dead, though, for there is a standing reward offered for him by two States. Why, it's the card-sharper, horse-thief and renegade-Lee Holly!"

"But who could have killed him?"

"That is Overton's knife," said one of the men.

"But Overton had not had it since noon," said 'Tana, speaking for the first time in explanation. "I borrowed it then."

"You borrowed it? For what?"

"Oh —I forget. To cut a stick with, I think."

"You think. I'm sorry to speak rough to a lady, miss but this is a time for knowing-not thinking."

"What do you mean by that?" demanded Lyster.

The man looked at him squarely.

"Nothing to offend innocent folks," he answered. "A murder has been done in this lady's room, with a knife she acknowledges she has had possession of. It's natural enough to question her first of all."

The color had crept into her face once more. She knew what the man meant, and knew that the longer they looked on her with suspicion, the more time Overton would have to escape. Then, when they learned they were on a false scent, it would be late-too late to start after him. She wished he had taken the money and the gold. She shuddered as she thought him a murderer-the murderer of that man; but, with what skill she could, she would keep them off his track.

Her thoughts ran fast, and a half smile touched her lips. Even with that dead body at her feet, she was almost happy at the hope of saving him. The others noticed it, and looked at her in wonder. Lyster said:

"You are right. But Miss Rivers could know nothing of this. She has been with us since the moon rose, and that is more than a half-hour."

"No, only fifteen minutes," said one of the men.

"Well, where were you for the half-hour before the moon rose?" asked the man who seemed examiner. "That is really the time most interesting to this case."

"Why, good heavens, man!" cried Lyster, but 'Tana interrupted:

"I was walking up on the hill about that time."

"Alone?"

"Alone."

Mrs. Huzzard groaned dismally, and Lyster caught 'Tana by the hand.

"'Tana! think what you are saying. You don't realize how serious this is."

"One more question," and the man looked at her very steadily. "Were you not expecting this man to-night?"

"I sha'n't answer any more of your questions," she answered, coldly.

Lyster turned on the man with clenched hands and a face white with anger.

"How dare you insult her with such a question?" he asked, hoarsely. "How could it be possible for Miss Rivers to know this renegade horse-thief?"

"Well, I'll tell you," said the man, drawing a long breath and looking at the girl. "It ain't a pleasant thing to do; but as we have no courts up here, we have to straighten out crimes in a camp the best way we can. My name is Saunders. That man over there is right-this is Lee Holly; and I am sure now that I saw him leave this cabin last night. I passed the cabin and heard voices-hers and a man's. I heard her say: 'While I can't quite decide to kill you myself, I hope some one else will.' The rest of their words were not so clear. I told Overton when he came back, but the man was gone then. You ask me how I dare think she could tell something of this if she chose. Well, I can't help it. She is wearing a ring I'll swear I saw Lee Holly wear three years ago, at a card table in Seattle. I'll swear it! And he is lying here dead in her room, with a knife sticking in him that she had possession of to-day. Now, gentlemen, what do you think of it yourselves?"

"Oh, 'Tana, it is awful-awful!" and poor Mrs. Huzzard rocked herself in a spasm of woe. "And to think that you won't say a word-not a single word! It just breaks my heart."

"Now, now! I'll say lots of things if you will talk of something besides murders. And I'll mend your broken heart when this trouble is all over, you will see!"

"Over! I'm mightily afraid it is only commencing. And you that cool and indifferent you are enough to put one crazy! Oh, if Dan Overton was only here."

The girl smiled. All the hours of the night had gone by. He had at least twelve hours' start, and the men of the camp had not yet suspected him for even a moment. They had questioned Harris, and he told them, by signs, that no man had gone through his cabin, no one had been in since dark; but he had heard a movement in the other room. The knife he had seen 'Tana take into the other room long before dark.

"And some one quarreling with this Holly-or following him-may have chanced on it and used it," contested Lyster, who was angered, dismayed, and puzzled at 'Tana, quite as much as at the finding of the body. Her answers to all questions were so persistently detrimental to her own cause.

"Don't be uneasy-they won't hang me," she assured him. "Think of them hanging any one for killing Lee Holly! The man who did it-if he knows whom he was settling for-was a fool not to face the camp and get credit for it. Every man would have shaken hands with him. But just because there is a little mystery about it, they try to make it out a crime. Pooh!"

"Oh, child!" exclaimed Mrs. Huzzard, totally scandalized. "A murder! Of course it is a crime-the greatest."

"I don't think so. It is a greater crime to bring a soul into the world and then neglect it-let it drift into any hell on earth that nets it-than it is to send a soul out of the world, to meet heaven, if it deserves it. There are times when murder is justifiable, but there are certain other crimes that nothing could ever justify."

"Why, 'Tana!" and Mrs. Huzzard looked at her helplessly. But Miss Slocum gave the girl a more understanding regard.

"You speak very bitterly for a young girl; as if you had thought a great deal on this question."

"I have," she acknowledged, promptly; "you think it is not a very nice question for girls to study about, don't you? Well, it isn't nice, but it's true. I happen to be one of the souls dragged into life by people who didn't think they had responsibilities. Miss Slocum, maybe that is why I am extra bitter on the subject."

"But not-not against your parents, 'Tana?" said Mrs. Huzzard, in dismay.

The girl's mouth drew hard and unlovely at the question.

"I don't know much about religion," she said, after a little, "and I don't know that it matters much-now don't faint, Mrs. Huzzard! but I'm pretty certain old married men who had families were the ones who laid down the law about children in the Bible. They say 'spare the rod and spoil the child,' and then say 'honor your father and mother.' They seem to think it a settled thing that all fathers and mothers are honorable-but they ain't; and that all children need beating-and they don't."

"Oh, 'Tana!"

"And I think it is that one-sided commandment that makes folks think that all the duty must go from children to the parents, and not a word is said of the duty people owe to the souls they bring into the world. I don't think it's a square deal."

"A square deal! Why, 'Tana!"

"Isn't it so?" she asked, moodily. "You think a girl is a pretty hard case if she doesn't give proper respect and duty to her parents, don't you? But suppose they are the sort of people no one can respect-what then? Seems to me the first duty is from the parent to the children-the duty of caring for them, loving them, and teaching them right. A child can't owe a debt of duty when it never received the duties it should have first. Oh, I may not say this clearly as I feel it."

"But you know, 'Tana," said Miss Slocum, "that if there is no commandment as to parents giving care to their children, it is only because it is so plainly a natural thing to do that it was unnecessary to command it."

"No more natural than for a child to honor any person who is honorable, or to love the parent who loves him, and teaches him rightly. Huh! If a child is not able to love and respect a parent, it is the child who loses the most."

Miss Slocum looked at her sadly.

"I can't scold you as I would try to scold many a one in your place," she said, "for I feel as if you must have traveled over some long, hard path of troubles, before you could reach this feeling you have. But, 'Tana, think of brighter things; young girls should never drift into those perplexing questions. They will make you melancholy if you brood on such things."

"Melancholy? Well, I think not," and she smiled and shrugged her shoulders. "Seems to me I'm the least gloomy person in camp this morning. All the rest of you look as though Mr. Holly had been your bosom friend."

She talked recklessly-they thought heartlessly-of the murder, and the two women were strongly inclined to think the shock of the affair had touched her brain, for she showed no concern whatever as to her own position, but treated it as a joke. And when she realized that she was to a certain extent under guard, she seemed to find amusement in that, too. Her expressions, when the cousins grew pitiful over the handsome face of Holly, were touched with ridicule.

"I wonder if there was ever a man too low and vile to get woman's pity, if he only had a pretty face," she said, caustically. "If he was an ugly, old, half-decent fellow, you wouldn't be making any soft-hearted surmises as to what he might have been under different circumstances. He has spoiled the lives of several tenderhearted women like you-yet you pity him!"

"'Tana, I never knew you to be so set against any one as you are against that poor dead man," declared Mrs. Huzzard. "Not so much wonder the folks think you know how it happened, for you always had a helping word for the worst old tramp or beggarly Indian that came around; but for this man you have nothing but unkindness."

"No," agreed the girl, "and you would like to think him a romantic victim of somebody, just because he is so good-looking. I'm going to talk to Harris. He won't sympathize with the wrong side, I am sure."

He looked up eagerly as she entered, his eyes full of anxious question. She touched his hand kindly and sat close beside him as she talked.

"You want to know all about it, don't you?" she asked, softly. "Well, it is all over. He was alive, after all, and I would not believe it. But now you need never trail him again, you can rest now, for he is dead. Somebody else has-has owed him a grudge, too. They think I am the somebody, but you don't believe that?"

He shook his head decidedly.

"No," she continued; "though for one moment, Joe, I thought that it might have been you. Yes, I did; for of course I knew it was only weakness would keep you from it, if you were in reach of him. But I remembered at once that it could not be, for the hand that struck him was strong."

He assented in his silent way, and watched her face closely, as if to read the shadows of thought thrown on it by her feelings.

"It's awful, ain't it?" she whispered. "It is what I said I hoped for, and just yet I can't be sorry —I can't! But, after this stir is all over, I know it will trouble me, make me sorry because I am not sorry now. I can't cry, but I do feel like screaming. And see! every once in a while my hands tremble; I tremble all over. Oh, it is awful!"

She buried her face in her hands. Only to him did she show any of the feeling with which the death of the man touched her.

"And you can't tell me anything of how it was done?" she said, at last. "You so near-did you see any one?"

She longed to ask if he had seen Overton, but dared not utter his name, lest he might suspect as she did. Each hour that went by was an added gain to her for him. Of course he had struck, not knowing who the man was. If he had known, it would have been so easy to say, "I found him robbing the cabin. I killed him," and there would have been no further question concerning it.

"But if all the other bars were beaten down between us, this one would keep me from ever shaking hands with him again. Why should it have been he out of all the camp? Oh, it makes my heart ache!"

While she sat thus, with miserable thoughts, others came to the door, and looking up, she saw Akkomi, who looked on her with keen, accusing eyes.

"No-it is not true, Akkomi," she said, in his own jargon. "Keep silent for a little while of the things these people do not know—a little while, and then I can tell you who it is I am shielding, but not yet."

"Him!" and the eyes of the Indian turned to the paralytic.

"No-not him; truly not," she said, earnestly. "It is some one you would want to help if you knew-some one who is going fast on the path from these people. They will learn soon it is not I; but till then, keep silence."

"Dan-where?" he asked, laconically, and her face paled at the question.

Had he any reason to suspect the dread in her own mind? But a moment's thought reassured her. He had asked simply because Overton seemed always to him the controlling spirit of the camp, and Overton was the one he would have speech with, if any.

"Overton left last night for the lake," explained Lyster, who had entered and heard the name of Dan and the interrogative tone. Then the blanket was brought to Akkomi-his blanket, in which the man had died.

"I sold it to the white man-that is all," he answered through 'Tana; and more than that he would not say except to inform them he would wait for Dan. Which was, in fact, the general desire of the committee organized to investigate.

They all appeared to be waiting for Dan. Lyster did not by any means fill his place, simply because Lyster's interest in 'Tana was too apparent, and there was little of the cool quality of reason in his attitude toward the mysterious case. He did not believe the ring she wore had belonged to Holly, though she refused to tell the source from which it had reached her. He did not believe the man who said he heard that war of words at her cabin in the evening-at least, when others were about, he acted as if he did not believe it. But when he and 'Tana chanced to be alone, she felt the doubt there must be in his mind, and a regret for him touched her. For his sake she was sorry, but not sorry enough to clear the mystery at the expense of that other man she thought she was shielding.

Captain Leek had been dispatched with all speed to the lake works, that Seldon, Haydon, and Overton might be informed of the trouble in camp, and hasten back to settle it. To send for them was the only thing Lyster thought of doing, for he himself felt powerless against the lot of men, who were not harsh or rude in any way, but who simply wanted to know "why" —so many "whys" that he could not answer.

Not less trying to him were the several who persisted in asserting that she had done a commendable thing-that the country ought to feel grateful to her, for the man had made trouble along the Columbia for years. He and his confederates had done ugly work along the border, etc., etc.

"Sorry you asked me, Max?" she said, seeing his face grow gloomy under their cheering (?) assertions.

He did not answer at once, afraid his impatience with her might make itself apparent in his speech.

"No, I'm not sorry," he said, at last; "but I shall be relieved when the others arrive from the lake. Since you utterly refuse to confide even in me, you render me useless as to serving you; and-well—I can't feel flattered that you confide in me no more than in the strangers here."

"I know," she agreed, with a little sigh, "it is hard on you, and it will be harder still if the story of this should ever creep out of the wilderness to the country where you come from-wouldn't it?" and she looked at him very sharply, noting the swift color flush his face, as though she had read his thoughts. "Yes-so it's lucky, Max, that we haven't talked to others about that little conditional promise, isn't it? So it will be easier to forget, and no one need know."

"You mean you think me the sort of fellow to break our engagement just because these fools have mixed you up with this horror?" he asked, angrily. "You've no right to think that of me; neither have you the right-in justice to me as well as yourself-to maintain this very suggestive manner about all things connected with the murder. Why can you not tell more clearly where your time was spent last evening? Why will you not tell where the ring came from? Why will you see me half-frantic over the whole miserable affair, when you could, I am sure, easily change it?"

"Oh, Max, I don't want to worry you-indeed I don't! But —" and she smiled mirthlessly. "I told you once I was a 'hoodoo.' The people who like me are always sure to have trouble brewing for them. That is why I say you had better give me up, Max; for this is only the beginning."

"Don't talk like that; it is folly," he said, in a sharp tone. "'Hoodoo!' Nonsense! When Overton and the others arrive, they will find a means of changing the ideas of these people, in spite of your reticence; and then maybe old Akkomi may find words, too. He sits outside the door as impassive as the clay image you gave me and bewitched me with."

She smiled faintly, thinking of those days-how very long ago they seemed, yet it was this same summer.

"I feel as if I had lived a long time since I played with that clay," she said, wistfully; "so many things have been made different for me."

Then she arose and walked about the little room restlessly, while the eyes of Harris never left her. Into the other room she had not gone at all, for in it was the dead stranger.

"When do you look for your uncle and Mr. Haydon?" she asked, at last, for the silences were hardest to endure.

She would laugh, or argue, or ridicule-do anything rather than sit silent with questioning eyes upon her. She even grew to fancy that Harris must accuse her-he watched her so!

"When do we look for them? Well, I don't dare let myself decide. I only hope they may have made a start back, and will meet the captain on his way. As to Dan-he had not so very much the start, and they ought to catch up with him, for there were the two Indian canoeists-the two best ones; and when they are racing over the water, with an object, they surely ought to make better time than he. I can't see that he had any very pressing reason for going at all."

"He doesn't talk much about his reasons," she answered.

"No; that's a fact," he agreed, "and less of late than when I knew him first. But he'll make Akkomi talk, maybe, when he arrives-and I hope you, too."

"When he arrives!"

She thought the words, but did not say them aloud. She sat long after Max had left her, and thought how many hours must elapse before they discovered that Dan had not followed the other men to the lake works. She felt sure that he was somewhere in the wilderness, avoiding the known paths, alone, and perhaps hating her as the cause of his isolation, because she would not confess what the man was to her, but left him blindly to keep his threat, and kill him when found in her room.

Ah! why not have trusted him with the whole truth? She asked herself the question as she sat there, but the mere thought of it made her face grow hot, and her jaws set defiantly.

She would not-she could not! so she told herself. Better-better far be suspected of a murder-live all her life under the blame of it for him-than to tell him of a past that was dead to her now, a past she hated, and from which she had determined to bar herself as far as silence could build the wall. And to tell him-him-she could not.

But even as she sat, with her burning face in her hands, quick, heavy steps came to the door, halted, and looking up she found Dan before her.

"Oh! you should not," she whispered, hurriedly. "Why did you come back? They do not suspect; they think I did it-and so —"

"What does this all mean? —what do you mean?" he asked. "Can't you speak?"

It seemed she could not find any more words, she stared at him so helplessly.

"Max, come here!" he called, to hasten steps already approaching. "Come, all of you; I had only a moment to listen to the captain when he caught up with me. But he told me she is suspected of murder-that a ring she wore last night helped the suspicion on. I didn't wait to hear any more, for I gave the little girl that snake ring-gave it to her weeks ago. I bought it from a miner, and he told me he got it from an Indian near Karlo. Now are you ready to suspect me, too, because I had it first?"

"The ring wasn't just the most important bit of circumstantial evidence, Mr. Overton," answered the man named Saunders; "and we are all mighty glad you've got here. It was in her room the man was found, and a knife she borrowed from you was what killed him; and of where she was just about the time the thing happened she won't say anything."

His face paled slightly as he looked at her and heard the brief summing up of the case.

"My knife?" he said, blankly.

"Yes, sir. When some one said it was your knife, she spoke up and said it was, but that you had not had it since noon, for she borrowed it then to cut a stick; but beyond that she don't tell a thing."

"Who is the man?"

"The renegade-Lee Holly."

"Lee Holly!" He turned a piercing glance on Harris, remembering the deep interest he had shown in that man Lee Holly and his partner, "Monte."

Harris met his gaze without flinching, and nodded his head as if in assent.

And that was the man found dead in her room!

The faces of the people seemed for a moment an indistinct blur before his eyes; then he rallied and turned to her.

"'Tana, you never did it," he said, reassuringly; "or if you did, it has been justifiable, and I know it. If it was necessary to do it in any self-defense, don't be afraid to tell it all plainly. No one would blame you. It is only this mystery that makes them want to hear the truth."

She only looked at him. Was he acting? Did he himself know nothing? The hope that it was so-that she had deceived herself-made her tremble as she had not at danger to herself. She had risen to her feet as he entered, but she swayed as if to fall, and he caught her, not knowing it was hope instead of despair that took the color from her face and left her helpless.

"Courage, 'Tana! Tell us what you can. I left you just as the moon came up. I saw you go to Mrs. Huzzard's tent. Now, where did you go after that?"

"What?" almost shouted Lyster. "You were with her when the moon rose. Are you sure?"

"Sure? Of course I am. Why?"

"And how long before that, Mr. Overton?" asked Saunders; "for that is a very important point."

"About a half-hour, I should say-maybe a little more," he answered, staring at them. "Now, what important thing does that prove?"

One of the men gave a cheer; three or four had come up to the door when they saw Overton, and they took the yell up with a will. Mrs. Huzzard started to run from the tent, but grew so nervous that she had to wait until Miss Slocum came to her aid.

"What in the world does it mean?" she gasped.

Saunders turned around with an honestly pleased look.

"It means that Mr. Overton here has brought word that clears Miss Rivers of being at the cabin when the murder was done-that's what it means; and we are all too glad over it to keep quiet. But why in the world didn't you tell us that, miss?"

But she did not say a word. All about Dan were exclamations and disjointed sentences, from which he could gain little actual knowledge, and he turned to Lyster, impatiently:

"Can't you tell me-can't some of you tell me, what I have cleared up for her? When was this killing supposed to be done?"

"At or a little before moonrise," said Max, his face radiant once more. "'Tana-don't you know what he has done for you? taken away all of that horribly mistaken suspicion you let rest on you. Where was she, Dan?"

"Last night? Oh, up above the bluff there-went up when the pretty red lights were in the sky, and staid until the moon rose. I came across her up there, and advised her not to range away alone; so, when she got good and ready, she walked back again, and went to the tent where you folks were. Then I struck the creek, decided I would take a run up the lake, and left without seeing any of you again. And all this time 'Tana has had a guard over her. Some of you must have been crazy."

"Well, then, I guess I was the worst lunatic of the lot," confessed Saunders. "But to tell the truth, Mr. Overton, it looks to me now as if she encouraged suspicion-yes, it does. 'Overton's knife,' said some one; but, quick as could be, she spoke up and said it was she who had it, and she didn't mind just where she left it. And as to where she was at that time, well, she just wouldn't give us a bit of satisfaction. Blest if I don't think she wanted us to suspect her."

"Oh!" he breathed, as if in understanding, and her first words swept back to him, her nervous —"Why did you come back? They suspect me!" Surely that cry was as a plea for his own safety; it spoke through eyes and voice as well as words. Some glimmer of the truth came to him.

"Come, 'Tana!" he said, and reached his hand to her. "Where is the man-Holly? I should like to go in. Will you come, too?"

She rose without a word, and no one attempted to follow them.

Mrs. Huzzard heaved a prodigious sigh of content.

"Oh, that girl Montana!" she exclaimed. "I declare she ain't like any girl I ever did see! This morning, when she was a suspected criminal, she was talky, and even laughed, and now that she's cleared, she won't lift her head to look at any one. I do wonder if that sort of queerness is catching in these woods. I declare I feel most scared enough to leave."

But Lyster reassured her.

"Remember how sick she has been; and think what a shock this whole affair has been to weak nerves," he said, for with Dan's revelations he had grown blissfully content once more, "and as for that fellow hearing voices in her cabin-nonsense! She had been reading some poem or play aloud. She is fond of reading so, and does it remarkably well. He heard her spouting in there for the benefit of Harris, and imagined she was making threats to some one. Poor little girl! I'm determined she sha'n't remain here any longer."

"Are you?" asked Mrs. Huzzard, dryly. "Well, Mr. Max, so long as I've known her, I've always found 'Tana makes her own determinations-and sticks to them, too."

"I'm glad to be reminded of that," he retorted, "for she promised me yesterday to marry me some time."

"Bless my soul!"

"If she didn't change her mind," he added, laughingly.

"To marry you! Well, well, well!" and she stared at him so queerly, that a shade of irritation crossed his face.

"Why not?" he asked. "Don't you think that a plain, ordinary man is good enough for your wild-flower of the Kootenai hills?"

"Oh, you're not plain at all, Mr. Max Lyster," she returned, "and I'll go bail many a woman who is smarter than either 'Tana or me has let you know it! It ain't the plainness-it's the difference. And-well, well! you know you've been quarreling ever since you met."

"But that is all over now," he promised; "and haven't you a good wish for us?"

"Indeed I have, then —a many of them, but you have surprised me. I used to think that's how it would end; and then-well, then, a different notion got in my head. Now that it's settled, I do hope you will be happy. Bless the child! I'll go and tell her so this minute."

"No," he said, quickly, "let her and Dan have their talk out-if she will talk to him. That fever left her queer in some things, and one of them is her avoidance of Dan. She hasn't been free and friendly with him as she used to be, and it is too bad; for he is such a good fellow, and would do anything for her."

"Yes, he would," assented Mrs. Huzzard.

"And she will be her own spirited self in a few weeks-when she gets away from here-and gets stronger. She'll appreciate Dan more after a while, for there are few like him. And so-as she is to go away so soon, I hope something will put them on their former confidential footing. Maybe this murder will be the something."

"You are a good friend, Mr. Max," said the woman, slowly, "and you deserve to be a lucky lover. I'm sure I hope so."

Within the cabin, those two of whom they spoke stood together beside the dead outlaw, and their words were low-so low that the paralyzed man in the next room listened in vain.

"And you believed that of me-of me?" he asked, and she answered, falteringly:

"How did I know? You said-you threatened-you would kill him-any man you found in here. So, when he was here dead, I —did not know."

"And you thought I had stuck that knife in him and left?"

She nodded her head.

"And you thought," he continued, in a voice slightly tremulous, "that you were giving me a chance to escape just so long as you let them suspect-you?"

She did not answer, but turned toward the door. He held his arm out and barred her way.

"Only a moment!" he said, pleadingly. "It never can be that-that I would be anything to you, little girl-never, never! But-just once-let me tell you a truth that shall never hurt you, I swear! I love you! No other word but that will tell your dearness to me. I —I never would have said it, but-but what you risked for me has broken me down. It has told me more than your words would tell me, and I —Oh, God! my God!"

She shrank from the passion in his words and tone, but the movement only made him catch her arm and hold her there. Tears were in his eyes as he looked at her, and his jaws were set firmly.

"You are afraid of me-of me?" he asked. "Don't be. Life will be hard enough now without leaving me that to remember. I'm not asking a word in return from you; I have no right. You will be happy somewhere else-and with some one else-and that is right."

He still held her wrist, and they stood in silence. She could utter no word; but her mouth trembled and she tried to smother a sob that arose in her throat.

But he heard it.

"Don't!" he said, almost in a whisper —"for God's sake, don't cry. I can't stand that-not your tears. Here! be brave! Look up at me, won't you? See! I don't ask you for a word or a kiss or a thought when you leave me-only let me see your eyes! Look at me!"

What he read in her trembling lips and her shrinking, shamed eyes made him draw his breath hard through his shut teeth.

"My brave little girl!" he said softly. "You will think harshly of me for this some day-if you ever know-know all. But what you did this morning made a coward of me-that and my longing for you. Try to forgive me. Or, no-you had better not. And when you are his wife-Oh, it's no use —I can't think or speak of that-yet. Good-by, little girl-good-by!"

Chapter XXIV
Leaving Camp

Afterward, 'Tana never could remember clearly the incidents of the few days that followed. Only once more she entered the cabin of death, and that was when Mr. Haydon and Mr. Seldon returned with all haste to the camp, after meeting with Captain Leek and the Indian boatman.

Then, as some of the men offered to go with them to view the remains of the outlaw, she came forward.

"No. I will take them," she said.

When Mr. Haydon demurred, feeling that a young girl should be kept as much as possible from such scenes, she had laid her hand on Seldon's arm.

"Come!" she said, and they went with her.

But when inside the door, she did not approach the blanket-covered form stretched on the couch; only pointed toward it, and stood herself like a guard at the entrance.

When Seldon lifted the Indian blanket from the face, he uttered a startled exclamation, and looked strangely at her. She never turned around.

"What is it?" asked Mr. Haydon.

No one replied, and as he looked with anxiety toward the form there, his face grew ashen in its horror.

"Lord in heaven!" he gasped; "first her on that bed and now *him*! I —I feel as if I was haunted in this camp. Seldon, is it-is it —"

"No mistake possible," answered the other man, decidedly. "I could swear to the identity. It is George Rankin!"

"And Holly, the renegade!" added Haydon, in consternation; "and Lord only knows how many other aliases he has worn. Oh, what a sensation the papers would make over this if they got hold of it all. My! my! it would be awful! And that girl, Montana, as she calls herself, she has been clever to keep it quiet as she has, for-Oh, Lord!"

"What is the matter now? You look fairly sick," said the other, impatiently. "I didn't fancy you'd grieve much over his death."

"No, it isn't that," said Haydon, huskily. "But that girl-don't you see she was accused of this? And-well seeing who he is, how do we know —"

He stopped awkwardly, unable to continue with the girl herself so near and with Seldon's warning glance directed to him.

She leaned against the wall, and apparently had not heard their words. Seldon's face softened as he looked at her; and, going over, he put his hand kindly on her hair.

"I am going to be your uncle, now," he said in a caressing tone. "You have kept up like a soldier under some terrible things here; but we will try to make things brighter for you now."

She smiled in a dreary way without looking at him. His knowledge of the terrible things she had endured seemed to her very limited.

"And you will go now with us-with Mr. Haydon-back to your mother's old home, won't you?" he said, in a persuasive way. "It is not good, you know, for a little girl not to know any of her relations, or to bear such shocking grudges," he added, in a lower tone.

But she gave him no answering smile.

"I will go to your house if you will have me," she said. "You and Max are my friends. I will go only with people I like."

"You know, my dear," said Mr. Haydon, who heard her last words. "You know I offered you a home in my house until such time as you got to school, and-and of course, I'll stick to it."

"Though you are a little afraid to risk it, aren't you?" she asked, with an unpleasant smile. "Haven't you an idea that I might murder you all in your beds some fine night? You know I belong to a country where they do such things for pastime. Aren't you afraid?"

"That is a very horrible sort of pleasantry," he answered, and moved away from the dead face he had been staring at. "I beg you will not indulge in it, especially when you move in a society more refined than these mining camps can afford. It will be a disadvantage to you if you carry with you customs and memories of this unfinished section. And after all, you do not belong here, your family was of the East. When you go back there, it would be policy for you to forget that you had ever lived anywhere else."

Mr. Haydon had never made so long a speech to her before, and it was delivered with a certain persistence, as if it was a matter of conscience he would be relieved to have off his mind.

"I think you are mistaken when you say I do not belong here," she answered, coolly. "Some of my family have been a good many things I don't intend to be. I was born in Montana; and I might have starved to death for any help my 'family' would have given me, if I hadn't struck luck and helped myself here in Idaho. So I think I belong out here, and if I live, I will come back again-some day."

She turned to Seldon and pointed to the dead form.

"They will take him away to-day —I heard them say so," she said quietly. "Let it be some-where away from the camp-not near-not where I can see."

"Can't you forget-even now, 'Tana?"

"Does anybody ever forget?" she asked. "When people say they can forget and forgive, I don't trust them, for I don't believe them."

"Have you any idea who killed him?" he asked. "It is certainly a strange affair. I thought you might suspect some one these people know nothing of."

But she shook her head. "No," she said. "There were several who would have liked to do it, I suppose-people he had wronged or ruined; for he had few friends left, or he would not have come across to these poor reds to hide. Give old Akkomi part of that gold; he was faithful to me-and to him, too. No, I don't know who did it. I don't care, now. I thought I knew once; but I was wrong. This way of dying is better than the rope; and that is what the law would have given him. He would have chosen this —I know."

"Did you ever in your life hear such cold-blooded words from a girl?" demanded Haydon, when she left them and went to Harris. "Afraid of her? Humph! Well, some people would be. No wonder they suspected her when she showed such indifference. Every word she says makes me regret more and more that I acknowledged her. But how was I to know? She was ill, and made me feel as if a ghost had come before me. I couldn't sleep till I had made up my mind to take the risk of her. Max sung her praises as if she was some rare untrained genius. Nothing gave me an idea that she would turn out this way."

"'This way' has not damaged you much so far," remarked Mr. Seldon, dryly. "And as she is not likely to be much of a charge on your hands, you had better not borrow trouble on that score."

"All very well-all very well for you to be indifferent," returned Mr. Haydon, with some impatience. "You have no family to consider, no matter what wild escapade she would be guilty of, you would not be touched by the disgrace of it, because she doesn't belong in any way to your family."

"Maybe she will, though," suggested Seldon.

Mr. Haydon shrugged his shoulders significantly.

"You mean through Max, don't you?" he asked. "Yes, I was simple enough to build on that myself-thought what a nice, quiet way it would be of arranging the whole affair; but after a talk with this ranger, Overton, whom you and Max unite in admiring, I concluded he might be in the way."

"Overton? Nonsense!"

"Well, maybe; but he made himself very autocratic when I attempted to discuss her future. He seemed to show a good deal of authority concerning her affairs."

"Not a bit more than he does over the affairs of their paralyzed partner in there," answered Seldon. "If she always makes as square friends as Dan Overton, I shan't quarrel with her judgment."

When 'Tana left them and went into the other cabin, she stood looking at Harris a long time in a curious, scrutinizing way, and his face changed from doubt to dread before she spoke.

"I am hardly able to think any more, Joe," she said at last, and her tired eyes accented the truth of her words; "but something like a thought keeps hammering in my head about you-about you and —" She pointed to the next room. "If you could walk, I should know you did it. If you could talk, I should know you had it done. I wouldn't tell on you; but I'd be glad I was going where I would not see you, for I never could touch your hand again. I am going away, Joe; won't you tell me true whether you know who did it? Do you?"

He shook his head with his eyes closed. He, too, looked pale and worn, and noticing it, she asked if he would not rather move to some other dwelling, since —

He nodded his head with a sort of eagerness. All of the two days and the night he had sat there, with only the folds of a blanket to separate him from the room where his dead foe lay.

"I will speak to them about it right away." She lifted his hand and stroked it with a sort of sympathy. "Joe, can you forgive him now?" she whispered.

He made her no reply; only closed his eyes as before.

"You can't, then? and I can't ask you to, though I suppose I ought to. Margaret would," and she smiled strangely. "You don't know Margaret, do you? Well, neither do I. But I guess she is the sort of girl I ought to be. Joe, I can't stay in camp any longer. Maybe I'll leave for the Ferry to-day. Will you miss me? Yes, I know you will," she added, "and I will miss you, too. Do you know-can you tell when Dan will come back?"

He shook his head, and an hour later she said to Max:

"Take me away from here, back to the Ferry-any place. Mrs. Huzzard will, maybe, come for a few days-or Miss Slocum. Ask them, and let me go soon."

And an hour after they had started, another canoe went slowly over the water toward the Kootenai River, a canoe guided by Akkomi; and in it lay the blanket-draped figure of the man whose death was yet a mystery to the camp. He was at least borne to his resting place by a friend, though what the reason for Akkomi's faithfulness, no one ever knew; for some favor in the past, no doubt. Seldon knew that 'Tana would rather Akkomi should be the one to cover his grave, though where it was made, no white man ever knew.

Chapter XXV
On Manhattan Island

"What do you intend to make of your life, Montana, since you avoid all questions of marriage? You will not go to school, and care nothing about fitting yourself for the society where by right you should belong."

A whole winter had gone, and the springtime had come again; and over all the Island of Manhattan, and on the heights back from the rivers, the green of the leaves was creeping over the boughs from which winter had swept all signs of life months ago.

In a very lovely little room, facing a park where the glitter of a tiny lake could be seen, 'Tana lounged and stared at the waving branches and the fettered water.

Not just the same 'Tana as when, a year ago, she had breasted the cold waves of the Kootenai. No one, to look at her now, would connect the taller, stylishly dressed figure, with that little half-savage who had scowled at Overton in the lodge of Akkomi. Her hair was no longer short and boyish in its arrangement. A silver comb held it in place, except where the tiny curls crept down to cluster about her neck. A gown of soft white wool was caught at her waist by a flat woven belt of silver, and an embroidered shoe of silvery gleam peeped from under the white folds.

No, it was not the same 'Tana. And the little gray-haired lady, who slipped ivory knitting needles in and out of silky flosses, watched her with troubled concern as she asked:

"And what do you intend to make of your life, Montana?"

"You are out of patience with me, are you not, Miss Seldon?" asked the girl. "Oh, yes, I know you are; and I don't blame you. Everything I have ever wanted in my life is in reach of me here-everything a girl should have; yet it doesn't mean so much to me as I thought it would."

"But if you would go to school, perhaps —"

"Perhaps I would learn to appreciate all this," and the girl glanced around at the fine fittings of the room, and then back to the point of her own slipper.

"But I do study hard at home. Doesn't Miss Ackerman give me credit for learning very quickly? and doesn't that music teacher hop around and wave his hands over my most excellent, ringing voice? They say I study well."

"Yes, yes; you do, too. But at a school, my dear, where you would have the association of other girls, you would naturally grow more-more girlish yourself, if I may say so; for you are old beyond your years in ways that are peculiar. Your ideas of things are not the ideas of girlhood; and yet you are very fond of girls."

"And how do you know that?" asked 'Tana.

"Why, my dear, you never go past one on the street that you don't give her more notice than the very handsomest man you might see. And at the matinees, if the play does not hold you very close, your eyes are always directed to the young girls in the audience. Yes, you are fond of them, yet you will not allow yourself to be intimate with any."

And the pretty, refined-looking lady smiled at her and nodded her head in a knowing way, as though she had made an important discovery.

The girl on the couch lay silent for a while, then she rose and went over to the window, gazing across to the park, where people were walking and riding along the green knolls and levels. Young girls were there, too, and she watched them a little while, with the old moody expression in her dark eyes.

"Perhaps it is because I don't like to make friends under false pretenses," she said, at last. "Your society is a very fine and very curious thing, and there is a great deal of false pretense about it. Individually, they would overlook the fact that I was accused of murder in Idaho-the gold mine would help some of them to do that! But if it should ever get in their papers here, they would collectively think it their duty to each other not to recognize me."

"Oh, Montana, my dear child, why do you not forget that horrible life, and leave your mind free to partake of the advantages now surrounding you?" and Miss Seldon sighed with real distress, and dropped her ivory needles despairingly. "It seems so strange that you care to remember that which was surely a terrible life."

"Much more so than you can know," answered the girl, coming over to her and drawing a velvet hassock to her side. "And, my dear, good, innocent little lady, just so long as you all try to persuade me that I should go out among young people of my own age, just so long must I be forced to think of how different my life has been to theirs. Some day they, too, might learn how different it has been, and resent my presence among them. I prefer not to run that risk. I might get to like some of them, and then it would hurt. Besides, the more I see of people since I came here, the more I feel that every one should remain with their own class in life."

"But, Montana, that is not an American sentiment at all!" said Miss Seldon, with some surprise. "But even that idea should not exclude from refined circles. By birth you are a lady."

The girl smiled bitterly. "You mean my mother was," she answered. "But she did not give me a gentleman for a father; and I don't believe the parents of any of those lovely girls we meet would like them to know the daughter of such a man, if they knew it. Now, do you understand how I feel about myself and this social question?"

"You are foolishly conscientious and morbid," exclaimed the older lady. "I declare, Montana, I don't know what to do with you. People like you-you are very clever, you have youth, wealth, and beauty-yes, the last, too! yet you shut yourself up here like a young nun. Only the theaters and the art galleries will you visit-never a person-not even Margaret."

"Not even Margaret," repeated the girl; "and that is the crowning sin in your eyes, isn't it? Well, I don't blame you, for she is very lovely; and how much she thinks of you!"

"Yes!" sighed the little lady. "Mrs. Haydon is a woman of very decided character, but not at all given to loving demonstrations to children. Long ago, when we lived closer, little Margie would come to me daily to be kissed and petted. Max was only a boy then, and they were great companions."

"Yes; and if he had been sensible, he would have fallen in love with her and made her Mrs. Lyster, instead of knocking around Western mining towns, and making queer friends," said the girl, smiling at the old lady's astonished face. "She is just the sort of girl to suit him."

"My dear," she said, solemnly, "do you really care for him a particle?"

"Who-Max? Of course I do. He is the best fellow I know, and was so good to me out there in the wilderness. There was no one out there to compare me with, so I suppose I loomed up big when compared with the average squaw. But everything is different here. I did not know how different. I know now, however, and I won't let him go on making a mistake."

"Oh, Montana!" cried the little lady, pleadingly.

Just then a maid entered with two cards, at which she glanced with a dismay that was comical.

"Margaret and Max! Why, is it not strange they should call at the same time, and at a time when —"

"When I was pairing them off so nicely, without their knowledge," added the girl. "Have them come up here, won't you? It is so much more cozy than that very elegant parlor. And I always feel as if poor Max had been turned out of his home since I came."

So they came to the little sitting room-pretty, dark-eyed Margaret, with her faultless manners and her real fondness for Miss Seldon, whom she kissed three times.

"For I have not seen you for three days," she explained, "and those two are back numbers." Then she turned to 'Tana and eyed her admiringly as they clasped hands.

"You look as though you had stepped from a picture of classic Greek," she declared. "Where in that pretty curly head of yours do you find the ideas for those artistic arrangements of form and color? You are an artist, Montana, and you don't know it."

"I will begin to believe it if people keep telling me so."

"Who else has told you?" asked Lyster, and she laughed at him.

"Not you," she replied; "at least not since you teased me about the clay Indians I made on the shores of the Kootenai. But some one else has told me-Mr. Roden."

"Roden, the sculptor! But how does he know?"

She glanced from one face to the other, and sighed with a serio-comic expression. "I might as well confess," she said, at last. "I am so glad you are here, Miss Margaret, for I may need an advocate. I have been working two hours a day in Mr. Roden's studio for over a month."

"Montana!" gasped Miss Seldon, "but-how-when?"

"Before you were awake in the morning," she said, and looked from one to the other of their blank faces. "You look as if it were a shock, instead of a surprise," she added. "I did not tell you at first, as it would seem only a whim. But he has told me I have reason for the whim, and that I should continue. So—I think I shall."

"But, my child-for you are a child, after all-don't you know it is a very strange thing for a girl to go alone like that, and-and-Oh, dear! Max, can't you tell her?"

But Max did not. There was a slight wrinkle between his brows, but she saw it and smiled.

"You can't scold me, though, can you?" she asked. "That is right, for it would be no use. I know you would say that in your set it would not be proper for a girl to do such independent things. But you see, I do not belong to any set. I have just been telling this dear little lady, who is trying to look stern, some of the reasons why society life and I can never agree. But I have found several reasons why Art life and I should agree perfectly. I like the freedom of it-the study of it. And, even if I never accomplish much, I shall at least have tried my best."

"But, Montana, it is not as though you had to learn such things," pleaded Miss Seldon. "You have plenty of money."

"Oh, money-money! But I have found there are a few things in this world money can not buy. Art study, little as I have attempted, has taught me that."

Lyster came over and sat beside her by the window.

"'Tana," he said, and looked at her with kindly directness, "can the Art study give you that which you crave, and which money can not buy?"

Her eyes fell to the floor. She could not but feel sorry to go against his wishes; and yet—

"No, it can not, entirely," she said, at last. "But it is all the substitute I know of, and, maybe, after a while, it will satisfy me."

Miss Seldon took Margaret from the room on some pretext, and Lyster rose and walked across to the other window. He was evidently much troubled or annoyed.

"Then you are not satisfied?" he asked. "The life that seemed possible to you, when out there in camp, is impossible to you now."

"Oh, Max! don't be angry-don't. Everything was all wrong out there. You were sorry for me out there; you thought me different from what I am. I could never be the sort of girl you should marry-not like Margaret—"

"Margaret!" and his face paled a little, "why do you speak of her?"

"I know, if you do not, Max," she answered, and smiled at him. "I have learned several things since I came here, and one of them is Mr. Haydon's reason for encouraging our friendship so much. It was to end any attachment between you and Margaret. Oh, I know, Max! If I had not looked just a little bit like her, you would never have fancied you loved me-for it was only a fancy."

"It was no fancy! I did love you. I was honest with you, and I have waited patiently, while you have grown more and more distant until now—"

"Now we had better end it all, Max. I could not make you happy, for I am not happy myself."

"Perhaps I—"

"No, you can not help me; and it is not your fault. You have been good to me-very good; but I can't marry any one."

"No one?" he asked, looking at her doubtfully. "'Tana, sometimes I have fancied you might have cared for some one else-some one before you met me."

"No, I cared for no one before I met you," she answered, slowly. "But I could not be happy in the social life of your people here. They are charming, but I am not suited to their life. And-and I can't go back to the hills. So, in a month, I am going to Italy."

"You have it all decided, then?"

"All-don't be angry, Max. You will thank me for it some day, though I know our friends will think badly of me just now."

"No, they shall not; you are breaking no promises. You took me only on trial, and it seems I don't suit," he said, with a grimace. "I will see that you are not blamed. And so long as you do not leave America, I should like you to remain here. Don't let anything be changed in our friendship, 'Tana."

She turned to him with tears in her eyes, and held out her hand.

"You are too good to me, Max," she said, brokenly, "God knows what will become of me when I leave you all and go among foreign faces, among whom I shall not have a friend. I hope to work and-be contented; but I shall never meet a friend like you again."

He drew her to him quickly.

"Don't go!" he whispered, pleadingly. "I can't let you go out into the world alone like that! I will love you-care for you —"

"Hush!" and she put her hand on his face to push it away; "it is no use, and don't do that-try to kiss me; you must not. No man has ever kissed me, and you —"

"And I sha'n't be the first," he added, shrugging his shoulders. "Well, I confess I hoped to be, and you are a greater temptation than you know, Miss Montana. And you ought to pardon me the attempt."

Her face was flushed and shamed. "I could pardon a great deal in you, Max," she answered; "but don't speak of it again. Talk to me of other things."

"Other things? Well, I haven't many other things in my mind just now. Still, I did see some one down town this morning whom you rather liked, and who asked after you. It was Mr. Harvey, the writer, whom we met first at Bonner's Ferry, up in the Kootenai land. Do you remember him?"

"Certainly. We met him afterward at one of the art galleries, and I have seen him several times at Roden's studio. They are great friends. He looked surprised to find me there, but, after I spoke to him, he talked to me a great deal. You know, Max, I always imagine he heard that suspicion of me up at the camp. Do you think so?"

"He never intimated it to me," answered Max; "though Haydon nearly went into spasms of fear lest he would put it all in some paper."

"I remember. He would scarcely allow me breathing space for fear the stranger would get near enough to speak to me again. I remember all that journey, because when I reached the end of it, the past seemed like a troubled dream, for this life of fineness and beauty and leisure was all so different."

"And yet you are not contented?"

"Oh, don't talk of that-of me!" she begged. "I am tired of myself. I just remembered another one on the train that journey-the little variety actress who had her dresses made to look cute and babyish-the one with bleached hair, and they called her Goldie. She looked scared to death when he-Overton-stopped at the window to say good-by. I often wondered why."

"Oh, you know Dan was a sort of sheriff, or law-and-order man, up there. He might have known her unfavorably, and she was afraid of being identified by him, or something of that sort. She belonged to the rougher element, no doubt."

"Max, it makes me homesick to think of that country," she confessed. "Ever since the grass has commenced to be green, and the buds to swell, it seems to me all the woods are calling me. All the sluggish water I see here in the parks and the rivers makes me dream of the rush of the clear Kootenai, and long for a canoe and paddle. Contrive something to make me forget it, won't you? Make up a party to go somewhere-anywhere. I will be cavalier to your lovely little aunt, and leave you to Margaret."

"I asked you before why you speak of Margaret and me in that tone?" he said. "Are you going to tell me? You have no reason but your own fancy."

"Haven't I? Well, this isn't fancy, Max-that I would like to see my cousin-you see, I claim them for this once-happy in her own way, instead of unhappy in the life her ambitious family are trying to arrange for her. And I promise to trade some surplus dust for a wedding present just as soon as you conclude to spoil their plans, and make yourself and that little girl and your aunt all happy by a few easily spoken words."

"But I have just told you I love you."

"You will know better some day," she said, and turned away. "Now go and pacify your aunt, won't you? She seemed so troubled about the modeling-bless her dear heart! I didn't want to trouble her, but the work-some work-was a necessity to me. I was growing so homesick for the woods."

After she was left alone, she drew a letter from her pocket, one she had got in the morning mail, and read over again the irregular lines sent by Mrs. Huzzard.

"I got Lavina to write you the letter at Christmas, because I was so tickled with all the things you sent me that I couldn't write a straight line to save me; and you know the rheumatiz in my finger makes it hard work for me sometimes. But maybe hard work and me is about done with each other, 'Tana; though I'll tell you more of that next time.

"I must tell you Mr. Harris has got better-can talk some and walk around; can't move his left arm any yet. But Mr. Dan sent for two fine doctors, and they tried to help him with electricity. And I was scared for fear lightning might strike camp after that; but it didn't. Lavina is here still, and likely to stay. She's a heap of company; and she and Captain Leek are better friends than they was.

"There is a new man in camp now; he found a silver mine down near Bonner's Ferry, and sold it out well. He was a farmer back in Indiana, and has been on a visit to our camp twice. Mr. Dan says it's my cooking fetches him. Everything is different here now. Mr. Dan got sawed lumber, and put me up a nice little house; and up above the bluff he has laid out a place where he is going to build a stone house, just as if he intends to live and die here. He doesn't ever seem to think that he has enough made now to rest all his days. Sometimes I think he ain't well. Sometimes, 'Tana, I think it would cheer him up if you would just write him a few lines from time to time. He always says, 'Is she well?' when I get a letter from you; and about the time I'm looking for your letters he's mighty regular about getting the mail here.

"That old Akkomi went south when winter set in, and we reckon he'll be back when the leaves get green. His whole village was drunk for days on the money you had Mr. Seldon give him, and he wore pink feathers from some millinery store the last time I saw him. But Mr. Dan is always patient with him whether he is drunk or sober.

"I guess that's all the news. Lavina sends her respects. And I must tell you that on Christmas they got some whisky, and all the boys drank your health-and drank it so often Mr. Dan had to give them a talking to. They think a heap of you. Yours with affection,

"Lorena Jane Huzzard.

"P. S. —William McCoy is the name of the stranger I spoke of. The boys call him Bill."

Chapter XXVI
Overton's Wife

A few hours later, 'Tana sat in a box at the theater; for the party she had suggested had been arranged, and pretty Miss Margaret was radiant over the evening planned for her, and 'Tana began to enjoy her rôle of matchmaker. She had even managed to tell Margaret, in a casual manner, that Miss Seldon's idea of a decided engagement between herself and Max had never a very solid foundation, and now had none at all. He was her good friend-that was all, and she was to leave for Italy in a month.

And Margaret went up to her and kissed her, looking at her with puzzled, admiring eyes.

"They tried at home to make me think very differently," she said. "But you are a queer girl, Miss Montana. You have told me this on purpose, and —"

"And I want to hear over in Italy that you are going to make a boy I like very happy some of these days. Remember, Margaret, you are-or will be —a millionairess, while he has not more than a comfortable income; and boys-even when they are in love-can be proud. Will you think of that?"

Margaret only blushed and turned away, but the answer was quite satisfying to 'Tana, and she felt freer because her determination had been put into words, and the last bond connecting her with the old life was to be broken. Ever since the snows had gone, some cord of her heart-string had been drawing all her thoughts to those Northern hills, and she felt the only safety was to put the ocean between them and her.

The home Mr. Seldon had offered her with his sister was a very lovely one, but to it there came each week letters about the mines and the people there. Mr. Seldon had already gone out, and would be gone all summer. As he was an enthusiast over the beauties and the returns of the country, his letters were full of material that she heard discussed each day. Therefore, the only safety for herself lay in flight; and if she did not go across the ocean to the East, she would surely grow weaker and more homesick until she would have to turn coward entirely and cross the mountains to her West.

Realizing it all, she sat in her dainty array of evening dress and watched with thoughts far away the mimic scene of love triumphant on the stage before her. When, on the painted canvas, a far-off snow-crowned mountain rose to their view, her heart seemed to creep to her throat and choke her, and when the orchestra breathed softly of the winds, music, and the twittering of birds, the tears rose to her eyes and a great longing in her heart for all the wild beauty of her Kootenai land.

Then, just as the curtain went down on the second act, some one entered their box.

"You, Harvey?" said Max, with genuine pleasure. "Good of you to look me up. Let me introduce you to my aunt and Miss Haydon. You and Miss Rivers are old acquaintances."

"Yes; and that fact alone has brought me here just now," he managed to say to Lyster. "To confess the truth, I have been to see Miss Rivers at her home this evening, having got her address from Roden, and then had the assurance to follow her here. You may be sure I would not have spoiled your evening for any trivial thing, but I come because of a woman who is dying."

"A woman who is dying?" repeated 'Tana, in wonder. "And why do you come to me?"

"She wants to see you. I think-to tell you something."

"But who is it?" asked Lyster. "Some beggar?"

"She is a beggar now at least," agreed Mr. Harvey —"a poor woman dying. She said only to tell Miss Rivers, and here is a line she sent."

He gave her a slip of paper, and on it was written:

"Come and take some word to Dan Overton for me. I am dying.

Overton's wife."

She arose, and Margaret exclaimed at the whiteness of her face.

"Oh, my dear," sighed Miss Seldon, "you know how I warned you not to give your charities individually among the beggars of a city. It is really a mistake. They have no consideration, and will send for you at all hours if you will go. It is so much better to distribute charity through some organization."

But 'Tana was tying her opera cloak, and moving toward the entrance.

"I am going," she said. "Don't worry. Is it far, Mr. Harvey? If not, perhaps I can be back to go home with you when the curtain goes down."

"It is not far," he answered. "Will you come, Lyster?"

"No!" said 'Tana; "you stay with the others, Max. Don't look vexed. Maybe I can be of some use, and that is what I need."

Many heads turned to look at the girl whose laces were so elegant, and whose beautiful face wore such a startled, questioning expression. But she hurried out of their sight, and gave a little nervous shiver as she wrapped her white velvet cloak close about her and sank into a corner of the carriage.

"Are you cold?" Harvey asked, but she shook her head.

"No. But tell me all."

"There is not much. I was with a doctor —a friend of mine-who was called in to see her. She recognized me. It is the little variety actress who came over the Great Northern, on our train."

"Oh! But how could she know me?"

"She did not know your name; she only described you, remembering that I had talked with you and your friends. When I told her you were in the city, she begged so for you to come that I could not refuse to try."

"You did right," she answered. "But it is very strange-very strange."

Then the carriage stopped before a dingy house in a row that had once belonged to a very fashionable quarter, but that was long ago. Boarding houses they were now, and their class was about number three.

"It is a horrible place to bring you to, Miss Rivers," confessed her guide; "and I am really glad Miss Seldon did not accompany you, for she never would have forgiven either of us. But I knew you would not be afraid."

"No, I am not afraid. But, oh, why don't they hurry?"

He had to ring the bell the second time ere any one came to the door. Then, as the harsh jangle died away, steps were heard descending the stairs, and a man without a coat and with a pipe in his mouth, shot back the bolt with much grumbling.

"I'll cut the blasted wire if some one in the shebang don't tend to this door better," he growled to a lady with a mug of beer, who just then emerged from the lower regions. "Me a-trying to get the lines of that new afterpiece in my head-chock-full of business, too! —and that bell clanging forever right under my room. I'll move!"

"I wish you would," remarked Harvey, when the door opened at last. "Move a little faster when you do condescend to open the door. Come, Miss Rivers-up this way."

And the lady of the beer mug and the gentleman of the pipe stared at each other, and at the white vision of girlhood going up the dark, bad-smelling stairway.

"Well, that's a new sort in this castle," remarked the man. "Do you guess the riddle of it?"

The woman did not answer, but listened to the footsteps as they went along the hall. Then a door opened and shut.

"They've gone to Goldie's room," she said. "That's queer. Goldie ain't the sort to have very high-toned friends, so it can't be a long-lost sister," and she smiled contemptuously.

"She's a beauty, anyway, and I'm going to see her when she makes her exit, if I have to sit up all night."

"Oh! And what about the afterpiece?"

"To the devil with the afterpiece! It hasn't any angels in it."

Inside Goldie's room, a big Dutch blonde in a soiled blue wrapper sat by the bed, and stared in open-mouthed surprise at the new-comers.

"Is it *you* she's been askin' for?" she asked, bluntly.

But 'Tana did not reply, and Harvey got the blonde to the door, and after a few whispered words, induced her to go out altogether, and closed the door behind her.

"I thought you'd come," whispered the little woman on the bed. "I thought the note would bring you. I saw you talk to him, and I dropped to the game. You're square, too, ain't you? That's the kind I want now. That swell who went for you is the right sort, too. I minded his face and yours. But tell him to go out for a minute. It won't take long-to tell you."

Harvey went, at a motion from 'Tana. She had not uttered a word yet. All she could do was to stare in wonder at the wreck of a woman before her —a painted wreck; for, even on her deathbed, the ghastly face was tinted with rouge.

"I can't get well-doctor says," she continued. "There was a baby; it died yesterday-three hours old; and I can't get well. But there is another one I want to tell you of. You tell him. It is two years old. Here is the address. Maybe he will take care of it for me. He was good-hearted — that's why he married me; thought I was only a little girl without a home. Any woman could fool him, for he thought all women were good. He thought I was only a little girl; and I had been married three years before."

She smiled at the idea of that past deception, while 'Tana's face grew hard and white.

"How you look!" said the dying woman. "Well, it's over now. He never cared for me much, though-not so much as others did. He was never my real husband, you know, for I never had a divorce. He thought he was, though; and even after he left me, he sent me money regular for me to live quiet in 'Frisco, but it didn't suit me. Then he got turned dead against me when I tried to make him think the child was his. He wouldn't do anything for me after that; I had cheated him once too often."

"And was it?" It was the first time 'Tana had spoken, and the woman smiled.

"You care, too, do you? Well, yes, it was. You tell him so; tell him I said so, and I was dying. He'll take care of her, I think. She's pretty, but not like me. He never saw her. She's with a woman in Chicago, where I boarded. I haven't paid her board now for months, but it's all right; the woman's a good soul. Dan Overton will pay when you tell him."

"You write an order for that child, and tell the woman to give it to me," said 'Tana, decidedly, and looked around for something to write with. A sheet of paper was found, and she went to Harvey for a pencil.

"'Most ready to go?" he asked, looking at her anxiously.

She nodded her head, and shut the door.

"But I can't write now; my hands are too weak," complained the woman. "I can't."

"You've *got* to!" answered the girl; and, taking her in her strong young hands, she raised her up higher on the pillow. "There is the paper and pencil-now write."

"It will kill me to lay like this."

"No matter if it does; you write."

"You're not a woman at all; you're like iron-white iron," whined the other. "Any woman with a heart —" and the weak tears came in her eyes.

"No, I have no heart to be touched by you," answered the girl. "You had a chance to live a decent life, and you wouldn't take it. You had an honest man to trust you and take care of you, and you paid him with deceit. Don't expect pity from me; but write that order."

She tried to write but could not, and the girl took the pencil.

"I will write it, and you can sign it," she said; "that will do as well."

Thus it was accomplished, and the woman was again laid lower in the bed.

"You are terrible hard on-on folks that ain't just square," she said. "You needn't be so proud; you ain't dead yet yourself. You don't know what may happen to you."

"I know," said the girl, coldly, "that if I ever brought children into the world, to be thrown on strangers' hands and brought up in the streets to live your sort of life, I would expect a very practical sort of hell prepared for me. Have you anything more to tell me? I'm going."

"Oh —h! I wish you hadn't said that about hell. I'm dreadful afraid of hell," moaned the woman.

"Yes," said the girl; "you ought to be."

"How hard you are! And the doctor said I would die to-night."

Then she lay still quite a while, and when she spoke again, her voice seemed weaker.

"You have that order for Gracie, and you are so hard-hearted. I don't know what you will do-and I don't want her to grow up like me."

"That is the first womanly thing I have heard you say," replied the girl.

She went over to the bed and took the woman's hands in hers, looking at her earnestly.

"Your child shall have a beautiful and a good home," she said, reassuringly. "I am going for her myself to-morrow, and she will never lack care again. Have you any other word to give me?"

The woman shook her head, and then as 'Tana turned away, she said:

"Not unless you would kiss me. You are not like other women; but-will you kiss me?"

And, with the pressure of the dying kiss on her lips, 'Tana went out the door.

"Please give her every care money can secure for her," she said to the woman at the door; while the man, minus the pipe, was there to open it.

"Mr. Harvey, can I trouble you to look after it for me? You know the doctor and can learn all that is needed. Have the bills sent to me; and let me know when it is all-over."

They reached the theater just as the curtain went down on the last act, and she remained in the carriage until her own party came out.

"I can hardly thank you enough for coming after me to-night," she said, as she shook hands very cordially with Harvey. "You can never be a mere acquaintance to me again. You are my friend."

"Have I ignorantly done some good?" he asked, and she smiled at him.

"Yes-more than you know-more than I can tell you."

"Then may I hope not to be forgotten when you are in Italy?"

"Oh!" and the color flushed over all the pallor caught from that deathbed. "But I —I don't think I will go to Italy after all, Mr. Harvey. I have changed my mind about that, and think I will go back to the Kootenai hills instead."

Chapter XXVII
Life at Twin Springs

Over all the land of the Kootenai the sun of early June was shining. Trees of wild fruits were white with blossoms, as if from far above on the mountains the snows had blown down and settled here and there on the new twigs of green.

And high up above the camp of the Twin Springs, Overton and Harris sat looking over the wide stretches of forest, and the younger man looked troubled.

"I think your fear is all an empty affair," he said, in an argumentative tone. "You eat well and sleep well. What gives you the idea you are to be called in soon?"

"Several things," said the other, slowly, and his speech was yet indistinct; "but most of all the feel of my feet and legs. A week ago my feet turned cold; this week the coldness is up to my knees, and it won't go away. I know what it means. When it gets as high as my heart I'll be done for. That won't take long, Dan; and I want to see her first."

"She can't help you."

"Yes, she can, too. You don't know. Dan, send for her."

"Things are all different with her now," protested the other. "She's with friends who are not of the diggings or the ranges, Joe. She is going to marry Max Lyster; and, altogether, is not the same little girl who made our coffee for us down there in the flat. You must not expect that she will change all her new, happy life to run back here just because you want to talk to her."

"She'll come if you telegraph I want her," insisted Harris. "I know her better than you do, Dan. The fine life will never spoil her. She would be happier here to-day in a canoe than she would be on a throne. I know her best."

"She wasn't very happy before she left here."

"No," he agreed; "but there were reasons, Dan. Why are you so set against her coming back?"

"Set against it? Oh, no."

"Yes, you are. Mrs. Huzzard and all the camp would be only too glad to see her; but you-you say no. What's your reason?"

"Joe, not many months ago you tried to make me suspicious of her," said Overton, not moving his eyes from a distant blue peak of the hills. "You remember the day you fell in a heap? Well, I've never asked you your reasons for that; though I've thought of it considerably. You changed your mind about her afterward, and trusted her with the plan of this gold field down here. Now, you had reasons for that, too; but I never have asked you what they are. Do the same for me, will you?"

The other man did not answer for a little while, but he watched Dan's moody face with a great deal of kindness in his own.

"You won't tell me?" he said at last. "Well, that's all right. But one of the reasons I want her back is to make clear to you all the unexplained things of last summer. There were things you should have been told-that would have made you two better friends, would have broken down the wall there always seemed to be between you-or nearly always. (She wouldn't tell you, and I couldn't.) It left her always under a cloud to you, and she felt it. Many a time, Dan, she has knelt beside me and cried over her troubles to me-and they were troubles, too! —telling them all to me just because I couldn't speak and tell them again. And I won't, unless she lets me. But I don't want to go over the range and know that you two, all your lives, will be apart and cold to each other on account of suspicions I could clear away."

"Suspicions? No, I have no suspicions against her."

"But you have had many a troubled hour because of that man found dead in her room, and his visit to her the night before, and that money she asked for that he was after. All such things that you could not clear her of in your own mind, when you cleared her of murder-they are things I want straightened out before I leave, Dan. You have both been good friends to me, and I don't want any bar between you."

"What does all that matter now, Joe? She is out of our lives, and in a happier one some one else is making for her. I am not likely ever to see her again. She won't come back here."

"I know her best; she will come if she is needed. I need her for once; and if you don't send for her, I will, Dan. Will you send?"

But Overton got up and walked away without answering. Harris thought he would turn back after a little while, but he did not. He watched him out of sight, and he was still going higher up in the hills.

"Trying to walk away from his desire for her," thought Joe, sadly. "Well, he never will. He thinks I don't know. Poor Dan!"

Then he whistled to a man down below him, and the man came and helped him down to camp, for his feet had grown helpless again in that strange chill of which he had spoken.

Mrs. Huzzard met him at the door of a sitting room, gorgeous as an apartment could well be in the Northern wilderness. All the luxuries obtainable were there; for, as Harris had to live so much of his time indoors, Overton seemed determined that he should get benefit from his new fortune in some way. The finest of furs and of weavings furnished the room, and a dainty little stand held a tea service of shell-pink china, from which the steam floated cheerily.

And Lorena Jane herself partook of the general air of prosperity, as she drew forward a great cushioned chair for the invalid and brought him a cup of fragrant tea.

"I just knew you was tired the minute I saw you coming down that hill," she said, filling a cup herself and sitting down to enjoy it. "I knew a cup of tea would do you good, for you ain't quite so brisk as you was a few weeks ago."

"No," he agreed, and gulped down the beverage with a dubious expression on his face. He very much preferred whisky as a tonic; but as Mrs. Huzzard was bound to use that new tea service every day for his benefit, he submitted without a protest and enjoyed most the number of cups she disposed of.

"I suppose, now, you got sight from up there on the hill of the two young folks going boat riding?" she remarked, with attempted indifference; and he looked at her questioningly.

"Oh, I mean Lavina and the captain! Yes, he did get up ambition enough to paddle a boat and ask her to ride in it; and away they went, giddy as you please!"

"I thought you had a high regard for the captain?" remarked Harris.

"Who? Me? Well, as Mr. Overton's relation, of course I show him respect," and her tone was almost as pompous as that of the captain used to be. "But I must say, sir, that to admire a man-for me to admire a man-he must have a certain lot of push and ambition. He must be a real American, who don't depend on the record of his dead relations to tell you how great he is —a man who will dig either gold or potatoes if he needs them, and not be afraid of spoiling his hands."

"Somebody like this new lucky man, McCoy," suggested Harris, and she smiled complacently but did not answer.

And out on the little creek, sure enough, Lavina and the captain were gliding with the current, and the current had got them into dangerous waters.

"And you won't say yes, Lavina?" he asked, and she tapped her foot impatiently on the bottom of the boat.

"I told you yes twenty-five years ago, Alf Leek," she answered.

He sighed helplessly. His old aggressive manner was all gone. The tactics he would adopt for any other woman were useless with this one. She knew him like a book. She had him completely cowed and miserable. No longer did he regale admiring friends with tales of the late war, and incidentally allow himself to be thought a hero. One look from Lavina would freeze the story of the hottest battle that ever was fought.

To be sure, she had as yet refrained from using words against him; but how long would she refrain? That question he had asked himself until, in despair, a loop-hole from her quiet vengeance had occurred to him, and he had asked her to marry him.

"You never could-would marry any one else," he said, pleadingly.

"Oh, couldn't I?"

"And I couldn't, either, Lavina," he continued, looking at her sentimentally. But Lavina knew better.

"You would, if anybody would have you," she retorted. "I know I reached here just in time to keep poor Lorena Jane from being made a victim of. You would have been a tyrant over her, with your great pretensions, if I hadn't stopped it. You always were tyrannical, Alf Leek; and the only time you're humble as you ought to be is when you meet some one who can tyrannize over you. You are one of the sort that needs it."

"That's why I asked you to marry me," he remarked, meekly.

And after a moment she said:

"Well, thinking of it from that point of view, I guess I will."

Far up on the heights, a man lying there alone saw the canoe with the man and the woman in it, and it brought back to him keen rushes of memory from the summer time that had been. It was only a year ago that 'Tana had stepped into his canoe, and gone with him to the new life of the settlement. How brave she had been! how daring! He liked best to remember her as she had been then, with all the storms and sunshine of her face. He liked to remember that she had said she would be cook for him, but for no other man. Of course her words were a child's words, soon forgotten by her. But all her words and looks and their journeys made him love the land he had known her in. They were all the treasures he had with which to comfort his loneliness.

And when in the twilight he descended to the camp, Joe-or his own longings-had won.

"I will send the telegram for you, old fellow," he said, and that was all.

Chapter XXVIII
Again on the Kootenai

Another canoe, with a woman in it, skimmed over the waters in the twilight that evening —a woman with all the gladness of youth in her bright eyes, and an eagerness for the north country that far outstripped the speed of the boat.

Each dark tree-trunk as it loomed up from the shores, each glint of the after-glow as it lighted the ripples, each whisper of the fresh, soft wind of the mountains, was to her as a special welcome. All of them touched her with the sense of a friendship that had been faithful. That she was no more to them than any of the strangers who came and went on the current, she could not believe; for they all meant so much, so very much to her.

She asked for a paddle, that she might once more feel against her strength the strong rush of the mountain river. She caressed its waves and reached out her hands to the bending boughs, and laughter and sighs touched her lips.

"Never again!" she whispered, as if a promise was being made; "never again! my wilderness!"

The man who had charge of the canoe —a stalwart, red-whiskered man of perhaps forty-five —looked at her a good deal in a cautious way. She was so unlike any of the girls he had ever seen-so gay, so free of speech with each stranger or Indian who came their way; so daintily garbed in a very correct creation of some city tailor; and, above all, so tenderly careful of a child who slept among the rugs at her feet, and looked like a bit of pink blossom against the dark furs.

"You are a stranger here, aren't you?" she asked the man. "I saw no one like you running a boat here last summer."

"No, no," he said, slowly; "I didn't then. My camp is east of Bonner's Ferry, quite a ways; but I get around here sometimes, too. I don't run a boat only for myself; but when they told me a lady wanted to get to Twin Springs, I didn't allow no scrub Indians to take her if my boat was good enough."

"It is a lovely boat," she said, admiringly; "the prettiest I ever saw on this river, and it is very good of you to bring me yourself. That is one of the things makes me realize I am in the West once more-to be helped simply because I am a girl alone. And you didn't even know my name when you offered to bring me."

"No, but I did before I left shore," he answered; "and then I counted myself kind of lucky. I —I've heard so much about you, miss, from folks up at Twin Springs; from one lady there in particular-Mrs. Huzzard."

"Oh! so you know her, do you?" she asked, and wondered at the self-conscious look with which he owned up that he did —a little.

"A little? Oh, that is not nearly enough," she said, good-naturedly. "Lorena Jane is worth knowing a good deal of."

"That's my opinion, too," he agreed; "but a fellow needs some help sometimes, if he ain't over handy with the gift of gab."

"Well, now, I should not think you would need much help," she answered. "You ought to be the sort she would make friends with quick enough."

"Oh, yes-friends," he said, and sent the canoe on with swifter, stronger strokes. The other boat, paddled by Indians and carrying baggage, was left far behind.

"You make this run often?" she asked, with a little wonder as to who the man was. His dress was much above the average, his boat was a beautiful and costly thing, and she had not learned, in the haste of her departure, who her boatman was.

"Not very often. Haven't been up this way for two weeks now."

"But that is often," she said. "Are you located in this country?"

"Well-yes, I have been. I struck a silver lode across the hills in yon direction. I've sold out and am only prospecting around just now, not settled anywhere yet. My name is McCoy."

"McCoy!" and like a flash she remembered the post-script of Mrs. Huzzard's letter. "Oh, yes —I've heard of you."

"You have? Well, that's funny. I didn't know my name had got beyond the ranges."

"Didn't you? Well, it got across the country to Manhattan Island-that's where I was when it reached me," and she smiled quizzically. "You know Mrs. Huzzard writes me letters sometimes."

"And do you mean-did she —"

"Yes, she did-mentioned your name very kindly, too," she said, as he hesitated in a confused way. Then, with all the gladness of home-coming in her heart and her desire that no heart should be left heavy, she added: "And, really, as I told you before, I don't think you need much help."

The kindly, smiling eyes of the man thanked her, as he drove the canoe through the clear waters. Above them the stars were commencing to gleam faintly, and all the sweet odors of the dusk floated by them, and the sweetest seemed to come to her from the north.

"We will not stop over-let us go on," she said, when he spoke of Sinna Ferry. "I can paddle while you rest at times, or we can float there on the current if we both grow tired; but let us keep going."

But ere they reached the little settlement, a canoe swept into sight ahead of them and when it came near, Captain Leek very nearly fell over the side of it in his anxiety to make himself known to Miss Rivers.

"Strangest thing in the world!" he declared. "Here I am, sent down to telegraph you and wait a week if need be until an answer comes; and half-way on my journey I meet you just as if the message had reached you in some way before it was even put on paper. Extraordinary thing-very!"

"You were going to telegraph me? What for?" and the lightness of her heart was chased away by fear. "Is-is any one hurt?"

"Hurt? Not a bit of it. But Harris thinks he is worse and wanted you, until Dan concluded to ask you to come. I have the message here somewhere," and he drew out a pocket-book.

"Dan asked me to come? Let me see it, please," and she unfolded the paper and read the words he had written-the only time she had ever seen his writing in a message to her.

A lighted match threw a flickering light over the page, on which he said:

"Joe is worse. He wants you. Will you come back?

"Dan Overton."

She folded it up and held it tight in her hand under the cloak she wore. He had sent for her! Ah! how long the night would be, for not until dawn could she answer his message.

"We will go on," she said. "Can't you spare us a boatman? Mr. McCoy has outstripped our Indian extras who have our outfit, and he needs a little rest, though he won't own up."

"Why, of course! Our errand is over, too, so we'll turn back with you. I just passed Akkomi a few miles back. He is coming North with the season, as usual. I thought the old fellow would freeze out with the winter; but there he was drifting North to a camping-place he wanted to reach before stopping. I suppose we'll have him for a neighbor all summer again."

The girl, remembering his antipathy to all of the red race, laughed and raised in her arms the child, that had awakened.

"All I needed to perfect my return to the Kootenai country was the presence of Akkomi," she confessed. "I should have missed him, for he was my first friend in the valley. And it may be, Mr. McCoy, that if he is inclined to be friendly to-night, I may ask him to take me the rest of the way. I want to talk to him. He is an old friend."

"Certainly," agreed McCoy; but he evidently thought her desire was a very peculiar one.

"But you will have a friend at court just the same-whether I go all the way with you or not," she said and smiled across at him knowingly.

Captain Leek heard the words, too, and must have understood them, for he stared stonily at the big, good-looking miner. Their greeting had been very brief; evidently they were not congenial spirits.

"Is that a —a child?" asked the captain, as the little creature drooped drowsily with its face against 'Tana's neck; "really a child?"

"Really a child," returned the girl, "and the sweetest, prettiest little thing in the world when her eyes are open." As he continued to stare at her in astonishment while their boats kept opposite each other, she added: "You would have sooner expected to see me with a pet bear, or wolf, wouldn't you?"

"Yes; I think I would," he confessed, and she drew the child closer and kissed it and laughed happily.

"That is because you only know one side of me," she said.

The stars were thick overhead, and their clear light made the night beautiful. When they reached the boats of Akkomi, only a short parley was held, and then an Indian canoe darted out ahead of the others. Two dark experts bent to the paddles and old Akkomi sat near the girl and the child. Looking in their dusky faces, 'Tana realized more fully that she was again in the land of the Kootenais.

It was just as she would have chosen to come back, and close against her heart was pressed the message by which he had called her.

The child slept, but she and the old Indian talked now and then in low tones all through the night. She felt no weariness. The air she breathed was as a tonic against fatigue, and when the canoe veered to the left and entered the creek leading to camp, she knew her journey was almost over.

The dusk was yet over the land, a faint whiteness touched the eastern edge of the night and told of the dawn to come, but it had not arrived.

The camp was wrapped in silence. Only the watch-man of the ore-sheds was awake, and came tramping down to the shore when their paddles dipped in the water and told him a boat was near. It was the man Saunders.

"Miss Rivers!" he exclaimed, incredulously. "Well, if this isn't luck! Harris will about drop dead with joy when he sees you. He took worse just after dark last night. He says he is worse, though he can talk yet. I was with him a little while, and how he did worry because you wouldn't get here before he was done for! Overton has been with him all night; went to bed only an hour ago. I'll call the folks up for you."

"No," said the girl, hastily; "call no one yet. I will go to Joe if you will take me. If he is so bad, that will be best. Let the rest sleep."

"Can I carry the-the baby?" he asked, doubtfully, and took the child in his arms with a sort of fear lest it should break. He was not the sort of man to be needlessly curious, so he showed no surprise at the rather strange adjunct to her outfit, but carried the little sleeper into the pretty sitting room, where he deposited it on a couch, and the girl arranged it comfortably, that it might at last have undisturbed rest.

A man in an adjoining room heard their voices and came to the door.

"You can come out for a while, Kelly," said Saunders. "This is Miss Rivers. She will want to see him."

A minute later the man in charge had left 'Tana alone beside Harris.

All the life in him seemed to gather in his eyes as he looked at her.

"You have come! I told him you would —I told Dan," he whispered, excitedly. "Come close; turn up the light; I want to see you plain. Just the same girl; but happier —a heap happier, ain't you?"

"A heap happier," she agreed.

"And I helped you about it some-about the mine, I mean. I like to think of that, to think I made some return for the harm I done you."

"But you never did me any harm, Joe."

"Yes, I did-lots. You didn't know-but I did. That's why I wanted you to come so bad. I wanted to square things-before I had to go."

"But you are all right, Joe. You are not going to die. You are much better than when I saw you last."

"Because I can talk, you think so," he answered. "But I am cold to my waist —I know what that means; and I ain't grumbling. It's all right, now that you have come. Queer that all the time we've known each other, this is the first time I've talked to you! 'Tana, you must let me tell Dan Overton all —"

"All! All what?"

"Where I saw you first, and —"

"No-no, I can't do that," she said, shrinking back. "Joe, I've tried often to think of it-of telling him, but I never could. He will have to trust or distrust me, but I can't tell him."

"I know how you feel; but you wrong yourself. Any one would give you credit instead of blaming you-don't you ever think of that? And then-then, 'Tana, I tried to tell him down at the Ferry, because I thought you were in some game against him. I managed to tell him you were Holly's partner, but hadn't got any farther when the paralysis caught me. I hadn't time to tell him that Holly was your father, and that he made you go where he said; or that you dressed as a boy and was called 'Monte,' because that disguise was the only safety possible for you in the gambling dens where he took you. Part of it I didn't understand clearly at that time. I didn't know you really thought he was dead, and that you tramped alone into this region in your boy's clothes, so you could get a new start where no white folks knew you. I told him just enough to wrong you in his eyes, and then could not tell him enough to right you again. Now do you know why I want you to let me tell him all-while I can?"

It had taken him a long time to say the words; his articulation had grown indistinct at times, and the excitement was wearing on him.

Once the door into the room where the child lay swung open noiselessly, and he had turned his eyes in that direction; but the girl's head was bowed on the arm of his chair, and she did not notice it.

"And then-there are other things," he continued. "He don't know you were the boy Fannie spoke of in that letter; or that she gave you the plot of this land; or, more-far more to me! —that you took care of her till she died. All that must give him many a worried thought, 'Tana, that you never counted on, for he liked you-and yet all along he has been made to think wrong of you."

"I know," she assented. "He blamed me for-for a man being in my cabin that night, and I —I wanted him to-think well of me; but I could not tell him the truth, I was ashamed of it all my life. And the shame has got in my blood till I can't change it. I want him to know, but I can't tell him."

"You don't need to," said a voice back of her, and she arose to see Overton standing in the door. "I did not mean to listen; but I stopped to look at the child, and I heard. I hope you are not sorry," and he came over to her with outstretched hand.

She could not speak at first. She had dreamed of so many ways in which she would meet him-of what she would say to him; and now she stood before him without a word.

"Don't be sorry, 'Tana," he said, and tightened his hand over her own. "I honor you for what I heard just now. You were wrong not to tell me; I might have saved you some troubles."

"I was ashamed-ashamed!" she said, and turned away.

"But it is not to me all this should be told," he said, more coldly. "Max is the one to know; or, maybe, he does know."

"He knows a little-not much. Seldon and Haydon recognized-Holly. So the family knew that, but no more."

It was so hard for her to talk to him there, where Harris looked from one to the other expectantly.

And then the child slipped from the couch and came toddling into the light and to the girl.

"Tana-bek-fas!" she lisped, imperatively. "Bek-fas."

"Yes, you shall have your breakfast very soon," promised the girl. "But come and shake hands with these gentlemen."

She surveyed them each with baby scrutiny, and refused. "Bek-fas" was all the world contained that she would give attention to just then.

"You with a baby, 'Tana?" said Harris. "Have you adopted one?"

"Not quite," and she wished-how she wished it was all over! "Her mother, who is dead, gave her to me. But she has a father. I have come up here to see what he will say."

"Up here!"

"Yes. But I must go and find some one to get her breakfast. Then-Dan —I would like to see you."

He bowed and started to follow her, but Harris called him back.

"This spurt of strength has about done for me," he said. "The cold is creeping up fast. I want to tell you something else. Don't tell her till I am gone, for she wouldn't touch my hand if she knew it. I killed Lee Holly!"

"You didn't —you couldn't!"

"I did. I was able to walk long before you knew it, but I lay low. I knew if he was living, he would come where she was, sooner or later, and I knew the gold would fetch him, so I waited. I could hardly keep from killing him as he left her cabin that first night, but she had told him to come back, and I knew that would be my time. She thought once it might be me, but changed her mind. Don't tell her till I am gone, Dan. And-listen! You are everything to her, and you don't know it. I knew it before she left, but-Oh, well, it's all square now, I guess. She won't blame me-after I'm dead. She knows he deserved it. She knew I meant to kill him, if ever I was able."

"But why?"

"Don't you know? He was the man-my partner-who took Fannie away. Don't you-understand?"

"Yes," and Overton, after a moment, shook hands with him.

"I didn't want 'Tana to go back on me-while I lived," he whispered. It was his one reason for keeping silence-the dread that she could never talk to him freely, nor ever clasp his hand again; and Overton promised his wish should be regarded.

When he went to find 'Tana, Mrs. Huzzard had possession of her, and the two women were seeing that the baby got her "bek-fas," and doing some talking at the same time.

"And he's got his new boat, has he?" she was saying. "Well, now! And it's to be a new house next, and a fine one, he says, if he can only get the right woman to live in it," and she smoothed her hair complacently. "He thinks a heap of fine manners in a woman, too; and right enough, for he'll have an elegant home to put one in and she never to wet her hands in dish-water! But he is so backward like; but maybe this time —"

"Oh, you must cure him of that," laughed the girl. "He is a splendid fellow, and I won't forgive you if you don't marry him before the summer is over."

At that instant Overton opened the door.

"If you are ready now to see me —" he began, and she nodded her head and went toward him, her face a little pale and visibly embarrassed.

Then she turned and went back.

"Come, Toddles," she said; "you come with 'Tana."

A faint flush was tingeing the east, and over the water-courses a silvery mist was spread. She looked out from the window and then up the mountain.

"Let us go out-up on the bluff," she suggested. "I have been shut up in houses so long! I want to feel that the trees are close to me again."

He assented in silence and the child, having appeased its hunger, was disposed to be more gracious, and the little hands were reached to him while she said:

"Up."

He lifted her to his shoulder, where she laughed down in high glee at the girl who walked beside in silence. It was so much easier to plan, while far away from him, what she would say, than to say it.

But he himself broke the silence.

"You call her Toddles," he remarked. "It is not a pretty name for so pretty a child. Has she no other one?"

They had reached the bluff above the camp that was almost a town now. She sat down on a log and wished she could keep from trembling so.

"Yes-she has another one —a pretty one, I think," she said, at last. "It is Gracie-Grace —"

She looked up at him appealingly.

But the emotion in her face made his lips tighten. He had heard so many revelations of her that morning. What was this last to be?

"Well," he said, coldly, "that is a pretty name, so far as it goes; but what is the rest of it?"

"Overton," she said, in a low voice, and his face flushed scarlet.

"What do you mean?" he asked, harshly, and the little one, disliking his tone, reached her arms to 'Tana. "Whose child is this?"

"Your child."

"It is not true."

"It is true," she answered, as decidedly as himself. "Her mother-the woman you married-told me so when she was dying."

He stared at her incredulously.

"I wouldn't believe her even then," he answered. "But how does it come that you —"

"You don't need to claim her, if you don't want to," she said, ignoring all his astonishment. "Her mother gave her to me. She is mine, unless you claim her. I don't care who her father was-or her mother, either. She is a helpless, innocent little child, thrown on the world-that is all the certificate of parentage I am asking for. She shall have what I never had —a childhood."

He walked back and forth several times, turning sometimes to look at the girl, whom the child was patting on the cheek while she put up her little red mouth every now and then for kisses.

"Her mother is dead?" he asked at last, halting and looking down at her.

She thought his face was very hard and stern, and did not know it was because he, too, longed to take her in his arms and ask for kisses.

"Her mother is dead."

"Then —I will take the child, if you will let me."

"I don't know," she said, and tried to smile up at him. "You don't seem very eager."

"And you came back here for that?" he said, slowly, regarding her. "'Tana, what of Max? What of your school?"

"Well, I guess I have money enough to have private teachers out here for the things I don't know-and there are several of them! And as for Max-he didn't say much. I saw Mr. Seldon in Chicago and he scolded me when I told him I was coming back to the woods to stay —"

"To stay?" and he took a step nearer to her. "'Tana!"

"Don't you want me to?" she asked. "I thought maybe-after what you said to me in the cabin-that day —"

"You'd better be careful!" he said. "Don't make me remember that unless-unless you are willing to tell me what I told you that day-unless you are willing to say that you-care for me-that you will be my wife. God knows I never hoped to say this to you. I have fought myself into the idea that you belong to Max. But now that it is said-answer me!"

She smiled up at him and kissed the child happily.

"What shall I say?" she asked. "You should know without words. I told you once I would make coffee for no man but you. Do you remember? Well, I have come back to you for that. And see! I don't wear Max's ring any longer. Don't you understand?"

"That you have come back to *me* —'Tana!"

"Now don't eat me! I may not always be a blessing, so don't be too jubilant. I have bad blood in my veins, but you have had fair warning."

He only laughed and drew her to him, and she could never again say no man had kissed her.

"'Tana!" said the child, "'ook."

She looked where the little hand pointed and saw all the clouds of the east flooded with gold, and higher up they lay blushing above the far hills.

A new day was creeping over the mountains to banish shadows from the Kootenai land.

www.ingramcontent.com/pod-product-compliance
Lightning Source LLC
Chambersburg PA
CBHW071422300726
48976CB00004B/1211